"*Nightshifted* is like a dark and twisted version of *Grey's Anatomy* with vampires, zombies, and werewolves taking up residence in County Hospital's Y4 wing . . . The story moves at a similar pace to a hospital setting where there are small lulls in action and with sudden, even frantic bursts of action. That sort of pacing made *Nightshifted* an exciting read as I was constantly on edge, waiting to see what was going to happen next."

—*All Things Urban Fantasy*

"I loved this book. What a breath of fresh air! A memorable scene with an STD-afflicted dragon (yup) had me on the edge of my seat, the budding romance with Ti (zombie firefighter!) is sweet and tender, and I just plain loved hanging out with Edie. *Nightshifted* is a very strong start to what promises to be a wonderful new series!"

—*My Bookish Ways*

Also by
Cassie Alexander

Nightshifted

MOONSHIFTED

CASSIE ALEXANDER

St. Martin's Paperbacks

This is a work of fiction. All of the characters, organizations, and events portrayed in this novel are either products of the author's imagination or are used fictitiously.

MOONSHIFTED

Copyright © 2012 by Erin Cashier.
Excerpt from *Shapeshifted* copyright © 2012 by Erin Cashier.

For information address St. Martin's Press, 175 Fifth Avenue, New York, NY 10010.

ISBN: 978-0-312-55340-1

Printed in the United States of America

St. Martin's Paperbacks edition / December 2012

St. Martin's Paperbacks are published by St. Martin's Press, 175 Fifth Avenue, New York, NY 10010.

10 9 8 7 6 5 4 3 2 1

ACKNOWLEDGMENTS

The final draft of *Moonshifted* owes a particularly large debt to the acumen and understanding of my editor, Rose Hilliard, who saw where I was going and helped to get me there. The 1st–13th drafts would not have been possible at all without the oversight, encouragement, and late-night phone calls from Daniel Starr. I also had the good fortune to run it (such as it was, at the time!) through the Blue Heaven 11 workshop where Sandra McDonald and Deb Coates provided invaluable feedback on it. And this book would not be here at all had not my lovely agent Michelle Brower sold it, or if my husband Paul had forgotten to feed and water me while I was sitting at my desk. I would also, belatedly, like to thank my copy editor Laura Jorstad, and the people who are translating me into other languages for their patience and time.

Veterinary advice was helpfully provided by Dr. Kim Carlson, although any mistakes are mine. And I'd also like to take a moment to thank the nurses on my opposite weekend (who accurately point out that they also have never let me kill anyone on accident, either)—especially B and C. B for making nursing look easy in a way I'm awed by, even when she's doing CPR, and C for the good stories and being a fan of mine right out of the gate.

Eternal thank-yous to both of you for introducing me to my second home.

And thanks to you, reader, for coming back for a second book. Thanks for taking a chance on the first one—I can't wait to show you the third.

I have no fear nor shrinking; I have seen death so often that it is not strange or fearful to me.
—Edith Cavell

CHAPTER ONE

"Who knew a Code Silver isn't when an old-timer tries to beat you with their walker?" Charles said as he double-looped his scarf around his neck.

I grinned at him as I pulled my gloves out of my pocket. "Technically, a walker's still a weapon." We'd been trapped in a cold, dark room watching safety-refresher videos all morning, an exquisite torture for nurses used to staying up all night. I wound up my scarf and pulled on a cap. "Why don't we get any cool codes, Charles?"

"We do. Code Fur. Code Fang." He patted through his pockets, maybe looking for his own set of gloves.

I hadn't been in on any admissions since I'd been hired as a nurse at County a few months ago. But the vampires, weres, and other assorted casualties our floor catered to had to come in from somewhere. Not that the rest of the hospital knew that we kept vampire-exposed humans—daytimers—in our beloved County Hospital's basement, but we must get advance notice somehow. I just wasn't sure how that happened. There was a lot of information I wasn't privy to yet.

I inhaled to ask another question, and then looked up at him. I could tell behind his scarf he was cracking a smile. "Awwww, you liar. Code Fang. As if."

"Nurse Edie is Code Gullible."

"Whatever, old-timer."

Charles laughed and held the building's front door open. "After you."

I braced myself and headed outside.

Winter air was like a slap in the face—the portions of my face that it could still get to. We were two days before Christmas, and the skies were bleak. My hairstyle had been hat head for what felt like weeks now, and I was swaddled up in my warmest coat. Between my own hips and the three layers of clothing I had on underneath my coat, I probably looked like a Jawa from the original *Star Wars*, only with blue eyes peering out.

Charles and I were going out to the Rock Ronalds for lunch. It was in front of the hospital on the next cross street down, and it was where our recently released patients would take their legally prescribed methadone to trade for illegal heroin and crack. I wouldn't go there alone at night, not even the drive-through, but during the day with a male co-worker I felt safe—plus I desperately needed caffeine if I was going to make it through the afternoon.

"So what really happened, anyhow?" Charles asked as he double-tapped the signal-change button on the light post.

"Um." I rocked up and down on my toes, watching the orange stop hand across the six-lane street. I knew what he was asking but I didn't want to rehash the past, so I shrugged without meeting his gaze. "You know. I got stabbed by vampires. My zombie boyfriend ditched me on his way out of town. That sort of thing."

"Too fresh?"

"Yeah." I inhaled and looked up. He was smiling again; it gave him crinkles around his eyes. Charles was a good nurse and maybe even a better friend, in a wholesome

father-figure kind of way, if I'd let him be. He'd been working at Y4 for longer than I'd been alive. I couldn't help but
smile back. "We have advanced life support recertification
coming up together in four months. Hit me up then."

"Gotcha."

The light changed, and we both looked both ways twice
before crossing the street.

The bell over the door of the 'Ronalds rang as we walked
in, and a color-coded height sticker measured us as we
passed through the door, just in case.

Charles ordered fries with a side of fries at the counter,
and I took off my gloves to hand him money for my Diet
Coke. I realized this was the first time I'd ever hung out
with a co-worker outside of work. It was our lunch break,
but still, it counted for something. I grinned at him as I
returned from the soda fountain.

"Code Fang," he said, and laughed. "You totally bought
it."

"Yeah, yeah, make fun of the new kid."

"We don't get enough new people for me to tease."

"Maybe if so many new hires didn't die—which no
one ever told me, by the way—you'd get more chances." I
followed him to the nearest table and sat across from him.

"Would you have believed us if we told you?"

I drank a deep gulp of my soda and considered this.
"Probably not."

"For the record, I told you not to go back into that guy's
room." He glanced meaningfully toward my left hand. It
had a semicircular scar across the back of it, from where
I'd been bitten by a vampire. It didn't ache, except for when
it was cold—which, since we were in the depths of winter,
was all the damn time.

I rubbed at my scar. "If in the future you have a choice

between blatantly warning me about possible death, versus vaguely warning me in a smug fashion, please go with the former."

He nodded. "Duly noted."

At my last job my biggest fear was being coughed on by someone with active TB. But at County, particularly on floor Y4, where Charles and I both worked, the opportunities to screw things up and maybe get killed were endless. Floor Y4 catered to the supernatural creatures that no one else knew about: werecreatures in their mortal phases, the daytime servants of the vampires, the sanctioned donors of the vampires, and shapeshifters that occasionally went insane. And sometimes zombies, whom nurses occasionally dated, with poor outcomes. At the thought of my now twice-dead love life, my urge to make small talk chilled.

Across from me, Charles was starting in on his second cone of fries. Funny how knowing exactly what a ton of salt and fat could do to your heart didn't stop you from wanting to eat them. Like nurses who worked in oncology and still smoked. Charles watched me watching him eat, and tilted the cone toward me. I waved away his offer—it still felt too early to eat, my stomach was on night shift even if I was awake—and he shrugged.

"You sure you don't want to talk?"

"Yeah."

Charles measured me as he polished off the fry cone. "Here," he said. He wiped his hands on his napkins, then opened his coat and reached for his shirt buttons.

"What are you doing?" I whispered, and glanced around to see if other restaurant patrons were looking.

"I'll show you mine if you show me yours." Three buttons down, he started pulling the fabric out and away from his neck. "Seven years ago. Were-attack. Shattered my clavicle. I couldn't lift my arm over my head for six months."

I couldn't see anything; it was shadowed by the clothing he'd bunched away to show me. But I believed him that the scars were there. Even if they didn't show—they were there. I shook my head. "I'm not showing you mine. Just trust me, it looks like I got a C-section from an epileptic."

Charles released his collar and straightened his shirt. "That sucks. But on the plus side, at least you didn't wind up needing to start a college fund."

"True, that." I helped myself to one of the loose fries on his tray.

"So now we're scar-buddies. Right?"

I nodded quickly, a little ashamed at how badly I wanted Charles and me to get along.

"Then listen to me, Edie. What I'm trying to say is this—I remember how it was to be you. All excited about the adventure—it's not a safe way to be. You have to protect yourself. You have to remember that to them, we're disposable."

I didn't need to ask who *them* was. *Them* was the vampires that'd tried to kill me. And also the zombie boyfriend who'd needed to leave town. I'd felt pretty disposable then. The new scars didn't help me to not feel like that either.

"So no heroics. Be safe. I want to keep you around."

I was genuinely glad someone unrelated to me did. "Thanks."

"You're welcome." He finished his soda and stood. "Let's get back. Only five hours of films to go."

We bundled up and pressed outside again. "What do you think the next film will be?" I should have gotten a Diet Coke for the road. Maybe then the need to pee would keep me awake through class.

"Ignoring Ebola: One Thousand Ways to Die," Charles suggested. "Or *Mr. Radiation, Uncle X-Ray's Spooky Friend.*" He did a little cartoon dance, and I laughed.

"I liked the one where they explained how to evacuate the hospital by taking people down the stairs one at a time." I wasn't even sure Y4 had stairs. I'd only ever taken the elevator in and out.

"God. If we did that, it'd end up being some sort of horrible Hurricane-Katrina thing. Some people would get left behind, others'd make bad choices. If it ever gets that bad, I'm staying home." Charles hit the button to change the intersection's light, and I decided to press my luck.

"So tell me about the were attack?"

Charles kept his eyes on the light across the street, but I could see him squinting into the past. "Ask me when we have advanced life support recertification. We can trade war stories then."

"Fair enough."

There was a man with tufts of white hair sticking out from under his snow cap six lanes across from us, pacing back and forth. At first I thought he was just trying to stay warm, but as he moved I could tell by his bearing that he was angry. The traffic between us slowed as the light changed. Charles and I stepped off the curb at the same time as the other man did. We were across half a lane when a truck that'd seemed to be slowing down for the red light sped up instead. I heard the engine shift gears, looked up, and saw the man coming toward us do the same.

It hit him.

He crumpled forward against the hood, arms out, like he was hugging it in a moment of game-show triumph. Then it launched him into the air. I stopped in the middle of the road, stunned, unable to believe that I was actually watching someone fly. He made an arc, landed, bounced, and skidded to a stop, smearing red behind himself.

Half a second for the impact to occur, another half a second for the landing, and then the sound of screeching brakes as all other rightful traffic through the intersection came to a halt—except for the truck, which kept going. It missed the man's landing body by inches, and drove away with his blood in its tire treads.

"Jesus Christ," Charles said, and started to run for the injured man. I ran after him.

CHAPTER TWO

"I've already called nine-one-one!" yelled a bystander. I could hear someone retching behind me as we reached the man's still form.

"Everybody back! We're nurses!" Charles yelled.

Fuck me fuck me fuck me. I was no paramedic. I was used to people whom the emergency department had already cleaned up and put tubes and lines in. He was so injured—where to even begin? Charles knelt down, putting his fingers on the man's neck. "He's got a pulse. He's breathing." I knelt down beside him. Dark bruises were blossoming around both the man's eyes.

"Raccoon eyes," I whispered, having only seen it once before, on a trauma test in nursing school.

"Brain shear, go figure." Charles spared me a dark glance.

We had no supplies. We couldn't move him and risk his spine. One of the man's legs was twisted the wrong way, denim torn open, exposing meat and bone below. A moment earlier, and we'd have seen the stuffing of him, ragged edges of skin, yellow-white subcutaneous fat, red stripes of muscle tissue. But that moment had let his blood catch up with his injuries, and now it welled out from arteries and leaked from veins. It filled up his wounds, overflowing their edges and spilling out like oil onto the ground. When it began to ebb, I gritted my teeth and reached in, pushing against his broken leg's femoral artery. Blood wicked through the fabric of my glove and was hot against my hand.

"Here's an old-timer trick." Charles knelt straight into the stranger's thigh, his knee almost into the groin, only pausing for me to pull my hands out of the way. The blood leaching out of the man's leg subsided—although that might've been because there wasn't much left. "It'll clamp down the artery completely."

I inhaled to complain now was not a good time for class—but I stopped when I realized teaching was what Charles did to cope. Our patient groaned and tried to move his head. I crawled through the gravel and broken glass up to the man's head. "Sir, you can't move right now. There's been a bad accident." I put my hands on either side of his head. His snow cap had been peeled off, along with part of his scalp, and his wispy white hair was sticky with blood. "I'm so sorry, just please stay still."

"Aren't you going to breathe for him?" someone behind me asked. I glanced back and saw a man with a cell phone jutting forward.

"What is wrong with you?" I swatted the phone out of his hand, sent it skittering into a slick of blood stained snow by the curb. "Show some respect!"

"Hey! That's my new phone!" The bystander started pawing gloved hands through the grimy snow to get what was his. There was a shadow there, cast by the man himself, and I saw it shudder, swallowing the phone inside its blackness like a throat. I wondered if it'd been a trick of the light.

The injured man moved again, reaching up a hand to fight me. "No no no no no," I said, but he continued to clutch my wrist with the strength of someone who had nothing left to lose. "Stay still, okay? It's all going to be fine," I said, knowing I was lying. "Just stay still."

He groaned and the shape of his jaw shifted, becoming narrow and more angular. His teeth pressed forward, stretching against the limits of his lips, lengthening, showing yellow enamel. His beard began to grow—just like fur. "Charles?" I asked, my voice rising in pitch. It was daytime, on a cloudy December day—but I looked over my shoulder and saw Charles's face turn dusky, like the surrounding gray sky.

"Code Fur, Edie. We need Domitor, now." He fished in his coat pocket for a phone. "I'm calling the floor." The sound of a distant ambulance began in the background. "Get back here before they do."

I stood, found my footing in the ice and blood, then I was gone.

I froggered through the rubberneckers on either side of the highway, then hit the edge of the hospital grounds, my feet pounding against cement. Fortunately we de-iced the sidewalks as a courtesy to our patient population, who frequently had to crutch, walker, or wheelchair themselves in. The frozen dead lawn was too slick and treacherous to run on.

I ran past the office complexes that kept our bureaucracy running, between twenty rows of cars in an employee parking lot, around the edge of our loading docks, and made a beeline for the main hospital doors.

Running through the hospital as a nurse in scrubs is easy—people get the hell out of your way, assuming you've got someplace important to be. Running into the lobby in civilian gear covered in blood, however—

"What's going on?" Our officer-guard held his hand up and looked behind me for pursuit.

"Emer-gen-cy—" I gasped. I yanked my badge out of

my back pocket, dangling it for inspection as I brushed past him. "Gotta go—"

"Not so fast—"

"Gotta go!" I yelled and ducked down the next hallway, running for the stairs.

I wasn't in shape at the best of times, and working at Y4 didn't pay enough for me to have a gym membership—and ever since I'd started working there, getting to the gym had been less of a priority than staying alive. But I raced as fast as I could, my knees and chest screaming—because I'd left Charles out there with a werewolf, in the middle of who knew how many gathering civilians, himself a prior victim of a werewolf attack.

There was a warren of hallways that led to my elevator. I took all of them at speed, and seemed to have lost the security officer behind me. I reached the elevator that led to Y4—running into it to stop myself. I swept my badge over the access pad, then braced my hands on my thighs and panted for air. Tiny electrical shocks were running up and down my hamstrings, and my knees kept trying to melt.

The elevator doors didn't open. I ran my badge over the access pad again. The light went green, but there was no opening sound.

"Come on." I flashed my badge a few more times, then scanned the recesses in the ceiling for the Shadows, the creatures that acted as the gatekeepers for our floor. "I know you're watching this. Hurry up!"

There was an audible metal *thunk* as the elevator arrived. The orange doors opened and a Y4 day-shift nurse I recognized handed a 60cc syringe out to me, with one alcohol wipe.

"Tell Dr. Carlson to get ready—" I told her as I snatched them from her.

"Will do."

I turned around and started running back down the hall, before spinning around again. "IV or IM?" I yelled out. I wasn't one of the vets on staff, how the hell should I know how we gave this med?

"Intramuscular!" she yelled back at me before the closing elevator doors cut her off.

I raced back outside. My lungs were on fire now. Each slap of my shoes against the pavement sent lightning bolts up my shins. I ran through a shadow, hit a patch of black ice and tripped, sprawling out of control on the ground. I curled around the medicine as I fell, protecting it, glad that the needle had a safety cap on—if I injected myself with a werewolf's dose of Domitor, I'd die, no doubt. I slid onto the grass, staining myself with water from the snow I'd melted. I was stunned for a second, then scrambled back to my feet and stepped onto the cement unsteady as a newborn calf. My knees were throbbing and an ankle felt twisted, but the medication was still in my hand, the syringe still full, the cap still on, and I had just a block and a half to go.

Amplified commands to *Pull Over!* fought with sirens, and traffic had slowed to open up the ambulance's path. I raced around the same cars I'd dodged originally, finally reaching Charles and handing him the syringe like a baton.

Then I dropped to my knees gasping for air, gulping in exhaust fumes from the cars dithering around us. My knee was in the stranger's cold blood, which didn't feel much different from the sweat freezing against my back. The stranger was still prone, still dying, brown eyes fixed in eye sockets that were black and blue.

"IM," I panted.

"Thanks." Charles uncapped the syringe and hunched over the man, covering his actions with his body. He sank the needle deep into the victim's good thigh, and the man spasmed. I grabbed his nearer hand and felt the strength surge through him as his change began, his nails growing to claw at my skin. I leaned forward, holding my badge between us. "We've got you. We know what you are. We're noncombatants. But there's a lot of civilians around here. Behave, okay?"

His shallow breathing continued. Just as his nails were about to break skin, the Domitor hit him, and his body went slack.

Charles turned to another person with their cell phone out, flicking blood in their direction. "What part of *don't take pictures* do you not understand?"

The offender sprang back away from the flow, into the slow-moving traffic, and got honked at. Just what we needed, someone else getting hit—

"Put your phone down, sir," said a cop, and the sullen bystander put his cell phone away.

The ambulance arrived. Paramedics scrambled out— the first one gestured me away. "Ma'am, you should step—"

"We're nurses. We tried to stop the bleeding," Charles said, pointing at his knee, still wedged into the werewolf's thigh.

"What happened?"

"Hit by a truck," I said. "Head and leg injury, I think." Diagnosis of the century there, Nurse Spence.

The paramedic reached back into the ambulance cab to grab the safety mover and a neck brace. The injured man was breathing even more shallowly now. Domitor, or impending death?

"Doesn't look good," the paramedic said, taking a spot by the man's neck, setting the brace against it.

I couldn't disagree.

CHAPTER THREE

There was no way to escape the feel of blood drying against my hands. I could take my gloves off, but then my hands would be cold—colder—and the gloves were biohazards, so where would I put them? I couldn't just litter them here, although that's what the EMS crew was doing, shedding paper and plastic all over the ground, small pieces getting caught up by the wind of passing cars like candy wrappers. The paramedics worked over the werewolf, efficiently doing what they could, straightening, rolling, scraping him up like he was a huge piece of dough. I stood stiffly, holding my gory hands out away from myself, watching them.

A second cop car pulled up just as the crew shut their doors. I had half a second to whisper to Charles, "We aren't infected, are we?"

"Tonight's not a full moon," he whispered back. The weres we treated waxed and waned with the moon—trapped in their animal form under its sway, and completely mortal when it was dark.

"You two saw this?" the cop said. Charles nodded, and he started asking more questions.

I doubted our statements would be helpful. The truck was black; that was all I knew. I hadn't thought to look at its plates, I'd been too busy watching the man fall and bounce. Same with Charles—and by then most of the other bystanders had disappeared.

"Did the truck slow down at all?"

I shook my head. "It happened so fast." There was a chance the truck hadn't seen him. A slim but possible chance. But there was no way that he hadn't known he'd hit someone. "He just kept driving," I said, with another mystified shake.

"Lucky guy," the officer said after writing down both our names. "Hit-and-runs aren't usually in front of hospitals." He put his notepad away. "My wife's a respiratory therapist. What floor do you guys work on?"

"Nursing office," Charles said.

"Pediatrics," I said at the same time, my usual lie.

"Well—if he lives, maybe we'll be able to figure things out."

Both Charles and I nodded as the officer got into his car and drove off.

"That was close, with that guy and the phone," I said, shivering. Now that I wasn't running, I was freezing in place.

"Yeah." Charles said. We'd watched the traffic unsnarl after the body was taken away. I wondered how long the traffic jam would have lasted after a werewolf sighting.

"What would have happened if we hadn't been here?"

"I don't know. The Shadows might have fixed things— they'd fix things eventually."

"Cops and all?"

"Cops, respiratory therapists, and all."

"Heh." The Shadows were dark amoeba-like creatures that lived beneath County Hospital, feeding on all the pain and sorrow the hospital provided. In trade for this, they "protected" our floor, so only people who worked on Y4 knew about Y4—the Shadows messed with everyone else's minds. Chances were we'd seen that cop's wife be-fore, and chances were she couldn't remember who we were, even if her life depended on it. "You sure we're not infected?" I asked him. I knew the rules, but I wanted to hear him say it.

"Positive. Were blood's only contagious on the full moon. You can still get the shots if you want, though."

"Are you?"

Charles looked down at his knees. "Depends on how fast I wash all this off me."

We walked in calmly, which got us past the security desk despite the blood. It was the running that was frowned upon—mere bleeding was fine. Charles and I feigned like we were going to the emergency room, and then doubled back toward our home floor. I felt bad at the mess we were leaving for the janitor, smeary red bootprints, but I was sure he'd cleaned worse before.

Reaching the elevator bank to Y4 again, I held up my badge and realized my name was obscured by a bloody thumbprint. "Gah. Each step gets more disgusting."

Charles faked being distracted. "What? I didn't hear you. I was too busy dreaming of a shower."

I grinned. "I'd go for a bleach bath."

"And rent a soap snorkel?"

"Is that a snorkel carved out of soap, or one that blows bubbles?"

"I hadn't really thought it that far through." Charles was stained worse than me. His pants were covered in a bull's-eye of blood, like someone had done a shitty tie-dye job beginning at his knees.

We got onto our floor, keyed ourselves into the bathroom–locker room area using a paper towel to pro-tect the keypad from our contaminated fingers, grabbed scrubs, and stopped in front of the unisex bathroom door.

"You start, Edie. I'll be right back."

While I wouldn't normally go along with chivalry, I was too disgusted with my current state to argue, and Charles went into the men's locker room besides. I hit the bathroom's lever door handle with my elbow to open it, and stepped inside.

Gloves went into the trash can, lined with a red biohazard bag. I threw away my shirt and jeans away, but remained hopeful about my coat. After washing up, I changed into scrubs, put my coat on, and emerged into the short hallway outside.

Charles stepped out of the men's locker room, in green scrubs just like me, holding his wallet and keys. I felt as fresh as an only slightly bloodstained daisy, but Charles smelled it. "Did you scrub yourself with Benza Quat?" I asked him.

"Yep."

"Isn't that stuff toxic?"

"One can only hope," he said, shouldering on his coat. "I'm out of here, Spence."

"But—don't you want to see him?"

Charles opened the door and held it for me, and we stepped into the hallway outside. "No. I leave work at work. That's the safest way to be." The elevator arrived behind him, and he went in, keeping one hand out to hold the door.

I was torn between taking Charles's advice for once, and seeing how our new patient was. Inside the elevator, Charles shook his head and sighed. "You look like you're ready for work. You'd better get out of here before they forget you're on night shift."

"I'll be fast."

"See you next shift." He pulled back his hand, the doors closed, and he was gone.

Left alone in the dim hallway, I felt a little lost. I knew the hallway on either side of me spiraled out, dotted with doors my badge wouldn't open. Behind me, there was only the elevator or the locker rooms. The double doors that led into Y4 were in front of me, bright fluorescent light beaming out through the wire-glass windows inside. Had I a kinder heart, narcotics on board, or been experiencing sudden blood loss, they might look like the entrance to heaven. But I knew better. Most of our staff was there not because they wanted to be, but because the Shadows had given them no other choice, and the patients we treated were both victimized by and propagators of an endless cycle of violence.

Despite that—or maybe because of it—I still felt like what I did here mattered. Which was why I didn't want to leave.

I'd helped to save a little girl recently, who also happened to be a vampire. I'd risked my life for her—it was what had gotten me broken up with and stabbed.

I hadn't heard from her since the Rose Throne had picked her up from my house a while ago. But that was okay, because I couldn't imagine my life not having helped her. I only hoped in helping her I hadn't taken her from a frying pan and pushed her into a fire.

I needed to know about this guy now too. I shoved my coat underneath my free arm and pushed the doors to Y4 open.

CHAPTER FOUR

During the day, Y4 was always loud.

I crept along the periphery of the semicircular room, past the intensive-care-level beds that we usually used for daytimers, toward the were-corral hallway, where all the shouting was coming from. I just wanted to look for a moment and read the monitors.

The stranger was in room one, and it was easier to see the machines than the patient—the monitor with vitals on it hung from the ceiling overhead, the ventilator sat beside the bed, and IV pumps on poles surrounded the bed, pushing in medication. They'd even gotten the machine that delivered high-pressure blood, that compressed blood bags like stepped-on grapes, to quickly shuttle their contents up IV lines.

People were swarming the stranger—he was draped in blue as doctors tried to do sterile things to close him up. When a doctor moved I could see a wrist restrained with a leather cuff to the bed frame below, and when a nurse left the area near his head, and I could see he had a collar on now, to keep his neck safe. A titanium-tipped endotracheal tube came out of his mouth—we couldn't use plastic here, our patients would bite them in two—and tubes attached to it went to the ventilator.

There were red medication warning labels on the hanging IV bags. We were giving him a blood pressure through a combination of transfusions and drugs, so while the pressure on the monitor was real for now, it wasn't something the patient was doing on his own. You couldn't give drugs forever; nor could you keep pouring blood through a sieve.

At his bedside another nurse had a tranquilizer gun out, aimed at the patient, ready to juice him with a dart of sedatives if he started to change again.

The day-shift charge nurse spotted me as she was coming out. "Are you going to help or just stand there?"

I shook my head hard and fast. "I just—no."

Her eyes squinted at me. "Charles called it in—you were with him?" I nodded. "What happened?"

"Hit-and-run." If the cop hadn't said it, I wouldn't have thought it—not at first. "He needs to be a No Info. Someone did this to him." No Info was how we protected patients injured via violence—people who needed to be hidden in case more violence followed them to the hospital door.

There was a muted roar from inside the room, and the gowned doctors and nurses present all jumped back. The patient thrashed in bed, finding all the leather restraints tight in place.

"Clear!" The nurse holding the gun took a step nearer, and the medical team stopped what they were doing to give her a shot. Other nurses went to the pumps and dialed up the sedatives. Everything was quiet for a tense five seconds as staff waited to make sure they were safe to continue.

"You'll make him a No Info, right?" I said, breaking the silence.

"Sure, fine." The charge nurse only had eyes for what was happening inside the room, with her team, which was as it should be.

I backed away down the hall. The nurse holding down

the fort at the front desk looked up from the monitor and recognized me. "Will he make it?" she asked.

If he was pissed off enough to fight, hopefully he was pissed off enough to live. "We'll see," I said.

I jogged out to my car, cold crawling up my shins. Thin cotton scrubs didn't keep any cold out, or heat in—by the time I made it to my little Chevy I was freezing. I cranked the engine on and dialed the heat up, holding naked hands out to the vents in supplication. When I'd thawed enough to operate my vehicle, I drove home, right past the accident site. Other ignorant cars drove over the stranger's blood, but not me. I changed lanes.

By the time I made it home I was warm, but I felt disgusting. The birdbath scrubbing I'd given myself in the bathroom sink wasn't cutting it anymore. I could feel the sweat and grime, not to mention blood, that I was sure was still there, trapped deep in my pores. Screw a bleach bath; if I ever got paid decently, I'd install a chlorhexidine shower.

I parked close to my apartment, ran inside, and locked the door behind me. My Siamese cat Minnie came up to greet me at the door. She sniffed me, then gave a disappointed yowl—she knew I'd been consorting with dogs. "I know, I know." As I shimmied off my clothing, German started chattering from the vicinity of my kitchen's countertop bar, from Grandfather's CD player.

"Not you too." It'd been a while since he'd last spoken to me, not that I ever knew what he was saying. I'd picked him up from a patient—or rather, he'd picked me out—and he only spoke German, a language I didn't comprehend. He lived in a CD player that didn't have a CD in it or batteries. I didn't want to say he was a ghost . . . but I didn't know what else he could be. Mostly I knew how he was feeling by his tone. Today it sounded like I was in trouble.

"I missed you too, Grandfather." I patted his player.

The lid didn't sit right, but the structural integrity wasn't important. He said something else that sounded snippy, and his on-light went to yellow.

"I didn't do anything bad, honest." I tossed my scrubs and coat into a trash bag. I'd be down one good bra until I laundered everything, dammit—but laundry could wait until after I'd showered.

I went into my bathroom and cranked the shower up to scalding, flicking my hand under it while I waited for the water to heat. Once I was under it, the hot water calmed me down. I concentrated on scrubbing myself clean, each and every part, more so than I usually bothered to, even after taking care of that one patient with active TB.

When I emerged, pink and dewy, I became aware of a vortex of cold air rushing in from beneath the door, trumping my bathroom's jungly shower clime. Plus—I heard Grandfather talking to himself again outside, sounding extremely displeased. It was December, and I knew I hadn't left any windows open—

Old Edie would have naively walked out into her living room, wondering what'd happened. New Edie sashed her robe tight, grabbed the toilet plunger to hold it like a club, and listened at the bathroom door before opening it.

CHAPTER FIVE

My apartment was small. My bathroom was across from my bedroom—I opened the door quietly, and peeked into the dark room, before hearing someone talking in my living room.

"Really now, the things you say," said a female voice. The German invectives continued.

I ran down the hall and leapt into my living room, the plunger held high. "Who's there?"

By the dim light of my reading lamp, I could see a young blond girl kneeling beside my couch. It took me a second to recognize her—Anna looked much older than when we'd last seen each other, ten days ago. Sweet sixteen was what the songs said, but what sixteen-year-old had ever thought that about themselves? She was playing tug-of-war with Minnie, using a piece of ribbon. She looked from the plunger to me and smiled, showing tiny triangles of fang.

She looked almost human, because she was. Kind of. Anna was a living vampire, the child of two daytimer parents, a vampire freak of nature, the girl whose life I'd helped to save.

Even though she was a vampire, I couldn't help it—I was damn happy to see her. I went in for a hug.

"Put the stake down!" said a male voice from my kitchen.

"What?" I heard the sound of a gun being cocked.

"Gideon!" Anna chastised sharply. "It's okay."

"It's okay? There's a man in my kitchen with a gun." I stood there, mid-lunge, holding my toilet plunger like a wizard's wand.

"I'm sorry, Edie—" Anna waved at the man. "Gideon, please."

The man, who was dressed so darkly I could barely differentiate him from my cabinets, let the gun slide release, tilting the gun's barrel down.

"Thank you," Anna said, nodding to him before looking back to me. Our huggy moment was gone. I set the plunger down.

"How'd you get in?"

"You invited me."

Back when she had looked nine, yes, I had. "But the door was locked."

"Gideon has many talents."

"You couldn't wait outside? Call? Knock?"

"We did knock. You didn't hear us. Well, that German-speaking thing you keep did."

"I was in the shower." Grandfather was quiet now—but I felt slightly safer with him still on my kitchen counter, between Gideon and me. Grandfather would say something if that guy came any closer. I closed the neck of my robe tighter and sat on the far end of my couch. "When did you get all old?"

She smiled. "Once they started to feed me decently. I can control it, some."

Anna looked like a student from a goth boarding school. A black clip held back her frizzy blond bangs, tamed for the first time since I'd met her, and she had a maroon turtleneck on, a pocket watch strung on a gold chain around her neck. A thick black felt skirt went down to her knees, where maroon tights began, sinking into warm winter boots. Most of the times I'd seen her before this, she'd been angry, wearing a ratty nightgown that had been spattered with other people's blood.

"You look good," I said, with a nod.

"I'm staying with Sike. She lets me borrow clothing." Sike was a model acquaintance of us both. She was a day-timer, the servant of a vampire both Anna and I knew, and she'd be as comfortable stabbing someone with a stiletto as with a shiv.

Anna rose up to sit beside me and crinkled her nose. "You're clean, but your house smells like blood and were-wolf."

No point in lying. "There's a reason for that, but I can't tell you about it. Patient privacy, et cetera." I looked over at the stranger in my kitchen. How about some nurse privacy too? "Why's he here?"

"Gideon's my driver."

"Oh." I didn't want to know why Anna needed a driver with a gun. Or rather, I did, but . . . Charles had had a point this afternoon. I wanted to ask her how she was, what had happened to her since she'd been gone, the sort of things you'd ask your friends if you hadn't seen them for a little while. But most people's friends weren't vampires. I had already bought her a Christmas gift, though, just in case—

"Wait here, okay?" I asked, and left the room. I put my plunger away first and then went to my bedroom to find something to wear.

I wasn't Christmas-coordinated enough to have a tree; there was hardly a point. When you lived alone plus worked night shift, the holidays just slid on by. But I had bought Anna a black scarf, because it seemed appropriate, and it was the kind of thing I would wear myself if I didn't see her again.

With my hair pulled up and warmer clothing on, I returned to the living room and turned on the lights.

Grandfather was still muttering at Gideon in the kitchen, who as far as I could see had put away his gun. I reached for the small pile of gifts on my kitchen countertop, and Gideon eyed me but didn't draw. I returned to my spot on the couch. "I bought you something."

"A gift?"

"For Christmas." I handed her the box. She carefully opened the wrapping paper at the taped corners and straightened the creases, just like my grandmother, saving it for later. "I just realized I don't even know if you get cold. But if you do, there you go," I said lamely, as she parted the gift box to reveal the scarf inside.

"The winter here is nothing compared with the winters of my childhood." She pulled the scarf out and wound it around her neck. Seeing as once upon a time she'd come from Russia, back when it was still called Russia, I believed her. She stroked the end of it and smiled at me. "I have something for you too." She reached for a bag at her end of my couch and rummaged inside.

This was unexpected. Anna was the nicest vampire I'd met so far, but as vampires go, that was like saying she was the least alcoholic attendee at an AA meeting. I glanced over at Gideon, and there was an emotion I couldn't name on his face—jealousy? Was he her daytimer? Why would a daytimer be jealous of me?

Anna turned back toward me, a small box on her lap. It was wooden and carved—it reminded me of the box the Evil Queen had given the hunter to put Snow White's heart in.

"It's not a gift, Edie. I'm sorry about that. I forgot it was Christmas," Anna said, holding the box out.

"I kind of figured vampires didn't go in for Christian holidays." I took the box. It was heavy and ornate. The wood was dark, and there was a rose crest carved on the top and inlaid with gold, gold that I suspected was real, having met assorted members of the Rose Throne before. I fumbled around with the lid until I found the mechanism that slid it off. Underneath was a cream envelope of thick paper, and inside of that was a note with calligraphy so ornate as to be almost unintelligible. I tilted the card back and forth. "Just tell me where you're registered."

She snorted. "It's a request for your attendance at my initiation ceremony. It's on New Year's Eve, at midnight."

"Initiation into what?" I hedged. Holiday shifts were time and a half. I was in peanut-butter-sandwich mode, after having been out injured recently. Working Christmas and New Year's were really going to help my bottom line.

"The Sanguine. They're the the ruling council for the Rose Throne. It's where they'll approve me to begin my own line. I'll be able to have my own House, under the auspices of the Rose Throne."

"Anna—"I looked up to explain to her all the reasons why I couldn't attend her vampire party, first and foremost being I didn't want to be the only hors d'oeuvre in attendance. Then I saw the look on her face. "Oh, God. This is important, isn't it?"

"I'm afraid so." She pointed at what was left in the box. I set the letter aside and reached in, finding a black velvet bag. I picked it up and a heavy object slid out.

It looked like a hunting knife. Its falling hilt made the box thump into my lap. The blade equaled the handle's size, and it was as ornate as the letter's calligraphy, with waves and flourishes curlicuing out, rendering it mostly useless, except for what I was sure was a very sharp tip. I picked it up gingerly. "This is one expensive party favor."

There was a real hourglass embedded in the hilt, but instead of being filled with sand, it was filled with blood. I tapped it, and it spun end-over-end, red fluid sloshing from side to side, to fill the lower chamber once the spinning stopped. The top chamber was still stained with blood, like a shaken test tube at County's lab. "Is this your blood?" I asked, even though I already knew the answer. She nodded. "I don't want to be a daytimer, Anna."

The man in my kitchen gave a derisive snort.

"That's why I've chosen you. Because I am part human, I have to bring a human to the ceremony with me. Not one I coerced—one I chose." She reached over to press the knife down so I would look at her. "This knife has to stay intact until my ceremony. The temptation of my blood is a test. And you're the only one I know who will pass it."

My gaze went back to Gideon. If he were given a vial of Anna's blood and she left the room, I wouldn't bet on him managing to count to thirty before drinking its contents to acquire its power. I knew from taking care of daytimers at the hospital that all of their motives were nefarious by default. "What else does this entail?"

"Technically, when this is done you'll belong to my court, as my Ambassador to the Sun."

"I don't suppose it pays?"

She snorted. "It's only a ceremonial position, and only for one night." She looked at me, her eyes softening. "I wouldn't ask you if I had anyone else I could ask."

I wondered how that made Gideon feel. I put the knife back into its bag very carefully, the bag into the box, and stared at its velvety softness. The man in my kitchen made a frustrated sound. He was hungry like all daytimers were hungry, for the power that their masters contained. Dogs on a leash, one and all.

"I know how you all fund yourselves. I won't be a part of it." Gambling, drugs, protection money—everything illicit trickled down into vampire pockets eventually. They were fat ticks on the neck of humanity. Anna's seeming goodness aside, I couldn't endorse that. I tried to hand the open box back to her, and she put up one hand to refuse it.

"Edie—you're the only human I trust." We'd both almost been killed recently, for the same end, by the same people. She'd rescued me then. It'd been more complicated than that, but—I looked from her to the box I held as she waited for me to decide. I wondered if she was holding her breath—if she even needed to breathe. She looked worried. Scared, even.

I couldn't say no. Not even if I ought to. I set the box down on my own lap. "Don't make me regret this, okay?"

"I won't. I promise you." She smiled at me, then stood and straightened her skirt, bending down to retrieve her hair ribbon from the ground. Minnie's disembodied paw swatted out after it from her hiding spot beneath the couch. Gideon rounded my bar, crowding us in my small living room.

"Do I need to do anything in the meantime?"

Anna shook her head. "I'll send my driver for you at eleven that night. I'll be in seclusion until then. Call Sike if you need anything." Anna reached out and grabbed my hand. Her skin was soft and cool as she squeezed it. "Thank you, Edie."

"You're welcome." I squeezed her hand back. Gideon wove through us to open up the door. They left, and Grandfather muttered something I was sure was unkind.

I'd just pledged my help to a teenage-looking but hundred-year-old vampire whom I knew had a temper and a half. There was no way this could end badly, right?

CHAPTER SIX

The next morning I woke up at eight. I got up, peed, brushed my teeth, and took an Ambien, because I had to work that night. I didn't like drugging myself to flip my sleep schedule back and forth, but it was better than being bleary all night. Or lying in bed, trying to sleep, and not managing to get any. My bed was warm, Minnie was nearby, and I already had food in the fridge for dinner and late dinner.

It was Christmas Eve day, not that you would know from looking at my house. It wasn't that I didn't celebrate holidays—although when you're working most of them, it's hard to get into a celebratory mood—I'd just been busy recently. There was a small fake tree at the top of my closet that I could have pulled out—but I'd missed my window right after Thanksgiving, and I'd been busy every day since then, mostly just trying to survive.

As I lay there, I could feel the sleep I'd just woke up from coming back for me. It was like the Ambien was lifting up the sheep-gate. Then my phone rang. I fumbled for it in the dark. "Hello?"

"Edie!"

Only my mother could sound that happy to talk to me. "Hey Momma."

"We've had a change of plans."

"Uh-huh." I nuzzled my head back into the pillow.

"I know you've had a bit of a rough time recently, so instead of you driving all the way out here on Christmas Day, Peter and I are going to drive in to your place."

I blinked into my mattress, then bit the inside of my lip to rouse myself. "What?"

"We're having Christmas in town. It'll make life so much easier for you."

"No, it won't. I'm working tonight, Mom. I was going to drive out to your place after my shift—"

"But see, this way you only have to come home—"

"And cook, and—" I rolled over in bed, now fighting to stay alert. "Mom, I don't even have a table."

"Jake told me about that. Said the glass on the old one had broken."

"Oh really?" I asked archly. What'd happened was that my heroin-addict brother had pawned it for cash to get high—but even in my slightly drugged state, I had the wisdom to keep that to myself.

"So we'll bring the card table in. There's only the four of us. We'll bring in everything we need. You don't have to worry about a thing."

Except for my mother and stepdad and junkie brother visiting my house, which had a ghost-possessed CD player and was a way stop for visiting vampires.

"Mom, really, it's easier—"

"Tell her we'll be there at eleven," I heard a male voice shout from the background.

"We'll be there at eleven A.M. I think that way we'll miss the traffic," my mother passed along.

"Mom, I not even going to remember this conversation when I get up."

"Then write it down, dear. Love you!" she said, and then hung up before I could protest further.

I stayed conscious and disappointedly aware of my

situation for another crucial alarm-setting thirty seconds. Then I drifted back to sleep.

When my alarm went off at five P.M., I had a few confused moments. Usually I set my alarm for six or seven. What time had I gone to bed the night before? I remembered Anna visiting, vaguely, and I could see the knife's dark box on my dresser like a pirate's treasure chest.

But there'd been something else. Something urgent.

"Oh, no."

Christmas.

I didn't care how trivial Mom pretended it would be. There was no way I would get off that easy.

I lurched upright in bed, shoving Minnie off the edge with my foot. "If I'm up, you're up, cat." I was still clean from the previous night's shower. I had work tonight—but before going there, I had other work to do.

First thing, I cleaned my bathroom. I wasn't usually very messy, but it'd been a long time since I'd cleaned like I cared. Second up—the bedroom. You could see right into it. And here, I had been lax. Clothing was strewn across my floor—the only clothes in the hamper were things that desperately needed to be cleaned. Like, say, my werewolf blood–stained coat from the day before. Fuck.

I pulled my clothing bag out of my hamper, shoved everything on the floor into it, grabbed the trash bag with my coat, and braced myself for an extreme investment of quarters as I lugged everything down to the laundry mat down the hall.

Returning, I went through the kitchen first. It wasn't like I had much to do in the fridge—I could organize approximately one package each of turkey slices and grape jelly just fine. I set a kettle to brewing for tea, so at least I'd have something to offer guests, and cleaned the inside of an old pitcher.

Last but not least, was my living room. Once upon a time I'd had a dining room set, which'd been nice. But the set was gone now, when the couch ought to be.

I inspected the bloodstained side of my couch, a souvenir of the time Anna had spent here. I'd tried to clean things up with hydrogen peroxide, but that'd ruined the ornamental floral pattern something fierce. So I'd turned the cushions over, but there was still a stain on part of the side, and a bleached spot to boot. Neither stain was blatant, but my mother had a way of seeing through things—with the exception of my brother, Jake. I knew I couldn't come up with a good-enough lie on the spot.

So that meant . . . shopping for a couch cover. With my last forty dollars from this paycheck. On Christmas Eve.

Dismayed, I set out for Target.

CHAPTER SEVEN

On my way out the door, I stopped and grabbed Anna's knife. My brother had a lifelong penchant for going through my things. New couch covers could be explained away, but fancy cutlery could not. I decided to toss it in my locker at work for a few nights. It was three times as secure there as anything in my house would be on Christmas Day. I left the fancy box behind on my dresser, settling the knife into the bottom of my purse, wrapped in a hand towel, and had a few crazy thoughts about how exactly I'd explain it away if I got pulled over on my drive in.

Only no one was out ticketing people on Christmas Eve night. They—and by *they*, I meant *everyone*—were at Target, desperately shopping.

Packed to the gills did not begin to describe it. I parked my Cavalier out in a satellite parking location, and then hiked into the store.

Throngs of shoppers milled around, none of them looking any happier than me. I was lucky, I supposed—I wasn't going to the toy aisle. I wove my way to homewares and stood in front of the couch cover zone, in do-it-yourself home-decorating land.

It would take a lot more than forty dollars to make my entire apartment look nice. But there were only so many extra shifts I could take and still maintain a life, by which

I meant feeling like I left the hospital often enough to see the sky.

Out of habit, I diagnosed people around me. Flat affect and slumped shoulders? Seasonal affective disorder. Red eyes and sneezing? The flu. I wondered what disorder people could read on my face, given both knowledge and half a chance.

"Hello, Edith."

No one had called me Edith since my grandmother'd died. No one except for—I had a sinking feeling in my stomach as I turned around.

A tall man was standing there—strike that, a vampire, one that I knew. "Dren." A Husker, in service to the Rose Throne. The last time I'd seen him was at the end of my trial when he'd tried to kill me. I'd cut off his hand in self-defense.

"What do you want?" I asked him. The other shoppers glanced at me when I spoke, but none of them looked at him. He had his vampire look-away high beams on; no one's consciousness could get a grasp on the fact that he was there.

He stared at me with his grass-green eyes. "I believe you owe me."

"For what?"

"My hand and my Hound."

His right hand sat on his sickle holster, his left wrist plunged into a coat pocket that subsequently stayed flat.

If he hadn't tried to hurt me, he'd have been fine. And I didn't even kill his lizard-person-Hound-thing—the Shadows did. We were very in the open here. Sure, I had an antique knife hidden inside my purse, but I didn't think I'd know how to use it, if I even got a chance to pull it out.

"Let me get this straight—say, if I had let you kill me, then would you, technically, owe me?"

"If that had happened, you would not be in a state to

ask for reparations," he said over a short blond woman's head.

"So my crime is really not that you lost your hand, but that I didn't finish the job?"

"That's one way of putting it."

All of the passing shoppers veered to the left, nearer me and farther from Dren. None of them could see him, and yet none of them wanted to come near him, either. Me, though, they could see and hear. They might not be able to diagnose me, but they knew that I was wrong. I started getting the stink eye, but it'd take a hell of a crazy show to get people off course on Christmas Eve.

The couch covers I so desperately needed were at my back. I looked up and down the aisle. I couldn't count on any of these people to help me—they all thought I was talking to myself. And even if I could have . . . I still couldn't. I couldn't put anyone else in danger.

"What do you want, Dren?" I asked, letting my weariness with the world seep into my voice. "I'm a noncombatant. You can't hurt me."

"I'm not supposed to hurt you. That doesn't mean I cannot."

And suddenly all the ways that Dren could hurt me came to mind. I'd be seeing them tomorrow. My horror must have flashed in my face. "So you see," he said.

I cleared my throat so my voice wouldn't crack. "How can I make good?"

"My hand is irreplaceable."

"I didn't know—" It was his own fault for attacking me. I hadn't meant to injure him.

"My Hound," he continued as if I hadn't spoken at all, "requires the use of a gifted victim."

"I didn't kill your Hound, Dren. The Shadows did."

"I do not have access to the Shadows. You do."

I had no urge to ever visit the Shadows' home, subterraneanly deep below the hospital, again—much less do anything else that would indebt them me to them further. We had a deal—they kept my brother clean, and I worked for subpar wages on Y4. I didn't have anything left to trade, other than matching organs. "We don't really get along."

Shoppers were positively arcing around Dren and I now, in broad ellipses that would have done colliding protons proud. Surely it was only a matter of time before security came and—what, kicked me out? So Dren and I could have this conversation out near my car, in the street? I clenched my hands into impotent fists.

"Regardless. You owe me. I need you to do a job," he said. I blinked, sure I didn't want to hear what he would ask of me next. "I have suspicions that need confirmation with blood," he went on.

"Hey there, pretty lady. Need any help shopping today?"

I was rescued from responding by a stranger. I turned, expecting to see someone in a uniform, maybe holding a white coat. What I found was a jovial-looking older man, his stomach stretching the confines of a red sweatshirt that had a Christmas tree stitched on it, LED lights and all.

I looked over to Dren, begging him *No civilians* with my gaze. "I'm fine—thanks for asking."

"You're fine, but you don't seem fine, if you catch my drift."

"I get that a lot," I said, feeling my lips purse. He came nearer, and I saw his eyes flare from dark brown to watery gray. The bridge of his nose changed, and the position of his eyebrows. "Asher?" I guessed, with hope.

He put his arm companionably around me and turned to look at Dren. "I don't believe we've met," he said, putting his hand out. I watched his skin flow from shade to shade—and so did the vampire.

Dren took a step back. "I want nothing to do with you, shapeshifter."

"Then you'd best be leaving," Asher said, taking his hand back.

"This does not end things, Nurse." Dren turned and started striding away.

"I know," I said after his departing form. But what would?

I supposed that Asher and I together, talking to the same blank spot, looked like we were doing performance art. But the tide of people looking for last-minute deals was unrelenting, and soon people trolling for sales forgot about us. Carts and customers angled around Dren without even thinking about it, until he vanished into the darkness outside.

I turned toward my pseudo-Santa. "How'd you get him to leave?"

"I wasn't born being called Asher. It's a nickname. The vampires think of my name like a verb."

"Oh." Asher had sort of saved my life once before. We'd also slept together, before I knew he was a shapeshifter, and before he knew that I knew what that meant. "Well, thanks. And thanks for the other time, too. And for the flowers at the hospital."

"You're welcome." He grinned at me. I hadn't seen him wear this face before. I wondered whose it'd originally been. I'd never seen him in less-than-superbly-chosen clothing before now.

"That shirt is hideous." Maybe it'd come with the face's original owner.

"It's seasonal," he protested. "And you look just as festive."

"I'm going to work tonight." I had on two pairs of long johns and one white turtleneck beneath my green hospital scrubs, and my coat. I'd decided to convince myself that the spots on it were pre-existing stains, and not dried were-wolf blood.

"Really? That's tragic."

I shook my head. "It's holiday pay. After this, there's a holiday drought till Martin Luther King."

"You forgot New Year's Eve."

Not in the least I didn't. "Yeah, well, I'll be busy that night, it seems."

"Kissing strange men under mistletoe?"

"Doubtful." I turned back toward the aisle to contemplate my couch cover choices.

"You're not worried about the psychotic and pissed-off vampire that you've irreparably damaged for the rest of his immortal life?"

"I'm guessing I'm safe for tonight. I'm more fearful of dealing with my family tomorrow." I pulled down a couch cover. It was large enough to cover my couch, but it had stripes. I didn't want to commit to stripes. Plus, it was fifty dollars.

"Wait, you're working, and they're still coming over? You're not cooking, are you?"

"No." I didn't cook ever, unless turkey sandwiches and peanut butter and jellies counted. "My mom's coming in. I'll only have to deal with my family on the most stressful day of the year after just two hours of sleep."

"That doesn't sound fun."

"It won't be." I went up on tiptoes and reached to the back. There was a black couch cover there. It wouldn't go with my decor, slight as it was, but it was cheaper. Thirty. I glanced over at Asher, watching me. "What're you doing for Christmas? Actually, why the hell are you here?"

"Would you believe Santa sent me?" He touched a spot on his shoulder, and the LED lights on his shirt blinked on, winking green and red.

I rolled my eyes. "No."

He shrugged. "I go where the people go. Where there are crowds. The more people I touch, the more options I have," he said, wiggling his fingers out toward me. I danced backward and he laughed. "Don't worry, you've got your badge on you somewhere," he said.

He was right, I did. The badge that got me into Y4 also proved I was a noncombatant to the creatures that honored such things. Remembering his arm around my waist. It hadn't been skin on skin, but: "You touched me!" I protested.

"Of course. But you've got a coat on." He looked around. "It's harder this time of year to find skin. That's why I go to the dance clubs."

Which was where we'd met. No one danced in thermals, not even in icy Port Cavell.

I started walking toward the register, and he followed. "How come it doesn't drive you mad?" The only other shapeshifter I'd had close contact with had been a patient at Y4, and they'd been driven insane after touching too many vampires. It'd overloaded whatever it was inside of them that kept them *them* . . . and what'd been left hadn't been pretty.

"I maintain a smug sense of superiority, no matter what form I am in. It helps." He offered me his elbow. "Want me to walk you to your car?"

I'd slept with him twice, when he'd been hot, olive-skinned, and vaguely British—and here he was looking like somebody's dad, maybe even somebody's grandpa. He was the opposite of sexy—doughy, and that shirt, oh, that shirt. I wasn't sure which of them was harder to deny. Sexy Asher was wicked and tempting. This Asher was more likely to be disappointed in me if I didn't take him up on his offer, which might be worse.

"Sure."

"Want me to get that for you?" he pressed, reaching for the couch cover and his wallet at the same time.

"No."

"You sure?" he said looking down at me. His eyes seemed his own, no matter what the rest of him looked like. He clearly remembered the cheap apartment complex where I lived.

I still had a full jar of peanut butter and jelly at home, half a loaf of bread, and my pride. "Yeah, I'm sure. Thanks."

Asher walked me to my car, and there were no angry vampires in sight. I stared at my shoes, concentrating on not slipping on patches of ice, and contemplated my chances of survival. It wasn't till I was almost at my car that I realized how tense Asher was—mostly by the fact that he wasn't being glib.

"You really think I'm in danger, don't you?" I asked him.

The expression on his current face said it all. "If you don't, you're not taking things seriously enough, Edie."

"No, I am. I'm just being quiet for once." My cold fingers fumbled through my keys.

"Where's your zombie boyfriend when you need him, then?"

I looked at the ground and frowned. "He said he had to go."

"Spend holidays with his zombie family?" Asher guessed, the note of sarcasm in his voice unmistakable. "Is he going to come back soon? You shouldn't really be alone—"

"I don't know. He didn't say." Without meeting his eyes, I finally found my car key and unlocked my door.

"What? Edie—"

"He said he had to leave town, okay? He didn't make any promises as to when he'd be back. Or if he'd be back.

At all." I shook my head, remembering the night when he'd left me—it still hurt. "Too many people saw him save me. So he had to go."

Asher's voice was soft. "That's not right, Edie. You're not the kind of girl—"

"How can I get Dren off my back?" I interrupted. I didn't want to pull off any more scabs just now.

This version of Asher made a disappointed face at my predicament, then answered me. "You'll have to find something that Dren really wants and give it to him."

Like my life, or someone else's. "There's just no way."

"You could get the Shadows involved again—"

I shook my head. "I hate those things."

Asher shrugged. "All right. I'd offer you my people's protection, but I think I know how you feel about that already. Can't you just get that killer vampire friend of yours to take care of him?" He held his hand low to indicate how tall Anna used to be.

"I suppose I could. Maybe. Hey, have you ever heard of the phrase *Ambassador of the Sun*?"

"What is that, a shitty metal band?"

I snorted. "No. My vampire friend has her vampire debutante ball soon. She'd like me to have a position in her court. I wasn't going to take it seriously, but—"

"If it'll get Dren off your back." Asher finished my thought as I ducked into my car. "I've never heard of it before, but I'll look into it and get back to you."

"Thanks, Asher."

He performed a hand-twirling bow. "What kind of Grinch would I be if I didn't escort lovely ladies safely to their cars?"

I gave him a wan smile and closed the door.

CHAPTER EIGHT

Most roads were empty, so hopefully the hospital would be slow. I'd noticed before my transfer to Y4 that on holidays our workloads seemed to go down. Even truly sick people would rather be at home than here.

I parked in the visitor lot and went in. Our Charlie Brown tree was slumped in the lobby, but there were some gift donations stacked beneath it, and somebody had thoughtfully added a pine-scented car freshener to its cheap ornaments and tinsel. I walked by and wound my way down to Y4.

There was a note from our nurse manager on my locker. *You didn't complete attendance of your mandatory safety class. Your new class is scheduled January 10.* The date was underlined in red. I could feel the disappointment in her cursive. "I was only helping to save some guy's life, and then covered in were-blood. Sheesh," I said to no one as I pulled the note off my locker and shoved it into my bag. Maybe Charles and I would be rescheduled together. That would be nice. I took the knife out and settled it onto the top shelf of my locker just as Gina came into the room. She smiled as soon as she saw me.

"Merry Christmas!" She rummaged in a large red gift

bag and pulled out a smaller one to give me. It said EDIE
RN on the card.

I grinned for a second as I took it from her—and then
realized I hadn't even thought about getting my co-workers
gifts. I should have. I'd been in denial about this entire
holiday season, and now I felt like a heel. "Gina, I can't
take—"

"It's nothing big." Her voice was muffled by her locker.
She began humming "Up on the Rooftop."

I peeked inside the bag. Saran-wrapped cookies, oat-
meal and chocolate chip. "Awww, Gina—"

"See? You're welcome."

I teased the edge of the wrap up, and the scent of home-
made cookies wafted out. "You're awesome, Gina."

"I know." She pulled off her dirty scrubs and began
pulling new ones on. "See you on the floor!" she sang after
me as I left the locker room. I ducked into the bathroom to
pull my hair into a ponytail in front of the mirror, my heart
swelling a little bit with the spirit of the holiday.

Y4 wasn't decorated for Christmas, but someone had found
a small boom box and carols were playing.

Meaty's head rose up as I came through the doors.
"Edie! Happy holidays!" My charge nurse was a massive
human being with an androgynous face and an indetermi-
nate gender. As far as I was concerned, it didn't matter—he/
she/it had saved my life twice now, and I was pleased to see
them.

"Merry Christmas yourself," I said with a grin. I sidled
up to see the assignment sheet. "Room one? I'm not a
vet—"

"He's two to one. You're spotting Gina. Winter is
strong as hell—and he's important. The Consortium will
be watching this one."

The Consortium was the insurance group in charge of us, some sort of HMO for the supernatural. I'd never seen any of their representatives, but I figured that was because I didn't work day shift. I glanced back at the doctors' charts behind Meaty. Room one still said NO INFO. "We know his name now?"

"Unofficially. He's been here before. I recognize him." Meaty's voice sounded unhappy about that fact. "Gina's already getting report. Tell her he's Karl Winter—but we're not allowed to tell anyone else that yet."

"He's seasonally appropriate at least," I said.

Meaty snorted. "Get down the hall."

I hovered outside room one. Gina was getting a report from the prior shift's vet-RN, and their spotter was inside the room, holding a tranquilizer gun. I knew what my job would be for the rest of the night.

"Psst, Lynn—" I whispered, and the gun-holding nurse looked back at me. Her back slumped in relief.

"Thank God, and it's about time." She backed out of the room as I rummaged through the isolation cart outside the door, pulling on all my gear—a thin cotton smock, hair bonnet, gloves, and mask. Heat billowed out of the room, and I started sweating. It was going to be a long night.

I took the gun from her. She stretched and her back popped twice. I waved the rifle a bit into the interior of the room. "Is this really necessary?"

"Do you want to find out?" She stripped out of her gown and tossed it into the soiled linen cart. "The Domitor slows the change, but it's not perfect. And every minute of the day the full moon gets nearer."

"True."

She caught me looking at her, instead of the patient. "Eyes on the prize there, Spence," she said, pointing at her eyes then back into the room with two fingers. "Always keep him line-of-sight."

I nodded quickly, and did what I was told.

From my position near the door, gun at my shoulder but barrel pointed down, I could hear the end of Gina's report. In a way, I was relived to be holding the rifle—despite my poor track record in shooting things on Y4 and at the range, it was easier than managing eight separate IV drips. We were supporting him in every way possible, keeping his blood pressure up but not too high, tracking his insulin every hour, running in antibiotics that I didn't even recognize the names of. It sounded like Winter had a lot more wrong with him than just a straight trauma.

And at the end of it, I heard the term *LKA*. I blinked, and looked harder at Winter. Sure enough, under the sheets, his left lower leg was gone, amputated below the knee. The accident had turned Karl Winter into a three-legged dog. It sounded like it ought to be the punch line of some joke, but I doubted Winter would find it funny when and if he woke.

There was the rustling of paper and the chart check behind me, and then the drawers of the metal isolation cart slamming as Gina pulled on her gear.

"I don't suppose you got any range time in between now and the last time we did this." Gina's voice didn't sound like she was kidding. She was in nurse mode now, and although we were something that almost passed for friends, I wouldn't press things tonight.

"I was a little too busy to go through my allotment of bullets this month," I admitted. Our jobs at Y4 came with access to ammo and free time at the range. We both knew I was an awful shot. "I'll make up for it by standing close."

"Sounds good," Gina said, though I noticed the first thing she did was dial Winter's sedation up.

I watched her check the lines and then check her patient. It was strange watching another nurse do her job while I was hampered by the gun. The nearer she got to him, the tighter my finger felt around the trigger.

"How is he?"

"Rough." She shone a bright light into each of his eyes. "There's some brain function—he's initiating some breaths on his own, but the ventilator's doing most of the work of breathing. It's hard to say if there's anybody home."

"When will we know?"

Gina shrugged. "Full moon?"

"Oy." I tried to imagine myself standing here, a rifle halfway up my shoulder, on and off for the next six nights. I'd wind up having a hunchback.

"They think the bleeding in his brain's stopped at least."

"Why'd they have to take his leg?"

"Were-limbs are hard as hell to reattach. Their stupid healing powers—it's like working with superglue, and gluing your fingers together instead of your project. You stick the limb on, it adheres, but none of the blood vessels talk to one another on the inside, and then it gets infected and just falls off . . ." Gina's voice drifted off as she leaned in, listening to him breathe. "It's one thing if the patient's awake and can control himself, slow it down. Entirely another if he's out and he's in shock."

I waited till she took the stethoscope out of her ears to ask my questions. "Wait. I'm confused. Why didn't he just heal himself up at the scene?"

"The brain injury stuff—I think that prevented him. The surprise, then the damage—who can say?" She gestured to her own head, then looped the stethoscope over one of the IV poles. "Plus, he's old."

"He doesn't look *that* old." Sure, he looked sixty, but that wasn't that old nowadays. Hell, there were whole wings of County that were filled with people over seventy-two.

"Edie, he's the oldest were I've ever seen alive." She stripped off her gear and stepped outside. I walked backward and set my back against the doorjamb. My left arm was already aching from holding the rifle at half-mast.

"How old is he?"

"Fifty-eight."

"My mom is fifty-eight. Fifty-eight is the new twenty."

Gina snorted, which was nice because it let me know she still had a sense of humor. "Werewolves run down as they age. The metabolic processes their transformations require of them—it's not easy running like that, always overhot. They live in dog years. Our No Info is way older than they usually get to be."

"Oh! That reminds me—Meaty told me to tell you his name is Karl Winter."

Behind me, I heard Gina suck air through her teeth. "No wonder he looks familiar. Shit."

"Why? What?"

"He's the werewolf king."

CHAPTER NINE

"And I'm the Nutcracker," I said. There was silence from behind me. "Hello, Gina, that was funny—"

Gina groaned. "He's not only a werewolf pack leader—he's the only pack leader in town. He calls it a coalition, but they're not exactly a democracy." She pulled out the doctor's charts from his admit the day before.

"How do you know?"

"I'm the were-vet. Of course I know. Now I've got to double-check everything." She flipped wildly through the charts, reading notes.

I'd taken care of someone who was related to a senator in my former nursing life, a fact that that patient managed to work into each and every conversation. Nothing like the threat of being sued by someone who actually knew lawyers to strike fear into the hearts of hospital employees. "But this guy's No Info, right? So no one will know."

"I give it forty-eight hours. The Deepest Snow pack leader doesn't just go missing—"

"Okay then, you've only been his nurse for forty-five minutes. I think you're safe so far."

"You'd think, but I really like my license. Hang on."

I was quiet while Gina reviewed her work, watching Winter breathe, his chest lift matching the corresponding line on the ventilator.

"Okay. I think we're all up to date," Gina said at last. "I don't need to make any changes."

"Good. Can I come out now?"

"Yeah, I think that's best." She looked up from her charting, and squinted into the room and our future. "I'd bet money that within a day there'll be guards on his door."

"Too bad for you I'm too smart to bet against you. Plus I'm poor." I came out of the room, and she sealed the door, turning on the camera feeds. We could still look up at what was happening in the room—and hear things, as it turned out, when a pump beeped to warn it was running dry—while remaining safely outside the room.

"I'm looking forward to the end of tonight," Gina said around three A.M.

"I'm going to be a cripple tomorrow." I held up my right arm. "This is my mashed-potato-whipping hand."

Gina snorted. "I keep forgetting that it's Christmas."

"Me too. I'm in denial."

There was a lull in our conversation while she wrote down Winter's latest set of vitals. I stared at the monitor showing Winter's sleeping form. "Brandon said he has something big to ask me tomorrow," Gina said from behind me.

"Brandon?"

"The guy I've been dating, whom I don't talk about, so people won't judge."

I glanced over my shoulder, and Gina was still charting, but also chewing on the inside of her lip. I tried to figure out why she'd be sharing information with me now, and it hit me like a hammer. "Oh, God. He's a former patient, isn't he?"

"No. His brother was."

I wasn't sure how I ought to take that news. Did she want me to be the blindly supportive friend? Or the wise friend who told her she knew better? "He's not a vampire, is he?"

Gina snorted. "No. He's a were-bear."

There was another long pause between us. I decided to feel things out. "How long have you been dating him?"

"A while."

"What do you think he's going to ask?"

"I don't know," she said without looking up.

I couldn't seriously endorse marriage, for myself or for just about anyone. But that probably said more about me and my hesitant attitude toward commitment—and the fact that I rarely bothered to learn the names of men who shared my bed. "Well, just because my track record's been bleak doesn't mean you shouldn't try," I said.

"Thanks. I think." She stood up and shook herself, a little like a wet dog. "It's on the hour. Ready to go?"

"As ready as I'm gonna be." We both suited up.

"The thing is, when you were sleeping with a zombie it wasn't particularly contagious," Gina said as she shone a light into Winter's eyes again, one at a time, in case the size of either pupil had changed. Bleeds in the head would apply pressure to the nerves in control of the pupils—a blown or uneven pupil meant a fresh bleed.

"I made sure he didn't bite me," I said sarcastically. To be honest, I didn't know all the ins and outs of becoming a zombie. And Ti, my erstwhile boyfriend, had been the cursed kind of zombie, not a mindless ghoul. "I showed him my bra but not my brains. I think that was the trick." I went around the room to stand opposite from her, so that she never blocked my shot. I'd actually shown him a lot more than my bra, but I didn't want to embroil Gina in a TMI.

"Do you miss him?"

"I don't appreciate being ditched." No matter how much it might have been for my own good. Ti had rescued me at the end of my trial, and I knew he'd felt he'd been seen by too many people there, even before that, when he'd been out acquiring extra . . . parts. We'd walked through the hospital lobby looking like we'd been through a bloodbath, and a lot of the blood had been mine. I could understand why he felt like he needed to lay low for a while, but I didn't like being left behind. Even though we hadn't been together very long, him choosing to keep his cover over me hurt. Especially when he hadn't made any promises about ever coming back.

I felt foolish about caring, and then feeling foolish made me feel angry again. That anger shone too brightly for me to think of very much else.

"With Brandon, it feels real. As close as I think it's ever felt for me." Gina walked away from Winter to put the flashlight down and scan the IV pumps. "But if I date him—if it goes farther than that—the Consortium will step in."

I hadn't realized our extracurricular activities were that closely monitored. By the Shadows, maybe. But the Consortium too? No. "Where were they when I was dating a zombie?"

She made a face. "I mean it a little different from dating—"

An intercom I didn't know we had in the room turned on, and I heard Meaty's voice over it. "Ladies, incoming."

Gina's tone went from familiar to professional in an instant. "I knew it." She reached back and snatched the gun from me. "Go outside."

"What? Protocol—"

Gina started sweeping me out with the butt of the rifle. "Go, fast, now."

Frowning and not entirely sure I should listen to her, I stepped out of Winter's room, gown and all. "Gina—" I protested again.

She shut the door, closing herself inside.

CHAPTER TEN

"Gina?" I beat on the door with one fist. The monitor set beside the door flickered off. "Are you kidding me?"

There were footsteps coming down the short hall. I pulled my mask up and hitched up my suit to sit down in the chair like I was in charge of whatever situation was going on inside the room in front of me. Just me, nursing no one in particular, in complete isolation gear, just sitting in the hall. Fuck this. I frowned at the open charts.

Someone addressed the back of my head. "Where is he?" I turned on my chair and saw a squat bald man wearing a bowling shirt underneath a black woolen peacoat. "Where? I know he's here—"

And this was why Gina'd shoved me outside. My innocence would make me a better liar. "I don't know who you're talking about, sir." I quickly folded paperwork and closed charts, so that no identifying information was showing.

"You know exactly who I'm talking about." He reached into his coat, pulled out a phone, and typed a quick text with stubby fingers. "He's here, and you're keeping us from him." When he was done texting, he looked up at me, eyes narrowed. "The longer you lie, the more there'll be hell to pay."

Awesome. Just awesome. I inhaled and exhaled, taking the part of myself that might have felt outrage and stuffing it into a separate mental box. He was entitled to his anger, just like we had every right to be cautious. "I'm sorry, sir. You'll need to come back tomorrow, when the social worker's here—"

"I cannot believe you're keeping us from him." He came nearer, looming. I pushed my chair back. Being right wasn't always a guarantee that you wouldn't get hit. Behind him, a man and a woman, clinging to each other, rounded the bend.

"Jorgen. Stop that at once," the woman commanded, and he stepped back. I reached forward, grabbed everything off the desk, and set it into my lap. Then I pushed back again, out of swinging range.

The woman was older, blond going gray, wearing a navy pantsuit. Her arms were wrapped around the younger man, like he was supporting her. She looked around and moaned.

"Oh, he's here, Jorgen—just as I was afraid of." She reached out to the bald man, and he held an arm out toward her. Like a swinging monkey changing vines, she switched the men she leaned on, coming closer to me. "How is he? Is he okay? What do we know?"

"Nothing," Jorgen spat at me. "She won't even admit his presence. Despite the fact that I can smell him here."

The younger man took a step forward. He was my age, wearing casual clothing: jeans, an army-green hoodie.

"What can you tell us?" he asked.

"Nothing." There wasn't much protecting me just now. Meaty was around the corner, Gina was still inside, and the Shadows weren't known for being timely unless it suited them. I held all of Winter's charting to my chest. "I'm sorry. I can't say a word."

As if she had no spine, the woman slid down from Jorgen to bring her eyes level with mine. "You have to save

him. You have to do everything you can." Her eyes were
icy blue, rimmed with the red of tears, and she put her hand
on my gowned knee. Her fingers knotted with restrained
strength. "Everything. Just give him till the moon," she
pleaded.

The young man put his hand on her shoulder, until she
stood up. "Jorgen, Helen—let's go."

"But she knows things—" Jorgen protested.

"I'm sure she does. But we're stopping her from doing
her job. If he is here, we don't want that." He cast a glance
down at me, wrapping his arms protectively around the
weeping woman. "Keep him safe—and alive."

All that was in me wanted to nod, or comfort them, but
I couldn't. Officially, he wasn't here—and beyond that,
only foolish nurses promised things they couldn't guarantee. I wasn't a were-vet, I had no ideas about his outcome—
more good reasons why Gina was the one on the inside,
not me.

Jorgen eyed the whole hallway with dismissal, then
looked again at me. "We'll be back," he said. And then he
howled. His form was human, so the howl was misshapen,
a rough imitation of a howl. Helen seemed startled at this,
and the young man surprised. Then they joined in, their
howls more wolf-sounding, hers an alto, his a tenor, sliding
together up and down an otherworldly scale. I'd never seen
humans make those noises before—and remembered a
camping trip from a long time ago, with my family, my
brother, and me sitting around a fire, mocking wolves from
afar, trying to join into their distant choir.

The wolves here closed their eyes as they howled, like
they were praying, sincere. The howls reverberated up and
down the short hallway after they stopped, their own
echoes answering them.

When they were done, Jorgen hung his head. "He would
have answered, if he could."

Helen sobbed, and the young man pulled her closer. Conjoined in their sorrow, they walked back up the hall.

I waited thirty seconds, then knocked on the closed door. "Gina, get back out here."

The monitor flicked on, and she stood in it, front and center. "Still in one piece?"

"No thanks to you, yes."

The door to Winter's were-corral opened. "Hey, I was the one in here with the sick werewolf."

"*You* were the one with the tranquilizer rifle," I said. She laughed and handed it back to me, pulling off her gown. "Did you see any of that?"

"Yeah. I made the cameras one-way. It was a regular telenovella out here." She tossed her gown into the linen cart.

"Are all weres so . . . emotional?"

"Depends on the were, and the animal. Wolves? Yes. Cats? Not so much. Depends on the pack, too, and the family, and the percentage were, major, minor, bitten or born—"

"Okay, okay. Sorry I asked. What did you make of all that?"

"Makes me glad I won't be the social worker here tomorrow morning—and that I have tomorrow night off."

Wishing I did, I set all the charts back down on the small desk. "What now?"

"Now, I need a new bag of neo. If pharmacy hasn't sent one, mix one up, will you?"

I was thrilled to be asked to perform concrete tasks instead of lying to visitors. "Sure. Be right back."

The rest of the night was slow and report to day shift went quickly. All us night-shift nurses waved at one another again at the elevator doors before going our separate ways.

I saw Charles in the lobby walking ahead of me—he must have caught the previous elevator up.

I jogged to catch up with him as he speed-walked out the lobby's front door. "Hey, stranger—where were you last night?"

"With my patients."

"And you didn't come down the hall, not once? What is it, I smell?" I shoulder-checked him in a companionable way.

Charles kept walking quickly, so I double-timed to keep up. "No. Just keeping my head down. As soon as Meaty told me who that patient was—they don't pay me enough to take care of him."

"They don't pay us enough to take care of anyone," I said, my voice light. Charles ignored me. "Really, Charles. What's wrong?"

"That scar I showed you—I got that during the last were-war. Trying to stop them from fighting in the hall. They always say later they don't know their own strength, and that they're sorry. It's a fucking lie."

"I'm sorry, Charles," I said, because I was, and because I didn't know what else to say.

"It's not your fault. But just don't ask me for anything more than saline flushes, okay? And even then, I might just throw them down the hall to you."

"Okay. I'm a good catcher."

We waited for the light to change so we could cross to the parking lots. "I'm parked legally today, Spence. See you later."

"Merry Christmas, Charles."

"You too." He waved at me and headed toward the staff parking garage.

CHAPTER ELEVEN

I didn't like feeling as if I couldn't count on Charles—and I was afraid of anything that frightened him, instinctively. Charles was brave, smart, and strong. He was the nurse I wanted to be when I grew up, when I eventually would know it all, or at least know better.

I picked my way out to the visitor parking lot in the dark morning. The visitor lot always looked like a war zone. There were bags of fast-food wrappers, dirty diapers, crushed soda cans—all the trash people couldn't possibly be bothered to carry twenty feet to one of the many available garbage cans. The few trees that survived had birthdates of children carved into them, gang signs, profanity. ID bands littered the ground, like patients had chewed them off, or dogs had escaped their collars. Mucky snow wasn't helping things. I concentrated on stepping around numerous slushy landmines until I reached my car—and there was someone leaning against its side. A man wearing a green hoodie.

I was conscious of the wind blowing at my back as he pulled his hood down and looked up at me. "I'm sorry for catching you here like this," he began. "I know it looks bad."

Random weres surprising me at my car? Yeah. I made a face as he went on. "Helen's distraught, and Jorgen is only bitten—he can't scent his own piss unless it's by the light of the moon. But I knew this was your car, and that you'd come out eventually."

"You've been standing here all night?"

"For the last four or so hours."

It was easier to see him out here in the daylight, not the fluorescent lighting of Y4's halls—maybe I because I found it easier to breathe, surrounded by so much more space. He would be a few inches taller than me when standing, with short wavy brown hair. He had a strong nose that had been broken before—what did it say about him that he hadn't used his ability to change into a wolf to heal it?—and he was lean. He looked a little like one of my brother's junkie friends: not the addicted part, but hungry, haunted.

He pushed himself off my car. "How is he?"

It wasn't that I was bad at lying, although I was. It was that I hated doing it. I looked down at the slushy ground. "I'm afraid I don't know what you're talking about."

"I just want to know if he's okay. That's it. It's Christmas. He's my uncle."

His grief and worry seemed earnest, plus the standing outside for five hours in December—but it didn't matter. There was nothing I could say. Hospital rules and privacy laws prevented it. There was no way to know if this man—werewolf, I corrected—didn't have some part in Winter's state. Sure, he felt genuine, but I'd been conned before. Recently, even. I turned my attention to my purse and pulled my keys out, then walked to my car door.

He didn't move. I was close enough to feel how warm he was as I unlocked my door, his excess heat bleeding through his cotton coat. I could see the melt line on my windshield that a few hours of his body's warmth had de-iced for me.

"Is it really going to be like this?" His eyes searched me for answers, lips pressed thin, as I got inside my car.

"For right now, I'm afraid so." Ignoring him, I closed my car's door. He stepped aside.

CHAPTER TWELVE

The look in his eyes haunted me all the way home. If someone I loved, say my mom or my brother, was alone in the hospital, and I wasn't allowed to see them—but no. I'd done the right thing, and more important I'd done the legally correct thing, which was crucial for someone who wanted to keep her job.

I lost more theoretical sleep that morning hauling my new couch cover onto my couch. The directions were in Chinese, and Grandfather offered a few comments in German; both were equally unhelpful. Then I went back to my bedroom, switched into my flannel pajamas, and snuggled under the electric blanket. I didn't set my alarm—I figured my family could wake me up when they got there, and if they were late for some reason, then I'd be lucky enough to have slept in.

I was fast asleep until the doorbell rang.

"Oh, man." I looked at my alarm clock. Ten thirty A.M. A full half hour earlier than I'd expected them. Unfair.

I lurched out of bed and made it to the hallway. Usually I'd brush my teeth first, but it was cold outside, and I'd brushed them before going to bed, oh, two hours before. I looked out the peephole and saw Jake standing there, waddling back and forth like a penguin.

"What's the password?" I yelled through the door, just like we used to do when we were kids.

"*It's fucking cold* is the password." He stuck his tongue out at the peephole.

"Hey, don't lick the door, you'll get stuck." I opened it with a grin. "Come on in."

"Thanks." He came in and stamped around in my hallway. Every time I saw him he looked cleaner than the time before. Admittedly, today he was helped by the slightly newer coat he was wearing since the last time I'd seen him—it made him look more filled out, possibly a trick of the extra down.

"That's a nice coat."

"It's a gift from some kind soul."

I listened for the irony in his voice, or ruefulness, but didn't hear it. Maybe he was happy living on someone else's hand-me-downs. I'd gotten him some sweaters and new gloves. What else did you give a homeless person? I'd given him a couch to sleep on often enough.

"I thought Mom and Peter would be here already?" He took off his coat and put it in my hall closet.

"They said eleven." I went to the thermostat and turned the heat up. "How's things?"

"The usual." He sat down on my couch, and picked at the couch cover. "It's better than the bloodstains."

"About that—" I walked into my kitchen to preheat the oven—the faster we could get Xmas over with, the better for me, sleepwise. "They don't need to know, okay?"

I saw a familiar light in his eyes. "What's it worth to you?"

Oh, had we played this game before. I gestured to the empty space where my dining room set had once been. "Me not telling Mom where my table and six chairs went."

Jake rocked back into the couch. "Deal."

I frowned. I shouldn't have to make deals with him. Or apologize to anyone about anything. But he'd seen me a bit ragged lately, and while I didn't owe him or anyone else answers, I didn't want this dinner to degrade into a he-said, she-said meal. We'd had enough of those in our past already.

There was a knock at the door. "I'll get it." Jake stood, and I went to go put on Christmas-morning-appropriate clothing that wasn't footie pajamas.

"Jakey!" I heard my mom crow from my bedroom. "Where's Edie?"

"Getting dressed—"

"Go help Peter, will you?"

I heard her coming down the hall, and of course she didn't knock. Doors were foreign concepts for my mother, which was perhaps why Jake and I played the password game, to prove that boundaries existed. She blustered into my room. "Edie!"

"Hey, Mom." My mother, Shelly-Rae Spence (now Grinder), was shorter than me and much more petite. She'd called me strapping, growing up—not because I actually was, but because I was compared with her. She'd meant it as a joke, but I'd been an emo teenager and always felt self-conscious about being a moose to her deer.

"Merry Christmas!" she said, arms flung wide. I barely made it into my shirt before she hugged me. I hugged her awkwardly back.

"Merry Christmas. I preheated the oven."

"Always thinking ahead! That's why you're my favorite!" she told me. Jake and I were always her favorite, often within earshot of each other. "Peter, put the turkey in!" she yelled back down my short hall. "We precooked it this morning, before we bought it over," she confessed to me in a quieter tone.

"Thanks, Mom."

She patted my arm. "I know how you like to sleep."

I inhaled to defend myself, but she left the room before I could. It wasn't that I liked to sleep so much as the fact that I'd gotten off work *two freaking hours* before. But my mother and I had had this conversation on multiple occasions, usually when she called me sometime during the day before three P.M. or from other time zones.

I counted to ten backward, then followed her back out.

Jake was wrestling with the card table my mother had brought in, while Peter was in the kitchen. I didn't think I'd ever had this many people in my tiny apartment simultaneously before.

"It's a shame about your dining room set, Edie." She was unfolding chairs and setting them in front of the couch.

Peter pointed out at me with a potato-covered spoon. "Did you look on the Internet? Was that glass breaking some sort of manufacturing flaw?"

"Uh—I didn't even think of that, to be honest."

"Well, at the very least you should write a letter."

Peter, my stepfather, was the letter-writing type. He was the type who, when the waiter asked how the meal was, was always honest instead of kind, like he thought the cooks behind the counter actually cared if his burger was a little dry. If you ever asked him if your ass was fat, it usually was. He wasn't mean—he'd just missed out on some sort of filtering apparatus that most of the people who were more socially greased for life came with. Seeing as my biological father's social lubricant had been alcohol, I supposed I should be pleased.

I looked over at Jake—he of the original table's mishaps—who chose that moment to look away. "I'll think about writing a letter."

"Do." Peter smiled and nodded. He swept my counter contents aside to get to a plug, and there was the sound of potatoes being whipped.

* * *

My mother suggested we open gifts while things were re-heating. I'd gotten her the usual, a sweater and a bottle of her favorite perfume. My brother earned socks and a new backpack from Peter. I could see the mild disappointment behind his smile. Nothing said *New on the streets* like nice things. He'd have to rough it up some, or trade it in for something else. Peter didn't have any idea what it was like to be mostly homeless, and I didn't really either, except what I'd gathered from watching my brother and County's clientele.

Peter gave me a belt with a huge abstractly shaped silver buckle. "It's sure to be fashionable soon," my mom said, patting my arm as I lifted it out of the box. I spotted a gift receipt below and grinned. Returned soon was more like it.

My mother saved her gift for last. It was big and fluffy in that way that was always disappointing as a kid: a pillow from your least favorite grandmother, or a stuffed animal from your aunt. I ripped into the wrapping paper with trepidation and found—a lovely new winter coat. It was teal with large gold buttons.

"She got it last spring when they were on sale," Peter said, so I would know.

It was utilitarian, sure. But every single other coat I owned right now had someone else's blood on it. I clutched it to my chest and beamed at her. "It's perfect."

We were all together there, having some sort of cookie-cutter Christmas, only things were really nice for once. Peter was passing the stuffing when Grandfather started up from his current location, in the kitchen next to the toaster.

"What's that?" Peter asked.

"A gift from a patient's family," I lied quickly, and raced over to the bar. "I didn't know any German."

"Well, that's very kind."

"Wasn't it, though?" Grandfather didn't talk unless—I patted his lid in what I hoped was a pacifying manner and started edging toward my door. There was a knock, and it nearly made me jump out of my skin.

"I'll get it, dear—" my mother began.

"No! No—no—I've got it." I raced around my kitchen's tiny bar and teetered up on my heels to look through the peephole. Someone I didn't know stood outside. He raised his hand to knock again. I opened the door just an inch, prepared to throw my entire weight behind it to close it again if I needed to.

CHAPTER THIRTEEN

"And you are?" I whispered through the crack.

"You know who I am, silly." And for a second, his eyes flared brown.

"Asher! You were not invited."

"I just came to bring you a gift," he explained as I opened the door wider. "I didn't know—"

"You knew." I planted a finger into Asher's chest. "I told you last night."

Asher scratched his chin in contemplation. His current chin, one I hadn't seen before. He was normal looking, just a little on this side of average, clean-cut handsome sliding toward middle age. The Asher I was used to was chiseled-handsome with a fancy car; this version was more the man-next-door who probably knew how to use power tools. "Did you mention it?" he asked.

I gritted out in a low voice, "For a shapeshifter, you're a really miserable liar."

"Only when I want to be." He leaned in and pecked me on the cheek. It was unexpected—both from him and from this new form.

"Who is it, Edie?"

"It's—" My voice caught. I wasn't sure what to tell them.

"I'm Kevin. Nice to meet you all." He waved from outside while scanning around the room to include everyone in his wave.

"Well, come on in, Kevin!" my mother said.

"Oh, no, Mom—"

"It's Christmas, Edie—"

"I was really just here to drop this off." He handed me a box. It was tiny, but had a weight to it when I hefted. "To drop this off for my special girl."

My eyes widened at him—in anger and panic. *"Asher,"* I said, under my breath.

"Really?" My mother's voice reached new heights. "Did you hear that, Peter?"

"Any friend of Edie's is a friend of ours. Come in, come in," he said, waving Asher in.

Jake was the only one who wasn't fooled. He'd spent a week with me recently, helping me out after I'd been stabbed. He'd had the wisdom not to ask questions—and to be honest, I'd been able to handle most of my own care—but he'd known I hadn't had any boyfriends calling, either on the phone or in person, during all of that time. He set his shoulders and gave Asher the once-over, subtly jerking up his chin in manly acknowledgment.

Jake being protective of *me*? Now, that was a change.

"We didn't bring enough chairs, I'm afraid—"

"That's fine, because Kevin was going—" I said, trying to close the door.

"Edie! Why didn't you ever tell us about him?" my mother pressed, unashamed to interrogate me in front of witnesses.

"We just started dating," Asher began, taking a step inside. "It was an office romance."

My mother's bearing straightened. "Are you a doctor?"

Asher laughed. "No. I do computer work for County. Someone downloaded a virus onto a computer on Edie's floor, and the rest was history."

"A very short history." I sighed and let him in. "Come in."

Asher grinned at me. "I thought you'd never ask."

What followed was fairly painless, as these things go. An extra folding chair was hauled from my hall closet. My mother's cooking was excellent, as always, Peter pontificated on random topics, and Jake kept his head down. Jake was off the drugs—one look at him and you could see it—but while he'd been using, he'd developed an almost vampire-like ability to deflect attention from himself. No one wanted to know anything about my job—and if they did, as a nurse, losing their interest was easy. Most people didn't want to talk about piss, blood, or shit. And besides, my mother was more interested in my nascent "relationship" with Kevin and the currently vacant status of my womb.

"She's always been concerned with her career, Kevin," my mother began, apologizing for me. "But I'm sure if she met a good man, she'd settle down. She could work a normal job—there are nursing jobs during the daytime, my friend Frances has one, and her hospital even provides day care, she told me a few months ago at church. Do you attend church, Kevin?"

Asher did a much better job of answering to a strange name than I would have—I wondered if the forms he took came complete with names imprinted, like those written on the back of T-shirts for summer camp—but it was nice to see that my mother's stream-of-consciousness way of speaking could derail even him. He swallowed slowly, looking a little pained, like the piece of mashed potatoes in his throat had corners. I grinned maliciously across the table at him.

"Well, Mrs. Spence," he began.

"Grinder," Peter corrected, not because he was mad, but because he couldn't help himself.

"Mrs. Grinder," Asher continued. "I haven't been to church in a long time. But I was raised—and this will sound odd, I admit—half Catholic, half Pentecostal."

"Really?"

"Really. I spent summers with my Catholic grandmother, but my father's family are foursquare all the way."

Somehow I doubted that was the case. Sure, someone who'd imprinted on him had probably gone to church once upon a time, but—my mother squinted at him, taking his measure, then she glanced at two-hours-of-sleep me. "Well. As long as you practice some sort of religion . . ." At this late stage in the baby game, as I crested twenty-five and slid down toward thirty, she apparently couldn't afford to be too picky.

Jake's phone rang, and he excused himself to take the call.

The whole table held their breath—at least the part of the table directly related to me. Who called someone else on Christmas Day? Family—though I knew both Jake and I would make our calls to Real Dad later—or junkies, who knew no boundaries when it came to the necessity of getting high.

My mother glared at me. If it were up to her, I'd inspect Jake's phone bill each month, tracing calls back to their sources, making sure that each and every one was church-approved. Unfortunately for her, I didn't have that much free time, or any inclination. Despite things I'd done in the past, I was not my brother's keeper. As long as his minutes were under the limit, he could be calling the Dalai Lama. Then again, my Evangelical mother'd hate that even more.

"No, you should come by. Really. There's already other people here," we heard Jake say from inside my bedroom.

Asher looked from person to person, wondering what the rest of us were cuing on. Oh, dear God—what if he touched Jake, and after this would be able to rearrange his features to look like him? Or my mother? Whom had he passed a plate to tonight? Just when things were feeling normal—I should have known not to let my guard relax. Then again, after only two hours of sleep, what guard did I have left? I felt the blood drain from my face.

"Edie?" Asher asked.

"It's okay," my mother said, putting her hand out toward Asher's to pat it, an attempt to dissipate the tension we all felt in the room.

"No it's not!" I lunged across the table to intercept.

"Edie!" Peter reprimanded.

"I'm sorry. It's just been a long day." I took Asher's far hand safely in my own and pulled him toward me. "My family just has some secrets, is all. I'm sure you understand."

He looked down at my hand clutching his beneath the table, my knuckles white. He squeezed my hand back. "Of course I do, dear."

"Thanks," I said, but I didn't feel it. For all I knew, it was already too late.

Jake returned to the table, gesturing with his phone. "Sorry, that was my ride."

"We could drop you off, Jake," my mother began.

"Nah, you guys need to make good time." He said the words like he was mocking them, because he was.

"Well, at least let us make your mysterious friend a to-go plate."

"I, for one, want to know what Edie got," Peter announced.

I glanced over at Asher. There was a slight yet possible chance that he really had forgotten my family would be here today and had bought me something frivolous and personal. I wouldn't put it past him to embarrass me. I looked around the table, and it was obvious I wasn't going to get out of this.

I steeled myself, picked up the box, and shook it. Something heavy thunked inside, and I sighed with relief. The wrapping came off quickly, revealing a simple silver cuff. I had no doubt it was real silver, and the look in Asher's eyes confirmed it.

"For just in case," he said. In case I needed to burn anything that was allergic to silver.

"How sweet!" my mother cooed.

"It is. Thanks." I set the cuff on my wrist.

Peter looked to Asher. "I bet Edie doesn't have a single jar of silver polish in this house."

The doorbell rang, saving me from more cleaning tips. "I've got it—" Jake announced as I stood. He walked over and beat me to the door. "Hey, Raymond," he announced. "Raymond, meet my family. My family, meet Raymond," Jake added in his casual cool-guy way.

While my nurse radar was only in its infant stages, it didn't take much skill to know the guy on my stoop was still using. Raymond was a white guy with dreadlocks, wearing fingerless gloves—he looked thin, picked at, and strung out. My heart sank.

"It's been great seeing you, Mom, Peter." Jake leaned down and gave my mother a kiss on her cheek.

"You've got your leftovers, right?" my mother asked him.

"Of course."

My mom beamed at him. "I'm very proud of you, Jake." I knew this was how it began. Him moving back in—thank God for Peter. He'd put an end to the previously endless cycle of Jake leaching off my mother, getting clean at expensive rehab centers, and then getting dirty and disappointing her all over again.

I knew it it was my time on Y4 that had gotten him clean and my continued employment that kept him that way. As long as I worked on Y4, the Shadows would stop him from getting high. Not that that had stopped him from trying. You could say my brother lived in hope.

Still, I'd almost been proud of him today too—until I'd found out who he'd be hanging out with tonight.

CHAPTER FOURTEEN

Asher stuck around to help load the card table and chairs into my mother's SUV. Then, confident she was leaving me in good hands—and probably warring with her twin urges for me to stay celibate until I was married, while being profoundly hungry for grandchildren—my mother and Peter took off, my mom waving wildly through the window until they were out of sight.

I sighed and looked back at Asher.

"Can you change into you?"

Asher shrugged. His shoulders widened and he became two inches taller. The shirt wasn't part of the show, and now it clung to him tighter than it had before, filled out by his chest instead of the beginnings of a potbelly.

I wanted to ask, *Is this really you?*—but that was the thing with Asher. I'd never know. I knew some girls went in for mystery, but Asher's ability to shapeshift went beyond.

I couldn't not think he was handsome, though. Beautiful dusky olive skin and coffee-dark eyes, and an English accent at will. I sighed. "If my mom had thought I was dating you—or this you—instead of Kevin, she'd never forgive me till the day I died."

"Is that a complicated way of saying you find me handsome?"

"It's a complicated way of saying it's complicated." I walked past him to sit on my couch. He sat down beside me. "Why is my brother hanging out with such losers?"

"You know that guy?"

"No. He's probably someone Jake met at the shelter. But I know his type. Not all of us need to touch people to know who they are."

"Who else is he going to be friends with? It's not like homeless people are upwardly mobile."

"You sound like Peter."

"I could."

I whirled on him. "You didn't, did you?" I wasn't sure what verb to use for Asher's ability to absorb other people's spirits—if that was even the word—and look like them.

"I meant I could talk like him. Something tells me he's pretty easy to imitate." Asher leaned forward. "Did you really think I'd copy your mom?"

I shook my head back and forth. I wasn't sure if I was negating him or negating me. "I didn't know. You didn't, right?"

"No, of course not."

"Would you tell me if you had?"

"Not if it would upset you. But I didn't, so it doesn't matter." He gave me a cryptic smile. "I found out what an Ambassador of the Sun is for you."

"Way to change the subject. Do tell."

"Keep in mind that my people can't impersonate vampires, just daytimers—and sometimes that gets us into places while other times it just gets us tortured and killed. Still, the last time anyone saw one of these ceremonies, from the periphery of the room, it looked like there was a lot of blood, and some churchy statements about the Ambassador being the vessel who kept the remnants of their humanity."

"In a jar? Or a scrapbook?"

"The memories are hazy. It was a long, long time ago."

"Is it in a record book I can read?" On the off chance I could make more sense of it, reading it personally.

"Shapeshifter records don't work like that. It's more of an oral tradition, let's say." He tugged at the confines of Kevin's shirt, pulling at a too-tight sleeve.

I realized that me forcing him to be something he wasn't just because it was what I was comfortable with was lame of me. "You can change into someone more comfortable, if you want to."

"No, it's okay. I need to go." He pulled his shirt down one more time, then paused. "Unless—" he said, looking at me, lips spreading into an easy, hopeful, smile.

I was flattered to have his attention, and then just as quickly ashamed to be pleased. I told myself there was nothing wrong with recognizing you were sitting next to someone beautiful. My recent loss hadn't frozen my heart or made me blind. And I knew from work that people expressed their grief in different ways. I could take him back to my bedroom and express quite a lot between now and the time I had to go back to work tonight. It might not be guilt-free later, but he was the type of partner to ensure that the ensuing guilt would be worthwhile.

My phone rang. I quickly went to answer it. It was County's automated system, asking me if I wanted to come in four hours early for a half shift. "Yes," I told it, and then hung up. "Work called. They need me to go in early tonight," I explained, apologetic, pocketing my phone.

Asher rocked to standing. "Some other time then, maybe."

I didn't want to promise anything, but I also didn't want to close any doors. "Maybe," I agreed, walking over to my front door. He pulled on the coat that he'd worn coming over, luckily Asher-sized. "Thanks for the information and the bracelet, Asher."

"You're welcome. Thanks for lunch."

We were both in my short hallway, crowded together as he passed. I didn't know what I ought to do, but I felt like I should do something. I leaned up and pecked him on the cheek, much as he had me when he first came into my home. He looked startled, then theatrically dismayed.

"How did I, the great Asher, fall into the friend zone?"

"By being a friend." I opened up my front door. "Don't worry. The sex zone still sometimes sends cookies and the occasional rescue ship."

He looked down at me, an amused smile lifting his beautiful chiseled cheeks. He stood close for a second, close enough for me to smell his vetiver cologne, and then stepped outside.

"Merry Christmas, Asher."

"See you around, Edie."

I stood in my doorway until he made it into his car safely, then watched him drive away. I wondered if I'd made the right decision. Sometimes the best way to get over being hurt was to rip the Band-Aid off, after all.

But there was nothing to do now but nap. I set my new bracelet into the box Anna's knife had come in, and then I tried to sleep.

CHAPTER FIFTEEN

Tons of people came down with the Christmas Flu. Other popular sick days included Thanksgiving, New Year's Eve, and the Fourth of July. If you couldn't personally come down with an illness, you could always count on a family member, or spontaneously need to care for an incontinent cat. I knew our nursing office wasn't allowed to ask why people called in sick, due to some union provision against doing so, which would be nice if I ever got to take a mental health day. I could blame blindness—I just couldn't see going in.

I was as tired as I thought I'd be when I got up, and drove to work in a blur. Reaching the visitor lot, I got a spot close to the door—unsurprising, since it was still the holiday—and pulled in. For the rest of the world, it was still Christmas Day. For me, Christmas felt like yesterday, and today felt like it was everyone else's tomorrow. Working night shifts did something awful to your sense of time if you didn't try to fight it, and it was especially hard in winter, when it was cloudy and dark. Today was no exception. The sun was almost gone, just a dull pressing lightness, like the beginning of a migraine, hiding behind thick clouds.

I got out of my car, locked it from the inside, closed my door, and headed toward the lobby. Someone was outside on the small patch of lawn, retching their guts out into a garbage can. Nothing like the holidays for alcohol poisoning. I picked up my pace before they could recover for long enough to stop me for directions.

The bright lights of the lobby made a man standing inside the first set of automatic doors cast a long shadow. He wore a high-collared trench coat and a wide hat with a low brim. At my approach, his head tilted up and I saw his face.

Shit. Dren.

"Hello, Nurse."

I was overwhelmed with a deep sense of unfairness, the earnest and befuddled kind that you usually only feel when you're a child. This was my home—sometimes even more than my apartment was. How dare he come here, now, threatening me. My jaw clenched.

"Your brother sleeps at the Armory every night," Dren informed me. "I suppose it's better there than the cold ground outside, but what's the matter, Nurse? Don't you love him? Or is he why you're here?" He looked back into the lobby beyond.

"Stay away from my family, Dren."

"Why should I?" His eyes glittered with amusement at my discomfiture. "You still owe me."

"I don't know how you expect me to repay you when I don't have anything to repay you with."

"Ah, but you do, and you'll pay the price I ask," Dren began. He leered, and I could see his fangs, longer than his other teeth. "We hear King Winter himself is in repose on your floor. Get me royal werewolf blood, or I'll drain your brother dry."

I swallowed and took a step back. "But—you can't—you're not allowed."

"Just because it's not allowed doesn't mean that anyone will stop me in time. Trust me, I can be quite fast."

He unholstered the sickle he wore and twirled its handle in his one good hand so the blade made a golden circle, spinning in the light. "I wonder if royal blood is really blue?" He rolled the *r* in *royal* with mocking condescension. "I've never eaten that high up the food chain before."

"But—why?"

He stopped spinning the blade and tilted his head to look at me in an insectile fashion, far removed from any humanity I knew. "It's that or your brother's life. Does your curiosity matter?"

If Jake fell by himself again, I could maybe stomach that. I'd been instrumental in keeping him afloat for so long, no one could blame me for being tired. But if I had a part in his death because of something I could have done here? I would never forgive myself. There was pride in my work, and honor . . . and then there was family. "How much?" I heard myself ask, before I'd even fully thought it through.

"That's my girl. Let's say a fat drop."

"Wet or dry?"

Dren laughed cruelly. "Surprise me."

I had no idea how I was going to smuggle blood out of a room where I wasn't the primary nurse—one that might, if Gina's guess was right, have guards outside the door by now. "If I do this, are we done?"

"Oh, no. You'll still owe me—but we can deal with those payments later." He holstered his weapon.

I inhaled. "Dren—tell me why?"

"If I told you now, I'd have to kill you, girl, and that's the truth." He pondered for a moment, for show, flipping the collar of his coat up against the dregs of the evening sun. "I would say I wouldn't enjoy it, but that would be a lie."

He tugged his hat brim lower and walked out into the last of the day.

* * *

Fuck fuck fuck. I considered things on the elevator ride to Y4. Luckily, since I was coming in for the end of a P.M. shift, the locker room was empty. I checked the bathroom too, just in case, then made a furtive call.

"Daytimer central, here for all your nefarious deeds," a woman's voice answered me in a singsong.

"Sike? Is Anna there?" I said.

"She's in seclusion," Sike said. It sounded like she was packing in the background—drawers were being opened, and fabric rustled.

"Sike, I saw Dren."

"Really?" She made a thoughtful purring noise. "I haven't seen him in a while. How is he? Does he seem lonely?"

"He wants me to get him a sample of werewolf blood from the hospital."

"Hrmph. No accounting for taste." The sounds of packing continued.

"He says if I don't do it, he'll drain my brother." I couldn't tell her precisely what was happening on Y4 right now, but surely she understood why I'd called. Just because I wanted Anna to thrive didn't mean I wanted to be bullied by the whims of every other vampire.

"That sounds like a moral quandary for you." There was the sound like the closing of a closet door.

"It's not." I frowned at the locker room floor. Should it be more of one? It should, and yet—"Sike, after Anna's ceremony, will you all be able to protect me from him?"

She paused in her actions again, on the far end of the line. "I don't know. We'll need to talk to Anna. But—"

"She's in seclusion. Great."

"You'll have your answer in less than a week. And what's a little blood between friends?" Sike said, hanging up. Sike and I hadn't gotten along the past few times we'd met. I don't know why I'd thought this phone call would be an exception.

My phone's screen jumped to show me the time. I was late. Fuck.

I changed scrubs and put my leftovers in the Y4 break room fridge, then ran up to trauma ICU, repeating a mantra to myself: *Only four hours, holiday pay, only four hours, holiday pay.*

It's always strange to be a float on another unit. I'd floated around enough to be able to find a saline flush within twenty feet of anywhere in the hospital, but each floor had its own peculiar habits, and its own people you learned you did not want to cross.

I knew from prior experience that the charge nurse for the trauma ICU was one of them. You know how some people played the game where they added the phrase *in bed* at the end of fortune cookies? You could add the phrase *are you stupid?* to everything she said. She just had that intonation.

I pushed through the doors and made my way to the charge nurse's desk.

"Edie Spence, I'm floating here tonight."

The charge nurse ignored me. "You're late." *Are you stupid?*

"Sorry. Traffic." We both knew on Christmas Day, it was a lie. She pointed without looking up.

"Your assignment's on the board, your break is at nine. Don't be late, or you won't get it."

"Gotcha. Thanks."

I wrote down the room number I was responsible for and trotted down the hall.

Trauma was always loud—even louder than Y4, and the noise here was around the clock. I'd never been here before when there wasn't an admit going on, and someone being discharged to make room for someone new. There were the normal hospital sounds, machines, pumps, ventilators, but above and beyond that—chatting, crying, chatcrying. Visitors. They were what sucked most about coming in early. Visitors were never good. Even when they were happy there'd always be something. It was one thing to consider yourself a highly skilled waitress with access to narcotics—it was another for someone else to treat you like it. Repeatedly.

Still, it was Christmas. And sad things were happening here, by virtue of the fact that it *was* trauma. You could ask visitors to tone it down, but you could hardly throw them all out.

I made my way down the floor to my assignment. I wasn't very surprised when my echolocation of the loudest visitors found them inside my room. Of course— because I was the float.

As a float nurse, you were either given the easiest patients because they didn't trust you, the hardest because they didn't care if you drowned, or the ones with the worst family members, because everyone else was over dealing with them. I stood in the doorway of my assigned room and looked inside.

There were rosaries hanging on all the IV poles. An entire Latino family was in here, but most of the noise came from one older woman crying, wailing the ancient refrain of *Why God, Why.* Everyone at the hospital wanted answers from God, and He was never around to give them. She looked up at my entrance, and I could see where her tears and overzealous use of Kleenex had completely wiped away one of her makeup eyebrows. An older man was pacing beside her, and a younger woman stood at the head of the bed, petting my patient's cheek. The nurse I was replacing was across from her, programming an IV pump.

"Hello?" I knocked on the doorway, and the nurse inside came out.

She kept her report brusque and devoid of emotion. *Seen it all, done it all* was the motto of the trauma ICU nurse. *Innocent bystander syndrome. Gangbanger fight. Gunshot wound to the spine. Paralyzed now, and losing sensation as the swelling continues. On pressors to keep his blood pressure high.*

The trauma from the gunshot, the bullet's cavitations, or the subsequent swelling had done an odd number on his spine. It had already rendered him unable to move, and as his injury progressed his ability to feel was being stolen away from him, one centimeter at a time. The outgoing nurse and I checked the IV drips together and probed along his side. When we found the spot where feeling ended, we drew another dot with a purple Sharpie, like we were turning him into a connect-the-dots paper doll, one dot after the next. The wailing in Spanish didn't stop.

I took advantage of the old nurse leaving the room to leave myself, co-signing the chart, rifling through the history and progress notes.

Truth was, I was hiding.

In nursing school we went to some cultural classes, but they weren't so much about learning about other cultures as they were Being Nice to people with different beliefs. That part had worked so well that I could now Be Nice to vampires, so surely I could deal with anything here. But part of me always remembered that time I'd asked a patient if he was *frijoles,* instead of *frío.*

I read the chart for a bit, trying to look official, and found out what I already knew: Javier Rodriguez, male, aged eighteen, was inside. And this would be the last night he had feeling below his neck.

I closed the chart, said a silent prayer hoping that the doctors had already answered all of the hard questions in eloquent Spanish, and went inside.

CHAPTER SIXTEEN

Javier had short dark hair and wide shoulders. He was dressed in a hospital gown and had a plastic collar on, protecting his neck from any pressure or torque.

Standing over him and stroking his hair was his sister—or maybe his girlfriend. She was strikingly beautiful. High, precise brows over wide, heavily made-up eyes; lips outlined in red, with the lipstick fading in between, from time spent kissing Javier's forehead. Her straight black hair spilled down the bed to his armpits.

"Hi. I'm Edie, I'm going to be your nurse for the next four hours," I said over the sound of his crying mother. He grunted.

I ran the blood pressure cuff, took his temperature, felt for pulses, listened to lungs. A small dressing beneath his right clavicle was stained with the color of old blood. I took a Sharpie and drew its boundaries, just in case it opened up again.

"Are you in any pain?"

Javier flicked dark eyes toward me, then back at the ceiling. "No. Never."

The woman standing beside him nodded and resumed petting him. His mom kept sobbing, wordless sounds.

"Is there anything I can do for you?" I asked him, then included the room at large.

"Café," said the not-crying woman. She was definitely the girlfriend. I knew from the way I saw her look at him now.

"Certainly," I said, and retreated out the door.

I walked down the row of other rooms on the trauma floor. None of them had happy people inside. That, multiplied by the time of year, made everything particularly grim. I went to the room labeled NUTRITION, like it was from *Star Trek,* and made an instant coffee. While I was loading up an extra Styrofoam cup with powdered creamer and sugar, the overhead intercom announced that visiting hours were over for the night.

The charge nurse called to me as I passed her desk on my way back. "Hey, float. Send all those people home."

It took me a second to realize who she meant. "All of them? Can't someone stay?"

"We don't allow that here."

I frowned at her. She didn't look up to see it. "He can feel things now but by tomorrow morning, he'll be insensate," I said.

"So?"

Seen it all, done it all, are you stupid? I tried another tack. "It's Christmas."

"Only till midnight. Then it's December twenty-sixth."

"So someone can stay till midnight?" I asked, trying to work in some innocence and charm. I really didn't want to be the bad guy. Not this time.

She stopped typing and turned toward me. "One person. And that person better have a ride home, we're out of bus passes."

I'd take what I could get. "Okay. Thanks."

She went back to typing on her computer, without response.

* * *

I slunk back to Javier's room with the good-bad news. "I got permission for one of you all to stay till midnight." I hated myself a little for hoping the designated visitor didn't wind up being his mom.

"Luz," Javier said, in a whisper. I was sure who he meant.

Javier's mother started crying again, and blotting at her face—at this rate, the other eyebrow didn't stand a chance. I stood outside the room while they said their good-byes. They hugged him. It would be the last time he was able to feel it. There was a knot at the back of my throat, and all the swallowing in the world couldn't get it to go away. I felt like I was spying, so I opened up my chart and tried to disappear.

"Pretty girl. Pity she's with him," said a person standing next to me. I startled and looked up.

Sike stood beside me. Sike was a Rose Throne day-timer, and while Anna trusted her, I did not.

In her day job, Sike was a model and as such professionally gorgeous, but right now she wore little makeup and her red hair was pulled into a high bun. A dour lab coat covered her slender frame's soft curves. The name VERONICA LAMBRIDGE was embroidered on the pocket over the words LABORATORY TECHNICIAN. I knew Sike was neither Veronica, nor a lab tech. She patted the white lapel. "Fits nice, doesn't it?"

I looked around at the floor. "You should have called."

"Oh, I'm not here for you." Sike smiled at me, and her face didn't match her tone. "Let's not be an idiot in public. I'm just your friend from the lab."

"Lab workers and nurses don't fraternize." I hoped that "Veronica" was merely off duty and not stuffed into a trunk. "If you're not helping me, then why are you here?"

"I need you to take me to Y4." She put her hand on my arm just as Javier's parents walked out, the father propelling the mother around my desk and toward the doors. We were both quiet until they passed.

"I can't leave till my break," I whispered.

"When's that?"

"Nine. You've got an hour to kill."

It was obvious from her bearing that this was untenable. But there was no way she could drag me off in front of so many people without causing a scene. She wasn't a full vampire, just a daytimer, she didn't have look-away yet. She let go of my arm.

"Just go yourself," I said, massaging blood back into my tricep.

"I can't. The elevator doors won't open for me."

I pretended to read Javier's chart. "Has that ever happened before?"

"No."

Well. Saying that was not good was probably an understatement. "There's a lobby behind those doors. Go wait by the fish tank." She looked down at me, full lips pursed in frustration. "I'll come as soon as I can," I added.

"You'd better."

If it wasn't one vampire, it was another . . . in a manner of speaking. I waited until I was sure she was gone, then went into Javier's room for his hourly feeling check.

"Can you feel this?" I poked the cap of my pen against the side of his ribs.

"No."

"This?" I asked, trying higher.

"No."

I looked up at his face and saw his jaw clench, between answers.

"This?"

"*Sí.*"

I marked it. Another half a centimeter of feeling, gone.

It was like he was slowly drowning, no way to turn around, walking farther and farther out into an inexorable sea.

"Is there anything—" I began, because I had to.

"Just go," his girlfriend said, then added, "Please."

I nodded, and did so.

I noted his new loss of feeling in his chart. The charge nurse came by, I thought to break me early, but she handed me a printout from a news website instead. *Two Injured in Drug Deal Gone Bad,* said the headline, and beneath it, *One died en route, and one went to County, in critical condition.* I folded it in half, and stuck it under the chart, realizing how easily their problems could have been Jake's. Thank God that at his worst, he was always a user, not a dealer, at least not that I knew. Okay, so maybe I did look at our shared cell phone bill some—but only to see if he'd been dumb enough to use it to make too many calls to strange numbers.

An hour is a long time, sitting outside of someone's room. On Y4, I could have made myself useful, restocking things, making bedrolls, reading charts, but here I didn't know the flow, and didn't want to get in anyone's way. I doodled some in the margin of my non-official report sheet, sketching a flaming heart. When I heard a strange beep from inside the room, I looked up. Luz was texting on her phone, and she walked toward the door.

"I have to answer this."

"Just pull the curtain. You can talk in the room." There were NO CELL PHONE signs up all over, but nurses and doctors talked on them all the time—I hadn't seen an iPhone make anyone's pacemaker give out yet.

"No. I have to go."

I stood in her way. My break was starting in fifteen minutes. Sike needed me, for some likely unpleasant reason, and I needed Sike for some guidance. But if Luz left now and there was a break relief nurse sitting out here when she tried to come back who wasn't a softie like me, chances were she wouldn't get to come back at all.

She must have read my thoughts on my face. "You know what it's like to have obligations?" she said, the last word like it was an anchor.

I inhaled and exhaled. "I do. You wouldn't know it to look at me, but I do."

She nodded. "Then you understand. I'll be back." She chugged the last of her coffee, and walked out.

I spent five minutes leaning on the doorjamb. Javier couldn't see me from the bed. He was my only patient, which was something of a miracle for a trauma float shift. He shouldn't be alone, and I didn't have any honest excuses to leave. I took Luz's spot by the head of the bed, hauling up a chair.

"Anything you want to talk about?" I asked him.

"Not with you." A pause. "Nothing personal."

There was a fine line between joyriding someone else's pain, and trying to maintain an open channel of communication. Even I wasn't always sure which side of it I was on. But I sat there to show I cared, just in case it mattered to him.

The second hand clicked away. Sike would come looking for me soon. I hoped she stayed tactful, or her definition thereof.

I could use this time here to read the article the charge nurse had given me. Would it change anything, knowing who else had gotten hurt, or why they'd died? Not really. I had a job to do here, no matter the circumstances beyond. But sometimes I did wonder where that job ended. Did I ever really throw my scrubs into the linen cart and get to just go home?

I hunched over and set my elbows on my knees, deep in thought, as Javier dozed beside me.

Luz's return startled us both. She eyed me with suspicion as she entered the room, coming to stand by my side.

"Did anything change?" she asked.

"No. I'm afraid whatever they already told you still stands." I looked up slowly and realized she was shaking. "Are you all right?"

"I'm fine," she said.

I wondered if she was in denial, or if she was so used to being strong that she couldn't stop, not even now.

"Tomorrow, he won't be able to feel me?" she asked. I nodded.

"I'm so sorry." I couldn't even begin to comprehend her loss. Her anger was so palpable, so strong, it was like I could feel her very atoms vibrating—if pushed wrong, there was a chance she might fly apart.

"It's not fair," she said.

"No, it isn't," I agreed, because she was right. I turned to walk out of the room.

I made it three steps before she caught my arm and pulled me back, toward the half of the room hidden by curtains, and I let her.

"What do you think will happen if I give him these?" she asked in a whisper, holding out her other hand. She held four small glass vials, with a clear fluid inside.

"Depends on what that is." I tapped one, and watched it slosh.

"Luna Lobos."

I knew enough Spanish to parse that. "Wolf Moon?" I said, and she nodded.

"That still doesn't tell me what it is." I picked one up. "You can't give him drugs, Luz. You don't know what they'll do to him—"

"It's not drugs." I stared at her, and she went on. "I swear it. It's a booster. Like—the Red Bull with vodka. It's not the Red Bull's fault that the vodka is alcohol."

"Even if that's true, it's not a good idea. He can't sit up to swallow right now. You give him that, and he'll choke," I said, trying to sound stern, setting the vial back down. Truth was, the sum total in those vials was maybe two tablespoons of fluid combined. Hard to see him aspirating on that.

"You don't know what I've seen. This stuff," she said, rolling the vials around in her palm. "Sometimes it's better than the high." She closed his hand suddenly, making all the vials clatter. "It might make him better."

"You can't bargain his injury away."

"I'm his *hyna*. I have to try."

I didn't know what a *hyna* was, and I was still within my rights to kick her out of the room. This was why I hated visitors. You gave them an inch, and they'd take a thousand miles.

"Sorry." I put my hand out. "Give it here."

"Awww, no—"

I shook my head. "Give it here, or I'll kick you out of the room." I hated being a hardass, but there was no way I was going to let her give him medication, vitamin supplements, anything that wasn't by the books tonight.

She squinted at me in anger and dropped the vials into my hand. I popped them into the sharps container on the wall and stepped outside.

"I'm going on break now," I told the charge nurse. Hopefully Luz would be less pissed off at me by the time I got back.

"Come back in fifteen," the charge nurse said as I pushed through the doors into the waiting lobby.

* * *

"Finally." Sike stood when she saw me. She walked ahead of me to the elevators and pushed the DOWN button.

"I still don't get why you can't get to Y4 on your own," I said as the elevator arrived.

"Me either," she said and stepped inside.

We went through the warren of hallways that led to Y4, and reached the final elevator bank. "This is the one that wouldn't work for me," she said, pointing. I waved my badge in front of the door. It arrived, and we stepped in.

"The Shadows control our access. You'd have to ask them." I looked up, toward the recesses behind the lights set above. "Maybe they didn't want you to come down?"

"But now it's fine?" Sike frowned. "What's changed?"

"I'm here?" I guessed. The Shadows never did anything the easy way, not when the hard way involved more pain for them to feed on. Shit. "Sike—why are you here?"

"There's been a small accident."

The elevator doors opened, releasing us onto Y4.

CHAPTER SEVENTEEN

My home floor was chaos. The P.M. shift charge nurse spotted me from behind her desk. "Did they call you to come in early?"

"I'm on break from trauma. What's going on?"

"New admit. If you want to keep your dinner down, stay outside." I didn't think I had that as an option. "Who's she?" the charge nurse asked as Sike came forward. Sike opened her stolen lab coat, pulling some paperwork out of the breast pocket.

"I have visitation rights for any members of the Rose Throne on this floor."

The charge nurse snorted. "Figures. Room four."

Sike put her forms away and walked across the floor. I could leave now, my escorting job done, but my stupid, foolish curiosity wouldn't let me. I followed her in.

Doctors barked orders and nurses swarmed the room like ants: finding IV sites, hanging meds, setting up sterile surgical trays.

"Did anyone find the fingers?" a doctor asked aloud. "Any of them?" he went on, his voice rising. No one answered.

The patient sat on the bed in the middle of everything, arms exposed, face bound up in gauze, seeping bright red blood. A nurse stood beside the bed, clamping her gloved hands over the gauze where his ears would be, to apply pressure.

"And not a drop to drink," Sike murmured, then strode into the room. "The Rose Throne demands recursion."

The doctor stopped where he was, Betadine staining his gloves and his patient's hand orange-brown. The doctor was willowy, too tall, folded over the bed like a number 3. When he looked over at Sike, his face was stern. "You can't take him—he needs profound medical care."

Sike took off her lab coat and folded it over her arm. "Gideon Strand is the Rose Throne's property."

I blinked. The man underneath all the gauze was Gideon? The daytimer from my kitchen, with Anna? I couldn't tell. With all the gauze, I couldn't see much of anything.

"We demand recursion. I'm here on behalf of Anna Arsov, the near-ascended."

"I don't care who you are, lady. You're not taking him."

"Gideon," Sike said, addressing their patient. The gauzed man groaned in response. "Come with me." She snapped her fingers.

And like King Kong on the Empire State Building, he started to swat staff away like tiny planes.

"Restraints!" the doctor ordered, and a nurse ran off to get them. Technically—I should have. Or could have. But I didn't know whose side I was on just then—"Ten milligrams of Haldol stat! And get me a trank gun!"

There was an isolation cart right outside the door. I took a step back outside and made my choice—I put the code into the isolation cart and hauled open the top drawer. It unlocked, freeing the trank gun. I grabbed and loaded two of the sedative darts.

I went back into the room with the trank gun ready,

even if I wasn't sure whom I was going to shoot. Sike and the doctor were in each other's faces.

"I have every right to take him. He belongs to my Throne. We are responsible for his care."

"You can't possibly care for him. He's staying here."

Gideon was wrestling with the nurses beyond. One of my P.M. shift co-workers yelped as he made contact with her ribs.

"Nobody get injured!" said the doctor, and the nurses stopped trying. Gideon pulled himself out of bed and stumbled, unable to see where he was at or where he was going.

"I promise he will be better off once relinquished into my care," Sike said. "I have all the official paperwork." She presented her papers again, folded neatly in two. "It's signed in triplicate, in her blood. You have to comply."

"He's covered in wounds. Infection is a given—"

"He'll get blood."

We all knew she didn't mean merely human. "Do it here then," the doctor challenged her.

Sike frowned. "Fine. Leave the room. Now." Sike turned toward me and handed me her lab coat, then pushed Gideon back to sitting. I made to follow my co-workers but she called after me. "Edie—stay."

My curiosity had curdled to guilt and horror, but I did as I was told.

Sike sat beside him on the bed and blotted away the Betadine distastefully with the corner of a sheet. Then she reached into her pocket and pulled out a makeup compact, flipping it open to reveal what appeared to be a crème blush.

"Gideon, give me your hand."

She smeared her right thumb in the substance, then ran it along the edges of his wounds. One knuckle at a time began to seal. Only the first knuckles remained on that hand. I wondered with a sick fascination what was left of the other one.

"Sike—what happened?" I didn't want to see what was under the bandages covering his face. "And why?"

"Becoming a member of the Sanguine is not without trials." She continued to paint what was clearly a vampire-blood-based substance onto Gideon's hand, like a salve.

The enormity of his situation settled in. He had no fingers. Lord only knew what the gauze around his face was concealing. "Who did this?"

"If I knew that, I'd be killing them right now. Anna was asleep when he was damaged, and he did not see his attackers." Finishing with his nearest hand, she reached up to unwrap his face. "He was her first daytimer. Her eyes, her ears," she said, as his face was uncovered—his eye sockets were empty, hollow, and the shells of his ears were gone. "And now he is as helpless as a baby bird."

"But why?"

"Because she chose him."

"I thought they revered Anna?"

"Our kind buys reverence with fear." She loaded up her thumb with the salve again and pressed it into the moist concavity of his eye sockets. I breathed deeply to keep my stomach straight.

"So the Rose Throne isn't all one big happy vampire family?"

"The words *happy* and *family* do not belong in the same sentence as *vampire*." She traced the outlines of his mutilated ears. "But this wasn't us. The Rose Throne is pleased about Anna's ascension. This was someone else."

"Who? And why?"

"I'll be trying to figure that out as soon as I leave here."

I swallowed. I didn't want to think of myself just now, but—"Whoever did this—could they come for me?"

Sike paused in her ministrations. "I suspect that this was done for show. Harming a daytimer's much more of an affront than killing a mere human. No offense."

"None taken," I said. "Somehow, your explanation doesn't make me feel any more safe."

"You don't understand, Edie. Even without your badge, you wouldn't. She can hear him inside her mind, crying." Sike unwound his other hand and started to treat it. "Not killing him is worse than death, in this case."

"Make him into a vampire then—" I prodded. It was what he'd wanted—what all daytimers did.

"With a human, vampire blood can only heal so much. And there are some things that becoming a vampire will not heal. You cannot regrow lost flesh—things lost in life, unhealed, stay gone. Would you want to live forever, like he is now?"

And I remembered Dren, eternally pissed at me for the loss of his hand, and his task for me tonight. I shook my head, and she nodded. "You see my point."

Sike flipped her compact closed and pocketed it. Then she rewound the gauze around him, still bloody from the first time through.

"I can get you clean gauze, at least."

"It doesn't matter now." She stood. "Gideon, follow me."

Gideon stood and hobbled forward, like a stiff but obedient dog.

"Where will you take him?" I asked her, stepping out of their way.

She smiled cruelly. "Home."

CHAPTER EIGHTEEN

Even if I had wanted to eat on my break, I didn't have any time. The rest of Y4's P.M. shift looked at me like I was some sort of traitor, which I supposed I was now. I put the trank gun away after taking out the darts, tossed Sike's stolen lab coat into my locker, and went to wait for the elevator to head back up to trauma.

The doors opened and I heard steps from Y4 behind me. I hit the elevator's CLOSE button and held it. I didn't want to hear it from anyone else on my floor. At the last moment, a jacketed hand jabbed between the closing doors, sending them open again.

"Hey—" It was the were from this morning, the one who'd been leaning on my car. He shouldered his way into the elevator. I ran to the rear, putting my back into the corner. "No—look," he said, then saw me and stopped where he was. "This is pretty threatening, isn't it?"

"Yes." My hands were up, pushing him away, even though I knew there'd be no way I could win a fight with him. He backed up, keeping his hands spread wide to hold the doors open.

"I'm sorry about this morning," he said. I stood straighter and put my hands down. "I just didn't expect for anything to ever happen to my uncle."

I had no idea if Winter's status had changed—I hadn't

looked at any charts on my way out the door. "I'm afraid I still don't know what you're talking about."

"I know that you know." He gave me an exhausted smile. "Thanks for keeping him alive, last night."

"You're welcome," I said, unsure precisely what I was taking credit for when Gina'd done most of the work. He stepped back, then doors of the elevator closed, and the elevator rose up to the ground floor.

How lovely it was to sound honorable when I was 99 percent I sure would be bleeding his uncle tonight.

I would have sat down in the elevator to think, if it didn't stink of were-piss from all the visitors that'd marked their territory as they rode up and down. A curl of gauze rode with me, Gideon's, from his exit. It was half covered in blood and stuck to the floor. I'd probably stepped on it on my way inside.

I had no doubt that Dren would make good on his promise to drain Jake if I didn't comply. Vampires were only honor-bound where other vampires were concerned— humans and daytimers were replaceable, as Gideon had found out.

It wasn't the getting blood, so much as the not knowing what it'd be used for. Winter probably had enough blood now to spare—I knew we'd tanked him up with transfusions, ever since he'd been hit. But what would Dren do with the blood once I gave it to him? Dren was a Husker, a kind of vampire bounty hunter, which gave him some mandate to go around messing with people's lives. I spent the duration of the elevator ride up pondering what Winter's blood could possibly mean to him.

In the end, I supposed it didn't matter—because what it meant to me was that Jake would be all right. I'd saved Jake from himself too many times for me to let him down now.

* * *

I walked into trauma past the charge nurse's desk.

"You're late," said the charge nurse. "Again."

"Sorry."

"Just because it's a holiday doesn't mean you can break the rules," she said. *Are you stupid?*

"Yeah."

I made my way back to my assigned room. Luz saw me and glared. I sighed and proceeded to ignore her through my next assessment of Javier. He'd only lost a quarter of a centimeter of feeling this time. Maybe the swelling in his spine was going down. The dots down his side hadn't always been regular up to this point. Who knew.

I bided my time until shift change. Luz tried to get the next nurse to let her spend the night, like I thought she would, and was refused, much to both their chagrin: my replacement's, that Luz was still there to ask, and Luz's because she hadn't gotten her way.

I listened to their heated argument as I co-signed the chart. Tonight was going to be long for everyone.

The thought of holiday pay was no longer enough to sustain me as I walked back down to Y4. Between being tired, being hungry, and being disgusted with myself over Gideon, Dren, and Jake, I had no strength left to hold up my head.

I slouched into the locker room and changed my scrubs quickly, so I wouldn't bring strange germs back down. As if anything I'd seen in trauma could be stranger than my job here.

Gina came in, all coats and cold from the outdoors. I was surprised to see her. "You do realize there's no holiday pay after midnight?" I asked.

"Yeah, I know."

"Um. So how was the thing with the thing?"

Gina hissed out air through pursed lips, hauling off her outdoor gear. "Spent Christmas with my folks. Avoided Brandon entirely. I got called into work, and here I am."

"If I didn't know better I'd say you were exhibiting classic avoidance behavior. Or oppositional defiance disorder. I always get those two confused."

Gina snorted as she opened her locker. "It's a good thing you don't know better then." I headed toward the door of the locker room. "Hey, Edie." Gina called after me. "Thanks for asking."

"Sure."

I went out to Y4. Meaty was nowhere to be seen, but there was a ton of talking from the were-corral side of the room, around the bend. I found my name on the assignment board—I was with Gina again, and Winter, same as last night.

Meaty came back from the corral side of the floor just as Gina came up behind me. "Spence, Martin—break room consult now," Meaty said and lumbered off the floor.

"Marteen?" I said, pronouncing Gina's name with the same accent Meaty had given it. "I always thought it was just Martin."

"Yeah, because you're white."

"Why didn't you ever correct me?"

"Because I'm lazy."

"Which is clearly why you've gone through more schooling than I have, Ms. Doctor of Veterinary Medicine."

Gina rolled her eyes. "All those extra letters mean is I get to be the one standing nearer the teeth."

We reached the break room door together. Meaty already occupied the far side of the table, waiting for us.

"We all need to be on the same page here," he began. "First thing—we're trying to set boundaries on visitors, but day shift was a freaking circus. Between family members, gawkers, and people paying their respects—" Meaty made a disgusted sound. Each of us knew gawkers/family/respectors were often the same thing. "We've told them visitors have to leave for the night, but I expect it'll start up early this morning again. Second thing—they've started posting guards at the door."

"They don't trust us?" Gina asked.

"Deepest Snow doesn't trust anyone. Don't take it personally. Just know they're going to look at your paperwork and watch you with the eyes of a hawk."

Gina hissed in disappointment. "I knew I should have ignored that call tonight."

"Do we have to talk to them?" I asked.

"Only to answer their questions. Don't go looking for additional topics of conversation." Meaty looked from one to the other of us. "Last but not least, the family's produced a DNR."

"Oh, fuck," Gina cursed, and I groaned.

At this late stage in the game, Do Not Resuscitates were slippery fish. Unless you had yours on you, say tattooed on your chest when you collapsed, by the time you got to the hospital it was usually too late. Tubes had been installed to make you breathe—it was one thing for everyone to make an informed decision about not putting tubes in in the first place. It was another thing, after that, for family members to agree on disconnecting them.

"Does everyone agree?" I asked. The other thing about DNRs was that anyone could tell you to ignore them—from a wife or firstborn, right on down to a distant cousin. Anyone who had any need for closure could say stop, and pull the brakes on the death train.

"The nephew is recusing himself. The daughter is undecided. We're having a family conference tomorrow. I suspect they'll want to hold off until the full moon."

"Shitty way to spend the day after Christmas," I said.

"Shitty way to spend the next eight hours," Gina said, giving me a glare.

She was right. We would spend the night keeping him keeping on, but not have much room for error. If he crashed and we did extraordinary things to save him—all our good work might be undone tomorrow. And who knew how long he'd hang on afterward? We would drive his body right past death's station, and who knew when the next stop would be? I'd seen people with DNRs continue living for weeks, not just days.

Or if he did die, and the family hadn't come to a resolution yet, they'd be looking at us firmly. People experiencing sudden tragedy usually wanted someone to blame. Couldn't punish death or fate, but you could definitely punish staff.

"This is the latest MRI from this morning." Meaty flipped open a folder on the table, revealing a brain scan. I didn't need to be a neurologist to know that it wasn't right. A huge white spot took up space where normal brain matter should be. "After the accident and bleed, there's no room in his skull for anybody to be left home inside there. But not everyone in the family is ready to hear that. Got it?"

"Guards at the door. Shaky DNR, bad bleed. Got it," I said.

Gina put her hand out, like we were in a high school football huddle. "One two three, don't get mauled. Goooo team!"

I could get behind that. I put my hand on top of hers, and we pounded them together onto the table.

CHAPTER NINETEEN

I gathered supplies for any and all assorted tasks we'd have to do tonight while Gina got report. Pleths, dressing change kits, biopatches, line labels, one of everything, putting them into a pillowcase like a demented Santa. Less running around if things went bad—and with all these extra supplies, I'd be better able to exploit any opportunity I had to get some blood.

I realized I should have felt bad about it, or at the very least torn—but were-problems were not my problems. Jake and Dren were. Besides, how much harm could one drop of blood really do?

As I rounded the floor, I spotted something near Winter's door, in addition to the nurses exchanging report outside. A small black wolf curled up in the doorway, tail-to-nose. It had a puppy look about it, with too-big feet, too-fuzzy fur, and copper-yellow eyes. Beside it, taped to the wall, was a handwritten note that said, *My mom said I could spend the night.*

"Oh, my God, it's a wolf puppy!" Its eyes opened up and focused on me.

"It's a wolf *person*," Lynn corrected me. She and Gina finished their chart checks, and the P.M. shift nurses exited the floor.

I waited until they left and set down my supply bag.

I crouched down to see it better, without touching. "It's the cutest thing ever, Gina."

"The cutest thing that can bite your face off." She looked down at the small wolf. "No offense."

The wolf closed its eyes again. Gina had enough experience to treat the wolf like a person. I didn't. I'd have to get over that. But the cute was making it hard. I looked over to Gina and opened my mouth.

"Don't ask to pet it. That's rude," she said, without looking up from Winter's flowsheet.

"Damn you and your telepathy."

Gina made a face at me. "Get ready to go in."

We suited up. I felt weird having a wolf puppy watch me from the doorway while I kept a rifle with tranquilizer darts aimed at its relative inside. Now that it was standing, I could tell that it was a little taller than knee height.

"How's things?" I asked Gina while the wolf's ears tracked us both.

Gina didn't answer, but she gave me a thumbs-down, hidden from the wolf's line of sight.

I walked closer to the pumps—I could see we'd gone up on his blood pressure medications—and that a new one had been added, because the old ones weren't working well enough. His sedation was much lighter too.

"Mr. Winter, can you hear me?" Gina said loudly, right to the side of the bed. She shook him a bit, then did a sternal rub, checking for response to pain. He didn't move. "Mr. Winter?" She looked to me, gave a half shrug, and went on with her assessment. The wolf in the doorway watched with intelligent eyes, sitting on its haunches. I wanted to talk to it, and bit my tongue. Having a wolf out here was a brilliant ploy. We—or at least I—would say all sorts of things in front of it, treating it like a pet or an animal, not a person. And wolves were probably better at reading people—I was sure it'd known from Gina's stance how poorly Winter was doing, even before she'd said anything. A relative might rationalize away a nurse's actions, desperate for good news, but a wolf would know better, I figured.

"Junior! What are you doing here?"

The hoodie-wearing were whom I'd already met twice today rounded the corner, looking sternly at the wolf puppy. The puppy startled up to all fours, seemed excited for a second, then tucked head and tail down at his approach.

"Did your mother say you could stay like this?" he asked.

The wolf puppy looked to the note, taped on the door.

"I am calling her to come get you." The puppy made a whining sound. "You're not in trouble. She should know better." He stepped away to make his call.

The wolf looked to Gina and me. Gina shrugged. "Sorry, kid."

He came back around the corner. "Your mother's on her way. Do you have any clothing to wear?" The wolf lowered its head. "Well, hopefully she'll remember."

"We have scrubs," Gina offered.

"Can you take him and go get some?"

Gina looked from me, to Winter, inside the room. "Sure. Edie, stay here."

"Aye-aye, Cap'n."

Gina left the hall, the wolf pup padding beside her. Now would have been a perfect blood-getting chance, only the other were was still out here, in the way. He sat down in Gina's vacant chair and set his elbows on his knees. "I guess you know I know he's here now, right?"

I gave him a weak smile. "Yeah."

"I'm Lucas." He put his hand out, and I shook it.

"I'm Edie." I wanted to look through things and do

some work, but I didn't want to do anything wrong in front
of him. Visitor-guards made me self-conscious. "Are you
going to be here all night? Guarding him?"

He half smiled. "Is that what they're calling it? We call
it a vigil."

"Ahh. Sorry." There was silence filled by the hissing of
pumps, the inflation and deflation of the sequential com-
pression device on his one good leg.

"Do you think he'll get better?" Lucas asked, after a
time.

I inhaled, then paused before speaking. Breaking people
into bad news was a process, like drawing a new swimmer
out into the deep end of the pool. Sometimes people had
to be confronted with it repeatedly before it sank in.

"Your silence says it all." Lucas snorted.

"I'm not a vet," I explained. "I'm only a nurse."

"He's a man now, not a wolf."

"I think what will happen soon is you all will have to
decide what kind of life he wanted for himself—and what
kind you all want for him now," I said, choosing my words
carefully, showing him the deep end.

Lucas stared into the room. "How tactful of you."

"Sorry."

"Don't be." Lucas inhaled and exhaled deeply, as if
waking himself from a dream. "He just needs to make
it to the full moon. And the moon needs to heal him. It
has to."

"Why?"

Lucas made a face I couldn't completely read. "His
pack needs him."

I would have asked more questions, only Gina came
back around the corner with a barefoot boy in tow. "Here
we go." The boy was in extra-small scrubs; the sleeves
hung down low, and Gina'd had to cuff the legs. The boy
had bone-straight black hair with uneven bangs. The

copper-yellow eyes that had looked fine on the wolf were now out of place—downright creepy. He seemed timid, hiding behind Gina's leg. "Edie, meet Fenris Jr. Fenris Jr, meet Edie."

"Hi, Edie," Junior said, then to Lucas, "Was Mommy mad?"

"Not at you." Lucas stood up and pointed to the chair. Junior sat down in it, and Lucas wheeled him away, so he couldn't see in the door. "Let's see if we can find another one of these. I bet they won't mind if we run some chair races in that hall outside."

Fenris Jr.'s face brightened at this. Lucas was driving him off in Gina's chair when Jorgen came around the bend. He eyed us and Lucas darkly.

"What's the meaning of this? I just got a call from Helen."

"You left Junior here, alone."

"I had some phone calls I needed to make in private. He was only alone for a bit."

"It's not that he was alone—it's that he was here at all. Even as a wolf, he's too young for this, Jorgen."

"He's his mother's child," he said. Lucas's lips straightened into a line.

Gina cleared her throat to get their attention. "We strongly discourage child visitors."

The bald man glanced at her, then back to Lucas. "We need to transfer Winter to a better facility. He's not getting the best care here."

I blinked. That was the first I'd heard of it. And to think, I hadn't even bled him yet. Beside me, Gina stiffened in anger. Lucas stood straighter, letting go of Junior's chair.

As if by magic, Meaty came around the corner to join us. "Is there a problem?"

Jorgen looked from one to the other of us. "She consorts

with were-bears, and she's employed by vampires. Neither of them is acceptable. They both should be replaced."

Meaty appeared unfazed. "I would let either one of them care for me, myself."

"You have poor taste then."

"Jorgen, you forget your place," Lucas said. "I know your loyalty to my uncle runs deep, but now is not the time."

Jorgen looked at Lucas, and I remembered what Lucas had said that morning, leaning on my car, about bitten versus born. God, that seemed a long time ago. Jorgen looked like he was going to take a step nearer Lucas, then exhaled roughly, deflating.

"This nurse was one of the ones who found him. She saw the accident herself," Meaty continued, as if nothing had gone on. "She's been involved in his care since he first came here, isn't that right?"

I nodded, because I knew Meaty expected it of me.

"Nurses found him?" Jorgen asked.

"Why do you think he's still alive?" Meaty said.

"Did you see who hit him?" Junior asked.

"No," I said to the boy. "I just saw the truck. I gave a report to the police at the time."

"They need to get back to work, Jorgen. Take Junior upstairs to wait for Helen." Lucas nudged the boy to Jorgen's side.

Jorgen was still eyeing daggers at us, but I got the sense that he couldn't disobey a direct command.

Junior peeked into Winter's room one last time. "Bye, Grandpa Winter," and then he looked up and to us. "Bye, Gina, bye, Edie. Sorry you didn't get to pet me."

I gave him a smile. "Me too."

CHAPTER TWENTY

Without the boy and Jorgen radiating disapproval, the climate outside Winter's room warmed again. Gina's shoulders slumped, and she sighed. "I'm gonna go to the bathroom. Anyone want coffee?"

"Yes, please," Lucas said.

"I'll be right back." She pushed away from her desk and stood.

"Anything I can do while you're gone?" I asked.

Gina glanced at her chart and shrugged. "You can do a fingerstick."

I nodded. "Sounds good."

I turned to the isolation cart as soon as I could to hide my smile. A fingerstick was perfect. I'd go in alone, get a blood sugar on him, and keep the test strip afterward for Dren's blood. I couldn't have planned it any better.

Lucas came to stand beside me, startling me from my nefarious thoughts.

"He's that bad, eh?"

"How do you mean?" I tried to sound innocent.

"He's gone down from two nurses, one with a trank gun, to one nurse without a trank gun." His eyes searched mine. "You all don't think he's getting up again, do you."

"Um." I inhaled, and exhaled, glad my expression was hidden by my mask.

"Let me guess. You can't tell me."

"It's not that I can't tell you, it's just not my place. I might do it wrong. Hell, I might be wrong. I don't know how the moon works on your kind."

"Can I come in with you?"

Dammit to hell. I didn't have a good excuse to keep him outside. "Sure. Why not?"

I got my supplies together at the edge of the room. Lucas walked in without gear on—what could happen to him if he got bitten, he'd become more were?—but being alone in the room with two werewolves made my cotton isolation smock feel a lot like a hooded red cape.

"So who was he to you?" I asked as I approached the bed.

"Frightening mostly." Lucas stood on Winter's right side, and I joined him there. "One Halloween as a kid I asked my mom if I could dress up as him."

"That bad?"

"Worse, really." Lucas looked down at Winter's still form and shook his head. "He was willing to do anything to get his way."

I didn't know what to say. "I'm . . . sorry?" I guessed.

"He was the perfect pack leader," Lucas said, going on like I wasn't there. "He didn't give a shit about anything else, anyone else—his life was the pack. Anything for the pack. He had to be tough. Cruel, even." Lucas reached out to touch Winter's face hesitantly. We hadn't shaved him since his arrival, and his five o'clock shadow was becoming a low beard. "Goddammit—he lived this long. He wasn't supposed to die."

I uncovered one of Winter's hands. I'd lance his finger

and get blood while Lucas was distracted by his grief and—"Oh, no."

"What?" Lucas's attention spun to me. "What's wrong?"

"It's probably in the chart already. I just didn't know—" Winter's fingertips were turning black. It was due to the blood pressure medication we gave people. At the volume he was getting it here, we were saving his vital organs at the expense of the rest of him. If we couldn't turn down his meds soon—if the moon didn't heal him, if he didn't wake up and the processes in him that regulated blood pressure begin to work again—his hands would go. His remaining foot too.

Lucas's eyes narrowed. "That's bad, isn't it."

"Yeah. I'm sorry."

Lucas leaned over the bed so that his face was over Winter's. "You're not supposed to die. Do you hear me? You're not supposed to die."

There was a small cough from the room's doorway. "Did I come at a bad time?"

Lucas and I both looked up. A man I hadn't met yet stood in the doorway, shadowed by the light outside. Lucas's hands clenched on the bed's side rail, so hard the bed shook. "Viktor."

"I take it now's a bad time?" The other man—were, I was guessing—stepped into the room.

It was my job as nurse to make them calm down—but this was the only window I'd have to get blood for Dren. I was torn for half a second, and then I jabbed the lancet into the edge of Winter's intact palm.

"How did you do this, Viktor?" Lucas released the bed, making it rattle. He rounded toward the door. "You couldn't just wait for him to keel over on his own?"

"Me? I know nothing." The visitor, Viktor, clutched an

innocent hand to his chest. "I only just found out about the great one's condition."

I squeezed Winter's hand hard to milk blood out. I just needed one drop. One stinking drop—

"He was my leader too," Viktor continued. "I have as much right to pay respects as you."

"Get out," Lucas said, his voice no more than a growl. "You did this. I don't know how, but you orchestrated this somehow—"

I didn't have to be supernatural to feel the tension filling the room, flowing out from whatever history the two weres shared. I could hit the CODE button on the wall and summon twenty other medical personnel here, but then I wouldn't get my blood—

One thick drop welled out of the lancet-made hole. I swiped the test strip across it. It was all I needed—and it'd better be all Dren needed—to keep my brother safe.

I slid it into the glucometer and looked up at the two men. "Lucas—sir—you—"

"This is shameful! I have rights! I am a member of the pack!"

"You also own a black truck. I'm not stupid, Viktor," Lucas said. Lucas crouched to jump—when Charles appeared in the hallway holding a trank gun behind both of them.

"No transformations on hospital grounds!" he shouted with a low voice. "Don't think for a second I won't shoot you both." He waved the gun between them to prove his point.

Lucas slowly relaxed, coming back to standing. "Viktor here was leaving."

"As a pack member, I have every right to pay respects," Viktor complained.

I moved around the bed to be out of the way of Charles's possible shots. Viktor was a young man—same age as Lucas, probably—but he dressed older, in a three-piece suit. He held a fedora over his chest, seemingly to calm his injured pride, and without the hat I could see one lock of white hair against the rest of his natural black.

"Family makes the rules here, not packs," Charles informed everyone, with the gun still held high.

Viktor sighed then and bowed elaborately—to Winter, not to Lucas, I realized—and reset his hat on his head. "Until full moon then?" he asked of Lucas.

"Oh yes," Lucas said, with a dangerous tone.

Viktor left, Charles stepping backward to follow him with the barrel of his gun. "You all right, Edie?" he called back to me.

"Yeah."

"Maybe your other friend in there better leave too," Charles said.

Lucas muttered something to himself. I wanted to stand up for his right to be there, but after their altercation I questioned the wisdom of it.

"Okay, now you, Edie," Charles said. I exited the room. It was just Charles and me in the hall. He set down the gun.

"That's bigger than a flush, Charles—" I tried to tease. My voice was too high, too tense.

Charles shook his head. "Don't do that again, Edie. I don't care how safe they seem. Never be alone with one of them."

"Okay." After that little show, I had to agree. I took a deep breath in and let it out slowly.

"Glad you're good," Charles said, and clapped my arm. "What's his blood sugar at?"

I hadn't realized I was still carrying the glucometer around. I looked down at its screen. "Two eighty-three."

* * *

Charles and I changed the insulin drip together since it was a medication you needed a co-sign for, and when Gina returned I explained what had happened and took Lucas's coffee in his stead. I wasn't about to go find him. The test strip with Winter's blood was safely in my pocket. That was all that mattered to me.

I had to go to the bathroom near shift change. I told Gina and waved at Meaty and Charles on my way out the door, and exited to find Lucas, sitting with his head between his knees outside in the hall.

I couldn't exactly avoid him. The door to Y4 slammed shut behind me. He didn't look up. He wasn't asleep, was he?

"Pretend I'm not here," he suggested without looking up.

I snorted. He'd been so frightening in the room, but now he just looked depressed. Winter was my patient . . . but that was the problem with visitors. Sometimes they needed nursing too. I walked over to him and knelt down. "Want to tell me what that was about?"

Lucas looked up at me, eyes full of sadness. "I'm next in line to lead the pack."

CHAPTER TWENTY-ONE

"Oh." I didn't know how to react. In my world, promotions were positive things.

"I never wanted this day to come." Lucas leaned forward and put his head back into his hands. "I'm not like Winter was."

At a loss for words, I continued the conversation the only way I knew how. "How do you mean?"

He looked up at me. "Winter would have killed Viktor back there. Hell, he would have killed Viktor the second he heard anyone got hit with a black truck."

"There's more than one black truck in this town."

"You don't know Viktor." Lucas shook his head. "But that's not the point. The point is I don't want to lead. I'm not like him. I don't even want to be like him."

"Is anyone else in line?"

"Fenris Jr. But that'll be a few years. The pack can't function without a leader for that long."

"Winter's not dead yet."

"Yet," Lucas repeated dourly. "Helen has access to all the group accounts—she got them when Fenris Sr. died. But any time without a leader is too long for creatures accustomed to having one. Long enough for people to get ideas. If he doesn't heal, then I'll have to take over on the next full moon night." He inhaled deeply. "I shouldn't be telling you all this."

"Don't worry. I'm good at keeping secrets." Like the fact that I had Winter's blood in my pocket right now.

Lucas stared at me with his light brown eyes. They were rimmed in a darker brown, almost red. I felt guilt flush my face. "Thank you."

The rest of the night was uneventful. Gina and I gave report to the same crew that'd had him yesterday, and went to the locker rooms together. I wanted to ask her privately about why she'd taken an extra shift, but by the time I'd slipped the test strip into my going-home scrubs' pocket and double-washed my hands, she'd already gone.

As I exited the Winter family was arriving. Helen, whom I assumed was the matriarch now, was dressed all in black with Fenris Jr. in tow.

"This place—" She drew up short and worry furrowed her brow. "It smells like Viktor. Was he here? Did he come here last night?"

I looked to Lucas, who stood exhaustedly behind her, for guidance.

"He was, but I sent him away," Lucas answered. "I knew it was what you would have wanted."

"Good." She turned toward me and reached for me like she knew me, her in her Sunday best and me in scrubs. I was startled into hugging her back. She ran her cheek against my own, breathing in my hair as she held tight. "Don't let that awful man see my father. Don't let him come down here. Ever."

Just what I wanted, to be the local were-guest bouncer. "You're going to see the social worker—you should tell him that," I told her.

She smiled up at me weakly. "Okay. I will." And then

she clung to me again, as though she needed my support. "Thank you so much for all you do."

"You're . . . welcome?" I said, and looked to Lucas for help. He reached for Helen and gently pulled her away from me.

"You'll keep him alive for us, won't you?" she asked me from Lucas's arms.

I didn't want to make any promises I couldn't keep. Plus, I wasn't even in charge of his care. But trapped there, with Junior looking hopefully on—my unwise mouth began to form the word *Okay*. Only our social worker's arrival saved me from myself. He waved the Winter family toward a meeting room down the hall. Jorgen was the last to go in. He paused and sniffed at me.

"Wash your hands, girl. You're not even fit to smell like him," he said as he passed. I grabbed my purse tighter and left, gritting the truth behind my teeth.

CHAPTER TWENTY-TWO

The story of Nurse Edie and the Very Long Shift was almost through, thank goodness. I wove through the visitors in the lobby, sleeping on the couches set up like pews. In inclement weather, homeless people sometimes set up shop there, claiming they were waiting for friends. It would be hard to differentiate between them and the family members who really were waiting. This morning was no different.

On my way out I saw Luz sound asleep at the end of a couch, arms crossed, leaning against a column. I wanted to go over to wake her and ask how Javier was—but she'd been out here for eight hours, she wouldn't know. I was off shift, I needed to stay that way. I needed to get home.

I drove home that morning in the dark. Dren wasn't lurking in the lobby, underneath the awning, near my car, under my car, inside my car—I even checked in the trunk. I'd watched too many horror movies to not look.

By the time I got home you could tell that it was daytime, and I figured I was safe. Twelve hours is a long time to be at work, even if you're not on your feet every minute of it. I unlocked my front door, already dreaming of the shower I was about to take.

Grandfather started ranting. I stopped in my entryway. "What's going on?" My keys were still in my hand—I slid the longest one between my fingers, so I could punch at someone with it if I had to. There was a groan in response, from inside my house.

Leaving the door wide open behind me, I took another step in. "Hello?"

Another groan. I made it to my living room and looked at my couch. It was currently occupied. Gideon waved a fingerless hand at me. My eyes slid up to his face, empty of eyes, ears, and lips, and I wanted to throw up, only I was too fucking tired.

"You have got to be kidding me. Hang on." Without taking my eyes off him, I found my phone in my purse and dialed Sike. She picked up on the fourth ring.

"Hello, Edie!" She sounded pleased to hear from me, which meant she was in on this.

"Why is there a Cenobite sitting on my couch?"

"What's a Cenobite?"

"Rent Hellraiser." I walked backward without taking my eyes off him and closed my apartment door behind me. "Was this really the fucking plan?"

"You didn't think they were coming home with me, did you?"

"They?" I sputtered, and looked down my short hall.

"In your closet."

I went back to my bedroom. There was a lightproof sheet over my bedroom's small window again. I'd kept it after the last time I needed it, for help hiding vampires. Being a night-shift nurse and all, lightproof curtains were a wonderful luxury. My bed was empty, but my shoes were cast out across my floor again. This didn't bode well. I slid my closet open and peeked inside. "Goddammit, Sike. I hate you." There was a woman inside my closet, on the floor. She wasn't breathing, but I knew she wasn't dead.

"Likewise, of course," Sike said.

I squatted down, the phone still pressed to my ear. I put fingers to the prone woman's wrist and felt no pulse, just flesh, soft and cool. "Who is this?"

"Veronica Lambridge. Gideon's girlfriend, and former laboratory technician."

She didn't look like a Veronica—she had mousy brown hair, close-cropped, like a ten-year-old boy's, and a smattering of freckles that made her look even younger. Her face was peaceful now, but who knew how she'd feel when she woke up.

"Anna changed her, after Gideon's attack, for her own protection. But Anna's not allowed to make new vampires yet, so we had to hide her."

I slid the closet door closed again. "My house is safest why?"

"No other vampires have access to it. You haven't been making more friends on the side, have you?"

"Of course not."

"Well then, there you go. You're the Ambassador of the Sun, they need a little baby-sitting, and your place is safer than ours till we figure out who did that to Gideon."

I was silent on the line. "Anna trusts you. I don't know why, but she trusts you," Sike went on, her voice bitter, mocking—jealous. "You might be the only one she trusts."

I pushed Veronica a little farther into my closet and slid the door closed. "How long will she be out?"

"Three days is the normal. We'll pick her up between now and then."

"Maybe you could call first?"

Sike laughed at me. "We'll come by at night." And then she hung up.

I stood in my bedroom, looking at my closed closet door. I was so tired. I was so scared. I was so tired of being scared.

But in my mind, I put all of my nurse armor on. I was going to do what needed doing. Again.

I went back out to living room, where Gideon sat, pantsless on my couch in a hospital gown.

"We're going to have to make the best of things, okay?" He was mute, of course. "Look, you were here beforehand, right? Did you give yourself a tour?"

He shook his head.

"Well, the bathroom is down the hall. But." I could not just have him sitting on my couch with no pants. I gave a slightly manic laugh at the thought, then breathed in deeply and went back to my bedroom.

Gideon was way taller than me. My old scrubs would be highwaters on him, but at least he'd be able to shimmy in and out of them, even without entire fingers. I silently blessed my new washable couch cover, which was keeping his boy parts from direct contact with my couch.

I brought the scrub pants out into my living room. "Okay, stand up. Right leg up. Left leg up." I hitched the pants onto him and drew them up. After I tied the drawstring in a loose bow, I put my hand to his elbow and directed him down my short hallway.

"So there's a bathroom over here, to your right." My toilet was against the back wall, but I didn't trust him to hit it in his state. I pulled him inside the small room. "There's a shower here"—I knocked on the glass door so he could hear it—"and I'll leave the door open. You can just pee in there. And if you have to do worse, just let me know. It won't be the first time I've wiped someone's ass, so don't be shy, okay?"

He made a cross between a grunt and a groan. I decided to take it as a yes.

"Are you hungry?"

He nodded. Without lips, there was only so much he

would be able to keep inside his mouth. Lips were one of those things that people didn't appreciate till they were gone—although most times that was due to a stroke, and not internecine vampire warfare. Thank God they'd let him keep his teeth. I inhaled and exhaled, drawing on additional strength and sanity hidden deep inside.

"I'll make some eggs."

I was tired as hell, but Gideon's day had been worse than mine. I scrambled the eggs up, cubing some leftover Christmas turkey to toss inside. He'd need all the protein he could get to heal.

I surrounded him with dish towels, and sat beside him to fork pieces of turkey and egg into his mouth. He gnashed at them, having a hard time moving them around without a tongue, without lips to hold them in. His gums weren't meant to be exposed like this. I knew his mouth would dry out. And then his teeth would go. I wondered if Anna knew what she'd gotten herself into. I knew I hadn't, really. And Gideon—damn.

In between Gideon's bites of food, I researched—if research online about werewolves can actually be called such—causes of werewolf-itis. It seemed only appropriate since I had been carrying Winter's blood in my pocket.

The Internet was its usual helpful-unhelpful self. Twenty standard ideas and fifty thousand nonstandard ones, complete with comments below the articles from twelve-year-old kids who swore they were going to go out to a national park and slaughter a wolf to try out that pelt-wearing thing *this weekend*. That'd wind up really well for anyone who tried to do it in the Deepest Snow pack's park.

The standard ideas were pretty standard, though, at least. Accidents of birth—being born on a full-moon night, the seventh son of a seventh son thing, or with a caul.

Then there were accidents of locale, being bitten by a werewolf personally, or just plain bad luck—putting on that old furry thing you found abandoned in the forest, witches' curses, and drinking water from a werewolf's paw print, which sounded ludicrously dumb.

Part of me being super Pollyanna with Gideon and nosy on the Internet was the fact that a baby vampire was asleep in my closet. I didn't want to go in there to sleep and hang out with her. I mean, daytime was safest for me and all—but what would she wake up as? And who? And how mad? I didn't know anything about her.

Had she wanted to become a vampire? Had she been a daytimer too? Or just someone whom Anna had thought it'd be a good idea to save? There was saving, and then there was this, me spooning eggs into the mouth of a man who had no lips.

Gideon would eventually need something to drink, too. Maybe I could feed him ice chips. Or in the shower, with his face turned up into the faucet like a bird.

I took a few deep breaths. "Are you okay for now, Gideon?"

He nodded. Perhaps if he'd been able to talk, he'd have told me how ironic that question was. *Okay* was a very relative term.

"I'll buy you some other food soon. But I gotta sleep. It's been a long day," I said, knowing I spoke for both of us. I put a station on my laptop's Internet radio, and I set Grandfather beside him. "Keep him company, okay?" I doubted Gideon spoke German, but hey. "I've got a cat too. Be nice to her, or else. I'll be asleep in the back. Don't be afraid to go to the bathroom. We'll work out a system, I swear."

I got him some blankets and left him there on my couch. I didn't want to go back into my room, but with him on the couch, I had little choice.

I crawled into bed, and Minnie hopped up on my bed to eye me once I'd gotten settled. "I know," I told her. "This is all incredibly bad." True to her Siamese ways, she meowed in agreement. Then she snuggled under the blankets with me, and despite both of us knowing it was a bad idea, we went to sleep.

CHAPTER TWENTY-THREE

The closet doors were still closed when I woke up. I lay in bed for a moment and contemplated my next move. Luckily for me, my underwear lived in my dresser, and I could just wear some things that weren't *that* dirty on the floor. I didn't want to open my closet up. I mean, what if I went in there for a shirt, and somehow the lightproof fabric fell off my window, and she dusted from the daylight, leaving a dust stain right there in my closet. How would I get my deposit back then?

I snorted, rolled upright, and hunted down some clothes.

Gideon was still in the living room, sitting on my couch. The Internet radio had paused out long ago. I glanced at my oven's clock—it was four. I'd only been asleep for six hours. Not enough to feel rested after the night I'd had. But it was still daylight out. Safer than night-time, for sure.

"Okay. I'm gonna go get us some food." I took my laptop back from Gideon and woke it up to check my bank account. My paycheck had autodeposited the evening before—somehow I never believed it was going to until I'd seen that it had. I breathed a little easier. I could make it for another two weeks just fine—rent wasn't due till the fifteenth. But I couldn't feed Gideon eggs forever. He'd get scurvy. "Do you like Chinese?" There was a take-out joint nearby I could hit. And it was all cut up into small bites already. He shrugged.

"Is that a no on Chinese?"

He shrugged again.

"We're going to have to get better on nodding or shaking our heads if we want this thing to work. Wait—egg rolls?" A nod. "Mushroom chicken." A large shake no. I breathed a sigh of relief. "Lemon chicken?" Another nod.

We played twenty questions till I had our menu figured out, and discovered that Gideon did not like mushrooms, kung pao, or hot-and-sour soup. Which was just as well because he wouldn't be able to drink it. Which gave me a thought.

I found the old mister I'd used with Minnie back in the day, to dissuade her from clawing up my couch, back when my couch had been worth attempting to save. I cleaned out the spigot, filled the bottle, and returned.

"Open up your mouth. I'm gonna mist you like a houseplant."

I think more water went on him than in his mouth. But he could almost hold it, and spray himself with it, if he smashed both his hands together, Hulk-style. It would keep him busy for a while. That would be the biggest damage he'd face, as time went on. Not being able to interact with the outside world could make him go insane. I'd seen it before, with long-term patients. They were mostly druggies before they got hurt, so they hadn't had much of a support structure to fall back on afterward. And Gideon didn't really either—just Anna, his now-a-vampire girlfriend, and me. I could barely manage owning a cat. Caring for an entire other human being long-term was out of the question.

I looked around my small living room, made smaller by the addition of Gideon. I spotted the boxes that were left here for me to deal with after Christmas morning. There was that ugly belt in one of them, the one Peter'd given me, which I had no chance in hell of ever wearing. I could return that, and maybe at least break even on the Chinese food.

"Okay, Gideon, I'm taking off now," I said while picking up the boxes to take out to the trash and/or return. Gideon nod-grunted from his spot on my couch.

Winter's test strip was still in my purse. I should have put it in a plastic bag, because ew, biohazards, but the blood was dry now, and I doubted my purse was going to become a were-purse come the full moon. I didn't want to touch it anyhow—I wouldn't until it came time to hand it over to Dren.

Daylight, such as it was, filtered through the clouds above. The constant gray of living in Port Cavell—at least during winter, and not in summer when all it was was too warm—wore on me. Each winter day, numbingly cold, wet, miserable, just like the last. No wonder vampires liked it here so much. I parked my car in a mostly vacant lot. Now that Christmas was over, all the weather-bleached decorations looked like grim little flags, flapping surrender in the wind.

I hit the Chinese food place first. I stood in line, ordered my takeout, and my phone rang. Jake. Normally I wouldn't pick up and be that person who talked in public, but with him I'd been trained to feel I was one phone call away from an emergency at all times.

"Hey, Sissy."

"Hey yourself." I stepped back and looked sheepish as I handed the Asian woman my credit card. "What are you up to tonight?"

"About five eleven," he said, and I snorted.

The lady at the counter handed my card back, and I

tipped her well, since I knew I was being rude. "What's going on?" I slid the food off the counter and made my way to the door.

"Just wondering if I could take you out for dinner tomorrow."

"Really?" I stepped outside, back into the cold.

"You don't have to sound so surprised."

I opened my mouth to say all the ways and reasons I could refute that, and then carefully closed it again.

"You don't have to be so stunned either," he said, during my pause.

"Sorry, Jakey. Just trying to walk outside and not trip in ice is all."

"Uh-huh. So? Are you in?"

"I'm in. What time?"

"Six?"

"Sure. Want me to pick you up?"

"Sounds good."

"Love you, Jake."

"Love you too."

I settled my and Gideon's dinner into the passenger seat of my car, and carefully walked around to the driver side. The mall was two exits down, and I bet they'd be doing a brisk business in other returns today—I couldn't have been the only one gifted the world's most hideous belt.

The mall was a U-shaped structure around a curb-to-curb parking lot. I parked near the middle, in a space that the mall's snowplow had cleared, prepared to walk the rest of the way in. I looked inside the box as soon as I'd gotten out of the car, to make sure the gift receipt was still at the bottom. God bless sensible Peter.

A car parked ahead of me. I closed the box and started walking for the store. The car's driver got out and started walking quickly toward the wing of the mall behind me—not so strange, considering it was cold outside. She was bundled up against the weather in a fashionable parka with a furry hood, and she held something to her cheek, like she was talking on a phone, but I couldn't see it.

I watched her, and I noticed she noticed me. Girls have to watch out for that sort of thing. Maybe not all girls, but I'd just checked my trunk for a vampire less than ten hours ago. My paranoia meter was at eleven. I didn't like how close she was coming, but cell phones made people act stupidly. It was a scientific fact.

We passed another row of cars, then rounded a tiny snowdrift the snowplow had made. That's when I saw another woman step out of the woman's car. I stopped, and as the first turned to look at the second, and I saw that she wasn't holding anything after all.

I turned and ran for my car.

CHAPTER TWENTY-FOUR

I was fumbling for my keys as they clattered behind. Some part of me still hoped I was overacting, but as I unlocked my door and caught the handle to open it, a hand grabbed my shoulder and yanked me back. One of my fingernails bent and broke inside my glove, and I hissed in pain as she shoved me to the ground.

"Fire!" I yelled, like I'd heard you were supposed to. "There's a fire!" I scrambled to my knees and put my back against my car door. Now, inside my pocket, my badge was glowing day-bright. Hell of a time to warn me.

The two women stood there, heads cocked sideways, as if they were listening to something I couldn't hear. "What do you want?"

Winter's blood? Shit. Did they know? I scrabbled for my dropped purse. "Look, I'll give it back to you—"

The first one, with the parka on, bent down, sniffing. She kept her eyes on me, breathing deeply.

"I'm sorry—my brother—you wouldn't understand—" I sputtered.

The second one didn't breathe at all. I saw her make a fist with a gloved hand and swing for me. I screamed and ducked lower—she hit my car instead, and I heard the door panel dent.

I crawled toward the front of my car. One of them

grabbed my ankles and hauled me back. Reaching out, I put my hand into Peter's gift box, tissue paper bleeding pink into the snow. The belt buckle rasped against asphalt as she yanked my deadweight again.

I flipped over, feeling the seams of everything that had just healed in my abdomen twist inside me, and punched out with the belt buckle by my fist. I caught the hoodless one's jaw, and the skin there burned away. She cupped her hand to the wound, and for the first time her lips opened— to bay.

"Oh fuck, fuck, fuck—" I curled into a ball, to try to protect myself. I was going to die here over a single dot of blood, in a mall parking lot, with Chinese food cooling in my poor dented car behind me.

The baying woman looked up. There was a loud *thump*, and my car shook up and down. I looked up, and a trench-coated figure stood on my hood.

Dren.

"Sun's down, girly-girl. Time to play." He squatted on his boot heels and looked at the two other women. "You've started without me. Tsk." Who would have thought this morning, when I was looking for him like he was Jimmy Hoffa, that I'd be so happy to see him now.

"Dren—they—" I panted.

His eyes narrowed, staring at them over me. "You're not bitten—or born. I would scent you if you were. Name your pack."

The women fell back at this, appearing disoriented and confused.

"No—" Dren leapt off my car hood and landed beside me in the muck, his good hand on his sickle.

"Who are you?" one of the women asked. Then she looked to her friend. "What is this place? Where are we?"

I didn't want to tell them they'd just been planning to kill me. I put my back against my car.

Dren kept himself between me and them, and he waved his sickle as if clearing the air of cobwebs between us. "You can see me. You know what I am. Go."

The women turned and ran. One fell to her knees in the ice, then scrambled back up to get away.

"I—I thought they were weres?" I said aloud.

"So did I. Stay here," he commanded, and rushed away as though he'd never been there to begin with.

I hoped he didn't mean stay precisely here, my ass in the snow. I got up with a groan, collected my purse and my belt, and gingerly sat inside my car. My gloves were ruined, and the back of my new coat was soaked through. I took it off, turned on the heater, and rolled the driver-side window down. I didn't want Dren sneaking up on me outside. Dren reappeared momentarily.

"Who were they?"

"What good does it do to share my suspicions with you?" He snapped his fingers as if beckoning a dog. "Did you get me what I desire?"

"I did—and it almost got me killed!" I pressed my hand to my stomach where I'd wrenched it wrong. My broken nail was throbbing, along with most of the rest of me.

Dren shook his head. "Which way is the wind blowing, Edie?" He pulled the glove off his good hand with his teeth, tucked it in his pocket, and licked his forefinger before holding it up.

I sank back into my car seat. "Just tell me, Dren. I don't know."

"North. All night." Dren put his hand inside his pocket and slipped on his glove. "Those things didn't scent you. They were sent after you. It's quite a different verb."

My lips pulled into a frown. I didn't know why any weres would currently hate me. Jorgen had seemed peeved this morning, yes, but that was his natural state—maybe Viktor? But if so, why? And why did they suddenly forget who they were when Dren appeared? That seemed more a compulsion to me.

"Solve your problems on your own time." Dren held his hand out. "Give me the blood. Now."

I pulled the little test strip out of my purse. He inspected it before putting it into his mouth like a strip of gum.

"Interesting. Very interesting." He rolled it around inside his mouth like the first sip of fine wine. Then he spit it out on the ground.

"What does it say?" I asked.

"It says your brother gets to live." Dren gave me a faint smile, hiding the calculations occurring behind it.

"Anything else?"

"Nothing you need to know right now."

"Nothing about all of this?"

"Go home, Edith."

"Thanks for saving my life, I guess," I said as ironically as possible.

Dren smiled cruelly, showing fangs. "You're welcome."

I hopped into my car. I'd check on the dent later—nothing in the door was going to affect my power steering, which was all I needed to get home right now. Before the engine took, Dren was gone. I didn't see where to—and as long as he wasn't riding along on my car's roof, I didn't care. Pulling out of the parking lot, I called Sike and got her voice mail.

"Hey. Two things that were allergic to silver just tried to kill me in a parking lot. Thought you might want to know," I said, and hung up.

My apartment complex's parking lot was empty, and my door was locked. I was very pleased to see the inside of my apartment again, even if that still included an eyeless aberration sitting on my couch.

"Who wants lemon chicken?" I asked as I walked in, and Gideon turned toward me. I smiled bravely, even though he couldn't see.

I wrapped up my finger and put on the abdominal binder I'd been sent home with after my stabbing. Its tension around my waist, a feeling that I'd chafed at while wearing it originally, felt comforting now, like a squeeze from a good friend. I didn't think I'd done any damage, but I wanted to make sure.

After the ceremony of setting out the many towels, it took a while to feed Gideon, and he was a horrible conversationalist. But it gave me a way to keep busy, even if it couldn't entirely still my thoughts.

Who were those ladies? And why were they after me? If Dren didn't know what pack they were from . . . what did that mean?

Gideon missed more food than went in, making a huge mess with each bite. Feeding a grown adult took a lot of time and reminded me of my nursing school days. Seemed like half my time was spent sitting in the rooms of elderly patients, feeding one half spoon of applesauce or pudding at a time. Sometimes those little old ladies were so hungry, and they hadn't been properly, patiently, fed in so long, it just made you want to cry. Once people lost the ability to feed themselves, that was the beginning of the end. But not for Gideon, which made me want to cry a little, too.

I fed him until he didn't want to eat anymore and I felt like a better person for it when I was done. At least one thing had gone right today, and for the past hour or so, no one had tried to kill me.

"Let's find out what our fortunes are," I said, like I did at the end of every Chinese meal, except most times I was talking to Minnie. I cracked open two cookies like walnuts and fished the slips of paper out of the cookie shards.

"Here's yours, Gideon," I said. "Now is not the time to circle mints."

Gideon tilted his head at me.

"I'm so not kidding. That's what it says. We should take it back." I snorted and pulled out mine. "You will meet a tall, dark stranger? So original. Thanks, fortune cookie."

I'd prefer not to meet any more strangers right now, maybe forever. I crumpled the fortune up and tossed it aside. At least it hadn't said anything about meeting them in an alley. Or with knives.

I set our dishes in the sink along with the ones I still needed to wash from Christmas, and tried to figure out how best to occupy my time. Gideon was a couch hog, and hanging out in my bedroom with Veronica only a closet door away didn't sound like much fun.

I decided to suck it up, take the folding chair out of my closet, and hang in the corner on the Internet. Minnie came along to agree that this suited her just fine, if only I'd magically create more lap space for her. I'd just about negotiated balancing a laptop and a cat when my phone rang.

"Sorry, Minnie." I set her down, and put the laptop down beside her. Maybe it'd be Anna or Sike calling me back with some decent explanations. About time. I found my phone, and didn't recognize the number.

"Hello?"

"Edie, it's Gina."

"Hey! What's up?" I immediately thought of everything I could have done wrong last night, when I'd been briefly in charge of Winter. "Did I screw something up?"

"Nooooo, this isn't one of those calls." Her voice was a little slurred. Then she was quiet.

"Are you all right?" I asked.

"Yes!" She protested. Then more silence. "No. I just

had a fight with Brandon." There was a hitch in her voice as she said his name. "I think we just broke up."

I winced. "Oh, Gina, I'm so sorry."

"It was the right thing to do, you know? There were extenuating circumstances but—"

"Where are you? You shouldn't be alone." There was the small matter of why she'd called me, instead of her other friends, assuming she had other friends, which she ought to. We couldn't all come from the island of misfit toys. There were loud noises in the background. Voices, music. She shouted an address over them. I plunked it into Google Maps. Just twenty minutes uptown. "Okay—I'll be there soon, all right?"

"All right. Thanks. I owe you."

"No problem." I'd almost gotten her killed once before. It was the least I could do.

CHAPTER TWENTY-FIVE

Before I left, I put on my silver-buckled belt over my older coat and silently thanked Peter. I didn't have a printer, and my phone's GPS was sketchy given winter clouds, so I wrote down the driving instructions instead, after doing a street view to make sure I'd recognize it when I got there. Online, it'd looked like a warehouse. In reality, it was a bar. The outside was nondescript—the only thing that gave away its barness was the presence of a single, large bouncer. I walked up to him, wondering how things were going to go.

I smiled hopefully up as he stared down. "You don't smell like us."

Of course. This was a were-bar. I should have thought to ask. What if the women I'd just fought off were in here somewhere? Foxes, meet chicken.

But if Gina was inside, maybe all was well. Or they'd kidnapped her and put her up to it. One of those two things. The bouncer was still giving me an eye—chances were if someone inside wanted me dead, they'd have told the muscle to let me through.

I'd taken to carrying my badge around, on the off chance I ran into any more pissed-off vampires, accident-prone weres, or promiscuous shapeshifters. I pulled it out of my purse. "I'm not. I'm here to pick up a friend."

"Oh. Her." He held open the door and didn't ask to see my ID.

Either he was telepathic, or he knew who I wanted to pick up already. Not good.

Inside, the bar was divetastic. It wasn't smoky, but my shoes stuck to the stairs, and I was glad I hadn't dressed up. The bar occupied an island in the center of the room, with a bartender stranded inside it; there were tables on one side and a dance floor on the other. In the back of the room, very private booths hugged the wall. It wasn't that big a place, but it was crowded. Four nights till the full moon on New Year's, and the locals were whooping it up. There was loud music playing, even if it seemed too early for them to dance.

I descended the steps to the floor, trying to not look as out of place as I felt. I didn't have to push through the crowd—the people standing made room for me while ignoring me. I wondered if this was what it felt like to have vampire-style look-away on.

I wove my way between clusters of people talking and drinking, with an electric feeling at my front and my back. Was this how sharks felt, swimming through the sea? I saw Gina, her head in her arms, at the bar.

I pulled up a chair. "Hey, sexy."

She tilted her head up. I could see where her eyeliner was smudged. The weres here didn't need to see her face to know she'd been crying—they could probably all smell the salt of her tears.

"Hey. Thanks."

"No problem." The bartender, from his spot behind Gina, eyed me inquisitively. I shook my head, and he went on to the next new patron. "So what happened? Want to talk?" I scooted my chair in closer.

"I ended things. It was rough." She finished off the

clear drink in front of her, slamming down the empty glass, making the ice clink inside.

"I'm sorry to hear that, Gina."

"Don't be. I don't know why I ever thought things would work out between us." She flagged the bartender down, and he obligingly took her glass to pour her another of whatever had been in it before. "He was so hurt, Edie. That's what was worst." I could smell the alcohol on her breath. "I really meant something to him. And he meant the world to me."

I scooted my bar stool closer. "Then what went wrong?"

"He wanted me to change for him." The bartender put down a fresh drink. "And not just lose-a-few-pounds change, but all the way change."

"You mean—" I said, and looked around at all the other patrons of the bar. "Change, change?"

"Yeah."

"He wanted to bite you?"

"He already did. It doesn't have to be bites, you know. There are less violent ways." I did not want to think of my co-worker having sex with a bear, so I kept my mind and mouth shut. "It takes a month to kick in—not a month really, but a moon. This moon coming up was supposed to be my moon. But I stopped it."

"How?"

"We've got shots. And since I'm a vet, I can prescribe them for myself. The laws are different, heh." She took hold of the drink and pounded it down. "And that was that."

I had a lot of questions about this process—why was anyone ever bitten if they didn't have to stay that way?— but I kept them to myself for now.

"Anyways. I'm not fit to drive." Gina pushed herself away from the bar and teetered a bit.

"How much have you had to drink?"

"Four or five."

"Of?"

"Vodka tonics."

"Jesus."

Gina gave me a morbid smile. "Perhaps also of interest to you, as my medical adviser for the evening, is that I usually abstain, and I can't go home like this. My parents think I'm at work tonight. Can I just come home with you to your place?" Her smile got tight, and I could hear the tears just waiting to come out in her voice.

"Oh, Gina—of course." My place was currently occupied to the gills. I ran through ideas. Credit-carded hotel rooms? The week between Christmas and New Year's was likely to be expensive, and/or booked. I did think of one person to call. "Hang on, and stay here. I'll be right back." I hopped off my stool and went back to the hopefully quieter bathroom to make a call.

Things got louder as I went down the hall to the bathroom— maybe I'd have to exit the building to get some peace. There were the two doors for the bathrooms on my right, a saloon door for a kitchen to my left, and at the end of the hall, a larger, thicker door. Which sounded like it had a sports stadium behind it. Inside the bathroom wasn't any better—the sound from outside came in through the wall and echoed around the bathroom's tile.

I didn't really want to walk past Gina and everyone I'd had to walk past on my way in and then come back inside to get her.

The sound stopped crisply, then seconds later then started again. Like driving underneath an overpass in rain. I stepped back into the bar's hallway, changed course, and went for the bigger door.

It swung open into another crowd. The air was choked with the scent of musk and sweat. People's attention was on something happening beyond, and none of them had a glance to spare for me. While I was tall, I wasn't quite tall enough to see what was happening. I made my way around the edge of the auditorium until I found a gap I could elbow myself into.

They were watching a wrestling match. Two men were circling each other, hands out and low. Bruises covered both of them, and one had a cauliflower ear. One of them was huge, with red hair down to his shoulders, and then a layer of red hair almost like fur, flowing down his back, arms, and chest. The other was smaller, leaner, covered in tattoos.

I didn't recognize him at first; I only had one of those feelings you get when you know you've seen someone before. It took me a moment to place him, and when I did I said his name.

"Lucas?" The surrounding spectators ignored me, wrapped up in the match. I recognized one of them too—the piebald man I'd seen that same morning, still wearing his fedora.

Lucas's tattoos covered his arms, tracing up from his wrists to his back where they met across his shoulders. I couldn't make out what they were because he kept moving, pressing in, darting out. He ran in, stayed there, and the bear clubbed him down.

Lucas rolled with the impact and resurfaced lightly behind the larger man. He lunged for his neck, and was again tossed away. He bounced as he landed, whirling upright with a manic grin. He knelt for a second, then leapt back in.

I couldn't tell who was winning—Lucas seemed on the offensive, but he appeared to be losing, repeatedly. In between attacks and defending himself, the Bear-man was overly still, like a kung fu master searching within to find inner peace. But Lucas's willingness to get thrown

around was interrupting whatever the Bear-man was trying to do—until the taller, furrier man's skin flushed
darker, and his chest widened in all directions, like an
expanding barrel. Then Lucas was there again, dancing
forward, only to be swatted back. Lucas rebounded and
the Bear-man raged—all progress toward his animal side
lost with his temper as he grabbed Lucas up and threw
him to the ground. Lucas skidded across the cement floor,
picked himself up, and rushed back at the Bear-man, who
still hadn't recovered from his turn.

In a flash he was a wolf. There was Lucas, who'd be-
gun the leap, and then the wolf who'd finished it. Lucas's
change had been fluid, magical, from one form into the
other. He had been a human, and now he was a wolf even
larger than I was, with fur the color of rust with streaks of
gray. He had paws as big as dinner plates, teeth as long as
my fingers. Lucas's wolf shoulder checked the Bear-man,
knocking him to the ground, and twisted to put fangs on
the Bear-man's throat.

"No!" I cried out, but all the other people in the crowd
were cheering. I pressed forward as they did, to somehow
stop what I thought was going to happen next. But the
Bear-man, still not fully changed, slammed his paw-like
hand against the ground, and wolf-Lucas let him go. Hop-
ping back on all fours, Lucas changed back into a man
again, instantly—all man, naked. The room was quiet as
he stood.

"Are you going to offer me fealty, minor bear?"

The Bear-man, his bear-side completely lost with his
defeat, got to his knees. "Not tonight, wolf." He slapped
the floor with both hands and laughed, shaking his head.
"But I will buy you a drink."

Lucas smiled and offered his opponent a hand. The
Bear-man took it, and clapped Lucas on the back as he
moved to stand.

I stood there, flushed at their nakedness, wondering what I'd just seen. And then I remembered Gina outside, and that I was definitely where I did not belong, even less than I had mere minutes ago. I dove out through the crowd of weres pushing in to congratulate Lucas, and made it to the bathroom, hopefully unseen.

CHAPTER TWENTY-SIX

Asher picked up on the second ring. The background wherever he was sounded like the background where I'd just been. "Hey, it's me," I shouted into the phone.

"This is a surprise. Hang on." The background noises, wherever he was at, lessened. "Let me guess—the single nurse needs a house call?"

"Um. In a manner of speaking."

"In that case, your wish is my command."

I thought about asking him for inappropriate things—then briefly remembered the naked men I'd just seen and Gideon's parts at home. I really didn't need any more random genitalia in my life, and Gina and I needed to go. I closed my eyes, and the words spilled out. "My wish is to come over to where you live—" Asher gave a malevolent chuckle as I continued"—with a drunken co-worker. Who can't go home. And I can't go home either."

"Dare I ask why?"

"There's no more room at the inn. It's a long story. Can I tell you when I get there?" I bit my tongue so I didn't add a *please*.

He paused to consider things, then told me his address, and I committed it to memory. "I'm downtown right now, though—"

I thought I might know the club he was at. "We're even downer-town. You'll beat us."

"See you there, then."

"Thanks, Asher."

I went back to the Gina and the bar. "We have a plan now. Let's go." I started to pull her gently off her seat.

"I don't know why I did it. I could have just gone through with it. I loved him. It wasn't his fault—" There were three more empty glasses in front of her, and I gave the bartender an angry look. He saw me and shrugged. "I could have gone along with things. If I'd just stayed strong," she went on.

Denial. I doubted Gina would make it through all the stages of grief in one night, but I wanted to get her out of here before she hit any more of them. "Come on, Gina."

We were lurching as one through the growing crowd, and now our fellow bar patrons were looking at us smugly. I glowered back at them. Then the back door opened and the crowd from the fight surged in.

The bear and the wolf led the way, in their human forms, now with clothes on. Lucas wore a tank top, totally inappropriate given the the weather outside. Beside him was the Bear-man, still with a cauliflower ear, and behind them both, Jorgen. I started hauling Gina away faster, hoping we hadn't been seen.

"Edie—" I heard a voice call from behind me. Gina started to turn around, and I pulled her closer. We were so close to the door. "Edie, wait—"

There was silence behind us, and the were-bouncer I'd seen outside blocked the door. He didn't need to have changed to be menacing. I looked behind me. If Lucas was the one who'd sicced those girls on me earlier today—my mind ran through options. I had my silver-buckled belt on. I could—Lucas reached out a placating hand.

"Hey." He was smiling, the first time I'd seen him look happy since I'd met him—although I realized that was less than forty-eight hours ago. "Why are you here?"

Lucas was close enough that I could see his tattoos. One arm was prison-style, dark and faded, the other Japanese-sleeved, expensive. He was glazed with sweat and still breathing a little rough. Jorgen stood by his side, radiating displeasure at me.

"I just came to get my friend." Everyone in the room who'd been pretending to ignore us finally stopped pretending. Being the center of attention was unnerving. It felt very much like being prey.

Gina swung forward and lunged for Jorgen. "Do I still smell like a consort to you now, asshole?"

Even though the bouncer was still blocking the way, I tried to haul her up the first stair. Gina fought to concentrate on Lucas, or on one Lucas out of the many I bet she saw. "I hate you," she said, pointing her finger at Jorgen. "And you," she said to Lucas, moving her finger down the line, "and you and you—" Gina took control of herself and took a step up of her own accord, using this small leverage to wave her hand like a fervent preacher and include the entire crowd. "You're all assholes! All of you men!"

I grabbed for her and pressed her to me. The room filled with a pregnant pause. Had anyone at County made a code for what to do when your co-worker was going to get you killed?

Booming laughter began nearby. I opened eyes I hadn't realized I'd closed, and saw Lucas grinning from ear to ear. "She does have a point," he said, looking out at the crowd of gawkers himself. "Half of you are dogs."

"And those that aren't are bitches!" someone else yelled from the back of the room.

There were snickers all around, and I could feel the tension in the room defuse. Lucas closed the gap between us. "Need some help?"

"Yes. Please." Anything to get out of here faster.

Muscles rippled up and down his arms as he picked up Gina and pulled her up into a fireman's cradle, like he was off to carry her over a threshold. Her chin lay on her chest, and if she was going to throw up, I prayed for her to wait until we'd gotten outside and nearer to my car.

"I'm parked nearby—" I led the way out. Lucas followed, and luckily Jorgen stayed behind.

"What was all that about?" He hefted Gina's weight easily—not that she wasn't thin, but he had no problem carrying her.

"A lover's spat. Nothing personal, I swear."

"I know."

I stopped, and he almost ran into me. "You do?"

"Sure we do. The second I found out you were caring for my uncle I asked around. She may fraternize—but she's damn good at what she does." He looked down at the woman he carried. "She couldn't fall in love with one of us if she didn't love us all a little bit, I suppose."

I started walking again, quickly in the cold. "And what did your background check tell you about me?"

"Like Jorgen said. You're the one the vampires employ."

"That's not true," I said as we reached my Chevy. Gina was snoring. I unlocked the passenger door, and Lucas set her gently inside. "There's just the one. She needs my help, but only for a little bit more."

"You are compelled?" he asked me as I rounded my car.

"No. She just needs my help."

"And you are good at helping people."

"Like a fucking Girl Scout."

He gave me a wolfish grin over my car's hood. "What an interesting image."

I snorted, unlocked my door, and sank inside. I leaned over Gina to buckle her seat belt and reached to close her door. He held it open.

"Where are you taking her?"

"Someplace where she can sleep it off."

"Take good care of her." He stood and made to close Gina's door.

"Lucas—" There was nothing about him that gave the vibe he'd sent attackers after me earlier. If he had, wouldn't he have let the patrons of the bar off their leash, so to speak? He ducked down to peer inside. The winter air was misting off his skin, and beneath his tattoos moved muscles that could have torn my car's door off. "I was attacked this afternoon. By two were-women."

His eyes narrowed, making his red-brown eyes look like angry embers. "When? Where?"

"The Woodbridge Mall. At five P.M., or thereabout. One of them wore a fur-lined parka, the other didn't. That's all I know."

"Viktor," Lucas growled. Anger washed across his entire body. I could almost see it flow over him, the water of humanity parting to let the wolf show through. His hand clenched around my car door, and I realized that between that and the dent I'd probably just hit my deductible. "How did you survive?"

"I hit one. With silver. She might still have a scar. And then a friend of mine showed up—a vampire friend." Calling Dren a friend was stretching things, but I was smart enough to know that if this was a were-ploy, it would be better to seem like I had protection. "Are you sure it was Viktor?"

"His pack and mine have a long history. He can't get to me, and now he can't get to Winter, but you'd be easy—"

"Nothing personal, but I don't even know you. Why would he attack me?" I interrupted.

"You know me well enough. He'll do anything to stir up resentment before the full moon."

"If I'd died, I'd be a little more than resentful," I said.

He snorted and shook his head. "We need to put guards on you, Edie."

"No way."

"My pack owes you. For my uncle's life, such as it is."

"I—I don't trust you," I blurted out. His anger seemed real, and I wanted to trust him, but I also wanted to trust everyone, and that instinct wasn't wise. "I want to, but I can't."

His eyes measured me, I could almost feel him weighing my resolve. He released my car door and took a step back. "I'll find out who they were, Edie. As soon as I can. I'll let you know."

"Thank you." I nodded and put my keys into the ignition, waiting for the engine to catch and turn over before reaching for the door.

Lucas stood there watching me, with his wild-wolf eyes. "Take care of yourself, Edie."

"I will. Promise."

He closed my passenger door, and let me go.

CHAPTER TWENTY-SEVEN

Gina groaned a few times during transit, and I felt for her. I didn't get drunk often, but I knew how she'd feel in the morning, physically at least. Emotionally—I blew air through half-parted lips. Dating a were-bear—almost becoming one? And I thought *I* had the market cornered on bad ideas.

I followed Asher's quick directions and reached a neighborhood I hadn't been to before.

It was genteel. Not new money, but comfortably old—the houses were sprawling two-story brick affairs with dormered attics, surrounded by full tall trees. This was the land of the normal, storybook almost—strange, considering I knew Asher was anything but. I pulled into the driveway and left the engine running for Gina.

Asher met me at the door, looking like the Asher I knew best. Olive skin, dark hair, dark brown eyes. He took one look at me, and then past me to Gina, still slumped over in my passenger seat. "You want to put her in a spare room, or a spare bathroom?"

"Someplace with a lot of tile."

He followed me out to my car, and we retrieved her. Gina kept murmuring things that sounded sad, while Asher helped me help her down his entry hall. We made it up the stairs together, and I arranged her inside a claw-

foot tub while Asher went to get extra towels. I sat on the
toilet beside her, petting her hair, and Asher returned to
lean against the wall.

"Do I want to know what happened?"

"Girl meets were-bear, girl falls for were-bear,
were-bear says if you love me you'll let me bite you, girl
says good-bye." I wished I had an IV start kit and a ba-
nana bag—IV fluids with vitamins and minerals—right
about then. We could've set her impending hangover
straight in no time.

Asher's eyebrows rose high up his forehead. "I meant
at your house."

I looked down at Gina. Chances were she wouldn't
remember any of this, so I told him. About Gideon, and
Veronica. He let out a low whistle.

"Good thing she waited until after Christmas to dump
them on you."

"You're telling me." The kind of leverage Jake would
have over me, if I'd had to have a sleeping vampire and a
mutilated daytimer hidden in my bedroom closet during
Christmas lunch. I shook my head at the thought.

"You think she's going to be all right here?"

"I hope so." She was propped up, and she looked pretty
cozy. Asher's house was warm against the winter, but I
knew the ceramic tub she was curled up in was cold enough
to feel good, in that way that you craved when you were
wasted. I sighed and put my hands to my head.

"Want a glass of water, or a glass of wine?"

Wine would have been lovely, if I hadn't had such a
shining example of the early stages of alcohol poisoning
lying nearby. "Water, please."

I followed Asher down the stairs. His front room had
been turned into a library, with a fireplace and a wide
desk. He'd already stoked a fire. "You're the only one who

lives here?" I was suddenly nervous about leaving Gina alone.

"Just me," he said, and disappeared into what I assumed was his kitchen.

I walked around, looking at the spines of all the books. Hardbacks and paperbacks, crammed together, sometimes two deep, or perpendicular to one another—I could see all the titles, or fragments thereof, peeking out. Ancient philosophy, science fiction, modern biographies, the lives of Catholic saints.

"You read?" I asked when he emerged again.

"All the time." He handed the water to me. I took it without looking and kept walking around as he sat down on a leather couch. "Stop looking at my things."

"I can't." I pulled out a hardback copy of *Quo Vadis* and saw two Stephen King novels stacked up behind. "It's like you're the Wizard of Oz."

"How so?"

"I'm behind the curtain now. All of this . . . makes you feel more humane."

"Don't you mean human?" he corrected me.

"That too." The couch he was on was long, more than enough room for him and three of me. But I was too restless tonight to sit down. "It's been a really long day. I need to think things through."

"You mean there was more?"

"Yeah. I got jumped by two weres this afternoon." Asher moved forward on the couch, but I waved him back. "Don't worry, Dren saved me. And who would have thought that I'd ever get to say that aloud."

"What the—just what are you getting into, Edie?"

"That's the thing. I don't know." I shook my head. "It's complicated, but I don't think I've pissed anyone off."

An eyebrow rose higher on his forehead. "Does it have to do with you being an Ambassador of the Sun?"

"I don't think so. But I can't honestly say. They acted weird, Asher, the weres. When Dren arrived, it was like they woke up."

His frown grew deeper. "When do you have to go back to work?"

"Tomorrow night. Which I'm actually okay with, seeing as I at least get to have tranquilizer guns there." I stopped pacing back and forth and leaned against a desk strewn with papers.

He cleared his throat for my attention. "Can your friend in the friend zone make a friendly suggestion?"

"Certainly."

"This time. For real. Get the fuck out of town."

I bit my lip and looked at the hardwood floor. "I still need my job to protect Jake, Asher."

"He looked pretty clean to me."

"Yeah, he's good at that." I put my hands up to my head and ran them through my hair. "There's just never any guarantee it will last."

"You know, some people who knew you might say your life was worth a little more than his."

I lifted my head up and glared at him. "Asher—"

"You're a nurse, you help people, you give back to the community—you pay taxes. What does he do?"

"He's my brother—" I protested.

"A lot of people start off life with siblings. But when you die, you die alone."

I inhaled and exhaled a few times. "I'm not ready to give up on him yet."

"I bet. It's fun feeling needed, until it gets you killed."

A large log in the fireplace broke and sizzled, as fresh wood was exposed to the heat of the flames. I turned to watch it, because it was easier than looking at him. "You sound a lot like a co-worker of mine."

"Whoever they are, they must be very wise." I heard

him stand, and he walked over to me, blocking my view of the fire. "I have to be what I am, Edie. I have to do what I do to survive. You—you can still get out."

"What would I be then? Who would I be?" The person I was before all this craziness started—I didn't want to go back to being her. To being like everyone else. The type of girl who'd never gotten to have any adventures or know that there were vampires, or have people count on her for life and death. As much as sometimes I hated or was scared of my current job—it made me feel alive in a way that I never had before. Leaving town wouldn't just mean giving up Jake. It would mean giving up my entire life.

"There's nothing wrong with normal," Asher continued.

I looked up at him. "Says the most abnormal man I know."

He gave me a bitter smile, then walked past me to sit at the chair behind his desk. "You're welcome to stay the night here, with your friend. I'm afraid I still have some work to do."

Despite the fact that I'd asked for it, his dismissal hurt. "Was that what you were doing earlier at the club when I called, working?" He'd met me once upon a time at a club, after all.

He tilted his head. "Does it matter if it was?"

I knew he had every excuse to be out. It wasn't like we were a thing. And for him, the more people he could touch, the more people he could be. I assumed touching people equaled power. I inhaled and shook my head. "Never mind. Thank you for your hospitality, for me and for Gina. I'll be upstairs." I started walking toward the stairs.

"Are you jealous of them? The ones that I touch just to touch, just to see?" he called after me, his voice low.

"Of course I am." I could have denied it, but why lie?

Asher and I had slipped through each other's fingers before we'd even known why. And I was angry that he was still here when if the world was a fairer place, I shouldn't have to be alone.

"You can't judge me for doing what I need to, to survive. If a wolf is a wolf, and a shark is a shark, then a shapeshifter is and will always be a shapeshifter. What do you need to survive, Nurse Spence?"

I turned around and his head was resting on folded hands, his coffee-dark eyes watching me. The fire behind him cast a glow, making him look devilish. I knew this room was warm enough that once you took your clothes off, you wouldn't remember how cold it was outside.

"Don't make me have to tell you," I said. "Just guess."

Asher stood and rounded his desk. He stood in front of me for a moment, looking down, and I felt that current of electricity that you get when you're prey, yes, but prey that can still say no. All the power to make us go forward or hold back was inside my hand.

I reached up and touched his cheek.

A knowing smile crept across his face. "You're still wearing your badge."

"Of course I am. I'm horny, not stupid."

He turned and kissed my palm, and then took it in his own hand. Stepping forward, he closed the space between us and wrapped his arms around my waist. His hands were strong, like I knew they would be—it would have been easy to relax into him and let him take control. But now that we were here—I reached up and kissed him, hard. Angry. He slid his hands up my back and held me tight while I fought to be in charge, lips rough against his, trying to drink him in. It wasn't sexy, I wasn't trying to be sexy—I just wanted a chance to be fierce.

My hands clawed up his chest, started undoing buttons, finding a thin cotton T-shirt on underneath his dress shirt—I yanked it up from his waistband, my mouth still locked on his. He was breathing harder, answering my mood, reaching his arms back to free himself of his shirt, lips only leaving mine for a second to pull his T-shirt off, coming back to my kiss like he was drowning and I was air. I ran my nails up his naked back, pressed my whole body against his, felt him hard inside his dress slacks, knew exactly what he would feel like hard in me, and then raked my nails down his back again at the thought. He shivered and reached between us to take off my foolish silver belt.

There was a retching sound from the top of the stairs. Then another. And a third.

I pulled back and thumped my head against his chest. I heard his heartbeat racing—no matter what form he was in, that was mine. I breathed in heavy, the scent of his sweat, with its undertone of vetiver.

"Let me guess," he said, after a long inhale. "The sound of retching is like a mating call to a wild nurse."

"If I leave her alone, she might puke in her hair."

"That's disgusting."

"It was supposed to be." I stepped back from him. Parts of my body ached with regret. He looked disheveled, like I'd mauled him, which I supposed I had. "I can't just leave her."

"You can't just leave anyone. It's one of your biggest virtues, and one of your worst flaws." He bent down, picked up his dress shirt from his floor, and pulled it on. "Go."

Unsure if he was mad at me, but sure I was doing the right thing regardless, I ran up the stairs before I could embarrass myself or screw up anything any further.

CHAPTER TWENTY-EIGHT

Gina had crawled out of the tub and made it to the toilet. She was laying there, her face pressed against its side. Thank God Asher's maid, or some personal OCD streak of his own, had left this bathroom spotless, almost sterile. I'd feel bad if I'd brought Gina to someplace strewn with pubic hairs to hurl. I flushed the toilet and turned on the air vents.

"Why did I do this to myself?" Gina mused aloud.

"Love?" I guessed, though I knew she was being rhetorical. I knelt beside her and stroked her hair back from her face.

"I never should have even gotten infected. I should have known better."

"Better to know now than change your mind after the moon." I got comfortable sitting on the floor, using some towels to buffer my ankles. "Let me get this straight. You were dating a were . . . bear?"

She nodded sorrowfully, her face cradled against the side of the porcelain bowl.

"I have to ask. Were there any brightly colored insignias on his chest? Like a rainbow, or an ice cream cone?"

"What?" she said, peering up.

"You know. Like a Care Bear."

"Fuck you, Edie." She closed her eyes, like that would make me disappear.

"I'm just saying that if I were dating a *were*-bear, I would carefully check him over for any lame tattoos. Like of candy canes. Or sunshine."

"Fuck you and fucking were-bears." She snorted. I thought it might have become a laugh if she hadn't thrown up again.

Asher knocked politely about ten minutes later, before opening up the door. "If I've learned anything from watching pornography, it's that women at slumber parties need blankets and pillows. And perhaps also empty garbage cans." He set everything he'd brought down on the bathroom counter. "I'll be in the bedroom down the hall. Please call me before you two start to wrestle."

"Will do," I promised as he shut the door.

"How do you know him?" Gina asked me.

"We saw each other, once or twice."

"You broke up with that?" she inferred. I was saved from explaining by her having another wave of nausea.

My phone was ringing when I woke up. I was on Asher's bathroom floor, stiff and store.

"Ugh." I pushed myself upright. Gina was still snoring, so I knew she'd survived the night. I fished for my phone—it was dark, except for a line of light coming underneath the bathroom door—and found out it was eight A.M., and it was Sike's number on the screen. "Hello?"

"Edie—Edie, you're safe." It was Anna's voice, not an answer, a question.

"Sometimes. Yeah." I pushed myself to standing and opened the door to creep out into the hall. "Why? Is there something else trying to kill me I should know about?"

"I should hope not." Wherever Anna was, it sounded

hollow in the background; her words were echoing. I thought I heard the drip of falling water. It'd be ironic if we'd both spent the night in bathrooms. "Is Gideon safe?"

"He was when I left him." I sank down onto the carpeting in Asher's hallway and put my back against the wall. I was comforted by the fact that she cared about Gideon. Most vampires wouldn't. It made me feel that I'd put my trust in the right place.

"Good. Things are more complicated than I had feared."

I wanted to say, *You think?* But I knew that would not be well received. "Why were those weres after me? Who were they?"

"Did Dren contact you?"

"Yes. To extort were-blood from me." That had better not have been part of the plan.

Anna made a growling sound. "He was supposed to ask you for help and offer you aid."

"You mean getting Winter's blood was your idea?"

"No. His. But he did clear it through me. He didn't say he'd threaten you for it, though."

I sighed. "I probably wouldn't have helped him otherwise. Still, he could have mentioned you."

"I'm sorry he did not. I will speak with him as soon as I'm free."

"You're trapped?"

"Being tested."

"Are you passing?"

"Of course." The sound of dripping in the background of wherever she was continued. "I can only assume the attacks on you are because of your association with me. But it's unlike weres to work with vampires. Most of them hate us fiercely."

"Maybe some vampires are using the weres to cover their tracks?"

"Possibly. It does appear that some other Rose Throne Houses fear me."

"I can't imagine why," I said, as flatly as possible. Anna laughed. I'd only seen her slaughter a dozen members of her former Throne. She'd had every right to do it at the time, but some Rose Throne vampires were there, and all of them had long memories. "Hey," I went on, "have you heard of a were called Viktor? Now that Deepest Snow's leadership is changing, he's angry. Another were I know thought my attackers might have been sent by him."

"No. I'll look into it, though," she said. "Do you have a were you can trust?"

"Depends. Why?"

"I need you to talk to the highest-ranking were you can find. Ask them for sanctuary."

"Sanctuary?"

"Sanctuary, on my behalf. Use my name. Do it in a public place, where there's more than one of them. Sound as official as possible. They will not be able to refuse you."

"Why?"

"It's an ancient pact from our persecuted days. If I make them responsible for your care, they have to protect you."

"From . . . themselves? Does it really work like that?"

"It's supposed to. You know how long it's been since there's been a nochnaya?" she asked me, using her original people's phrase for what she was, a living vampire. "The time in which anyone's asked for sanctuary's slightly longer than that."

"Longer . . . or are you all only counting the times it was successful?"

She snorted on the far end of the line. "Just do it, Edie. I'm not there, Dren can't watch you during the day, and Sike won't survive a fight with a were this close to the full moon. It's supposed to be too humiliating for a vampire to have to ask for were-help for anyone to do it. One way in which my humanity helps me—I'm too emotionally wrapped up in your survival to care about my pride."

"I can't decide if that's comforting or not."

"I can't tell you if it should be." Behind her, I heard the sucking sound of an emptying drain.

"Where the hell are you?" I asked her.

"In a charnel house. I've spent the last three nights hung suspended in blood. The first test is always hunger." She inhaled and exhaled deeply. "I have to sleep now, Edie. The dawn comes, and tomorrow promises to be just as long as today."

And what did someone say to a teenage vampire whose fate was intertwined with her own? I shrugged at Asher's hallway wall. "Good luck, Anna."

"I hope not to need it."

The line went dead.

I pushed myself to standing again, stretched out my back's kinks, and descended to the first floor. When I didn't find Asher, I decided to give myself a tour.

It was weird to be at his home without him in it. First, because I expected him to spring out and catch me snooping, and second, because without him, it seemed as sterile as the bathroom had the night before. With the exception of the library below, his bedroom was plain: a huge closet full of clothing—mostly nice, but there were some strange costumey pieces, a few additional tragic holiday-themed sweaters—but no photos on the walls. His bathroom was dull too, all white tile, wood, and chrome. I even looked in his medicine cabinet, but it only had extra tubes of toothpaste, not unlabeled bottles of Ativan. As I went from room to room, it looked like an open-house home, ready for show. You could put yourself into this house pretty

easily. Just like last night I'd tried to put myself into
Asher, via mouth-to-mouth.

There was one locked door, but I was a little ashamed
about looking through all his other things, so it didn't
bother me, much.

I grabbed what I hoped was an extra shirt of his and
rousted Gina, helping her to strip and turn on the shower.
She needed it. I found a tray of bagels in his kitchen, a
half-full tub of cream cheese, and a note saying *Help
yourself* in clean block handwriting. A fresh pot of coffee, still warm, was the only thing to prove Asher'd been
there.

I was on my second bagel when Gina made it down the
stairs. "God, I'm so embarrassed." On her, one of Asher's
shirts hung almost to her knees.

"Don't be. Everyone's been there."

"I know. It's just that I'm not supposed to be that person. I didn't go to vet school for this."

I proffered the bagels, and she shook her head, looking
a little green. "I'm just glad you called me."

"I didn't mean to interrupt your date," she said, and I
stared blankly at her. "That guy who was here. This is his
house, right?"

I snorted. "The only person I slept with last night was
you. I have the tile prints on my ass to prove it."

She made her way around the kitchen and poured herself a glass of water. "If you're not dating him, can I have
his phone number?"

"He's not really rebound material." Though I would
bet that Asher wouldn't be above helping someone out
with revenge sex. "He's a shapeshifter."

Gina made a face. "Oh."

"Yeah." The clock on the microwave said it was ten
A.M. I needed to get back home. Gideon was less indepen-

dent than a houseplant, and the only reason I remembered to feed Minnie was because she'd tell me to. "Gina—"

"It's just that they're going to ask. That's what sucks." She set her glass into the sink. "I introduced him to my parents, Edie. I thought he was the one."

I didn't know what to say. I didn't think I'd ever felt like that. I'd stood on the edge of The Oneness before, and maybe peeked into the valley below, but I'd never made the final jump. I'd learned that if you thought of people as disposable, it hurt less when they disposed of you.

But that didn't stop me from putting an awkward arm around Gina as she slumped over Asher's kitchen sink and cried.

We gathered ourselves into my car not long after she stopped crying. As I drove she narrated a tangled web of semi-plausibility. She'd told her parents she was working last night, and now she'd pretend she had car problems and had to wait for the mechanics and a tow.

"Why's it so complicated?"

"I'm the baby of the family. I live with my parents. I just tell them I'm working when I go out on spend-the-night dates."

"I'm the baby of my family too. When I turned eighteen, my mother flung open the doors and kicked me out of the nest."

Gina sighed. "It's different for me. I was working and going to vet school when my mother got early-onset Alzheimer's. One of my brothers died in the war. The other moved away. My sister has four kids—taking care of Mom and Dad just fell to me. One day I was living at home to save money, the next I was stuck there because my dad couldn't convince my mom to take a shower otherwise."

"God. That's tough, Gina."

"Tell me about it." She shook her head. "That's what I traded. The Shadows keep her from getting any worse, and they get me, on Y4." I winced, but she was looking out the window. She went on. "I've never actually gotten to be a real vet. What I would give someday to just take care of a yippy dog. Even just a hamster. Turn here." She pointed in front of me. "If I'd stayed bitten, I wouldn't have been able to keep my job. Y4 fires you if you fraternize too much—the Consortium won't allow it. It might make you too biased, I guess."

"Nah—probably because then everyone would do it, and there'd be no one left to work on the full moon," I teased.

She gave me a halfhearted smile. "Really, if I lost my job, where would my mom and dad be? Part of me is afraid the Shadows will keep her alive forever, just to keep me trapped."

"That's a reasonable fear."

"I know. Anyhow. It is what it is now. I'll get out someday, just not today. Or tomorrow. Or four days from now."

I turned into a neighborhood where all the homes were packed together tightly, and she directed me into her driveway. "You going to be okay?"

"Yeah. I'll catch the bus into work tonight. I'll be fine."

That wasn't exactly what I'd meant, but I nodded. "Call me if you need anything else, Gina."

"I will." She gave me a tight smile. Her hand was on the door handle, but she didn't move to open the door. I could see her steeling herself to face her parents, haunted by the memories of what could have been, fighting the depression that came with realizing you made the wrong choice, even if you're not entirely sure which one it was.

"He doesn't deserve you, Gina. You know that, right?"

"I know. Doesn't make it hurt any less." She reached

over and hugged me before jumping out of my car. I watched her till her front door opened, then waved as I pulled out of her driveway.

I wished I could have helped her out more, but I had problems of my own to get home to.

CHAPTER TWENTY-NINE

"Honey, I'm home!" I announced as I walked into my house. There was a groan from the vicinity of my bathroom, and an accusatory meow from Minnie.

I walked around the bar and into my kitchen. I put an extra bagel into my fridge, noticing an empty space on my small kitchen counter where my toaster oven had been. Huh. Over by the couch, the mister bottle was empty. Hopefully some of that had gotten into Gideon's mouth. I paused and listened for more noise. Gideon would be dead if Veronica had woken up—and God help Sike if she didn't take Gideon with her when they took Veronica. I walked down my hall and pressed my ear to the bathroom door. There was silence beyond.

"Hey, I really want to take a shower." Speaking of which, he probably needed one too. Goddammit, if I had to shower people on my off days, I should at least be getting paid minimum wage.

Another groan. Gideon always sounded like an end-stage liver failure patient, with too many toxins in his brain to think straight. Like a seal having sex on a beach. "One for yes, two for no," I said. "Are you okay in there?"

Silence.

Fuck.

"I'm coming in." I opened up the door—it stopped

when it hit my electric scale. Which was on the floor and, for some reason, dismembered. "Gideon?"

Gideon stood in front of the mirror, his naked back to me, blocking his own reflection. I shoved the scale away with my toe and stepped inside. "You okay?" I asked, then gasped. The floor around my sink was spattered with blood, and Gideon's image in the mirror was not the same.

"What happened to you?"

With the mirror I could see his face—his eyelids still dangled over empty sockets, and his teeth were still exposed—but in his chest there was a piece of plastic, embedded in his flesh. There were raised welts where it had inserted itself—or where he had inserted it himself. *Oh, my, God.* There were other fragments elsewhere, like a jigsaw puzzle scattered on his chest. I felt a small part of my brain just shut off at the horror.

"Gideon . . . what did you do?"

Things that were not veins ran inside his chest; I could see them looping, curled, creating new circulatory paths. I reached out to turn him around, and he put up his hands to stop me—the ends of his fingers were spiked with pieces of metal, tines from something. My brain slowly parsed them—they were from the grill from my toaster oven.

"What. Happened."

A red light turned on near the apex of his shoulder. Like a webcam. Say, from my laptop. And I knew who'd been behind all of this.

"Grandfather."

Gideon didn't answer me. He couldn't while missing a tongue. But German muttered out from Gideon's chest, where the CD player rode under Gideon's skin like a pacemaker, the edges ragged and raw.

"How the hell did this happen?"

I'd only been gone for a night. One night. And Grand-father had taken all the electronics in my house and shoved them under Gideon's skin, like he was a fucking piñata. I wanted to throw up, but Gideon was blocking my path to the toilet, and I didn't want to step in his blood.

"What? How?" I sputtered. I let go of Gideon, and ad-dressed the vicinity of his chest. "Did you even give him a choice?"

"Wir sind beide zufrieden."

"Did he actually give you a choice?" I asked Gideon, my voice rising.

"Unsere Wahl war offensichtlich." The man—the hu-man beneath whatever the hell Grandfather had done—nodded. But maybe Grandfather was controlling him. Who knew. Who would ever know again.

I made to reach for the sink, and stopped myself before I put my hand into a smear of blood.

Gideon's hands weren't completely articulated, but he'd managed to get the hot water on. "That toaster oven was a graduation gift," I said.

Grandfather continued talking.

"I could try to translate what you're saying, but you ate my laptop." My brain was trying to get a wrap around what had happened. I could feel it revving up, and then spinning out of control. It was one thing keeping Grand-father around, thinking he was some moody German ghost—and another to have him blacksmith himself into a cyborg.

"I need a shower." I took some deep breaths. "This will all make more sense after a shower." Surely it couldn't get worse. I stepped aside, so Gideon could get past me.

He didn't move.

"A shower, by myself. Out. Now," I clarified.

Gideon held up his right forefinger, which had been replaced by the temperature-dialing rheostat from my toaster oven. And then he turned toward my bathroom mirror and sketched out something upon the fogging glass.

"Out!" I yelled.

He turned and squeezed by me, leaving the sink's water still on.

Written in the fog, before more fog could replace it, I saw two words: RADIO SHACK.

Not surprisingly, a shower didn't help. I couldn't really wash my troubles right out of my hair, when *What the hell had happened to Gideon* was continually at the forefront of my mind.

Gideon had been horrifying before, but my brain could grasp the ways he was damaged—I'd seen other people injured similarly at work. Now he was changed in ways I couldn't comprehend. I almost stepped out onto bloody tiles. Then I grabbed an extra towel and threw it down to step on instead. I didn't have the strength to clean anything else just now. Bleach would have to wait.

I walked into my bedroom. It would be day for a few more hours. I wanted to feel safe, but it was getting hard in between all the crazy. There was too much going on, and nothing I could do about it. Maybe once Anna's ceremony was done, and Gideon and Veronica were out of my house, it would all start making sense. Then I'd only have to worry about stalkery vampires and stalkery weres. It would mean that my problems had been halved.

I picked up the box Anna had given me. At least Grandfather hadn't assimilated Asher's silver bracelet. I put the bracelet on, feeling a bit like Wonder Woman, pulled the sheets back on my bed, and tucked myself inside.

I didn't set my alarm clock, and it felt late when I woke up. I blinked and reached for my phone. It was five P.M.

I was still safe, inside my house. As safe as could be expected anyway. I remembered today's To Do list: dinner with Jake, ask a were-leader for help.

I went toward my bathroom to brush my teeth, then remembered the huge bloodstain on the floor, and my apartment's other, non-feline, non-vampire occupant.

"Hey, Gideon——" I said, walking into my living room. He stood with his back to me, against the far wall. His shoulders were slumped—it looked like he was urinating, only I didn't smell pee and there was no corresponding sound. "Grandfather?" I tried instead.

Him having his back to me, with no hint he'd heard either name, was creepy. I walked over, feeling like that chick in a horror movie who always does what she shouldn't, no matter how many times you throw popcorn or yell at the screen. As I sidled around him, I saw he was plugged into the wall simultaneously via an outlet and a phone jack.

"I'm still not okay with this," I said. The cords looked umbilical—I tried not to follow them too far into the shadows my bathrobe created on his chest. Wait—my bathrobe. "Gideon," I said, my voice low. Was nothing sacred? He'd taken the shoulder and torn it, so that my laptop's webcam could peek through. I took a step nearer. "Do you even need food now? Water?" I asked, and got no response. "Okay. Fine. I'll just be in the bathroom, cleaning up your mess." I resisted the urge to poke him, to see if he would move or what he would do, and went under my kitchen sink to get bleach.

I'd need a new jug of bleach soon and some additional cheap towels. Hopefully that trip could wait until after the holidays. I wondered exactly how Grandfather-Gideon was communing with the outside world just now, and to what effect—I imagined him lodging serious complaints on assorted message boards and snorted. Honestly, it seemed like the sort of thing I ought to tell—or warn—someone about, but I wasn't entirely sure who, and since so far the only detriment was that he was probably using electricity like I was harboring a grow-light, it could wait.

I scrubbed until no one would know that my bathroom had been a crime scene unless they possessed a forensic degree. Empowered by cleanliness, high on bleach fumes, I got ready to go out to dinner with Jake.

I pulled on my scrubs and all the silver that I currently owned. Between my belt, bracelet, and badge—which might warn me a second or two before any attack—I'd give myself even odds on surviving for five seconds once I was outside my door. Five whole seconds, although not necessarily painless ones. Hooray for me. I estimated where I'd parked was about ten seconds away, and technically being in my car wasn't any safer than being outside it, really. If a certain crazed unknown someone in a black truck decided to run me over, my little Chevy Cavalier wouldn't stand a chance.

While I was standing there waiting, measuring assorted odds, Gideon came up behind me, looming.

"I've got to get to my car. Are you willing to spot me?" I wasn't sure what Gideon could do precisely—but once upon a time, I'd seen Grandfather laser out from the inside of a pissed-off dragon. Gideon nodded, then pointed at the doorknob with his chin.

It took me a second to catch his drift. "Ah. Opposable thumbs must be high on your To Do list."

Gideon nodded.

"Once I leave, don't open the door up for anyone but me, okay?"

Gideon nodded again, and with one last look at my badge, I opened the door.

CHAPTER THIRTY

The only thing I had to be afraid of on my way to my car was ice. The weather wasn't letting up—instead of snowing enough to run the city into the ground, it kept warming just enough to put a slick sheet of ice over everything as it refroze. I hopped inside and my engine took quickly. With a moment of forethought, I took my ibuprofen out of my purse and tossed it into my glove box—I'd hate to find out Jake had swiped it two weeks from now, when I was on my period.

Jake was waiting for me on the curb outside the Armory. When he saw my car, he put his thumb out like a hitchhiker, and I flashed my high beams at him.

"Hey, Sissy!" he said as he got in.

"To what do I owe the honor?" I said, pulling away from the curb.

"The usual. Your good taste in siblings, the fact that we share a mom." He grinned at me in the rearview mirror. "How's it going?"

"Eh. I'm tired."

"You work night shift. You're always tired."

"True."

"But I have a surprise for you."

"Really? What?"

"Dinner's on me tonight."

I flipped the right-hand turn signal on in my car.

"What?" he asked.

"I'm driving toward the nearest Burger King."

He snorted. "Go straight two lights, before making a left."

I did what he said, and there were directions after that. We wound up in a diner at an area just this side of decent. I'd been here before, long ago, when Mom would drop Jake and me off at a forgotten arcade with a fistful of quarters to kill an afternoon. The arcade was gone now, but the diner remained.

"Well, this is a blast from the past," I said, pulling into a small parking lot nearby.

"I thought you'd like it."

"Thanks. I think I do." He held the door for me as we went inside.

As I passed, I could see he was wearing nice clothes—he looked pulled together. It was hard for me to wrap my mind around this version of Jake: clean, polite, kind. The waitress took us to a booth.

"Just like old times. Want a chocolate milk shake?" Jake asked as the waitress waited for our drink order.

"Maybe a hot chocolate, instead. And a burger, please."

"Me too. A double."

The waitress took our order and went away.

"So," I said, looking at Jake.

"Soooo?"

"Really, Jake. What is up." I took my hat off and set it down. It was nice and warm in here at least. Plus, there were no eyeless cyborgs.

"Does there always have to be something up?"

"With you, yes."

"I just wish you could trust me again."

"How many times have you stolen things from me, Jake?"

"I don't want to hash over the past."

"How convenient."

"Do we have to have the same conversation every single time we hang out?"

I squinted at him. "Unless we're not talking that day."

He crossed his arms, and childishly stuck out his tongue. I couldn't help but laugh. The waitress came by with our hot chocolates, and we busied ourselves stirring in marshmallows.

"I can't blame you," Jake began, and I expected one of the reversals that had followed the last few times he'd said those words. *I can't blame you for whatever problems you have, like not trusting me,* he'd say, without ever owning up to his own flaws. But instead he continued, "I can't blame you for being mad at me. But I want you to know, I've turned over a new leaf."

The irony that it was the dead of winter, and we wouldn't see any new foliage till late spring didn't avoid me. "How so?"

"For starters, I'm buying us dinner tonight. And then next month, I'll be paying for my half of the cell phone bill."

I pursed my lips. If we were normal, these things would have pleased me; they'd be signs my erstwhile brother was getting back up on his feet. But if Jake had taught me one thing, it was that everything always came with a hitch. "How are you affording it?"

Jake shrugged nonchalantly.

"No. Seriously, Jake. I need to know."

"I've been working very hard lately is all."

"About that, Jake." I couldn't very well tell my brother to quit hanging out with other homeless people—just white guys with dreadlocks who probably sold drugs. "What is it that you do?"

"This and that."

"Selling drugs," I guessed, getting ready to scoot out of the booth. Was this the right time to make a scene? Was there ever a right time? Of all the things I would have thought that Jake could do to push me away, this was the last, biggest, final, straw.

"No. Energy supplements."

"Is that what they're calling meth these days?"

He inhaled and exhaled. "I knew you would make this difficult, Edie."

"I'm sorry. I'm glad you're doing well. But if you're taking money for running drugs, and then trying to buy me dinner with it, I just can't stand for that."

"It's not drugs," he protested. I stood up, and he stood up too. Other patrons were looking at us now.

"Why can't you just have faith in me?"

"Are you really asking me that?" My voice rose as I asked him. He held out his hands, palms up, pleading.

"Edie. I love you. I just need you to believe in me. One more time."

I stood there, looking down at him, torn between running away and running toward him. I breathed heavy, deep, then sat back down.

"Energy supplements," I repeated, trying to talk myself into it.

He nodded. "They're really popular. I'll cover the phone bill next month. The whole bill. Not just my half. I owe you."

"Okay," I said to him, and to myself. "Okay."

Our dinner came out. Jake opened up his burger and reached into his pocket, under my watchful stare, pulled out a palmful of glass vials.

I'd seen them before. Luna Lobos. Like the ones Luz

had, which she may or may not have given to Javier when my back was turned. Jake's vials held no such Schrodingerian duality—he popped off their caps and poured the contents onto his burger, where they pooled on the cheese. He saw me curl my lip in disgust. "Hey, I'm not just the owner, I'm also a member." He put the top bun back on and gestured grandly, like he'd done a magic trick, then pulled another full vial out of his pocket and put it on the table in front of me.

"What's in that? Vitamins and Windex?"

"Vitamins and caffeine probably." He took a few bites of his burger, smiled, and set it down. "You know, Edie—I really think this stuff is what's given me a new lease on life."

"How so?" I held it up and inspected his face, refracted through its blue-tinged contents. There were a few grains of what looked like pepper suspended inside.

"It's just—things have gotten easier, since I started this . . ." His voice faded, unsure what word to use, trying, I was sure, to pick one that wouldn't piss me off. ". . . multilevel marketing opportunity," he decided on.

"Uh-huh."

"I don't have the cravings I once did. I bought one of these, and as soon as I started taking it, all those other urges were gone."

I remembered all the money I'd spotted him while he'd been taking "care" of me, post-stabbing. Clearly he'd spent it on more than just lunch.

"Once I found out who to talk to, so I could start selling them myself, and taking a cut—it's been great, really. I have money now. I don't want to get high anymore. The only high I'm after is that performance high." I watched the light of memory go on in his eyes. "God, I haven't felt this good since I used to run track."

"You and I both know that was a long time ago. We're not in high school anymore, Jakey."

"But it's the same thing. I want to see how far I can go. How well I can do. Just like running track, back in the day."

Jake wouldn't be the first junkie I'd seen kick one habit, only to replace it with another. I'd seen addicts who had burned away the septum between their nostrils become addicted to purchasing expensive shoes once the coke had lost its kick. There always had to be something to fill that aching need.

"Just try one. Really. You'll like it, I swear." And here he was, still trying to convince me, all over again. I remember the first time he'd handed over a glass pipe with a full bowl, and how hard he'd laughed at me as I coughed out hot smoke.

"You know, Jake—" I put the vial back on the table. "I'm glad you're happier now, but it's really not my thing."

"This is what's stopping me from trying to score, Edie. It's like magic."

"Yeah. Well." I looked down at my unadulterated burger, and then picked it up. It wouldn't do any good to tell him anything, and so I wouldn't. I shoved the burger in my mouth and took a huge bite. Anything to keep from saying something I'd regret.

Jake sighed at me, shook his head, and then polished off the rest of the fries on his plate. When the waitress came by with a to-go box, he took the check, and he had the gall to flirt with her in front of me. She even flirted back.

I tried to see him as she must have—not as someone participating in a customer service transaction but as a person. He looked clean. Hell, he looked good. He had our dad's brown eyes, and his shaggy brown hair needed a cut, but looking a little rugged around the edges was almost a rare thing in this town. Holing up for winter after winter made most people soft and doughy. He looked like he'd been outside recently, like he might know how to use a football, or a rake. He put down cash for both our meals and tipped her well, like a true adult.

I had to admit, weird water in little blue vials or not, I was impressed. And really glad I'd kept shoveling in fries.

"Here, Edie, keep this, in case you change your mind," he said as we stood.

I inhaled to argue, then realized I was tired of fighting him. The thing with Jake was that he always wound up doing what he wanted to anyway. A salesman to the end, there was no way not to lose. I just wished he'd found this calling earlier.

"Sure, fine." I pocketed the blue vial, and together we walked out to my car.

CHAPTER THIRTY-ONE

We drove to the Armory in silence. I was concentrating on the road—the snowplows hadn't hit these streets since dawn, and it was getting treacherous. Jake seemed pleased with himself, like he'd won some argument I didn't know we'd had.

I pulled against the curb a block from the shelter, where I could manage to parallel-park without putting anyone else's life or vehicle on the line. Jake grinned over at me, in the street's half-light.

"Hey—I'd been meaning to ask, but I forgot. Can you see if someone's at the hospital for me? You met him on Christmas—Raymond." He saw the question on my face, and spoke more quickly than I could respond. "He didn't come home to the shelter last night, and I'm worried he got hurt."

"Caught in the crossfire of an energy supplement war?" I said sarcastically.

"Or frozen to death, after being beaten by asshole college kids," Jake replied, just as sarcastic.

"I'll keep an eye out."

"All right," he said, reaching over. We hugged in the front seat of my car, clumsy with coats and no-practice. He refastened all the layers of his sturdy new coat. "You know, Edie—" he began, and looked outside. "It wasn't so bad living with you."

I was glad it was dark inside my car, with the engine off—I hoped it hid the emotions running across my face.

"I could pay you this time," he went on. "I know things are rough for you right now—I don't know how come, but you can't hide it from me, they are. I'm not talking put me on the lease or anything, but I could pay for half your rent, and we could share things again—"

I knew the thousand and one ways that having Jake live with me would be a bad idea—above and beyond the fact that a cyborg and a sleeping vampire had temporary residence. When the bottom fell out of whatever he was currently selling, and he wasn't flush with cash, and he tried to use, or sell other, worse, things, then I'd be the bad sister who kicked him out, all over again . . .

"It was just a thought, Edie," Jake said.

Just a thought, but painful nonetheless. "I'm sorry, Jake. I need to get my own life straightened out right now."

"Yeah. I hear that." He reached over and knuckled my head like we were kids again, then opened my car door. Winter air rushed in and took my breath away. I was sending him out into the cold. Again. "Bye, Sissy."

"Bye, Jake."

I watched him get out of my car and walk down the street while my heart broke in two.

It wasn't a long drive back to the freeway, except that I missed the exit because I wasn't paying full attention. I wished, not for the first time, that I could tell Jake everything. That I could trust him again, like when we were kids. But there was nothing I could do to change the past, and the future was hazy right now. I made three right-hand turns instead of one left and wound up going past the Armory again.

I slowed down to see if I could see Jake inside. The first floor of the structure had bank-window-type glass and was brightly lit. Warm, I hoped, and safe.

"Hey!"

I heard the voice even though both my windows were rolled up. I startled, looking around, even though surely whoever it was wasn't talking to me.

"Hey!"

I spotted him, racing down the street—a man in a fedora. Viktor, the were from the other night. "Hey!" he yelled again, swinging his arms over his head, as if he was trying to flag me down.

I hit the gas, trying to outrun him, but my Chevy didn't have much get-up-and-go. It lurched forward, and he ran from the sidewalk out into the street at me. I had to hammer my brakes not to hit him, and I slammed my car into reverse and started rolling backward, blind down the street.

"I just want to talk to you!" He ran alongside me, pounding on my car hood. Leaving dents.

"Jesus Christ!" I braced my arm on the passenger seat and looked behind me. There was an alley coming up. I wasn't a stunt driver, but—

"I just want to talk!"

I yanked my steering wheel down and prayed there wasn't any oncoming traffic. My car spun into the alley, and I put it into drive again, and then this time floored it. I traced my way down the dark street, watching him race behind me, arms still waving like an air traffic controller, until he gave up and the night made him disappear.

I caught the exit onto the freeway this time and drove straight in to work.

I parked nearby in the visitor lot, trusting the Shadows to keep me safe once I was on hospital grounds. What was

Viktor doing skulking downtown? Was that a coincidence, or had he followed me there? Would Jake be safe? I should have asked Anna to protect him, too. The next time I paid attention to my surroundings I was in the elevator, dropping down to Y4.

On an impulse, I hit the STOP button and looked up. "Hey." I rapped on the wall with my free hand. "Are you there, Shadows? It's me, Edie," I said. I waited in silence, then sighed. "Which is it, you have no sense of humor, or no knowledge of popular literature?"

More silence. I felt sure they were listening in, though. "You'd better protect him from weres, too," I told the ceiling. And then I let the STOP button go.

I arrived on Y4 an hour early. Charles came into the break room while I was fishing in the back of the fridge for my emergency Diet Coke.

"Hey, Edie! Did they call you in, too?"

"I was down here already, and the weather was bad, so there was no point in driving home," I lied. "Why? We busy?"

"When aren't we," Charles said, and passed by me to take a Hot Pocket out of the freezer, popping it into the microwave as I cracked open my Coke. "So many donors came in last night. What the hell did they need all that blood for?"

After my chat with Anna this A.M., I had a suspicion. I sat down, since technically I wasn't on yet. "Charles, have the Shadows ever let you down?"

He turned around from the microwave. "Why do you ask?"

"Your scar. The one you showed me. They didn't protect you then, right? But—whatever they're trading you, to keep you here, surely they've made good on that."

"Yeah," he said, and behind him, the microwave counted down backward, seconds ticking away.

"What is it? If I can ask?"

He made a thoughtful face and let out a huge sigh. "My wife needed a heart transplant. She was low on the list."

"So . . . the Shadows moved her up?"

"Nope. She just got better."

"Oh. God." His wife—that'd mean he could never stop working at Y4. I mean, he could, but if he did . . . there was a distinct chance she'd die. That was an entire level of horror above the way they'd trapped me into working there. There was always the slim but possible chance that Jake might someday decide to stay clean. There was a ding, and Charles retrieved his Hot Pocket from inside the oven. "Damn."

"Exactly. How'd they get you?"

"My brother's a mess. Junkie. Homeless. Clueless as hell." I wished I could confide in Charles, but I knew I shouldn't. He had enough on his plate—plus he'd already warned me away from the weres. "There's just so much stuff going on right now, I get worried about him."

"Well, I don't like the Shadows, but I don't think they'll abandon ship just yet. This place is prime feeding territory. Where else would they go?" He bit into his Hot Pocket, hissing as it released steam.

"I can't believe you're a grown man, and you still eat those."

"If you ever meet my wife, don't rat me out. She makes me sandwiches, but I always pick up one of these on the way in." His phone rang from his pocket. "Speaking of," he said with a grin, reaching for it.

"She waits up for you every night?"

"She's a night owl too. We make a good team."

I smiled at him. It was nice to see that sometimes relationships worked. I took my Coke and ducked out the door.

* * *

If I stayed down in Y4, they'd put me to work. I hopped back into the elevator, made it take me to trauma ICU.

I'd get in trouble if I keyed myself into the computer looking up patient data on Jake's behalf, but with an exposed badge and a couple of open windows, I could make a thorough snoop. There couldn't be that many white guys with dreadlocks at the hospital. Javier and Luz were gone; their room held a woman colored Oompa Loompa orange with liver failure instead. I bet she sounded like Gideon. And I bet Javier was at a skilled nursing facility, and Luz was still being strong for him, at least for now. She was tough, but it was young love, so it wouldn't last— said me, the person who refused to admit she'd ever been in love before.

I quickly walked through all the ICUs. Satisfied that at least I'd tried on Jake's behalf, I texted him as I waited for another elevator.

Ur friend isn't here. And then, before I could think things through or regret it, I typed, *& still thinking about ur idea.*

Faster than I would have been able to type it myself I got, *Thanks Sissy. I owe you,* back from him in return.

Par for the course. The elevator arrived and I went back to Y4.

I changed into scrubs after my time skirting the HIPAA privacy line, and was just about on time.

Meaty saw me coming out of the locker room hallway. "I just made the assignments. You'll be around the corner tonight. Gina called in sick."

"I bet she did."

Meaty's eyebrows raised with a silent question, and I shook my head. "Never mind." I couldn't blame Gina for wanting a shift off after the night she'd had. "Who am I up with?"

"Rachel."

I made a face after Meaty passed by. Rachel was a four-legs-good, two-legs-bad kind of vet. She worked opposite weekends from Charles and me. On the rare shifts I had had with her, I'd never seen her hang out her co-workers much—so much so that I got the opinion that she hated us. Being in the were-corral corner with only her to talk to for eight hours would be hell.

As if mentioning her had summoned her, Rachel swung open Y4's double doors. "Edie, I need help. There's visitors."

My first reaction was to be surprised she knew my name. After that I paused for a moment, waiting for her complaint to go farther, then realized that was her complaint in its entirety. Visitors. Outside her patient's door. I nodded. "I'll be there in a second."

CHAPTER THIRTY-TWO

Rachel was standing near Lynn, the P.M. shift outgoing nurse, giving very meaningful looks toward Helen, who also stood nearby. She was dressed in head-to-toe black, the color of mourning, and it didn't suit her; it made her look too pale.

"Hey there," I said, giving Helen a smile. "Want to go get coffee?" She was a high-ranking were—I wondered if talking to her would count? There weren't any other weres around. I wondered how many needed to be listening in to officially kick-start the sanctuary engines of public humiliation and shame. At least where shame was concerned, I didn't have any.

I watched Helen resurfacing from her distant thoughts, to focus slowly on me. "Hmm? Oh—it's you. I don't think I ever got your name."

"Edie," I said, putting my hand out.

"Helen," she said, which I already knew. She shook my hand, hers warm but limp. Behind her, Rachel kept making furtive shoving gestures off to the side. "Do you think I'll miss anything?"

"I doubt it. And I bet you need a break. Let's take a walk," I suggested to Helen, reaching for her arm.

She reached back to me, and clung around me. I was startled by how near she was comfortable being—my personal bubble for strangers was a little farther out, unless I was about to sleep with them. But I didn't want to miss my chance to ask her for sanctuary, plus I felt sure that Rachel's happiness with me would be in direct proportion to how long I managed to keep Helen off the floor.

"Fenris Jr. is in bed, and I didn't have anywhere else to be," Helen said once we reached the double doors together, walking arm in arm. I nodded, even though I didn't think she could see me. "Have you lost someone before?" she went on.

No. I did know what it felt like to watch assorted someones leave, again and again and again. But not death, not yet. "No."

"It's awful." She squeezed me around my waist and arm as if to emphasize that fact, her hot hand on my arm's skin. I didn't like it when people touched me at the hospital, especially when I didn't know the last time they'd used hand sanitizer. I tried to keep that to myself, though. She was going through a lot, watching her father die slowly—just because I was jaded didn't mean everyone else had to be. I didn't squeeze her back, but I held her a little more firmly, and she relaxed into me. I assumed we'd hug, and that would be that.

"My husband's death was tragic, but at least it was quick. My father's death is a whole new kind of pain." She didn't step away.

I felt a little trapped, but I still made a sympathetic sound. She inhaled deeply, sniffing. Oh, God, if she started crying, what would I do? She sighed aloud and settled even closer to me, her head upon my chest, making walking almost impossible.

"Do—you want me to go get coffee and bring it back to you?" Rachel's desires and requests for sanctuary be damned, I wasn't going to haul a crying woman across half the hospital to the vending machines and back.

"No. It's good for me to walk a bit. To get away," she said from the vicinity of my right breast, and then raised her head, and took a step back. "I don't mean to frighten you. I apologize."

"It's okay." *Frighten* wasn't the precise word I'd have gone with—*creepy* or *overclose,* yes—but it'd do.

"We find comfort in one another. I am not often alone. I haven't been alone for the majority of my life." Helen looked over my shoulder, back from where we'd come. "And now—things change."

"I'm sorry." Where she'd been against me was warm. In other circumstances, her closeness would have been nice, say if she were a relative of mine. I wanted to do what was right, even if it felt weird. I reached out for her arm and gave her a comforting pat. I didn't know how else to help.

She put her hand to mine, pulled it down to her own, and gave me a weak smile. "Just a hand to hold, okay?"

I could deal with that. "Okay."

We walked hand in hand like schoolgirls to the cafeteria. It was closed but there were vending machines outside. I stood by Helen as she ordered coffee, and together we watched the machine pour. "When you're a child, they tell you parables about the moon."

"Like what?"

"Like the moon sees all, knows all, heals all. Whatever's convenient for them—that's how they are, adults," she said, as though she weren't among their number. "Up until tonight, I always thought that last part was true. I'd never had a wound the moon couldn't touch. But you don't need to be much of a were to smell the stink of death on Father now."

I hadn't smelled anything yet, but she was the wolf, not me. "We call that necrosis."

"How do you ever get the smell out of your nose?"

"The hospital's full of bad smells. You get used to it," I lied. People put toothpaste inside their masks, or told you to breathe through your mouth not your nose. You learned how to wash homeless people's feet with shaving cream, to cut the smell down, or set out a hospital-provided jar of clove oil in certain rooms, up high where the likely alcoholic occupants wouldn't find it until they were sober enough to know better than to drink the stuff. But necrosis was the worst, and there was no solution for it other than debridement or amputation. It was like a refrigerator full of already rotting food, left out for days in the sun. In humid June. The scent of it clung to the inside of your nose once you left. You didn't get used to necrosis, you just got as far away from it as quickly as you could.

I couldn't imagine what it would be like to have a far more sensitive nose in the hospital, walking to and from our floor. The drunks who came in in their own filth, the visitors with deodorant and cologne, the floor polish here alone—"It must be awful for you," I said.

"It is. Kindness helps, though." Helen took a long smell of her coffee, as though it were oxygen, and smiled at me. "Kindness, and other more pleasant things to smell."

The way she was looking at me right now, so open and trusting—I didn't want to ask her for her help, it wasn't fair of me. She was as much a patient here as Winter was. Maybe I could just put Gideon in my car trunk and rely on the sight of him to scare any other attackers away. I shook myself and blurted out a question before I could say of or think of anything else dumb. "How old is Fenris?"

"Junior's twelve. He's in fifth grade."

"He's a pretty cute—I mean, handsome wolf."

Helen laughed. "Thank you. He's a handful, but I love him dearly. Everyone does. It's very kind of Lucas to travel here to hold his place."

We made our way down the stairs near the cafeteria, then cut down toward the lobby. "Do you all homeschool?"

"No. My pack's philosophy requires forced integration, coupled with strict control. Packs that isolate themselves lose the economic means to survive. We may play in the parks come the full moon, but on a day-to-day basis we're out there being productive citizens, paying taxes, driving on public roads." She sounded like she'd given this talk before, and she was walking by herself now. It seemed our conversation had given her strength—that or the coffee.

Speaking of roads—"Where was your father coming from the day that he got hit?"

She reached the bottom of the stairs and turned toward me with a shrug. "I don't know. I wish I did."

"It looked like he was coming from the hospital." He'd been on the same corner that Charles and I had on our way to the Rock Ronalds.

"Did it?" she asked, her voice surprised.

"Kind of, yeah." Not that there weren't other buildings on our block.

Her head bowed and her posture slumped. "I guess now we'll never know," she said sadly.

We reached the lobby together. It was full as usual with visitors and vagrants—and a few of them stood at Helen's arrival. I heard someone whisper "Mother Helen!" and a handful of people crowded up, reaching out to Helen with their hands like she was a lost pop star. "How is he? Is there anything new?" They were an eclectic group: one looked like a biker, another looked nearly homeless, a third was a soccer mom, and three others were varying shades of gray.

Their attention seemed to bring fresh life to her. Like a wilting flower put in water, she revived to stand tall.

I wondered how much of it was real—being surrounded by friends in bad times helped—and how much of it was her feeling like she needed to put on a strong act. Maybe there wasn't that much different between Helen and Luz.

The guard up near the front of the lobby glanced our way, but he had obviously seen everything before. It wasn't his job to be the bad cop, even though he wore a badge—he was just supposed to keep the peace, and the visitors weren't misbehaving, even though I thought they were crowding Helen. I bet it helped that I was wearing scrubs, and they were all acting like they were about to get bad news. Guards gave bad news wide berth.

Helen reached out among them like Mother Teresa, hugging and petting them, individually and together.

I likely wasn't going to get a better chance than this to ask for her protection, even if it felt like I was invading a private moment between her and her people. This was not my place, these were clearly not my friends—I could tell by the looks they were giving me. More than I hated visitors—I hated feeling like one.

I stood to the side of the group and cleared my throat. "Helen—I know this is a bad time for you—but—"

The lobby doors opened and a woman in a parka came in, hood up. She walked past the guard's desk and slowly turned. The badge on my lanyard lit up like candles on a birthday cake.

I shoved into the group of weres and grabbed hold of Helen's arm. "Sanctuary—please!"

Helen turned her head to look at me in surprise. Behind her I could see the parka woman lower to all fours. Humans were not supposed to move like that. She didn't lope awkwardly like a werewolf from a horror movie—she glided, picking up speed, jumping over orange couches in the way. Her mouth opened, so wide I could see teeth,

teeth that were not right, teeth that were racing out as quickly as their owner to meet me.

"No running!" the guard yelled after her.

"Sanctuary!" I pleaded.

"Sanctuary?" Helen said, as though she hadn't heard me, then looked behind herself. I didn't know if the wind in the lobby shifted, or her were-senses tingled, but she shoved her nearest packmates away, sent them sprawling, and changed.

In the time it took for her coffee to fall to the ground, a blond middle-aged woman going sour with repeated loss turned into a yellow-gray wolf. In this new form, Helen crouched as the parka-woman leapt into the air to meet her.

The lobby strobed.

For a fraction of a second it was full color—orange couches, pieces of bright abstract art framed on the walls— and the next it was black. A were near me started howling. Moonlight filtered in through the skylights I always forgot our lobby had. The blackness was like a mist—I could see it—a cold, damp fog that smelled faintly of digestive juices. And then color resolved anew.

Helen was the only one who completed her leap. Her wolf form hit the ground, legs splayed out to catch itself, claws grating on linoleum tile. The parka-wearing woman was gone.

"No killing fights on feeding grounds," whispered something that was not human before the acrid tang of stomach acid went away.

Neither the guard nor any of the other visitors in the lobby reacted—just the weres, who clustered around a now naked Helen, kicking away an empty paper cup. Nice of the Shadows to clean up the spill hazard too. Always thinking about safety, that was them. I put a hand to my mouth and let out a squeak into my palm.

Naked yet still self-possessed, Helen made a thoughtful growl. "One of Viktor's women. I'm sure of it."

"I saw him earlier on today. Downtown," I said. "Near the Armory."

Helen looked to her people. "Three of you—go."

Three people at the back of her group peeled away and ran for the door, ignoring the security guard.

The rest of them continued as though nothing unusual had happened. They took off parts of their own winter clothing, handing them over to Helen. One gave her a knee-length trench coat, and between that and a black wool sweater she looked pretty normal, until you got down to the fact that her legs and feet were bare.

"Now, Edie, you were asking for Sanctuary?" she said.

I remembered Anna's suggestion to make it sound official, and cribbed my words from Sike the other night. "On behalf of Anna Arsov, the near-ascended, yes."

"Helen, the mother of the Deepest Snow pack, grants it." She looked to her were-friends surrounding us. "Protect her as though she were me. Both of you—" she pointed at two more weres in the group.

I had an image of returning to Y4 with two weres in tow. Charles would hate me for sure, then. "No—I'm safe while I'm here—the Shadows—you saw."

She petted the collar of her loaned coat and gave a smug smile. "Indeed. I'll send someone to wait for you at the end of your shift in this lobby," she said, then switched from regal to tired again. "I should get home. You'll call me if anything changes with my father, right?"

"Of course," I said, and nodded fast.

Helen and her retinue left then, her people clustered around her. The guard returned from outside, where the weres sent to chase Viktor had lost him. He panted, hands on knees, and watched the rest of the pack depart. None of them were running, so it was fine. Even if that one lady didn't have on shoes. I could see it on his face, him thinking that he'd seen crazier stuff.

I knew for sure he had. Even if he couldn't quite remember it.

CHAPTER THIRTY-THREE

"Back so soon?" Meaty asked as I walked past the nursing station.

"You have no idea." I rounded the bend, and Rachel looked up at my return.

"You got her to go home?" Rachel craned back in her chair, as though I were hiding a full-grown woman behind me.

"Yeah. Can I go on break?" I leaned forward to look at the clock inside Winter's room. "I know it's early but—"

"Sure, fine." Rachel waved me away too. To her I looked like another kind of visitor, me and my two legs.

I walked back out the way I'd come. I wasn't hungry, but I didn't want to sit down and be normal just yet.

First, I wanted to change my scrubs. Helen's coffee had stained the ankle of my pants when it'd fallen, and I still smelled tangy like stomach contents, at least to my mind. Maybe the Shadows' vapor had singed my nose. Where had the parka-wearing woman gone? I didn't think I wanted to know.

Did I feel safer about things now? I hadn't ever done anything to Viktor—but between the dents in my car and the were-women, I didn't know. Maybe he was insane. Since two weres had attacked me in the mall parking lot, and the Shadows had only killed one tonight, I didn't feel safer, really. I pulled off my scrub top angrily.

Helen had been so controlled when she'd been attacked. It must be fabulous to have a power you could call on when you needed it, just wrap it around you like a cloak—or know that you were already dead, or partially dead, and therefore mostly invulnerable. I yanked off my pants and threw them into the soiled linen cart forcefully.

I liked my job. I liked knowing things. I didn't think I'd like being normal. But I wasn't so sure I wanted this anymore, worrying about my life and smelling like puke. I opened my locker and redid my ponytail in the little mirror magnetized inside. On the top shelf inside I saw my dish towel holding Anna's ceremonial knife.

I'd made a promise. I'd see it through. But after that— who knew. I straightened my scrubs, pulled my lanyard to hang outside them, and slammed my locker shut.

The rest of the night passed in a haze. Winter's care was like moving deck chairs on the *Titanic.* When we turned him, he didn't resist, and the blackening of his toes and fingers was creeping higher, slowly but inevitably. I helped Rachel, I helped Charles, I helped Meaty—I couldn't wait for morning to come.

Since I didn't have a report to give, I snuck out as soon as I could. How would I know if the were-escort for me was safe or not? I should have asked Helen for a password.

I got out of the last elevator and started walking toward the lobby doors, scanning the couches full of unfamiliar faces.

"Looking for someone?" said a voice I almost knew. I turned around, and Lucas unfolded out of one of the lobby's chairs.

"Oh—it's you."

"Yeah." He looked as rumpled as I felt. His clothing

was wrinkled, his face was haggard, and he reeked of sweat.

"Have you been here all night?"

"I came straight from the fights. I was worried I'd miss you if I slept in my car." He swung his arms around fluidly, waking dull limbs up, and grinned. "Thank God the moon's near or I'd need you to go get me ibuprofen, Nurse."

I snorted. "So sorry to inconvenience you. There've only been two measly attacks on my life." If that woman had gotten to me last night, I'd have needed something stronger than an ibo to ease my pain.

"Sorry. I guess that wasn't funny." He jerked his head toward the lobby doors. "Let's get out to the parking lot and away from all these people. Then we can figure out our plan."

I followed him out toward the visitor parking lot, past the late day shift workers and bureaucrats coming in. Timekeepers and social workers, doctors and lawyers, all the bees that kept the hive running.

The visitor lot was nearly empty as we reached my car. "Did you find anything out the other night?"

Lucas shook his head. "Not yet. We're still running Viktor down."

"And you're sure it's him?"

"Viktor ran Winter down. You saw him do it, even if you don't remember seeing it. Viktor's after you because he feels guilty, and he's scared you'll tell," Lucas explained with a shrug.

"You're sure about all of that?" I asked. I sure as hell wasn't.

"Trust me. Viktor and I have a lot of history. More than either of us would like." He stared into the snow beside my car, then shook himself, almost dog-like, and his gaze rose to meet my own. He smiled. "Besides—do you have any other enemies I should know about?"

"Do you want the long list, or the short list?" I said, and leaned back against my cold car. "It's just that I wonder if he's working with vampires."

Lucas's face froze in surprise, then he laughed at me. "Weres and vampires? No. Never."

"You're sure?"

"Positive. We hate them. Viktor may hate us, but he's still a were—he hates vampires more. We just have to protect you until my pack finds him, is all. I'm glad you asked us for our help."

And despite the cold outside, and the fact that there were still mysterious weres after me and possibly vampires as well, I said, "Me too."

Tiredness hit me like a wall, and maybe, although I wouldn't have liked to admit it aloud, I did feel safer with Lucas around. I was glad Helen had sent him and not some were I didn't know.

"Now you look like you could use an ibuprofen," Lucas said gently, teasing.

"It's been a long night."

He thumped the truck he leaned on. "I already knew which car was yours, so I parked beside you. I'll escort you home."

My bed and a shower sounded like a fabulous idea—and then I had a vision of him expecting to guard me from inside my home, complete with Gideon and Veronica. "Okay. But you can't come inside."

"You mean your boyfriend doesn't know?"

"What?"

"You always smell like a strange man. I just assumed."

"Yeah—no." I had not yet gotten so desperate that I needed to Frankenstein a half-man, half-parts-liberated-from-my-kitchen boyfriend. I'd be buying fresh batteries long before that. "He's just a friend."

"You have a lot of strange friends."

"Don't I know it," I said, and grinned at him. "So—I guess I'll drive, and—" I began, hunting for my keys.

"Do you eat?"

"Yes," I answered without thinking.

"Good. I can guard you at a restaurant just as easily as I can at your house. When will you be up?"

Keys found, I looked up. "That's cheating," I protested.

"Unless you wanted to cook for me. I don't mind eating in," he pressed with half a shrug. "It's the fights you know. Have to keep up my strength. I'll even take a shower."

"Wow. A shower. That's it. I'm in," I said, deadpan. He waited, grinning. I realized I wouldn't win if I didn't muster up more energy to fight—and I might just not mind losing, anyhow. "If I say I'll see you at seven, can I finally go home?"

"Sure thing."

"I'll see you at seven then, Lucas. Good-bye." I waited until he got into his car before I got into my own.

Lucas's truck followed me all the way home, and he didn't get out of it, good to his word. Any more people hanging out in my apartment, and I'd have to start charging rent.

Minnie greeted me at the door, and Gideon was still communing electronically with my wall. "You'd better not be stealing cable," I told him and went into the back.

A shower washed the last of the potentially imaginary vaporized puke smell out of my hair, I ate the very end of Christmas's leftover mashed potatoes, and I crawled into bed at a quarter to nine.

I think I slept like the dead. Not as dead as Veronica, but close. I woke at six P.M. to a dark house, and a snuggling happy cat. Out the window I saw a dark sky and falling snow.

One hour to kill before dinner. I wondered how tonight

would go. Company I could talk to, that wasn't plugged into my wall or resting inside of my closet, might be nice, even if it was under duress.

It was in the silent dark when I was home alone, dealing with all my problems by myself, that I could admit that I missed Ti. He was the last man I'd dated. Zombie, really . . . but he'd felt like a man. Like a grown-up. Someone I could count on and rely on, up until when he'd left me. He had reasons for going, and they'd sounded valid, but I couldn't rationalize away feeling left behind, especially when there was no guarantee he'd be coming back. There'd been a brief, so brief, window when I thought I wouldn't have to be alone again, and that made my current loneliness sharp, nestled against my breast like a viper.

I decided not to feel bad about going out on my not-a-date tonight. Instead of tricky potential feelings with Asher, Lucas would be a better, less entangled, way to feel in control. He was handsome, and hey, it wouldn't be the first time I'd gone out with a dog.

"What do you think about that, Minnie?" I asked, and reached over to knuckle her head.

My phone rang, and UNKNOWN NUMBER lit up its screen. A part of me got excited, and then another part of me squashed that part back into the box with the tight lid where it belonged.

"Hello?"

"Edie Spence?"

It wasn't a voice I knew. Unknown really meant unknown. "Yes," I answered, swallowing down a small knot of disappointment in my throat, trying to pretend it'd never been there anyhow.

"Are you alone right now?"

"Is this a prank?"

"It's Viktor. Don't hang up." I waited on the other end

of the line. "You have to listen to me—I'm not the one trying to kill you, I'm being set up. They just need an excuse to kill me, the same way they killed my father. Anything a member of the Deepest Snow pack has to tell you is a lie."

I sat quietly in bed. "How do you expect me to believe you?"

"How can I prove it?" Viktor gave a rueful laugh. "If I could, don't you think I would? But they've set me up—and there's orders now to slaughter me on sight. I don't have time or opportunity to come up with proof. I only know how they are, how they've been in the past. They murdered my father, and killed half my father's pack. They'll kill you too."

"Why would they need to kill me to get to you?"

"Either you're a convenient excuse to do away with me—or you have something they want."

"They're weres. We don't run in the same circles."

"Then whose circles do you run in?"

I pulled my phone away and frowned at it. Employed by vampires, indeed. "I thought vampires hated weres, and vice versa."

"Oh, we do. But seven years ago a vampire from House Grey met with my father, and after that he met Winter to talk about a truce. That truce was the last time he was seen alive. Winter killed him, and his own son too, to hide whatever my father learned. They said he'd killed Fenris and then fused our packs—they stole my birthright from me!"

I blinked, trying to understand—wondering if I should even try, since Viktor sounded increasingly wild as he went on.

"Why the hell were you downtown yesterday?"

"I was following Jorgen. I'd like to slit his throat."

And he was supposed to be the good guy? Only in his

own mind. "Viktor—" I said, and started pulling the phone away from my ear.

"Don't hang up on me! You're lucky! No one warned my father. He didn't know how ruthless they could be." Viktor snarled on the far end of the line, an animal sound. "There'll come a time, soon, when Deepest Snow will rue the day, I promise you. Next time you see one of them, tell them that."

He hung up on me, and my phone showed me the time. It was six fifteen, and I still had to get ready for a date.

CHAPTER THIRTY-FOUR

The first thing I did was text Sike. "Heard of House Grey?" I waited while brushing my teeth and then gave up on a response.

Lucas knocked on my door precisely at seven P.M. I opened my door and sidled out so he couldn't see behind me.

"See? I showered." He looked like he'd tried far harder than I had, wearing a white dress shirt, black suit jacket, and skinny tie. Compared with him I was significantly underdressed. I had on jeans and a baggy sweater that hid my silver belt buckle underneath.

I looked him up and down. "Did I miss where you invited me to prom? Or were you going to tell me about the Book of Mormon?"

He winced, picking at a sleeve. "I haven't had much time to shop for new clothing since I got here, what with the fighting, the leading my new pack, the dealing with my family, and the guarding you. To be fair, someone else guarded you today while I slept, showered, and found this at the bottom of my suitcase. I think the last time I wore this was at a funeral. Which I realize is morbid, now that I've said it out loud." He took a step back, making room for me to walk forward. "Where are we going to eat?"

I would have punted the decision back to him, but he

was new to town, and for someone who was allegedly full of lies and possibly wanted to kill me, he appeared really uncomfortable in his old suit. I took pity on him. "There's a burger place up a few exits, not too far. If you're not afraid of getting ketchup on your shirt, that is."

"Sounds fine to me."

I waited till we were buckled in and on the road to ask questions. "So tell me about Viktor."

Lucas shook his head. "We haven't caught him yet. We're still looking."

"Every ship but your four fastest," I murmured to myself. Not that I was sure I wanted Viktor to get caught. "What's his history?"

"His father's pack and my uncle's pack were in a territory war. Not as humans, but as wolves—every moon, vicious, vicious fights. They threatened to spill over into human time, and neither one of them would back down. My uncle Winter and Fenris Sr. called a truce, and Viktor's father went along with them into a room. Only Winter came out."

"Take the exit here. See the sign up there? That's where we're going." I pointed, and Lucas nodded as he hit his turn signal. "Do you think Winter was on the up-and-up?"

"Are you asking me if I think he killed his own son and lied about it to stay in power?"

"I suppose I am."

I could almost hear the gears turning in Lucas's mind before he next spoke. "It's what the gossips have always said. He was my father's brother. He must have at least considered it."

"That's harsh."

"You should meet my dad." Lucas's hands tightened around the steering wheel for a fraction of a second.

"Would you have done that, if you were him? If you needed to? To clear the field?"

Lucas's head pulled back like he'd been hit. "No. Or I want to say no now." He looked over at me. "Being pack leader—they say it changes you. But Winter's always been an angry man." Lucas snorted. "It's probably what's keeping him alive now, the two extra decades of hate."

The light changed; Lucas turned and went on. "I can't say what went on in that room. I know what happened afterward, though. Winter said Viktor's father attacked and killed Fenris Sr., and we had to believe him. We killed all their high-ranking wolves and assimilated the rest by force. Viktor was only ten. Younger than Fenris Jr. is now. It's why we let him live. A symbolic gesture toward peace—a fragile figurehead."

"Not so fragile anymore."

"No. Not if he's attacking you." The neon light of the burger joint was shining down on us orange and friendly as we parked. A car with booming bass parked beside us, full of humans with normal lives. Lucas hit his parking brake, then turned toward me. "You're not the only one with questions tonight, Edie."

"That's good." Between the two of us, I hoped we'd get some answers.

I hopped out of the cab and walked around to meet him. He held the door of the restaurant open for me, and the throng of kids home from college rushed the door. One of them forcibly bumped into Lucas and didn't apologize. I watched him carefully for any signs of anger, but he merely seemed resigned.

"There are days when I wonder about my commitment to staying a member of society," he said as we entered together.

"Helen told me about that. Something about public roads and paying taxes?"

"Deepest Snow's philosophy. One of the reasons for

friction between them and Viktor's pack. Winter had a point there. If you cut yourself off, you forget why you shouldn't kill everyone when you get the chance."

He let me lead into the restaurant, which I knew was seat-yourself. I angled us toward the back, booths far away from the college kids on furlough.

"You know, you're not any older than they are," I said, sliding to the inside of a booth.

"Only deep inside my heart."

At the front of the restaurant, the college kids started to make a ruckus. They squirmed around, changed seats, and threw things. I had no doubt they were already drunk and suspected they'd go on to drink more.

From the darkness of our booth, Lucas watched them with glittering eyes. I wondered if he was trapped inside his past, angry about not ever having the chance to openly misbehave—and then I realized it was different. Feral. Something I'd only seen illicitly when he was naked, at the fights. Like how Minnie was when she saw a flickering laser cat toy—ready to pounce.

He came back to attention at the table. "You were saying?"

"I wasn't." Suddenly Viktor didn't seem so crazy after all.

The waitress came by. We both ordered burgers, and when she left, he looked to me. "How did you know to ask for sanctuary?"

"The vampire I'm friends with suggested it."

"He couldn't guard you himself?"

"She," I corrected, "is a little indisposed. Plus, she'd be asleep during the day."

"Ah. Her being a woman . . . makes more sense. I couldn't see a male vampire swallowing his pride. You say she's your friend?" His eyebrows rose at the term as the waitress came by with our drinks.

"We've been through a lot, she and I." I could tell him that we were friends, but I knew he wouldn't believe it. "Why do vampires and weres hate each other?"

"We used to be their favorite food. We'd last a lot longer than normal humans would, with less outlay of funds. It was easier for them to hide their habits using us, back in darker times, before Winter's roads and taxes. Another way that civilization has benefited the were." He tilted his beer toward me in a small toast. "So why are you her friend, and not a daytimer, or donor—or living in a small tight box?"

Without answering, I shrugged. He gave another look around. "You picked the right booth. This one has its back to the wall. Not another booth. And you can see both the kitchen and main entrances from here. Windows too. Good call. How did you know to pick this one?"

I frowned, unsure where he was going with his demonstration. "Because." Because I'd been in patients' rooms before where I needed a clear shot through to the door—even before working on Y4.

"I know why, even if you don't."

"Illuminate me, then."

"Because to me, and maybe to others, although hopefully you'll never know—you're prey. You've always felt it a bit. A little paranoid, a little overworried. Perhaps jealous of people with more freedom and less care. But that feeling inside you that you've carried your whole life—it's actually quite profound." Lucas slowly sank back into the booth and looked at me with his red-brown eyes. I wondered if it was the nearness of the full moon that made him seem relaxed, languorous. As a predator, he knew his time was near. "That sense of the world, and your place in it, that's what's currently keeping you afloat." He rested his forearms on the table, and his attention on me felt eerie. The waitress saved me, bringing out our plates of food.

"What's it like, being a werewolf?" I asked, trying to make easy conversation.

Lucas leaned back. "Depends a lot on what kind of were you are. Major weres like my family that can switch anytime are rare. Minor ones, with diluted blood, that only get pulled by the moon are more common. Bitten ones look like the weres from the movies, half man, half wolf, that sort of thing. Each has its pros and cons. We're all mortal without the moon in the sky—after that, it depends on how much were is in your blood."

"But you don't live forever."

"As my uncle is illustrating." Lucas gave me another knowing look. "What's the connection between your people and him?"

"I don't know. And neither do they. But—just as your weres aren't all cohesive, neither are the vampires. I only have contact with the one, really."

"Is she important?"

I watched Lucas's face for any hint of lies. Did he really not know who Anna was? He was from out of town. "She's important to me," I hedged.

"Are you worried about hurting her, if you talk plainly?" he asked, and I nodded. He visibly relaxed. "That makes me feel better at least. I get family. It's like pack."

I shoved my fries around on my plate, feeling guilty about not sharing. But talking too much had never done me any favors. My phone rang, saving me from myself, and as rude as it was, I went to answer it. It was probably Sike. "Hello?"

A groan answered me. "Who is this?" I asked, as Lucas perked up. "Gideon?"

The phone hung up. "A friend of yours?" Lucas guessed.

"More family. We have to go."

CHAPTER THIRTY-FIVE

I danced from foot to foot while Lucas found a waitress he could hand two twenties to before we left. I didn't care if he paid, I just needed to leave. Maybe Viktor had cracked, or maybe this dinner was a ruse to get me away from home—or maybe Grandfather'd discovered how to tap into cellular service and had had Gideon prank-call me. It could be a false alarm, but I doubted it.

Lucas caught up with me when I was halfway to his truck. We hopped inside. "Who's Gideon?"

"He's injured."

"It didn't sound like he told you that. I only heard a groan."

Damn weres and their good hearing. I tried to think of a way to explain Gideon's injuries. "He's handicapped."

"Oh. Shit." The truck hit the freeway, and Lucas pressed the gas.

The tires only lost traction twice, and Lucas's heavier truck found it again faster than my Chevy would have. He parked near my apartment, and together we ran toward my place. "Edie, I smell blood."

"Please—go." I didn't know what Lucas would find, but right now I didn't have anything to hide. In an instant, he ran ahead.

* * *

I stopped to wonder why he hadn't had to open my door when I reached it myself, already unlocked and open. I walked into my dark apartment. I heard movement in the darkness beyond.

"Gideon?" I stood in the short hallway. Hands grabbed me and pulled me sideways into my hall closet.

I tried to scream, but a hand covered my mouth, and I felt cold metal on my cheek. I made some noises, but nothing came through, my lips were pressed into someone's salty palm. I started thrashing, until I realized that whoever was holding me was only keeping me still. I calmed down and felt around with my hands, found skin that had wires braided in. The salt and cold resolved into something I knew—Gideon's hand.

I sagged with relief and he let me go.

"What happened?" I whispered. I could hear the struggles out in the apartment beyond. The red ON light of my webcam gleamed from Gideon's shoulder. I saw it bob as he shrugged, unable to tell me. We were beyond yes/no questions again.

There was a low animal sound from my living room. Then flesh hit flesh, and a wild squealing began. I cracked open the closet door and stepped out.

In the dim glow from the parking lot that seeped into my apartment, I could see Lucas wrestling with someone. I hit the hallway light switch, and something or someone in my living room hissed.

"Don't hurt her!" I cried out as I saw who.

Lucas had Veronica pinned. She was thrashing beneath him, muttering strange words, completely wild. He was strong this close to the moon, and she was weak, being newly made. But if she'd fed on whatever it was that'd made the bloodstain they were rolling in—she might have the advantage of him eventually. He would tire, and she didn't care if he died.

"Veronica. Veronica! Snap out of it!" I knelt down, snapping my fingers to get her to look at me. I didn't dare slap her; I'd get a hand full of teeth. "Veronica—you used to be Veronica. Don't you remember?"

"She's wild—we should—" Lucas said, pressing down on her even tighter.

"No!" My purse was in his truck, with my phone and Sike's number and my badge that might have helped. "Just try not to hurt her, okay? I'll be right back."

To get up I planted a hand into my carpeting, felt it stick in something dark and cold. I wiped it on my jeans as I ran for my open door.

A graceful female form appeared, blocking my path. She held a collar in one hand, a coat in the other. Sike.

"Well, this was unexpected." Sike picked her way in, stepping lightly around the bloodstains on the floor.

"Something you didn't plan for? Unlikely," I said, but thank goodness she was here. Maybe she would be able to make some sense of this mess. I willed myself not to dust off my bloodstained knees.

"Cross my heart and swear to die," Sike said, unconvincingly. She reached a hand out to Veronica, where Lucas still had her pinned to the floor. "Unhand my sister," she told Lucas, and he looked to me before responding.

"You know her?"

"Too well."

He released Veronica slowly, ready for her to pounce at him. Sike blocked her way.

"I'm from her. Shhh, now. I'm from her." Sike rubbed her hands over Veronica's head like she was petting a cat, and the newly born vampire responded like one, bending toward her. "They're all mad for a few nights," Sike said, by way of explanation. "It's quite the change, or so I've been told." She ran her hand through Veronica's short hair, kneading the other woman's neck. Sike brought Veronica's head to her chest, cooing at her as one might at a newborn child, and slipped the coat and collar on in one fluid motion, buckling the collar tight. "Smells like wolf in here," she said, and glared at Lucas.

"Not me," he said, rocking up to a stand. "It's why I rushed in." Lucas stepped and moved around Sike and Veronica, never showing them his back. Then he glanced into my kitchen. "And that would explain it."

I stood and followed. There was a man on my kitchen floor, shadowed by my counter. A white guy wearing a blue tracksuit with a hood. Gnawed. Dead. "Did you know him?" Lucas asked me.

"I've never seen him before in my life. Why is he here?" I hissed, trying not to sound hysterical.

"I don't know who he is, but I know what she fed on," Sike said, bringing Veronica up to a stand. She left blood-stained indentions on my carpet in the shape of her high heels, like tiny hoofprints. "We're going. Where's the gimp?"

I almost ran my hands through my hair, which would've carried blood and worse with them. "He's in the closet. But you can't take him if he doesn't want to go."

Lucas turned toward me with a raised eyebrow.

"I don't keep him in there. He was hiding there from her," I explained, realizing as I did so that it only made me sound more insane. "Gideon—" I called out, and he slid open my hall closet door.

He was wearing my bathrobe, the webcam looking out from where he'd cut a hole into the shoulder. And his fingers were still metal twigs, reclaimed from my toaster oven.

"What. Is. That," Lucas asked.

"Long story." I said. "Gideon—do you want to go with her?"

"What did you do to him?" Sike asked, looking him up and down.

I ignored her. "Gideon, it's up to you. Honest." I knew I wanted him to want to go with her, but I wouldn't send anyone with her who didn't want to go. Gideon turned to look at Sike. Then he nodded.

"All right then. Would all the circus freaks in the room please follow me?" Sike held Veronica up and began pulling the woman toward my door.

"Aren't you going to do anything about him?" I said, pointing toward my kitchen floor. My voice rose with each syllable. I was having to fight hard to keep it down.

"Not my problem. Ask your new boyfriend for help."

"Wait—what about what—" I looked from her to Lucas, not sure how much I should confide. "What about what I texted you about?"

Sike also glanced back in Lucas's direction. "I'll call you later." Then she escorted Veronica out the door. Gideon followed her, my bathrobe fluttering in the night.

I stood there, looking at a corpse in my kitchen and a bloodstain on my floor, with a man—no, werewolf—I hardly knew.

"Are you sure you don't know him?" Lucas asked. He leaned down and tossed the corpse for his wallet and keys, like someone familiar with the chore. He pulled the man's hoodie down so I could get a closer look.

I knelt down. "Still no idea who he is."

"I bet you have a strong stomach—but you might want to look away," Lucas warned. I didn't. He reached up, put his hand into the corpse's mouth, and yanked down on the jaw. I heard it pop as it dislocated, and then a wet snapping sound as tendons and muscles inside tore free. Once the jaw hung loose, he ran a finger along the teeth.

"What are you doing?"

"He has fillings. I don't. Weres don't get cavities—the moon heals all when you transform, even teeth. So he was made less than a moon ago."

"He's a were?"

"Was." Lucas touched the blood and then put it up to his nose. "I can't scent his pack, though. Which is strange."

Dren had said as much about the women who'd been chasing me. Lucas wiped the man's blood on his thigh. "This would have been his first moon, if he'd lived to see it." Lucas rocked up to his feet and offered me a gore-covered hand. "This violence is fresh. If you'd left dinner any sooner, or not come out at all—" He didn't have to finish his thought.

I looked around my kitchen. It was thrashed—not just the aftermath of a fight but completely tossed, high shelves emptied of their contents, a spout of flour from a torn bag still trickling white powder onto my floor. Lucas followed my gaze.

"He wasn't just out to get you. Clearly, you weren't hiding in your cabinets." He turned toward me. "What were you hiding in here?"

"Nothing," I said. It was even the truth.

There was a plaintive meow from my bedroom, and I ran back.

CHAPTER THIRTY-SIX

"Minnie?"

There was another sad meow, from behind my dresser. I walked over to it and crouched down. It'd been shoved away from the wall as whoever had tossed my room had looked behind it. Minnie was back there, wedged in, hiding and unhappy.

"Oh, Minnie—" If anything had happened to her, that'd be it. I'd be through.

Lucas followed behind me and whistled from my doorway at the mess. All the drawers were out of my dresser, my underwear and bras strewn across the floor. I assumed the were had done that—and it'd been Veronica who'd taken my closet door off its hinges when she'd woken up. I scruffed Minnie and pulled her out of hiding, holding her to my chest.

Lucas pulled his cell phone out of his pocket. "You should pack. I'm calling you a cleaner."

"A cleaner's not going to cut this," I said, squeezing Minnie tight.

"My pack's cleaner. He understands. I'll be out there, measuring your carpet." Lucas tilted his head toward my living room and left the door.

I should have asked some questions, like *Where are we going?* or *For how long?* But I stumbled around my bedroom in a state of shock. The mattress of my bed was pushed sideways and knifed open, stuffing poking out, looking like subcutaneous fat pushing out of skin.

The dark wood box Anna's knife had been in was shattered into large splinters on my floor. The knife was still in my locker at work. That was the only thing I could imagine the were had been looking for. A vampire-thing. So much for Lucas's assertions that weres and vampires were completely distinct.

I almost tripped over Asher's silver bracelet. I picked it up, put it on, and went for my closet door—I had an overnight bag inside.

Minnie's cat carrier was at the top of my closet. I put her into it, grabbed enough clothing off my floor for overnight and walked out into my living room. Lucas was walking around my living room in a very precise way, sending multiple texts. I stood in the hallway, watching him pace.

"Minnie can come, right?"

"I'm not sure if Marguerite will approve."

And this would be when I found out he had a jealous werewolf girlfriend. "Who's that?"

"My cat." He glanced over at my disbelieving face. "What, you think werewolves can't have pets? Plenty of people have dogs and cats that live together." His phone chirped, and he looked at it before nodding to me. "My cleaner will be here soon. Leave the door open for him. Of course you can bring her. Let's go."

All the locks on the door were busted in. I had no choice but to leave it open. Me and Minnie followed Lucas out the front door, and we all got into his truck.

"Where are we going?" I asked, once I had Minnie's carrier settled on my lap.

"My place. Just for a while. My cleaner's fast." I was thinking about this, and maybe he took my silence for fear, as he continued. "You couldn't stay there. Not with all the blood."

"Yeah. I'd totally lose my deposit."

He snorted. We took a turn, and Minnie growled.

"I feel awful putting her through this." God only knew how long she'd been hiding behind my dresser.

"Doesn't it occur to you to be mad? Your vampire friend just got you into a lot of trouble."

"Yeah, only somehow all the things attacking me are weres."

"True." His hands wrung the steering wheel. It occurred to me that a vampire couldn't get into my place without permission, but a were could. Lucas went on. "He didn't smell like Viktor. Which doesn't mean Viktor's off the hook."

"No, it just means I don't really know who's attacking me," I said. He was silent after that.

The buildings outside passed by like fence posts in the dark. After an uncomfortable silence, I spoke. "Won't you miss your fights tonight?"

"I've been there every night for the past two weeks. I think I can skip one."

Minnie's fear had subsided to a low growl by the time we got to Lucas's home. It was a huge, sprawling two-story—the kind of place you assumed would have a pool behind it, and it did, I realized, as we went up the driveway and around. There was a smaller home in the back, and when we got out of the truck, I realized that's where Lucas was leading us. I picked up the carrier and my overnight bag and followed him inside.

"My uncle is—was—a contractor. The main house is his. Helen lives there now, with Fenris Jr. This one is mine." He tossed his keys on the counter and pulled his phone out of his pocket. "I have to make some more calls.

You can take the first bedroom down the hall. There's a bathroom the next door past it, with a shower."

I set my stuff down in the spare room, then went into the bathroom and calculated the risks of showering in a strange house with a strange man in it versus being sticky with strange blood for the rest of the night. Disgust won over sanity, and I stripped out of everything, except for my silver bracelet, and hopped into the shower stall.

The hot water made it easier to think, but it didn't solve any of my problems. Everything I owned was torn, broken, covered in blood, or absorbed into a creepy cyborg. I still owed a vampire a new hand. Weres were attacking me, and I had a date with a vampire on New Year's Eve night. My thoughts spiraled like the water down the drain. I lost track of time.

There was a knock on the bathroom door. "Did you drown?"

"No."

The door opened up, and I prepared to be scared, tried to scrape together some adrenaline left over somewhere, deep down inside, but Lucas just set down extra towels on the counter and closed the door again. I turned off the shower and dried myself off—remembering that Gideon had worn my bathrobe out the door, one more thing I'd never see again—and carefully picked up all of my bloodstained clothes. I walked down the hall to the room where I'd relocated Minnie. The door to her cat carrier was open, but she still sat inside, like Lucas's carpeting was lava.

"I know. Boy, do I know." I dried out my hair as best I could, and thoroughly dried off my body. Then I hunted through the clean things I'd brought—sweatpants and baggy shirt. Asher's cuff didn't go with these, and I didn't want to be unkind. If Lucas was going to kill me, he would have done it in the shower to keep the carpet clean.

I snorted at my morbid self and put the cuff inside Minnie's cat carrier. Then I lassoed my silver belt around my waist one more time and untucked my shirt, so I could be a little protected but not openly rude. As armored as I was going to get, I went back outside.

"Hey."

"Hey." Lucas stood in his kitchen, not much bigger than my own. "I made coffee. I didn't know what else to do."

"Thanks." I took the mug from him. Might as well drink coffee and stay up. It was at least one thing I was good at.

"How's Minnie?"

"Unhappy."

"I believe that's tonight's theme. Cream? Sugar?"

"Both," I said, and he handed them over one at a time. Once I'd doctored my coffee to within an inch of its life, I walked out into his living room and sat down in a chair covered in cat fur. Of course.

"How are you feeling?" he asked. He sat across from me on a couch with his own coffee mug. He was wearing a white tank top now, which made it easy to see his tattoos. The one sleeve was blurry, covered in old work, but the newer sleeve was still fresh, ornate, gorgeous. "Are you shell-shocked?"

"I've seen people die before. Not in my living room, but—" I shrugged, attempting to be cavalier.

"Sure you don't want to tell me what was he looking for?" Lucas said, with his head tilted forward. His tone was casual, kind. Downright friendly.

"What does it matter, when he was a were?" I asked back.

Lucas's eyebrows rose at this. "You make a good point."

"How is it that there are weres you don't know about?

My vampire friend can't make new vampires without permission from her people." I didn't tell him that Veronica had technically been illegal. "How does that work for weres?"

"Viktor's family still has connections. He could have brought them in from out of town—Helen told me that he'd be a problem, even before I moved out." He gave his coffee a rueful smile. "I wished I'd listened to her."

"And what, killed him?"

"Maybe. If that's what it would have taken to avoid all this. Winter would have done it. Winter would have killed him the first day. He didn't appreciate other contenders." Lucas leaned back. "That's why I worry I don't have it in me."

"Viktor called me yesterday. He said you all were setting him up." I watched him carefully for any reaction, but Lucas was only surprised.

"He called you?"

"Have you ever heard of House Grey?" I decided to press whatever small advantage I'd gained.

Lucas looked baffled. "No. That's a vampire naming convention, isn't it? I can ask around." His phone beeped, and he glanced at it. "Just as I thought. Jorgen is pissed."

"He can't fight in your stead?"

"Hardly. He's only bitten."

Like the guy on my living room floor. "Can bitten people bite other people and change them?"

"No. It doesn't work like that. Only major weres can make more weres. There's not many loopholes. Unless you want to skin me and wear my pelt, that is." Lucas gave me a look. "What they were looking for at your place—did they find it?"

"I'm sorry, Lucas." I shrugged without answering him. Anna, I trusted, even if she was currently bathing in blood. Lucas, not so much.

"What can I do to change your mind?" he went on.

For all I knew his cleaner was right now tearing through my house again. I suddenly felt trapped in his small living room, wearing nothing but one silver-buckled belt for protection. Drinking a drink he'd made for me that could have been roofied or poisoned or—

"No—don't." He put his hand out. "I didn't mean to frighten you. You're safe here. I swear."

I squinted at him. "Are were-promises like vampire-promises?"

He gave me a roguish smile. "Depends on the were." His phone rang this time. He looked at who was calling, and hung up. "Sorry. Jorgen again. I have to leave it on for when the cleaner calls. But I don't want to hear it from Jorgen."

I imagined Jorgen back at that were-bar, discovering Lucas's absence and frothing at the mouth. "I don't get why you have to fight so much."

"To prove my ability to lead. Miss me on one night? Catch me on the next. It's not a match, really, it's a performance. Like I'm a magician and my wolf's the rabbit. How many times can I pull it out of the hat?" Lucas turned his phone's screen off. "It's a miracle Winter lived to see his amazingly old age, with them doing this to him."

I leaned forward, fascinated. "What's it cost you to change?"

"Pride? No, not really. I'm sure one of those vets you work with told you." He looked at me, and I waited quietly for his answer. "Each time you change it eats minutes off your life. It's like tapping into the bottom of the hourglass God gave you, draining out the grains of sand."

I hadn't thought of it like that, when Gina first explained it. It made everything seem more horrific. "Is it worth it?"

"On the nights when it's not for show, when you're

outside as you were meant to be, yes. I can't imagine how frightening it was for little Fenris at the hospital, without a pack, being out of place. But in the land where you belong, it's perfect. You can feel it's what you were meant to do, to be. Through the pads on all your paws." He jerked his chin at me. "What'd it cost you to be a nurse?"

"My sanity. Three years of school. A lot of student loans."

"Not literally. The parts when you're in it, when you're there."

"Heh." I stared down at the end of my coffee. "Most nights there's a lot of people being unhappy with you. They've heard news they don't want to hear, and you can't change that for them. You spend a lot of nights pushing dying people like boulders up very steep hills."

"What's it like when it works, when you feel it?"

I thought about it. "Those parts don't happen as often as I might like." The most recent one involved his uncle, on the pavement, but I didn't think I would tell him that. Because sometimes you could do everything right, and it still didn't turn out well. "When you see something that needs doing, and you know you're the right one to do it, even if you're scared—it's good. There's a lot of charting around those times, though. And sometimes being yelled at by drunks."

Lucas snorted. "My dad was a drunk."

"Really?"

"Yeah. I never was sure which came first, the alcohol, or the asshole. He did this to me." Lucas stroked a finger along the dent on his nose. "Said if I changed into a wolf to heal it, he'd rip off my arm and beat me with it. I believed him."

"How old were you?"

"Fifteen. He always preferred to fight me as a human.

He said the wolf would know how to fight when the time came—it was the human half that needed training," Lucas said, his voice an imitation of his father's. "It took me years before I realized he did it so he'd be bigger than me for most of my life."

"That's awful."

"Yeah, it was. I spent a lot of time in JV after that. He always waited until the day of the full moon to spring me. Thought he was punishing me. Little did he know, I preferred staying in jail."

"Lucas—" I set my coffee mug down on the ground and drew an equation in the air between us. "You've had a rough life, you don't have an education, you're not from here. And you're going to lead the Deepest Snow wolf pack why again, exactly?"

"I'm of age, and I'm the closest related male blood. It's how our system works." He shrugged. "I'm only holding the spot until Fenris Jr. comes of age. Believe me, I don't want it."

"I just don't see why you're more competent than, say, Jorgen."

"He's bitten. He doesn't know what being a wolf is like. He's still chained by what made him a man."

"Then why don't you give them shots to cure him and the others? Or do they really all opt in?"

Lucas gawked at me, then laughed. "I'm just imagining you interrogating my uncle. Jorgen would tell you his service to my family is an honor—he was bitten by the old man himself. And as for opting in—the world is full of paths, Edie." He leaned forward, even with me, and his voice went rough, otherworldly, like the wolf was pushing through. "Sometimes you take one, and it gets you lost in the woods."

I sat very still, and for a moment I felt like a rabbit

must feel when a hawk's shadow crosses above. Then Lucas laughed and shook his head. "I'm teasing, of course."

"Of course," I readily agreed. I held my mug out. "More coffee, please?"

CHAPTER THIRTY-SEVEN

I watched him as he walked back to his kitchen, barefoot on the tile floor. He poured more coffee, and I wondered how far I'd get if I flung it into his face and ran for the door. Consciously, I didn't feel like I was in danger, but my subconscious had other opinions something fierce. Maybe it was the predator-and-prey thing I was picking up on—he the spider, I the fly.

On his way back with my mug, his phone chirped from the kitchen table. He got the message, and brought the phone with him. "They're done with your place now." He handed the mug and the phone over at the same time, with the screen still lit. "So you can see they're not telling me anything other than that."

I took the coffee and sipped it—he'd put in sugar and cream for me already, made it just the way I'd had it before. "For all I know, this could be an elaborate code." I was only half teasing.

"Don't give my people so much credit. In the wild, a dumb wolf would starve or get killed. But as humans nine-tenths of the time, a higher percentage of us are able to bumble on day-to-day than you'd think."

"Well. Thanks for the coffee. I should probably be getting home now."

He frowned down at me. "Or you could just stay here tonight. It'd be easy for me to protect you here."

I looked around the confines of Lucas's small living room. "I don't think that's a good idea."

"You still don't trust me?"

"I don't know how I can. Sorry."

If he'd looked angry, I'd have been scared. Instead he seemed bemused, and he reached for his phone. "Fine. I'll call you a cab. He's one of ours—he can stay outside your apartment for the rest of the night."

His phone call sounded very real. He gave them an address and everything. I packed my stuff, after getting another trash bag for my stained clothing—maybe I should carry around trash bags just in case, at the rate I was going—and Minnie was still in the carrier, still growling her displeasure. After that, I didn't know how long we had to kill until the cab arrived.

"You're still sure I can't change your mind?" he asked when I was in the living room again, Minnie at my side. His eyes searched my face. "I promise no harm will come to you tonight."

"You just told me people wander off and get lost in dark woods. That makes it hard to believe you."

Lucas snorted and looked at the ground. "That was a mistake."

"Lucas, I want to believe you—which is probably why I should go."

I reached down and picked up my mug to carry it into the kitchen, and Minnie hissed behind me. I looked over, and she wasn't looking at me—

I turned around and Lucas was gone. In his place was a wolf as big as the couch. I stepped back. It took up so much space I felt like there was little room left to breathe. Not it—he. Lucas. His fur was the color of a worn penny, dull red, with streaks of gray. Minnie kept hissing.

"Is frightening my cat really the best way to convince me?" I picked her up and set her on the couch, away from him. When I looked back, he was sitting on his haunches, watching me with copper eyes. He got down on all fours and stretched toward me, head low. He crept nearer, bowed down, until he was an arm's length away. He kept looking, and I did my best not to move.

He could have attacked. He would have won. But he kept coming closer until his wet nose almost touched my kneeling thigh.

I reached one finger out, to trace the fine hairs on his muzzle the wrong direction. Lucas the wolf closed his eyes. Bolder, I stroked a path up to his eyebrow. The fur wasn't soft, but tactilely different than I expected. Somewhere between bristles and fur, both thick and springy. I ran the palm of my hand down the back of his neck, pressed it into his fur, felt it give, and then the solid muscle hidden underneath.

His head turned slowly to the side, and his teeth caught my wrist. His rough, warm tongue ran over my hand.

There was a knock at the door. My ride.

I pulled my hand away slowly, and he bit down a little more, pulling me toward him. His teeth were like the ends of blunt pens—not needle-sharp, but his jaw could crush my wrist and I would never chart again.

Then he let me go.

There was another knock at the door. Louder, insistent.

"If the world is full of paths, why does yours have to be the one lined with puppies?"

Lucas's eyebrows, and lips, pulled up into a literally wolfish grin. He sat up and bit my bicep with his frightening-not-frightening teeth, and then licked at my throat. I closed my eyes and laughed and pushed him away, and found myself touching skin.

"I'm a wolf, not a dog." He was sitting on the floor very near me now, completely naked. My hands were on his chest, and I pulled them back with a yelp. "Are you really so frightened of me?"

"No. But I should be. That's the problem."

"Edie, I don't want you to be afraid." He was near enough that I could feel the heat radiating off him, feverish. He was beautiful, and I could see all of him now, his tattoos scrolling up and down both arms, his stomach lean, his cock hard.

I'd spent the past few weeks angry, frustrated, over-thinking things, running scared. Here was something I could do that would be so simple, and feel so good, if I just let it. I was tired of fighting, I was lonely—and I was hungry. "I don't want to be afraid either."

The door knocked one final, last time, and I could hear someone cursing behind it as they walked away. I didn't jump up to follow.

Lucas reached out for me, ran his hand into my wet hair, caught a fistful, and gently pulled. His eyes—they were still his wolf's eyes, bright, searching my own, as he leaned in near and breathed deeply. His hand in my hair tightened, and he pulled away to look at me. His chest rose and fell, breathing hard, like he'd been fighting, and I felt the same sensation, mirrored in my own. I twisted my head and my wet hair slid through the fingers of his hand.

"I can smell you," he said, his voice deeper, more rough. "Still afraid—but curious. Ready."

I felt more naked than I had in the shower, even though I still had on clothes. "You're not wrong," I said, my voice low.

"Once we start, this close to the moon—" he said, and I could see the tension flow through him. He was as hungry as I was, but he was still tempered with restraint. "There's no going back."

I sighed and almost laughed at him. "Don't worry. You can't hurt me."

Then he fell on me, with a kiss.

CHAPTER THIRTY-EIGHT

Kissing was great and all, but—I kicked out of my sweat-pants beneath him. He left my mouth to bend back and grabbed the ankles of them, dragging them off me, dropping me to the floor. My underwear were the next to go; he grabbed each hip and tore them free. The shirt I already had halfway off when he started to help, and I could feel his chest against mine, each touch hot like flame. He stopped and stared. I had those stupid girl thoughts that you can get when foreplay downshifts gears without warning—what if he didn't like what he saw, what if he changed his mind about sex with me—but he was staring at the belt buckled around my waist. "What's this?"

"Don't touch it—it's silver." I reached for it, to unfasten it myself. "It'll burn you."

Lucas looked down at me, his cock still aching hard. Seeing it made me hurt deep inside, where I wanted it to be. He pushed my hands away from the buckle, lowered himself nearer to me, whispering against my neck. "Do you think I mind?"

A sizzling sound, and the belt was free. He sat up. I was on my back in his living room, and he knelt beside me, the belt in his hand. He held the belt buckle like a badge, and touched it, cold, to both my nipples till they were hard. Stroked it down the center of me, using it to push my legs open, grinding its rough design against my clit, and then he held up his hand where it should have been burned, and I saw it heal, as if by magic, which I supposed it was. I reached for him then, for his cock. His lips parted as my fingers wrapped around his flesh, found it hot, and stroked up. A growl rumbled, from the wolf hidden in him, now not very deep inside.

"I'm going to take you like I own you, Edie," he said, and his eyes almost weren't his own.

"Just for tonight," I amended, my hand sliding back down his cock. He laughed at my clarification—or maybe the fact that I thought I could clarify—and the wolf in him disappeared, leaving only Lucas behind.

"On your knees," he said, his face torn between smug and challenging. "That is, if you would be so kind as to agree."

"I think I can be convinced to go along."

I felt foolish on all fours, and wished that maybe for once I'd kept my mouth shut. He waited, and a second before I would have changed my mind and called everything off, he reached out and touched my back with his soft-rough hand. The touch startled me, disturbed me from my thoughts. When his hand trailed off me, after following the curves of my body, he reached up to start touching me again. He leaned in and rubbed his cheek against my side. I could feel the stubble scratch along my ribs, winding up in my armpit. I laughed. He bared his teeth and nipped me, the outside of my breast, the curve of my waist. His hands and arms kept flowing over me, from the nape of my neck, down my back, buttocks, the backs of my thighs. His mouth bit awkward places, sharp jolts of pain I didn't expect. Sensations I couldn't fight against or prepare for, smooth, rough, sharp, washing over me like waves. Keeping my eyes closed only added to the effect, and suddenly I was where I'd been before, only more so. I knew he was behind me now, his hands dipping beneath me to grab my breasts, rolling my nipples between fingers as he bit at my shoulders and neck, his chest hot against my back.

All sane thoughts fled my mind. There was only now, and what I wanted, and how would I get there. I became a beast. I pushed back, my hips against his, and he growled, his mouth near my ear. I pushed back again and he moved with me, using a hand to angle his cock down. The head of him slid across me and I moaned. He held himself there, perilously close to what I wanted, playing himself against my folds. I whined then, an animal sound, frustrated, heavy, sore. The second I gave up, he pushed himself inside.

It was like taking a hot spear. I cried out in surprise and triumph and he growled his ownership again. He pulled out of me, his hands clawing down my back, then shoved himself back in. Each stroke encompassed the length of him, so I could feel just how empty I would be when we were through, how full I was when he was deep inside. I made wild noises with each of his thrusts into me, I didn't care.

He leaned over and picked up the belt, flicking it down and around my neck. He held both ends like reins behind me. With each thrust forward, he pulled me back onto his cock. There was no physical pain, just leather chafing against my collarbones, no problems breathing. There was only the knowing that I'd been caught, the knowledge that he was riding me like the animal that I was.

I reached one hand between my legs and felt the solidness of him there, sliding in and out of me. My fingers found myself and rubbed. I could feel my orgasm build. I was flush with blood, with weight, with raw need—I didn't look back, I wasn't sure who I'd see fucking me, him or his wolf. I didn't want to know. All I wanted was to come.

The belt pulled me back again and my hand and his cock—it lit a fuse on something deep inside. "Don't stop," I begged, and he only growled and fucked me harder.

My orgasm rose and swelled and I could feel it coming and then it crashed over me, roiling through me. I cried out with each wave as it swept across me, pulling him deeper. I leaned back for even more of him, trying to keep us whole. His cock stiffened in me like an arrow, and then he growled long and low, giving quick short thrusts, until he was quiet, and I knew he was spent.

The belt fell from my neck, and he slid out of me. I fell to the ground, and he collapsed beside me, panting, exhausted.

He was all Lucas now, broken nose, short hair, eyes brown-red. He reached over to me and pulled me against him, roughly. I smiled at him. "And to think you thought tonight you wouldn't have to wrestle."

He laughed, and kissed me again.

CHAPTER THIRTY-NINE

He kept kissing me, and we weren't even fucking anymore. I didn't know what to do. As I lay beside him, his body was hot like a furnace, and the smell of sweat and sex filled the room. I pulled away from him, and he smiled at me. "Come on. If we sleep here, we'll wind up sore." Lucas stood and offered me his hand.

"More sore," I corrected him.

Concern flashed in his eyes. "I didn't hurt you, did I?"

I stood up on my own without taking his hand. "Not in any way I minded at the time." I picked my clothes up off the floor and pulled them on. "I'll be in my room, thanks."

He tilted his head and looked at me. "Edie, what just happened?"

I couldn't explain it to him—I just needed some space, fast. I didn't want to hope ever again. It wasn't even about him, it was about how my life would probably be better if I never let anyone in. I grabbed Minnie's cat carrier—she was asleep inside it, long since used to my conquests—walked quickly down the hall, and shut myself inside the room he'd given me. There were NASCAR posters on the walls. And the sheets on the bed were blue, with yellow stars and rocket ships. It felt like I was in the room of a child. I lay down on the bed and closed my eyes.

Lucas knocked on the door. "Edie, are you okay?"

"Can you just guard me from out there, please?" I asked through the door.

I didn't get an answer. After a few minutes of silence, there was one whine, then another. I waited and they didn't stop.

"Please, Lucas, stop." There was the sound of scratching at the bottom of the door. "You'll ruin the carpet." The scratching continued. I gave up and opened the door.

The wolf came into the room and bounded up onto the bed, the mattress springs groaning with his weight. He lay there, still, his head in his paws. He yawned a soundless question, stared at me, then closed his eyes. I waited, trying to figure out what I should do.

I turned off the light and crawled into bed beside him. He stayed a wolf. Furry, warm, with hot moist breath. His tongue licked my neck, once. I wrapped my arms around his neck, buried my face in his fur, and cried.

When I woke up, sun was coming in through the plaid curtains, and there was a strange cat lying beside me, colored peach and gray. It opened one lazy eye. "Marguerite?" I guessed. The eye closed.

The rest of the room wasn't my room, and all of a sudden I remembered everything that'd happened the night before—before the sex, and my subsequent shutdown.

I elbowed myself up to sitting. "Lucas?" He would want to talk this morning, and I would have to be nice about it.

Marguerite woke up and licked a paw. I looked down, and Minnie was still sitting in her cat carrier, ruling her small roost. I got out of bed. I really needed a toothbrush, and not having showered after sex made me feel gross. I opened my bedroom door, wrapped a blanket around me like a robe, and made my way to the living room. "Lucas?"

Jorgen was sitting on Lucas's couch, his bald head reminding me of a snake's. "The princess finally awakens."

"Hello, Jorgen."

"Helen wants to speak with you. She's in the main house." My belt was still on the living room floor. I waited until Jorgen left before I bent down to retrieve it.

I made most of an outfit, between what I'd brought and what I'd been wearing when I came in. My jeans from the prior night were cleaned, waiting for me, folded on the couch. I wondered if Lucas had done that, or if other pack members took care of the laundry. I pulled on my boots and went outside. At least the cold air felt clean.

I tromped up to the back door of the main house, and Jorgen opened it. While Lucas's guest home had felt like the epitome of prefabricated America, the inside of the main house was much nicer. The floors and the furniture were dark wood, and Jorgen led me into a dining room that was ornate. It was decorated in marble and more wood, with brass fixtures hanging from the ceiling to hold iron pots and pans. Helen looked up at my entrance from where she was pouring a cup of tea.

"Edie—thanks for coming. I hope you slept well?" Helen said, giving me a sly smile and handing over a delicate china cup. It looked too fragile to be used, much less by werewolves. I took it and sat down.

"I, uh, did. Thanks."

She went and got another cup out of a cupboard, and I looked back to check—Jorgen was gone. "I can't blame you for liking Lucas. He's a very handsome man. And wolf," she went on.

"It's not like that." This was pretty much what I'd been afraid of, inside and out.

"Really? Because—don't think I'm awful, because I'm

not—you're just not like us. These things—I've seen them before. They only end in tears."

I took the tea she offered and gulped it. It was weird being inside her delicate house, with so many delicate things. I knew I must look bedraggled after last night. "It was just a one-night stand. We were both lonely. Bored."

One of her eyebrows rose. "Really?"

I nodded. "Completely. One night."

"All right then." She took a delicate sip of her tea, then set the china down. "I can tell tea's not your thing—you're no good at drinking it."

"I prefer iced, to be honest." I set my china cup down with a guilty shrug.

Helen smiled. "Run along then. I've got a kingdom to run until he grows up—"

I was so glad to be dismissed, sitting on silk in my sweatpants, smelling of sex, that it wasn't until I left the room that I found myself wondering if she meant Lucas or Junior.

I went back to Lucas's place and packed my things back up. Lucas knocked on the door before entering. "Hey. Are you okay?"

"I'm fine. Thanks." I had everything ready to go on his couch, waiting.

"I got us lunch." Lucas held up a take-out bag, and he had a hopeful look on his face.

"Maybe you could just take me home?"

His face looked hurt as he looked me up and down, then nodded. "Okay."

We loaded back into his truck in silence, and the drive was quiet, except for Minnie, who was over this. Her growls went up and down like a siren, registering disappointment at every turn. When we pulled into my parking lot, he waited.

"I didn't mean to hurt you, whatever it was that I did."

"It's not that." I tried not to look at his face, but I couldn't ignore him. He looked sincerely concerned. "For me, last night wasn't about starting things with you. It was about me ending them with someone else."

His face clouded with confusion. "You said you didn't have a boyfriend."

"Because I don't anymore." I opened the truck door and hopped out of the cab, reaching back for Minnie and my things. "Thanks for the ride, Lucas. Last night was fantastic. I'm sorry I'm a mess."

He leaned over and caught my hand. "You smell like Helen. She warned you away, didn't she."

"She did, but it's not that."

Lucas frowned. "I'm only taking charge till Fenris grows up. They don't own me, Edie. Once he's of age, the rest of my life is mine."

"I believe you. And I'm sure you'll find someone really fabulous to appreciate you at that time."

Emotions ran across his face. Anger, betrayal, disbelief—I wondered if he'd ever been broken up with before, or refused. Then he went quiet. I could see him bottling everything up inside. I knew precisely what that looked like, and how it felt. "I have things to do. Someone else will be guarding you today." He reached into the center console and pulled out paper and a pen. "You should take my phone number. In case anything happens."

"Okay."

I wanted to say thanks again, or good-bye, but the best way to get out of things like this was to just leave. I knew that, too, from personal experience. I turned and walked away.

CHAPTER FORTY

I pulled out my keys and found my front door still open. Of course. I hesitantly looked inside.

It had that new-carpet smell. I hadn't smelled that since I'd been a temp in an office complex between semesters of nursing school. It was clean, and not exactly the same as what had been there before, but I didn't think my landlord could complain. I took a step in, closed the door, and set Minnie down.

The carpet actually had cushioning underneath. And hadn't been downtrodden by the feet of a hundred tenants. I waddled from side to side, just glorying in the niceness of it all before turning on the lights and looking in.

A brand-new couch. Not a shitty bloodstained old one with a couch cover to hide its hideousness, but one all the way from a store somewhere—I hesitated to think where Lucas's shady cleaning service been able to find a furniture store open at four A.M.—and I didn't care if it'd fallen off a truck. Taking up most of my apartment's wall, it was a shade of brown that matched the carpeting without being hideous—it was lovely. It was mine.

Minnie meowed, and I unzipped her carrier so she could escape. She leapt out and hightailed it to the bedroom, while I completed my short tour.

The kitchen was the same, only cleaner—all the dishes

done. If it weren't still winter, I'd open up the small
window to let out the remaining scent of bleach. I went
back down the hall, found my bathroom same as it'd
been left, and then turned toward my bedroom. It, too,
was the same. Gah. I had a suspicion that the cleaner had
been too busy dealing with traceable evidence. The DNA
was gone, but my trashed closet was left up to me.

It'd take me all afternoon to clean—I wondered what
time it was. I dug my phone out of my purse and texted
Sike—*Home now. Is this safe?*—on the off chance that she
would finally be helpful or supportive, and Lucas—*Nice
couch. Thanks*—even though I knew it was probably a
bad idea. Then I set to picking things up in my room.

I decided to wash anything that the intruder or Veronica might have touched. So I wandered around my room,
putting all the clothing he'd pulled out into a huge laundry bag, and hauled it down to the laundry. Numerous
quarters later, when I came back, Jake was waiting outside my door.

My heart dropped. "Jake? Are you okay?"

"I just wanted to say hi was all." He was carrying his
new backpack and a large duffel bag. "How's it going?"

"Busy." We couldn't stand outside talking forever—I
wasn't dressed warmly enough for the occasion.

"Can I come in?" he asked.

I wanted nothing less, but I said, "Sure," and I reluc-
tantly opened my door.

Jake let out a low whistle behind me. "What is this?"

"My landlord remodeled." Because there'd been a dead
body on my floor less than a day ago. But don't worry, the
vampire and daytimer left, so it's fine.

"Four days after Christmas? And two days before New
Year's Eve? In the winter?" Jake asked. He walked over
to my new couch. "He get you a new couch, too?"

"Don't ask questions, Jake."

"Why not? You get to feel high and mighty all the time. It's my turn now." He sat down, patting the cushion beside him. "How could you afford this, Edie?"

"Not now, Jake."

"It's never a good time for you, is it? But it's always a grand time to interrogate me." He leaned back, clearly feeling superior.

"Look, I'm not the one who stole things from you before. So I still get to have the upper hand." He opened his mouth to say something else. I cut him off. "Why are you here, Jake?"

"I was just going to give you money for the phone bill. Like I said I would. Business is brisk." His face softened a little. "Plus, I was worried. You've been strange for a while."

"Worried about me? Wow." I was taken aback. No drug worth selling would be handing out empathy to Jake like that. "I was worried about me, too. But things are getting better," I lied.

He looked around my living room, and then shook his head. "If you get into trouble, you can tell me, you know. No one's gotten into as much trouble as I have."

"I know." I stood a little straighter. "I've got a lot of laundry I have to wash today—"

He jerked his head at me. "I don't suppose—" he began and swung his bags around, like he should set them down. After all, I did have a fabulous new couch for him to sleep on.

"Not yet, Jake, okay? After the holidays maybe."

"Okay."

"Can you get home on your own?"

"Yeah. See you around, Sissy."

It wasn't until after he left that I realized he hadn't gotten around to pitching in for his share of the phone bill.

* * *

I spent the rest of the morning picking things up in my bedroom and putting them away, then I got another load into the laundry.

I threw clothing in willy-nilly—there wasn't a single thing I owned that couldn't be laundered on high—and heard something clink. I reached in and felt around.

The vials of Luna Lobos that Jake had given me. Goddammit. I had to convince him to get off this stuff. Selling energy supplements wasn't going to give him a normal life. I put the vials into my purse so I could take them to work and put them in the incinerator box.

Lucas had been right, it wouldn't be the safest thing ever to sleep at my house right now, but the locks on my door worked. I latched it—the dead bolt and the chain bolt. Then I took my step stool and unfolded it underneath the door handle to block further entry, and slept with my phone nearby.

I didn't wake up till eight P.M. There was a lump on my mattress where the strange were had knifed through it, and I could feel it under my left knee. Minnie was sprawled alongside me, the trespasses of the night before seemingly forgiven.

I got up, showered again, and got ready to leave. I needed to eat, and I needed food for late dinner tonight. I didn't look in the parking lot for a guard, but a black foreign car followed me from my lot to the grocery store, and out again from it, until I found myself on hospital grounds.

I was in the locker room when Gina came in, humming a happy tune. I confronted her. "You're cheerful tonight."

"And you're not. It's like we traded places."

"I had a long night off."

"Me too. But in a good way. I talked things out with Brandon. He doesn't care if I don't change."

"For how long?"

"He says, for forever."

"For real, forever?"

"For long enough." She smiled at me. "I knew I didn't screw up falling for him, Edie. I knew it."

I found a smile somewhere deep inside me—probably pulled it out of another fucking dimension—to share with her. "I'm really glad for you, Gina."

She hugged me tight and let me go. "Come on. Let's have a great night."

I walked out to the floor without her to see who we were getting stuck with tonight.

"Meaty—is there any other possible assignment?" Gina and I were with Winter. Again.

My charge nurse shifted behind the desk to give me a look. "Charles gets the daytimers, you two get the weres. It's only for two more nights, Spence. Suck it up."

I muttered, "Fine."

I braced myself to go around the corner and see Lucas there—but he had to fight again tonight. Of course. I peeked around, and for once there were no visitors. None at all. I felt myself relax, and Gina joined me for report.

Everything we were doing now for Winter was entirely for show. Either the moon would heal him—right down to his cavities, apparently—or it wouldn't. I checked orders with Gina and co-signed all the changes. We didn't bother to use the rifle anymore, not even when she was near. The Domitor was turned off—if the moon was going to work, we didn't want to prevent his change—but there was nothing frightening about him now. The bleed in his brain had taken care of that.

* * *

At three A.M. Gina was on break in the extra corral next
door, and I was reading a book outside Winter's room.
Things were peaceful. I should have known it wouldn't
last.

"Incoming, Edie!" Meaty shouted from around the
bend. I put my book down and tried to look official.

Lucas came around the bend, wearing his hoodie again,
looking rough, smelling like sweat. He seemed bigger than
he had last night, and he was breathing hard. When he saw
me he stopped, his face hard to read. "I just want to talk
to the old man."

"Okay." I pushed my desk out of the way and let him
go inside. Technically, he should have put isolation gear
on, and technically I shouldn't have let him go in alone. I
stood to hover near the door where I could see them both.

Lucas went over to Winter's bedside, staring down at
the king in repose. "No wonder my father hated you,
Uncle. He knew he'd never feel like this." He touched his
own chest. "I can feel their hearts, beating inside me.
This is what it feels like to lead a pack." He moved his
hand to Winter's chest, and I took another step inside the
door. "I can feel it coming—the moon has chosen me."

"Lucas—"

He looked over to me, and the shadows in the room
made his eyes glow copper, like an animal's in the night.
"Don't worry. I won't hurt him. He's already as good as
dead."

He patted Winter's chest again and came back toward
the door. Instead of passing me, he grabbed my shoulders
and spun me sideways to press me against the room's
wall, pinning me there. To call for help would be humiliating at best, injurious at worst. I remembered Charles's
story about weres saying they didn't know their own
strength afterward, and completely believed him.

I squeaked out, "How were the fights?" like a normal conversation with him would be possible now.

His face an inch away from mine, he said, "Easy."

He kissed me like he owned me. My head was pressed against the wall behind me, and his tongue ran deep inside my mouth. He only pulled back to tease, his hot breath gentle on my lips, before kissing me again.

Half of me wanted to leap outside my skin and run away, or scream. The other half wanted everything else from him, here, now, forget propriety, forget the disgusting hospital floor.

He planted his hand against my mouth so I couldn't scream, and licked up the side of my face. His other hand trailed down my body outside my thin cotton scrubs, stroking my breast, diving between my legs.

"You still want me," he said, finally letting me go.

I wiped his spit off my cheek. "People often want what they can't have."

"Sometimes it makes them want it all the more." He took a step back from me, inhaled, exhaled, deflating, becoming less of a monster, more of the Lucas that I knew. "We've found five of Viktor's men. We're on the hunt for the rest of them."

"That's good, I guess." I was breathing heavy, scared and turned on, mad at my body for betraying me.

"I have pack business from now until the moon. But after it, Edie—"

"You'll be a pack leader then." I wasn't going to fall for another guy who would have to leave me. I pushed him away, and he took an obliging step back.

"Don't think that this is over, Edie." And then he looked past me, back at Winter. "And as for you, old man—your pack is mine."

CHAPTER FORTY-ONE

I waited near my desk for five minutes, and then went out to the bathroom to wash my face and clean myself up. Luckily I'd started the evening looking disheveled, so Lucas mauling me didn't make a huge change.

Meaty was standing, yelling into the phone on my return. "We're a hospital, not a prison—no, I don't care, that's not what you pay us for."

By the time I got to the nursing station, Meaty'd hung up. "What happened?"

"Edie—go wake up Gina. Tell her we've got to open the extra were-wing."

Waking Gina was easy—convincing her that's what Meaty'd said was harder. "You're kidding—why?"

"I don't know." I didn't want to repeat half-heard conversations, but, "Something about us being a prison?"

"Oh, God." Gina flung herself out of the empty room's bed.

I followed Gina back into the hallway. She went to the back wall, which had a keypad and a metal doorplate set up beside it. She ran her badge over the doorplate and entered a combination on the keys. What I'd assumed was a wall for my entire career at Y4 lifted up, like a garage door.

"How many rooms will we need, Meaty?" Gina hollered.

"Half a dozen or so!" came the shouted answer from the main floor.

"Extra help, girl," Gina said, addressing me. "Linen and supplies for six rooms. Stat."

"You got it."

I ran back and forth, putting supplies into the six nearest rooms—the ones at the end of the hall were covered in dust.

"When's the last time we used these?" I asked on one of my treks back and forth.

"Last were-war," Charles said with disgust from his post at the front desk.

I had just about everything done by the time our occupants arrived. Jorgen led them in, one by one.

Each of them looked more forlorn than the last—unwashed, shuffling men and women who said nothing and kept their eyes locked on the ground.

"Who are they, Jorgen?" They all looked homeless to me.

Jorgen waited awhile before speaking to me, as though he had to muster up the strength. "These are your attackers. Viktor's mob. They attacked some of us too—only they didn't get very far."

The women who'd attacked me had been well dressed and able to drive a car. The people Jorgen led in, whom we placed in rooms one by one, didn't look like they could manage to take an escalator.

Gina emerged from the third room with her arms crossed. "Are they under custody?"

"Until we get some answers, yes," Jorgen answered.

"They can't stay here indefinitely just because you're mad at them. None of them is sick."

"Humanity at large needs to be protected from them, and the moon is near. Do you want all these unmanaged new weres out on the streets?"

"So your pack's assuming control of medical decisions for them? If something goes bad?"

"Sure. Why not?" Jorgen said with a shrug.

"I need to talk to Meaty." She walked back to the main floor while I stood in the hallway with Jorgen. As soon as she was out of earshot, he turned to me.

"Don't you have any shame, girl?"

I blinked and stepped back, unsure what he was accusing me of, unsure what to say. We were interrupted by Meaty, who came back with Gina.

"I don't like it any better than you, Gina. I'll ask the Consortium in the morning." Meaty pierced Jorgen with a look. "Are there going to be any more surprises tonight?"

"Doubtful." Jorgen made a gesture to indicate all of us. "Good day, ladies."

Meaty snorted.

I helped Gina where I could. None of the new admits ever spoke. They'd go where you told them to go, sit, stand, lie, like obedient dogs, but they seemed as uninterested in living as Winter down the hall.

I assessed the first one while Gina sorted out the rest. I ran a blood pressure and took a temperature, and then realized I had no idea what the normal ranges were for weres anyhow. As the thermometer beeped, I nervously pulled the were's mouth open, hoping he wouldn't bite me.

He had fillings. He was brand-new, just like the weres that had attacked me.

Keeping a wary eye on him, I cataloged his belongings. Coat, shoes, no wallet or any other ID—and a vial of Lobos Luna in his pocket. I finished what I was doing as fast as I could and got out of the room.

"It's creepy," Gina said, meeting me outside.

"Where did they come from?"

"One of them had a voucher from the Armory," Gina said with a shrug. "I should call a few shelters, figure out where they came from. It's a raw deal to be homeless and then get forced into a pack."

The combination of the Armory and the Lobos Luna was all I needed to hear. "About that—I need to go call my brother," I said.

Gina's eyebrows rose. "I didn't know that your brother—"

"Your mom, my brother, it's the same sort of thing." I interrupted. At least for right now, the Shadows were still doing their job of keeping him safe.

"Sorry, Edie," Gina said, with the empathy that only someone else trapped working on Y4 could properly express for my situation.

"Thanks," I said and ran down the hall.

I made it into the locker room and dialed up Jake. He was tired when he answered but he still sounded like himself. "Hey, Sissy. You want me to move in today?"

"No—not yet—Jake—you need to stop selling that stuff. Right now."

I could hear him rearranging himself, fabric rustling in the background as he hunkered down wherever he was sleeping tonight, to talk more quietly to me.

"Is this about the cell phone? Because I realized I forgot the second I got on the bus—"

"It's not. It's not at all." I tried to think of things I could tell him that would warn him off. "There's been some Lobos Luna poisonings at the hospital. That stuff is cut with something, Jake."

"No way. I use it every day."

Internally, I groaned. "Are any of the people who used, or sold it with you, missing?"

Jake made a thoughtful noise. "Raymond's still gone. Maybe some other guys. It's hard to tell, though. It's winter out, Edie."

"I know, I know. Just promise me, Jake, you'll stop selling—and stop using it, too."

"No."

"Jake—"

"For the first time in my life, I'm goddamn successful at something. And you can't handle it, Edie. You can't control me, and you can't tell me what to do."

I pulled my phone away from my face and stared at it in anger for a moment. "Which is why you want to move in with me? Because you're so successful?"

"Edie, don't go there. It's late. I'm tired."

He hung up on me. Dismayed, I walked back onto the floor.

Gina and I worked quietly until dawn together, and then went our separate ways. I went to find my keys, and found Jake's vials of Luna Lobos in my purse. I snuck back onto the floor while day-shift nurses were getting report, and grabbed a lab sheet when I thought no one was looking.

"Unknown sample. Unknown source," I jotted down. It was the kind of sample that made the lab want to come down from wherever they were and kill us—they weren't keen on doing work that couldn't be billed to anyone later. But maybe the Consortium had a slush fund for these sorts of occasions. Only the fact that I could say it came from Y4 gave me hope. Surely there was someone on our team down in the lab. Surely.

I put the lab slip and bagged-up sample into the pneumatic tube system, punched in the code for the lab, and wished it well as it got lifted and sucked off to wherever the lab was.

I walked straight through the lobby and out to my car. When another car left the parking lot at the same time, I knew I was still being guarded, especially once they followed me home. I let myself into my apartment, marveled at my carpeting and my couch's newness again. I fed Minnie and walked back to my bedroom—to find someone who wasn't me sleeping in my bed. It was Sike, and she was under a fur sheet, or maybe it was a fur coat. I could see her bare feet sticking out from underneath it, and her long red hair streaked across half my bed.

"Sike?" I asked from the doorway. I didn't want to walk across the room and touch her, just in case she would be violent when she woke. "Sike?" I said, a little louder.

Her eyes opened, and she took a deep breath. Pushing herself up on her elbows, she focused on me. "You were gone half the night!"

"It's called work. You should try it sometime."

She sat up, stretched, and pulled her coat around herself. "I am working. You have no idea. Planning a Sanguine ascension ceremony is like planning a wedding, only all the guests could kill you."

I walked into my room. "So to what do I owe the honor?"

"House Grey. Who told you about them?"

"A frightened were." I sat down on the edge of my bed beside her to tell her Viktor's story, but made sure her strange furry coat didn't touch my leg. "About seven years ago, someone from House Grey visited his father and ruined this guy's life."

"That does sound like them. And makes everything infinitely more complicated for us."

"Who are they?"

"A guild of vampires dedicated to their own causes, whatever and wherever they may be. Assassins, mostly."

"And they're part of the Rose Throne?"

"No. They're part of every Throne, whether that Throne knows it or not. The best assassin is the one you least expect. The Rose Throne is continually at war with them."

"Really?" I'd figured that since Y4 was in the business of caring for injured daytimers, if there was a war on, we would know. "Why haven't I met any of them before?"

Sike narrowed her eyes at me. "Because when their people get injured, they let them die. Or rather—they make sure they die. They never leave any witnesses." She snorted. "They don't keep lipless freaks around, at any rate."

Suddenly having released Gideon into her care didn't seem like that great an idea. "Is Gideon okay?"

She gathered her coat to herself and put her arms through its sleeves. "As well as he can be. We found out who hurt him. House Bathory. Bunch of ingrates, trying to show her up. I wouldn't be surprised if House Grey put them up to it, just to see how Anna would react." Sike looked around my bedroom. "Your knife is still safe, isn't it? Is it here?"

I inhaled to tell her, and then closed my mouth. I didn't really expect Sike to kill me, but—she laughed. "Look how fast you learn! Don't tell me. Whatever you're doing, keep doing it. Keep it safe."

"Why's the knife important to them?"

"It's not, and you're not—they're only interested in fucking Anna over without showing their hand. How they got weres to go along with them, I'll never know." She slid her feet into her cast-off heels. "Just two more nights. Anna's ascension is happening, if I have to make it happen myself."

"That coat is hideous." There were patches of skin on

it that had no fur; the fur that was there was uneven in length.

"Thank you. It was made for me by an admirer." She stroked a hand along her side and stuck a hip out to model it briefly. "I brought it here for show-and-tell, in case your boyfriend was spending the night. It might have been a friend of his once upon a time."

I put two and two together, and thought I was going to be sick. "It's werewolf fur?"

"The trick is to keep them alive when you skin them, so their pelts don't go back. And also to not wear it on a full-moon night. They're very rare."

Bile rose up in my throat. "I'm going to pretend I didn't hear that, Sike," I said as she walked out my bedroom door.

"Do what you like. See you two nights from now. Cheers!" she called from down the hall.

I waited until she was gone, locked my front door, took the comforter and anything else her coat might have touched off my bed, put it into my laundry basket, turned up my thermostat, and went to sleep.

CHAPTER FORTY-TWO

I woke up thinking I only had two more nights of chaos to go. I showered and got ready for work robotically, hit a grocery store, and drove in. The black import car followed me again.

When I reached Y4, the assignment board had twice as many patients on it as usual—there were rooms A through H, holding John and Jane Decembers.

"They're all still here, huh?" I said, looking over the board.

"Yeah, once this guy goes home—I'm going home too." Charles pointed at his assignment, the one lone daytimer. All the donors that needed blood had dried up, so to speak. "Rachel's coming in to help you guys."

"Great."

I got report from Lynn, who'd had rooms A through D during P.M. shift. "Have you ever seen anything like this?" I asked as we were co-signing charts together.

"No, and I've been here for fifteen years. They're creepy." She signed her name and clicked her pen shut. "Have a good night—I'm going to go home and try not to dream."

My first patient was female. She was a little cleaner than the rest, but she stood like Gideon had not long ago, with her back toward me, staring at a point on the wall.

"Do you know what's happening to you right now?" I came up beside her and pushed her gently to sit on the bed. "Has anyone talked to you about the choices you've made?" I kept trying. "Can you tell me your name?"

I saw movement outside the room and looked up— Gina was waiting for me by the door.

I pushed the woman back into the bed, then lifted up her feet, forcing her to lie down. I tucked her in and went to meet Gina outside.

"It's the same up and down the line. Depressing," Gina said.

"Is this normally how it goes?" I asked her. When Gina had infected herself for Brandon's sake, she'd seemed to manage fine. It certainly hadn't made her comatose.

"Not in the least. Usually weres are more full of life. Vibrant. Brash."

I wasn't sure those were the terms I'd have used to describe Lucas groping me last night. "Can we give them shots? Like the ones that cured you?"

"No. As the local pack, Deepest Snow assumed responsibility for them, as of this morning."

"So?"

"You need consent for shots. None of them can give it right now, seeing as they can't talk. And Deepest Snow won't agree. They asked on day shift and Helen said no. Said she'll integrate them somehow." Because that worked so well with Viktor. Gina saw my frown. "I don't like it any better than you do. Maybe they'll straighten out by the end of the night. Lock all their doors, okay?"

"Okay." I went to do it. I didn't like it, but the only thing that'd make me feel worse than locking them inside their rooms would be having them out here with me.

Taking care of people who only sat and stared and breathed began to wear at my soul. It felt like someone was performing a cruel psychological test, and I was the lab rat. I hooked all of my people up to their oxygen saturation monitors, not because I was afraid they'd stop breathing, but because it'd tell me if they moved. I went out to the main nursing station, where Charles was, and sat in front of the main monitor to watch all their oscillating blue lines. Meaty sat across from us, doing paperwork.

"I needed to get out of crazy corner," I explained to Charles.

"You shouldn't have let them sucker you into so much were-stuff in the first place."

"Gee, thanks." I made a sour face. "Who're you taking care of?"

"My one lone, lovely daytimer. He got a blood transfusion—vampire blood, half a cc—earlier today. He'll be healed by dawn. It's looking like I can take tomorrow night off." Charles kicked his chair and wheeled aside.

"Don't think I'm not jealous of you," I told him.

"Why? You have it off too. Almost everyone will. Those weres should get better, and it won't take a whole team to watch Winter die."

"I have some other stuff to take care of tomorrow night."

"I hope you have some fun, too. You've been serious lately, Spence. Too much work is taking the spirit out of you."

"Don't I know it." I charted each of my patient's oxygenations and heart rates for the hour. It was almost two. "How come you get to pick your assignment?"

"Because I'm the oldest nurse on the floor. Meanest, too, if you count that time I beat Meaty arm wrestling."

Meaty snorted, but didn't stop printing off medication reconciliation forms.

A phone rang. Not one of our normal phones, but an old-fashioned ring, like you heard in the background on old TV shows. Meaty started up, but Charles was closer and dug behind a tangle of power cords for the monitors and computers to bring out a dusty red phone.

"That's the emergency phone, right?" I asked, guessing from the color, and Meaty nodded. I'd seen them on other floors—been in surgical ICU once on a float when they'd turned off the phones to work on them, but left that one on just in case. It looked like a child's plaything, for kids who didn't get to play with cell phones.

Charles's face went dark. He handed the phone over to Meaty and then left the floor.

I wanted to run after Charles—but I didn't want to leave Meaty alone.

"That's unacceptable," Meaty told whoever was on the other end of the line, then cupped a hand over the receiver. "Edie—fire drill. Now."

Fire-drill protocol was to close all the doors just in case. I went down the hall to tell Rachel and Gina, and then went from room to room for the rest of the floor, starting with Charles's daytimer. The man waved at me as I closed his door. I halfheartedly waved back.

When I returned, I gave Meaty a thumbs-up sign. Still on the phone, Meaty nodded and continued to frown. "No. I don't care who you have to find. We have a contract with you." Meaty's voice dropped as the conversation continued. "I shouldn't have to remind you about our agreement—the Consortium requires you," Meaty said, then stopped and pulled the receiver away to glare at it.

"Meaty—what's going on?"

Meaty slammed the red phone down in disgust. "They're leaving."

"Who?"

"The Shadows. A prisoner of theirs escaped, and they're giving chase." Meaty glared at the phone as if sheer anger could change things.

"Leaving?" I whispered.

Meaty's gaze rose to mine. "No one else can know of this. Go get Charles."

I wanted to ask more questions, but I ran off the floor.

I found Charles in the men's locker room. I entered after I knocked on the door. "Charles—"

"Don't even try to stop me, Edie." I'd never been into the men's locker room before. It looked a lot like the women's, only there were a ton more empty lockers here. I looked away while Charles finished pulling on his clothing for outdoors. "If they're gone, there's no reason to stay."

"Maybe they'll be back fast," I said, aware of how lame it sounded.

"Are you willing to bet your life on it?" The inside of Charles's locker was decorated with black-and-white photos of a lovely middle-aged woman. He pulled out all his belongings and started taking down the pictures.

"She's beautiful," I said.

"She is. And I'm going to go spend some time with her now." The photos he carefully pressed into an ancient nursing care book, then put this into a bag. "If the Shadows are gone, I don't know how long we have left. I'm taking her, and I'm going away. Someplace warm—someplace safe."

"You'll take your cell phone with you, right?"

"Sure. But don't bother texting me until this is through." He pushed his feet into winter boots and reached for the door behind me. "It's been nice knowing you, Spence. Don't get any more scars."

After that, he left. I walked back onto the floor in a

daze. Charles had been my anchor on Y4. Knowing I could turn to him for help allowed me to feel safe. Now?

"Edie, your assignment's changed. You've got Charles's daytimer, too. Don't worry, I'll help." Meaty's voice was reasonable, even.

Don't worry? I repeated inside my head. There was no way I could help it.

CHAPTER FORTY-THREE

"Just let me go to the bathroom first," I told Meaty.

"All right. I'll see you when you get back," Meaty said, with an emphasis on the word *back*. We couldn't all abandon ship tonight. If word that the Shadows were gone got out—traveled into one of our patient rooms, wafted up the elevator, went around the corner—we'd all be sitting ducks for whatever came our way. Charles's sudden absence we could explain, but not Charles's and mine together.

"I'll be back," I promised, and then rushed back off the floor. I ran into the locker room, pulled out my purse, and dialed Jake. He didn't answer. I tried him again, and again. Who else could I call? I thought about dialing Sike—but even if she wasn't an assassin, she wasn't likely to care. I scrolled through the names on my phone's contact list—the only one who would understand the gravity of the situation, and might be able to do anything about it, was Asher. I hated to ask him for a favor again, but I dialed him anyway. He answered on the second ring.

"Edie?"

"Asher—thanks for the other night," I started off strong, then paused. How best to explain it? It was quiet on the far end of the line this time. I imagined him in his library, lying on his couch, reading a book.

"You're welcome. What's wrong now? You only call me when you want something."

I was abashed. He was right. "I'm sorry, Asher."

"It's fine for now. Just know that someday soon when I want something, I'm going to call you." He didn't sound like he was teasing.

"Anything. Just ask it. Only help me out one last time."

"Okay."

"You remember my brother? He's selling drugs. He's in trouble. I'm trapped here for the rest of my shift—I don't know what to do."

"What about the Shadows?" Asher asked.

"They're not reliable," I said, choosing my descriptor carefully.

He made a thoughtful noise. "How unreliable currently are they?"

"I can't tell you."

"Are you in danger?"

"No. I just need Jake to be safe." It was what I'd always needed, for almost as long as I could remember. "He's homeless. He stays at the Armory, downtown. He's selling this stuff called Luna Lobos, which has something to do with the weres. Plus he's an idiot. You know what he looks like. That's pretty much all you need to know."

"All right, Edie. I'll get on it." It sounded like he was setting a book down and standing up.

"Thank you so much, Asher."

"You're welcome. You'll owe me after this, though. We'll figure out how much for, later."

"Like I said. Anything."

"I may take you up on that." He hung up on me before I could say anything back.

I felt a little better, going back onto the floor, and found Meaty waiting for me, just in case.

"I'm back. Like I said I would be," I said.

Meaty nodded solemnly. "Thanks."

So now I had Charles's patient, and no report, on top of the other four. I flipped through the charts and caught myself up to speed—Mr. Hale was also the victim of a gunshot wound, much as Javier had been. Because Mr. Hale was some vampire's daytimer, though, he was eligible for vampire blood to heal him. I found the authorization from from the Throne that signed off on it—I'd never seen an actual order before. It was written on vellum, like Anna's party invitation. I wondered if all the vampires had the same stationery, with a snort. On the bottom was an imprint into something that I hoped was wax, but looked more like a scab. There was a design in the center of it that looked roughly like a dagger or some kind of handled tool. I scraped at it with a fingernail, and a crusty piece came off.

"Ew."

The County transfusion lab kept donations of elder vampire blood for Y4. Vampire blood was a rare commodity—despite all the blood they drank in, very little of it ever came out again. The metabolic processes that created blood had slowed in death like the rest of them. Anna, as a living vampire, seemed to be the only known exception.

I set the chart aside and sat up to look over the nurses' station. Our daytimer patient was watching me. When he caught me looking, he waved for me to come in.

I walked over to his room and stood in the door. He looked as sketchy as the mute weres down the hall, face riddled with old pockmarks and a sheen of grease. He smelled rank, like old sweat and urine. A scrub-down with mere shaving cream wasn't going to save my nose from him, assuming he'd even let me. "Hey lady—where'd my other nurse go?"

"His wife got sick, he had to leave."

The daytimer shrugged, then winced. "Can you give me anything for pain? I got pain, bad."

"Let me look at your chart."

I hoped that Charles had caught things up before he left so I didn't double-med the guy. Then again, there was almost no way he could die on my shift. Him getting vampire blood was almost the reverse of a Do Not Resuscitate code. Nothing I could do to him tonight would kill him, except if maybe I was carrying a bottle of holy water across his room and tripped on top of him.

I grabbed five milligrams of morphine out of the Pyxis, his max dose, drew it up, and took it in to him. My badge with my name on it was in my scrub pocket; I'd put it there so it wouldn't dangle over the weres as I tucked them into bed. I was supposed to pull it out and hang it outside the isolation suit so that patients could ID us. I decided not to bother with that this time. I'd be fine being *hey lady* for the rest of the night.

"Whole syringe, eh?" he asked when I came in. "You sweet on me?"

I ignored him. "How badly do you hurt, on a scale from one to ten?"

"Bad. Baaaaad," he said, writhing in bed to illustrate it. "I got shot, lady." He flipped the covers back to show me his bandaged leg.

"Didn't you get vampire blood this morning?"

He laughed at his own lame joke. "Aw, lady, you caught me. But how many times can I get morphine for free?"

"Why would you want morphine, if you can get vampire blood?"

"You think I get vampire blood for free?" He rolled his eyes and flipped his covers back.

I prepped a saline flush in the room, and gave him all of the morphine. He wasn't going to die tonight, and I didn't want to hear from him again.

I finished all of the charting on my weird patients by the end of the night. Report was minimal, since none of them had done anything. I was on my way to the elevator when Gina caught me.

"Hey, where'd Charles go?"

"Food poisoning," I lied, and felt awful for it.

Gina made a face. "That's what he gets for eating all those Hot Pockets."

I wondered who would guard me safely home this morning—and how everything would go down tonight. Just as I made it to the lobby, Helen and a twenty-person entourage were coming in. She smiled at the sight of me, and separated herself from her group.

"Go on ahead, everyone," she said, gesturing them onward. "You too, Fenris." She shooed her son, who'd tried staying behind. He gave me a quick wave, behind her back. "There'll be a lot of visitors today. Many want to pay their last respects to their leader."

I was sure Winter's day-shift nurse would love that. I couldn't blame them, though; this might be their last chance to see him alive, if his current condition could even be called that. Helen's guests walked around us, all in different shades of black. I was very glad Lucas wasn't in their number.

"You called it off with him, I assume?" She smiled at me indulgently once we were alone.

"There was never anything to call off, really."

"Says you. Wolves can be surprisingly sentimental.

Still, it was for the best. He's going to be a pack leader—it's a complicated life."

"No one would know that better than you," I said without thinking. She tilted her head at me as though I'd spoken words in a foreign tongue. "I've heard," I added.

"Well, I can't speak to what you've heard. But things will be over tonight." She reached out to take my hand. "If he doesn't get better when the moon comes, we'll—" she began, and paused.

"Withdraw care," I filled in for her, because it sounded less callous than *pull the plug*.

She nodded, her face grim. "Yes. I'll be signing some paperwork to that effect this afternoon, and then staying until the end. Moonrise is at five fifteen tonight. The rest of my pack will have to be afield with Lucas, ringing his time in. Even little Fenris will be gone. My father's death will be my burden alone." Her hand squeezed mine a little tighter. "Would you like to be there? You were at the beginning, it's only fitting you would be at the end, too."

I really didn't want to—but I didn't know how I could tell her no. My ride to Anna's ascension wouldn't come until eleven at night. Still, though—

"It would mean the world to me, not to have to be alone."

I swallowed my refusal. No one should have to be alone and in pain when they didn't want to be. "Okay." I gave her a weak smile. "I just need to go home and sleep some now, then."

"Thank you, Edie. Thank you a lot." She reached out and patted a flyaway of hair from my ponytail down in a maternal fashion before going on down the hall.

CHAPTER FORTY-FOUR

I wonder what the person in the black foreign car following me thought I was doing, cruising the alleyways and homeless shelters of downtown that morning. I'd left a message on Asher's phone, and on Jake's, and neither one of them had gotten back to me yet. I didn't know where else to check. I'd hit all the big shelters I'd heard of, and I didn't know all the smaller ones. The people inside them were all nice, letting me look—my wearing scrubs and the slight tone of panic in my voice helped. Maybe they thought I was looking to make good on a New Year's resolution, one day early.

Exhausted and beaten, I went home. The car parked nearby in my parking lot, but no one got out. I went into my apartment and stared disconsolately at my phone. I took a shower so I wouldn't have to take one tonight, and crawled into bed after setting a four thirty P.M. alarm. I was almost asleep when a text buzzed my phone.

All's well. From Asher.

Thank u, thank u, thank u, I texted back. One weight of many lifted, I fell asleep.

Four thirty came earlier than I'd have liked. I put scrubs back on, then pulled my car out onto the freeway. It being New Year's Eve, there was some traffic, but no one was driving drunk yet. The weather wasn't cooperating, the sky was full of ominous clouds, and the morning's gentle snow had turned into freezing sleet.

When I parked in the hospital lot, the black car parked behind me.

I didn't want to be down on Y4 during the day. None of my co-workers would be there, just people from the P.M. shift, and my co-workers didn't usually appreciate people from other shifts lingering. Most people were smart enough not to, like Charles. I hoped that the poor weather hadn't grounded their plane and that by now he and his wife were someplace safe and far away.

The elevators let me off, and I walked onto Y4. I nodded at the charge nurse, walked around, and found Helen standing near Winter's door. When I arrived, she reached out and leaned into me.

"Thanks for coming, Edie."

"You're welcome."

Lynn gave me a wide-eyed look at Helen's actions. I gave her a helpless shrug and wrapped my arms around the clinging were.

"I hate to ask right now, Helen—but what's Deepest Snow going to do with the rest of the weres in the hall?"

"It's possible the moon will help with their problems too. We'll incorporate them into our group—just because they were Viktor's doesn't mean they can't be ours."

"Wouldn't it be easier to just give them the shots?" I said from the vicinity of her hair.

"No. They made their choices. They have to live with them."

"But—" I started.

She pulled away and looked up at me. "Life isn't always fair." I didn't know what to say to that, as she nestled back into my neck. "Don't worry. We'll treat them kindly."

* * *

Time passed slowly. I couldn't see a clock from where I was, pinned by Helen just inside Winter's room. I could see the monitor, though—his numbers continued as they had, circling one tier above the drain. We were maxed out on Levophed, dopamine, and Neo-Synephrine—there wasn't anything else we could give.

Helen knew when it was time. "When things are done—if he doesn't get better—can you close the door? And just leave him in peace all night, until we can return, tomorrow?" she asked. I nodded against her. She held me close then released me, stepping farther into the room. The change took her, and this time I saw it—she bent over, as if cramped. Her hands slid into paws, like there'd been furred gloves waiting for her all along, and her feet pushed out of shoes like they were kicking into paw-boots. Her clothing slid away, vanished, and she was naked for the blink of an eye before her fur caught up with her, sliding like a sheet down her back. Her face was the last to go, and she was facing away from me, so I didn't see it change—I only saw when she trotted up to Winter, on all fours, and nudged him with her muzzle. She put her front paws up on the table, and if it hadn't been meant for weres it might not have taken her weight—she leaned over him, gray in the room's light, licking his face with a whine.

We all waited, Helen beside him in the room, me at the door, Lynn outside. Nothing happened.

Helen shook the bed with her paws, twice, rough, and then stepped off it and turned around. Her head was bowed—she sat down and let out a baleful howl. I imagined I could hear the loneliness in it like a distant train, traveling out of reach. She howled again and again, until the entire room, no, floor, echoed with her cries, one chasing another, filled with awareness that Winter would never chase anything, again.

When she was done, she sat there, looking at me and Lynn. Lynn came in. "I'll do it." Helen came over to me and leaned her wolf-form against my side.

When you withdraw care, you slide the drugs up as you slide the ventilator down. If you do it right, no one sees the patient, their relative, gasp for air. If you're lucky, they take one big breath in, and let one big breath out, and that's it, it's done. Lynn turned off the alarms and the blood pressure pumps one by one. Then she stood by the ventilator, dialing the oxygen down as she ran the fentanyl dose up. His blood pressure dropped; his heart rate became uneven and slowed. Three breaths later—each one like a protracted sigh—and it was through.

Helen bowed her head, almost touching the ground.

"Did you want to stay?" I asked her. Sometimes relatives liked to wait nearby.

She shook her head.

"We can put her in the family conference room, overnight. I've got the keys right here. It's three doors down, to the left, in the outside hall." Lynn handed the keys over to me, and I took them. Helen and I exited the room together, and she stopped to look back.

"When we're done, I promise we'll shut the door."

Helen nodded, in her wolf's form, and I took her out into the hall. It took me a moment to find the right key, and then I let Helen into an empty room holding a conference table, chairs, and a bench. "We'll come get you in the morning. We'll bring scrubs."

Helen went into the room and lay down on all fours. I closed the door on her, and took the keys back to Lynn.

Protocol was to leave all lines in where they were, and not to touch the body. "The coroner might be running late. It's a holiday," Lynn said.

"Not for everyone." I handed the keys back to her. "I need to get home."

* * *

I was halfway up in the elevator when I realized I'd forgotten it. I hit the DOWN button a few times to see if it'd change course, and it didn't. I had to ride all the way up and back down again. That's usually the sort of thing the Shadows would have found entertaining, the myriad small frustrations that ate into people's time. Where had they gone, and when were they coming back? I didn't envy Gina and Rachel working tonight. I hoped Meaty would keep them safe.

I let myself into the locker room and popped open my locker. Anna's ceremonial knife was where I'd put it almost a week ago, dish towel and all. I slid it into my purse and headed out the door.

The black car followed me home. I didn't think to question who was driving it—maybe the weres had human helpers too, like vampires. I didn't care. It was pushing seven by the time I got home. I had hit holiday traffic on the roads, people heading to New Year's Eve parties that would be vastly different from mine.

CHAPTER FORTY-FIVE

I didn't know what to wear to a vampire party, so I decided to be comfortable. More jeans, and a bulky sweater. I put my silver bracelet on, and my silver-buckled belt underneath the sweater. I tried not to think about the last time I'd seen either of them.

At eleven, I presented myself outside. There was already a limousine waiting. Vampires had style, I'd give them that.

I walked around the limo, wondering if I was supposed to. In movies they always had people opening the doors for you, and I'd skipped prom.

There was a body dressed in a driver's uniform lying by the open front door, and blood like a streak of tar against the fresh snow. Something not entirely human, and not entirely wolf either, crouched, waiting for me.

"Human whore," said a gravelly voice.

"Jorgen?" He was still wearing a bowling shirt, and still bald, but his face protruded, his nose and jaw muzzle-like.

"I don't think I need protection anymore." I backed up.

"Oh, yes, you do," he said, and leapt.

My feet went out from under me in the snow as I ran backward, and that was what saved me. He sailed over me as I fell, and I whirled on my ass, trying to kick out at him. He grabbed my ankles and yanked me nearer to him.

"Now that the moon is out, we no longer have to pretend," he said, looming over me. He leaned down, and I tried to punch him in the face.

He pulled back and to the side. His teeth scraped the knuckles of my hand, and my bracelet slid up his cheek as I followed through. He howled, reaching for his face with one hand, and swatting claws down my left thigh with his other.

I saw my purse and scrabbled backward. The knife was in it, if only I was able—I reached for it, cold slush sliding up my side. I grabbed the strap and yanked it to me.

Jorgen grabbed and pulled again on my leg as I clutched my purse to my chest.

"Why? Why this? Why me?" I tried to sound panicked—not hard—and hoped he'd bother to answer. My other things spilled out as my hand found the knife's hilt in my bag.

"Because." His face, undecided between man and beast, was gruesome. "Because life isn't fair," he said, sounding like Helen. "I shouldn't have been bitten. I should have been born. And because your Lucas is unfit to rule."

"I don't understand—" I protested, trying to scoot back.

Jorgen laughed at this. "Do you think I care?" Then he leapt.

We were so close it was like a body slam. All I had time to do was hold the knife up inside my purse, like a cartoon funeral rose. There was the sensation of impact. All over my body, a crushing physical blow. The hilt of the knife pounded into my stomach and knocked all the wind out of me. But it was wedged up. Caught on something.

Jorgen's sternum.

"Get off me—" I shoved at him and he groaned. His hands found purchase and he rolled himself away. I let the knife go and it sliced my purse free as it rolled with him. I sat up, holding the leather shreds of my purse, stunned, watching blood pour out of Jorgen like he was a fountain.

He tried to pull at it. There was an electric snap from the blade as he touched it, repelling his hand.

"Get it out—" he begged.

If I took it out of him, there was a chance he'd heal. If I didn't take it with me, I'd let Anna down tonight. I didn't think vampires believed in extenuating circumstances.

I squatted beside him, still catching my breath. "Tell me why."

"You saw me hit him with my truck." Jorgen's hands played through the blood he was losing, trying to keep some from spilling out.

I hadn't seen the driver of the car that hit Winter . . . but Jorgen assumed I had. Because it had been him.

Why would Jorgen hit Winter? Wasn't Jorgen bitten—a faithful were-follower? I swallowed. What could possibly change his mind?

"Tell Helen I love her. I've always loved her," he said, reaching a bloody hand out to me, then lowering it to the ground.

"Why'd you hit him, Jorgen?" The wolfman didn't respond. "Jorgen?" I resisted the temptation to shake him, to try to wake him up. There was so much blood, and Jorgen's breathing was shallow.

I could kill him for sure with the knife. Carve it down and slice his intestines through. But I knew what a stab wound through the gut felt like. I didn't have it in me. I stood, shaking.

"Don't follow me if you get up." I reached down, yanked out the knife, and headed for the limousine.

* * *

I stepped on my ID badge on the way to the limo. I freed it from the muck and shoved it into my pocket, lanyard and all, and then got into my ride.

Most of the blood on me wasn't mine, but my knuckles and thighs throbbed. The heat was on in the limo, keys still in the ignition, so I revved it up and pulled away.

The limo had GPS, and the driver, now dead and gnawed on in my parking lot, had been kind enough to enter in his final destination before he left.

Driving it was like driving a boat. Luckily it was automatic, not stick.

I didn't look at myself in the rearview mirror. I knew that would be a bad idea. I knew bruises were welting up all over my body, that my jeans were torn, that my sweater was covered in were-blood, and what else, who goddamn knew.

No matter how much I might have loved a monster once—I didn't sign up for this.

If I let go of the steering wheel, the limo would slide to the side of the road, into a snowbank, and I would cry, and be frozen there like a woolly mammoth until a snowplow happened by or the first thaw of spring. No, I would not look up, and I would not look down. I would only watch the road and the little blue dot on the GPS's screen that meant we were heading toward something, somewhere else. I followed that little blue dot, went out of town, and out into the countryside, until it pulled me into a parking lot circled by a white picket fence. I looked out.

It had once been a church.

I pulled the limo up. This parking lot was huge, so the church must have been prestigious, before . . . the fire. I nodded to myself. Snow didn't hide all the charred blackness of the roof, and I could see blue tarps underneath it, trying to keep some of the weather out. I bet the congregation hadn't had enough money or time to rebuild before winter, and now, this.

I parked the limousine. I didn't want to leave it. It was warm here, and it was safe, and I was starting to stick to the seat. A knock on the window startled me.

"You're late!" Sike said as I opened the door. I could tell she didn't expect to see me driving. "You stink of were-blood. What happened?"

"Your driver got jumped."

"How are you?" she said, and for the first time, I felt she meant it. She put out her hand.

I stood even with her, so she could see all of me. "I'm fine. But after this, I'm fucking through. You're getting me out." I knew she had no say in the matter, but saying it firmed my resolve.

"When you're done here, you should probably go to Y4. To get were-shots." She touched a hand to an earpiece I hadn't realized she had. "We need a disposal team at the Ambassador's personal residence. Driver two is gone." Then she gestured. "Please, follow me."

Some Ambassador I was tonight. Limping, I followed.

Seeing as the church had holes in some walls, it was freaking cold inside. It wouldn't bother the vampires, but it irritated me. I'd been through enough already tonight, I didn't need to freeze too.

The inside of the church had at one time been a Catholic affair. There was a clean space on a blackened wall where a crucifix had been removed, like an inverse cross. The rest of the inside was hollowed out, gutted by the fire. After that, I bet congregants had taken everything they could salvage. Construction lights made everything cast long shadows.

"Why the hell are we here?" I asked Sike.

"We wanted the most neutral ground possible. Churches make all vampires uncomfortable," she said as she led me in. "Plus, it has a sense of flair."

"Remind me to never go shopping with you," I muttered, following behind her, holding Anna's knife.

Because the pews were gone, vampires stood where the congregation should be, clustered together in their tribes. Sike led me around them and up to the raised altar at the front. I recognized the other people standing there. Gideon, Veronica, Mr. Galeman—a prior patient of mine whom Anna had bitten—Sike and I took our place by their side. Veronica still looked as feral as she had at my house, and as if to make up for it, Gideon was eerily calm.

"How'd they rope you into this," I asked Mr. Galeman, who stood beside me.

"Free beer," he whispered back. Sike hissed down the line at us, then glared at us to keep quiet.

Well. That. Was. Encouraging. I stood there, exhausted, and my legs kept complaining, each claw mark stung—I wasn't going to need just rabies shots, but tetanus as well. I looked like that chick from *Carrie,* or one of any number of segments from *Battle Royale.*

"Now the ceremony can begin," said a vampire I didn't recognize from the side. Organ music welled up, pretentious, dramatic.

"Is it always like this?" I asked Sike.

She glared at me. "Shut it."

Anna walked in from off stage. She was dressed simply, in white. It made her already fair skin paler; her blond hair gave her the only color she had.

She made her way down us, like she was in a receiving line. She spoke to Veronica and Gideon first, then Mr. Galeman, then me.

Anna looked me up and down. "You're magnificent."

"I'm not feeling it right now."

She slipped her hand into mine briefly. Then she smiled at Sike and went to the front of the stage.

"Bathory isn't here," Sike whispered, barely breathing beside me. She took her earpiece out of her ear.

"What does that mean?"

"They're not voting."

I tried to stare out past the lights, to figure out by the crowds where the lines of allegiances ran.

A vampire who appeared to be the master of ceremonies took the stage. He gestured for Anna to join him. "Anna Arsov, begin."

Anna opened up her arms to include everyone in the gathering. She looked so young beside him, and with all the lights shining down, her shadow was slight. "I have passed every test that you've given me. I have shown grand restraint, and I have known grave thirst. All the positions on my court have been filled. Who here would dispute my right to ascend?"

"House Arachne!" A lone vampire in the middle of an empty area of seats stood. "House Arachne does not recognize the right of the Arsinov to ascend to the Sanguine of the Rose Throne!"

"Old, but not as old as we are," Sike murmured just for my ear. "Powers include insect and small animal servants. Spiders, birds, and the like."

"And why would you dispute me?"

"You picked this place, so you have no taste. Worse yet, you picked these people—"

Anna cut her off. "It was within my rights to choose the locale, and to choose my own people. I have done nothing wrong."

"Many of them hate the church. They believe in the power it holds over them." Sike continued her narration.

"And you?" I asked of Sike.

"I believe in her," she whispered back.

"Does anyone else dispute?" the vampire overseeing the proceedings intoned.

A young woman in a tight burgundy velvet dress with swooping sleeves came forward. "The House of Bathory is undecided. We choose to abstain."

"Nouveau riche pretenders," Sike murmured to me. "Weak."

"Is that all?" the ceremony master asked, taking a moment to look around. "Together, two Houses cannot sway the vote. Sanguine rules of order say we should proceed." He turned toward me. "Human, can you present your knife?"

I'd forgotten I had it. I held it out. He took it with a gloved hand and spun the hourglass in the hilt.

"There's blood on it—but none of it's in you. That's what counts." He put it in his own robe. "We may begin," he said, and snapped his fingers.

One of the hovering observers came up with a small brass box. It had a crank handle and was set on a silver tray.

Anna turned to me and pointed at the box. "Edie, please."

I didn't want to ask what it was. I wish she'd told me more. I picked it up carefully and looked at the handle, then the sides, and finally underneath. There were grooves cut into the bottom, lined with tiny blades. The metal was old. The blades were unclean.

A scarificator. I recognized it from our introduction to nursing class, when our teachers had explained how far medical practices had come, and how far it had to go, and how we, the nurses of the next generation, were going to take it there. It was meant to bleed people, from olden times, when just lancing someone wouldn't do. Shown to be medically useless, despite the esteem it once held. Just like cocaine-spiked Coke, magnet treatments, and the benefits of smoking.

No one made them anymore—because no one believed in the health benefits of bleeding.

Except for vampires.

Anna rolled up her white sleeve and proffered me her wrist. Another observer brought up a golden urn that had been fitted with a delicate tap.

"I trust you," she said, looking down at me. I knew what the stakes were, but—"Edie. It will be okay. I trust you."

I knew I couldn't hurt her—doing this wouldn't hurt her. And many times vampires, and even sometimes me, found pleasure inside pain. But still.

Where was the difference between piercing someone's skin with a needle, for their own good, and setting this thing's blackened grinding blades onto her? How many times had I hurt to make things better—hurt other people, and hurt myself?

She wanted me to do it. If I didn't, it might be the end of her. And the end of us.

I set the box on her skin. Then I stabilized it with my thumb, holding it still, my fingers cupping her wrist. I could feel the smoothness of her skin.

And then, God help me, I spun the handle around. The blades dug down. I didn't dare look up.

CHAPTER FORTY-SIX

She didn't flinch.

The blades were dull—it'd been a century since they were sharp. At least sterility didn't matter—this predated the idea of germs, much less the autoclave—since there was nothing Anna could contract. I pressed the box harder and spun the handle with more force. I felt like a perverted organ grinder's monkey, paid a pittance to liberate someone's blood.

The first drops emerged. Snaking down her arm in red tributaries, joining on her wrist to become a river, following the same path of least resistance to pool in the palm of her hand.

Warm in a way their blood would never be, hot as it rolled down to drip drip drip into the urn. I could hear the first few drops ting, like rain on a cheap window, before there was enough blood to make it sound like slow running water.

I couldn't see the vampires in attendance, but I felt their attention, rapt. How much blood did one body hold? Her size, her slight weight? I knew the answer, somewhere. I tried not to think about it. Hard.

Those who were helping with the ceremony came up and twisted the tap, decanting Anna's blood into trays of small glasses, which I realized with a shock were communion cups. Some of them were precise, catching every drop. Others were wasteful, overfilling glasses, letting blood drip down between. Anna ignored them, I almost said something, and she put her free hand on my shoulder before I could speak.

"I heal quickly, even now. Keep going," she said.

I hadn't counted the congregants before. I wished I had. Tray after tray of glasses was filled, dispensed, and filled again. Anna's hand on my shoulder didn't change; it didn't claw me with pain or fade away with the urge to faint.

I wanted to think I would have stopped all this if it had.

After what seemed like hours, the last tray was full, and there was no one else in line. Anna stood there, still white and gleaming, if you ignored the carnage down her right arm. Sensing things were through, I lifted the scarficator, saw where it had ripped through the skin and into the muscles of her forearm, the shreds of exposed white tendon, the dull gleam of living bone. Just as quickly, she began to heal, tendons reknitting, muscle sheaths regrowing.

I had never seen the process up close before. I gasped aloud. It was genuinely miraculous.

From the front of the stage I could finally see the crowd—and I knew now why I had been chosen. They were rapt with lust. The room was silent, charged.

"So you see," Anna announced to the group before us, rolling her sleeve back down her arm. "I have passed the final test. I thank you for those who donated to my trials. Drink now, and think well of me."

Some vampires darted long tongues into the small cups, others tipped them back to drink each drop, and still others swirled elegant fingers inside, pulling out drops of blood to lick like cake batter. So cruel to be limited to just a sip of her blood, when they could take—and she would make—so much more. If one of them had been here, instead of me, and she hadn't been absolutely sure of their loyalty as she was of mine—

There was a commotion at the back of the room. A group of vampires forced their way in, jostling one another and the already seated host, each of them dressed as elaborately as the lone Bathory speaker before. None of them wore their attire like they were born to it, like they shared its age. Instead they looked like a well-funded Renaissance fair troupe had gotten loose.

"The House of Bathory will now decide!"

"Your time has passed," the master of ceremonies intoned.

"We have the right!" said a man, one of those entering late. "I am the leader of this House. I get to have a vote."

"The votes have already been counted." The master of ceremonies grew before me, the shadows around him gathering, taking up more space, crowding out the air.

"What would you find acceptable?" Anna said, stepping in front of me. At her intrusion, the master of ceremonies seemed to shrink and withdraw. All fights tonight were hers.

The man, dressed as an imitation of Henry the Eighth with a stomach to match, stepped forward. "We would prefer enough blood to bathe in, of course." Only members of his retinue laughed at his joke. "But we will accept a small sacrifice. One of your court, perhaps. Or more blood from your wrist divine."

I realized that as a whole, they lacked bargaining power, knowing she wouldn't let them slaughter us, her court, off one by one. But their dissent could cause chaos, and if she was low on blood, no true vampire would think twice about sacrificing a pawn for their cause.

How much had she bled? How much more could she

make? How fast? The longer this took, the more they would know she was stalling for time, and there were thirty vampires that still needed sating.

"I accept your challenge." She took another step forward. "I am afraid I cannot put my Ambassador again through such stress." She gave me a look overly full of pity, and then turned back to them. "I am forced to let you all drink from the source."

She crossed the distance between them and held her wrist up for the taller man who neared. He was looking for a trap. To drink was to put yourself in danger. Everyone here had also, if only in distant memory, been a gazelle.

"Drink deeply," she demanded, shaking her wrist as the last of the scarificator marks healed. He grabbed her arm, steadied himself and her, and bit her.

They were like sharks when they fed, eyes open, dark, then rolling back. His teeth fastened into her wrist, both sides. I could hear the force of his bite, fangs cutting into her. Behind him, the members of Bathory House leered. He couldn't even drink all of her blood—it seeped beyond the edges of his pulled-back lips, and dripped onto the floor.

Other jealous vampires were becoming restless—and not all of them were Bathory.

It would not go well for me in a bloodbath.

I watched him as they watched her. He closed his eyes.

She beheaded him. Without changing position or alerting him in any way, her free hand punched through his neck. Maybe he was drunk on blood, entranced by power—one second he was drinking, hunched over, and the next his head was still attached to her arm while the rest of his body staggered to the floor.

Instead of dusting, blood spurted out of his neck's open wound, on both sides. House Bathory crowded, stunned, dismayed, and she kicked his body toward them.

"You may drink of him, and through him, drink of me. When my blood in him is gone, all you will get is dust, and those of you who are not mine will die."

They fell on him like wolves. I heard fabric shred, then the sound of tearing meat, the break of bones. Anna pried his head off her wrist, where it sat whole, latched on, like a rattlesnake. As it fell it started crumbling to dust, peppering her clothes. The rest of the body crumbled accordingly, and the Bathory vampires who hadn't fed yet wailed.

Anna turned to the master of ceremonies. "Am I a member of the Sanguine, or am I not?"

A cruel smile played across his lips. He looked around to the others whom I had thought were mere servants, stuck holding trays, and I watched them nod one by one—the other members of the Sanguine, walking among us all along. The vampires had known, of course, but not me, till now. When he spoke, he showed black-stained teeth. "If you were not when you walked in, you have become so." He turned toward the Bathory vampires, now licking at drops of blood in the carpeting, eating fistfuls of dust. "We will handle the herd."

I closed my eyes. I didn't want to see what came next.

CHAPTER FORTY-SEVEN

I didn't know I was pressing my hands to my ears until I felt someone tugging at them. I'd been through too much tonight, done too much, seen too much blood.

"Did we break you?" Sike was holding my hands now, and shaking me. I focused on her again. Her face was clean, her smile high and bright. She raised a hand between us and snapped her fingers. "She's going to be very busy for a while now." We both knew she meant Anna. I didn't want to look around.

I'd never hurt someone intentionally like that before. And then I remembered how I'd stabbed Jorgen, and was still covered in his blood, and the blood of the driver before him, and—

"Do not throw up." Sike put her arm around my shoulder. Where she could have been angry or demanding, instead she finally seemed sympathetic. She led me through the groups of vampires still congregating. Tonight had changed things between us. She and I were finally on the same team.

This whole thing now seemed like some Hollywood-Halloween-themed wedding reception. The glamorous people in charge, those who toadied up to them, from all apparent walks of life and day jobs. Men in suits, trench coats, women in latex, necks strung with pearls. But then there were the off-kilter ones who looked like they'd just come in from the gym, or were just going out to a punk show.

I'd have sworn I saw a woman in sweatpants with something I could only see half of written across her ass, talking earnestly to one of the men with anime hair. I saw a glimpse of white—Anna was the only one wearing it— but then she was whisked away.

"You still need to get to the hospital for were-shots," Sike said. She propelled me toward the church's front, helping me as I limped. She nodded to the people who were guarding the entrance, and they opened the doors. "I'll call a car," she said once she'd gotten me to where I could lean against the wall. Her earpiece in again, she rattled off commands, then returned her attention to me. "You look like hell. Don't go were on me out here. It would make us look bad."

I plucked at the bloody shirt that I was currently freezing in. "Gee, thanks."

She shook her head and started fishing for a cigarette. "Sorry." When she found one, she looked up. "So what happened to you tonight?"

"How nice of you to ask." I watched her light up, wishing I had a bad habit to count on in stressful times. "Jorgen—a bitten member of the Deepest Snow pack— came after me."

Sike's eyes narrowed. "Anna's going to have words with them then. Now that her place is assured—we can't allow that kind of affront."

"Why them, though? It was supposed to be some other were. Viktor."

She took a deep drag and exhaled smoke. "I checked him out. He's too young. Too brash. House Grey would never make use of him. And if they were orchestrating things against Anna—they would have done it here." She drew a circle in the air to indicate the church behind us, her cigarette leaving a tracer of light behind. "She's in. She can make her own House now."

"Yay?" I asked with sarcasm.

"You're so small-minded. You don't even realize what that means." She blew smoke out of her nose like a dragon. "Because she's alive she can make more blood whenever she wants. People who belong to her will never have to go to Y4 and beg." She smiled, and I could imagine a time in the near future when the act would show the world her fangs. "Blood is power, and Anna's a fountain of it."

"So you're saying I'm safe now?" I asked her, my hands tucked into my armpits. She was calm and glamorous, dressed up for the occasion, smoking dramatic, and not shivering. I was her opposite, and becoming too cold to care.

"I'm saying get to Y4, get the shots, and stay there until we come and get you. Don't worry, the Shadows can protect you until dawn."

I inhaled her secondhand smoke deeply and leaned forward. "About that—"

A rush of vampires came out the doors, talking among themselves. And a car pulled up behind Sike. She turned and knocked on its hood twice, then smiled at me. "See? Good as my word. What were you going to say?"

I couldn't tell her what I wanted to, with so many vampires in earshot. "You shouldn't smoke. It's bad for you."

"What's it matter? Soon I'll be dead." She pursed her red lips and took another drag.

"You're not dead yet."

She looked at the cigarette she held and gave me a sour grin. Then she dropped it and stomped it out with a snort.

* * *

Sike flagged down Gideon and put him in the car with me. Our driver was under strict orders—from people who were far more frightening than I could hope to be—to take me to the hospital. The claw marks on my leg were screaming as I got inside, and I hoped that was all mechanical injury and not were-infection starting.

"Fancy meeting you here," I told Gideon in the backseat. He was wearing gloves and a leather coat now. It looked like he'd upgraded his webcam for a lens that sat on his forehead like a third eye. He groaned an acknowledgment and put a hat on his head.

The limo driver took off without asking where we were going; I figured he already knew. I tried not to move, and cursed vampires for getting me into these messes.

I wanted to call ahead and warn Y4 we were coming—and also text Lucas and ask him what the fuck was going on. I didn't want to believe that he could be in on it. And with the cuts on my leg, it was impossible to get comfortable.

Gideon saw me fidgeting, reached into his coat, pulled out a new-looking phone, and offered it to me.

"Thanks." Maybe people looking for cigarettes and people wishing they had their phones fidgeted the same. "I don't know his number, though."

Gideon kept holding it out. I took it, turned it on, went for the call icon, and hopped onto the contact list. "When did you get this?"

Gideon grunted. Jake's name, my parents' names, old nursing school friends—"You backed up my phone for me?"

Gideon shrugged. To think I'd been only worried about my brother making long-distance calls before now. I pulled up Lucas's information and sent him a text message. *Jorgen attacked me. What the fuck?* He would be a wolf until dawn, but maybe I'd hear from him in the morning.

* * *

We drove along, in from the countryside until we hit the freeway, and then the freeway to the less good part of town. Two exits away from County, the driver looked up.

"So where's your house?" He peered at us through his rearview mirror.

"What?"

"Your house. It's around here somewhere, right?"

I tensed in the backseat, and then hissed in pain. "I thought you were taking me to the hospital."

"Oh, I can't. The weather's just awful." The limo began to slow.

I looked out the window. It was snowing, but no more than it'd been an hour ago, and the road ahead of us was empty. In other circumstances, it would have been pretty in the moonlight. The driver braked the limo to a stop.

"I can't drive in this ice, lady." His reflection frowned at me. "I don't want to get trapped down here in this weather. You need to make up your mind."

"What are you talking about?" I leaned forward, gritting my teeth, and Gideon grabbed my hand. The driver reached to put the limo in reverse.

"Never mind. We're here." I opened my door, hopped out, and Gideon followed. The limo driver did a U-turn in the middle of the intersection and drove away.

"Maybe I can change into a were, heal up, and then get shots," I muttered to myself as we hobbled on our way in. Gideon offered me his arm, and I took it. "This is bullshit."

It was eerie in the moonlight, walking in the middle of the road. A crunching sound began ahead of us, and I kept waiting for headlights to shine and force us to dive away. The crunching sound continued until we crested a small hill, and then its source was revealed.

People were hobbling toward us. Some of them had

walkers that they were using in the ice. Others had crutches, wheelchairs, knee braces, walking alone or in pairs, pushing strollers, clutching one another for support.

They weren't on the way to some fabulous New Year's Eve party—they were leaving County, in nothing more than hospital gowns. It was a mass exodus, and we were in their way.

Gideon put his arm out and buffeted most of them aside. I tried to get some of them to talk, but they were as silent as the weres had been the night before—no, just this afternoon.

"Something's wrong, Gideon," I said. Gideon turned and looked at me with his eyeless-camera-lensed face. From somewhere near his chest, Grandfather said, *"Du hast jetzt sehen?"*

I was pretty sure he was agreeing.

County loomed on the horizon as we I neared. Hundreds of people passed us—I saw employees in their number. Lab techs with coats on, nurses and doctors in scrubs. I hoped none of them had left anyone behind in surgery.

In the moonlight County's squat cement exterior made it look like a factory. I remembered a simpler time at another hospital, when I'd worked aboveground, and I'd check for lights in certain rooms as I walked in to work my shifts—a light on meant my prior night's patient was still alive. I wasn't sure what the lights inside County stood for now.

Gideon and I hobbled to the emergency entrance doors together. The doors slid open, and boy did the heat feel good. Gideon pulled his hat lower as the security officer arrived. It made sense—if I saw me wandering in from the street, looking like this, I'd wonder who got shot.

"Miss, I'm afraid we can't see you tonight." The officer blocked my path.

"I'm in need of emergency medical treatment." The magic words that should get me through the door.

He stared over my shoulder, as if I weren't even there. "We're full—"

I pulled my badge out from my pocket, bloody lanyard and all. "I'm a hospital employee."

"Then you know. It's a Code Triage, we can't take any more—" He kept talking. Whatever he was seeing, it wasn't me. "You'll have to go to another facility."

Behind him, nurses and doctors and their assistants, my distant co-workers, were hustling a critical-looking patient out the door. That almost never happened. We were a level one trauma center. We could do it all. We didn't discharge vented patients at—I looked up at a clock—three A.M.

"I'm going to my home floor. I work here." I held up my badge in his field of vision. It glowed briefly before dimming again.

"Please go to your home floor to help with the immediate evacuation," the officer said. I nodded.

"Will do."

As much as it hurt me to walk, we took the back way, through the empty halls, so we wouldn't be confronted again before we reached Y4.

CHAPTER FORTY-EIGHT

Gideon and I could hear howls when the elevator doors opened. He helped me limp toward the double doors.

Meaty looked up from the main desk as I came in. "Edie? Are you okay? You look like hell."

Gina came around the corner with a smile for me, and then pointed at Gideon. "Who's he?"

"A friend. It'll take too long to explain." I hobbled over to the desk. Gideon took off his hat and started walking around the unit, looking at things.

"What's going on?" Meaty asked as I slowly sat in a chair.

"The whole rest of the hospital is evacuating up there. It's Code Triage—they're not taking new people in, and they're sending everyone inside out."

Meaty said, "Tell me everything. Now."

I whitecapped my past two days of events. They didn't need to know about Gideon or Veronica, sex with Lucas, or the details of the whole ordeal I'd just been through. But they deserved to know why I had blood on me. It would be enough.

"So I came here to get were-shots, only then I saw all the chaos up above—"

"Did they get you?" Gina asked.

"Define *get*?" I held up my hand, where Jorgen's teeth

had grazed me. Two knuckles were open, raw. And the claw marks on my thighs . . .

"Shit," she cursed. "On a full-moon night? You're going to need the full series." She stood and went over to the Pyxis to pull out meds.

Meaty sighed deeply. "Protocol says to lock the doors and sit tight. Access to our floor is regulated anyhow—it's not like they can come barging in."

"Even when the Shadows are gone?" I asked Meaty.

Gina interrupted. "The Shadows are gone? What?"

Meaty looked away. "We thought it best not to tell anyone."

I didn't remember getting a vote, but it was spilled milk now. Behind us, in the newly expanded were-wing, the full moon was working on its children. In between howls, I could hear scrabbling claws, digging at tile—and the occasional thump as a wolf-person threw itself at its room doors. I wasn't so worried about what might barge in, as what was trying to barge out.

"Who's watching the zoo?" I asked.

"Rachel," Gina answered, returning with a box of shots. I pulled out my cell phone.

"Do I have permission to call friends?"

"Are you sure they're friends?" Meaty asked.

"After the night I've had, they'd better fucking be."

I didn't call, I texted—Sike, then Lucas. *Something's wrong at work. Can you come?*

Sike responded shortly. "On my way." From probably phoneless and definitely thumbless Lucas, more silence.

Gina stabbed the first were-vaccination into my upper arm, smack into my deltoid muscle.

"That really freaking hurts." It wasn't the needle so much as the sensation of burning that spread out from the injection site. It felt like being slapped.

"Just be glad it's not in the stomach anymore."

Meaty was checking news links online. "I don't see anything about our Code Triage here. Gina, start barricading doors."

Gina moved behind Meaty, reaching up into the pneumatic tube system like she was searching for a flue. She pulled a metal sheet down, latched it into place, and pulled down a plastic sheet after it. She went from room to room after that, pulling down hidden latches and bars.

"Where'd Mr. Hale go?" I asked her. Charles's daytimer wasn't in his room.

"Out for a cigarette, about an hour ago. As soon as he left, that's when they started howling."

From around the bend, Rachel screamed. Gina startled and ran down the hall. Meaty did too. I followed, much more slowly.

"Who is this? Why is he by my rooms?" Rachel asked, pointing at Gideon. Fluorescent light was not doing him any favors. It highlighted the strange curlings of things that shouldn't have been traveling under his skin.

"Sorry. He's helping. Honest," I said, and Gideon walked back over to me, again offering me his arm.

"All of these rooms are secure?" Meaty asked.

"Of course."

I could see their occupants in the monitors, the quiet men and women of yesterday, now half human, half beast, all furious. At the sound of our voices in the hall, they redoubled their efforts to come out and play with us.

"It's too late to give them shots now, isn't it?" I asked.

Rachel eyed me pragmatically. "Do you want to open up a door?"

"No." But speaking of. I jerked my chin at Winter's locked room. "Did the coroner ever come?"

"It's a holiday. We called twice," Gina said.

There had to be connections among everything—the attacks on me, the attacks on Anna, Viktor's past, Lucas's future. Either Winter had taken them to the grave with him, or the answer was behind his door.

"Gideon—" I said, and we walked over to Winter's room together.

I turned on all the lights once we got inside—there was no reason not to see clearly now. I pulled the sheets off the bed, and the smell of necrosis that the weres had commented on was battled by the scent of shit, the final indignity of death, staining both him and middle of the bed like wet cement.

"What are we looking for?" Gina asked me.

"I'm not sure."

"Wouldn't want to have to give you twice the shots." She handed me gloves, and I pulled them on. Only another nurse could joke in the face of death, and I loved her for it.

His naked body was free of the bite-mark scars that vampire-sanctioned donors had, zones where too many injuries had left keloided scars, neck, armpit, groin. All his lines were still in the same places, his ET tube too. What was it? What were we missing?

I ran my gloved hands over his chest, down his arms, down his legs, down to his one remaining big toe. I hit the bottom of his necrotic foot, expecting to find it like a rotting overripe tomato.

Instead, it dusted. Not the whole thing, but the topmost tips of his toes. I hit it again, and another line of dust flew off—like I was beating an old rug outside in the spring.

"Did you see that?" I asked Gina and did it again.

"He's part daytimer," Gina whispered. "No wonder he lived to be so old."

"How come we didn't know?"

"Do you give men pregnancy tests? We just assume that weres are not also part vampires. Up until now, we were right." She reached out to hit his foot for herself, then reached back to hit his hand. Another cloud of dust came up, and a chunk of his wrist dusted away.

"Shit. This is it. What they were protecting," Gina said.

"He still died, though. What does this change?"

"His whole family—if this got out, they'd be humiliated. They'd lose control of the pack." Gina started pacing and talked as she thought. "But they already have lost control—I mean, Lucas will be pack leader now."

"Only for the interim, until Fenris Jr. is of age," I corrected her.

"Five years from now. A lot of things can change."

Rachel returned to the doorway of the room. "I went and checked the conference room—Helen's gone. She broke down the door."

"Which vampire was giving him blood, is what I want to know," Gina said. Gideon stood by the head of the bed, looking down at Winter. He leaned forward, almost like he was going in for a lipless kiss, and then stood straight again.

Gina kept pacing. I would have paced too, only my thighs were still on fire if I moved, and thanks to the were-vaccination my shoulder felt like someone had run a truck into it.

"Winter was leaving from here when he got hit—Charles and I saw him. Why the hell was he here to begin with?"

Gina stopped. "Which floors have security cams?"

I looked over at Gideon. "I think I know someone who can find out."

We installed Gideon behind the fastest computer on the floor, and he pulled a USB cable out from a pocket and plugged it in. I didn't know where the end of the cable was located, and I didn't want to ask.

"Is that really happening?" Rachel said.

"Yeah. Ask him if he gets cable."

Gideon communed with the computer, but nothing showed on the screen.

"By the way, Spence, this is for you. It came in earlier today." Meaty held up a printout—I could see the lab's insignia in the corner, from underneath. "Unknown specimen report. Hydrogen dioxide. Smectite. Feldspar." Meaty shook the paper. "What sample did you send them? It wasn't even spit."

"It was this drug my brother's been selling downtown." I took the paper from Meaty to read it myself. "I don't even know what smectite is."

Images began appearing on the monitor in front of Gideon, and we all crowded around. There was a man who looked like Winter, having a fight in the hallway with a person wearing a lab coat. The security cameras didn't have great resolution, and I couldn't read lips. "Dammit."

"I know where that is," Gina said, pointing at something flowy and metal monopolizing half the screen. "I recognize that crappy statue. They're outside the transfusion center. Weres visit the transfusion center all the time. They donate a lot of blood, to cover them during their mortal times."

"He was probably just donating," Rachel said, and squinted, leaning forward. "Why would you get mad about not being able to donate?"

The onscreen fight between Winter and a tech continued. "When you want to make a withdrawal instead," I said.

Gideon switched screens. The monitor view divided into eight quadrants, each of them showing gray squares outside. It was snowing lightly in all of them, and black shadows were coming toward the screen.

"Is that now?" I asked him, and he nodded. "Is Triage over? Are those patients, returning?"

Gideon didn't respond to me. He opened up one of the smaller rectangles so that it occupied the whole screen. The people coming toward the camera were not the helpless crutching group Gideon and I had seen leaving. These new people ran, strong, on two and four legs both. "Look at the way they move," Gina said. "Weres."

"Smectite and feldspar are types of clay," Meaty said from behind us. "Your brother was selling water and dirt."

"What? The way he talked that stuff up—it was like magic. And it wasn't just him. I confiscated a vial of it from one of the weres here, too." I was sure it had something to do with things—

Gina took the sheet from me and gasped. "No way." And then she groaned. "He was selling it? To how many people?"

"I don't know. He said business was good—" As I talked the color drained from her face. "Why?"

"Your brother was selling water from a werewolf's paw print."

"So?" I asked—but the reading I'd done came flooding back to me. "You mean everyone he sold to—is going to become were?"

"This'll be their first moon." Gina leaned forward and tapped the monitor screen. "That's them. Coming here, now."

"Paw prints—that's old. Older than me, even." Meaty maneuvered around the station table and came to look at the screen with us. My own brother had been selling werewolf-water. And it was a full moon. And some of his clients, and probably other "dealers" and their clients, of the Luna Lobos were coming here too. More people crowded the camera's angles all the time.

"Shit. How fast does it work?"

"Not how fast, how much. Depends on how much you

drank." We all watched the screens, aghast, and Gina shook her head. "Who the hell was hooking them up?"

"Doesn't matter. We're sitting ducks here, people. Grab as many trank rifles and as much ammo as you can," Meaty said. "It's time to leave."

CHAPTER FORTY-NINE

"Why are they coming here?" I asked Meaty while Gina and Rachel raided the isolation carts for guns and ammo. The weres in the distant rooms were still trying to escape.

"Someone's controlling them," Meaty answered. We both watched over Gideon's shoulder as the weres became more numerous, zooming closer. I almost wanted him to turn off the feed.

"But—why here? Why now?" Behind us, there was a wall-rattling *thump* as the weres in the distant rooms still tried to escape. Thank God they'd reinforced after the dragon. Thank God.

"There's only three things that are valuable at this hospital." Meaty ticked off thick fingers. "Vampire blood, were blood, and a shitload of narcotics. I'd bet those things are after the first two. As for why now—who knows? Maybe because the Shadows are gone. I'd like to know how they found that out, though." Meaty glared at me.

"If I had talked, do you think I would have been stupid enough come back here?" I said.

Meaty grunted. "Charles didn't talk. He's already in Bermuda."

"So whoever's running this show did something to set the Shadows off. It doesn't change what we're dealing with right now," Gina said, frowning as she returned. "I can't believe you didn't tell me, though."

I did feel bad. I'd been making the best of bad situations for the past month. I looked to Meaty.

"All right. Let's go." My charge nurse started for the door. On the computer screen, the weres had reached the hospital lobby doors.

"Wait! What about the blood? You can't just let those things take it."

"My interest here is in saving my skin and yours. I haven't lived this long to die now," Meaty said, loading up their gun with darts.

It didn't feel right, just abandoning the ship. I knew Meaty knew better than I did, but—"I'll call Sike again. She's bound to almost be here." The confirmation site hadn't seemed that far away.

"And then what?"

"I don't know." But I had my answer to my why-now question. If what Sike had said about Anna's ability to make endless blood was true—maybe this was the other angle on that game. Maybe Anna was so threatening to the status quo that someone wanted to make a run on all the other vampire blood in the county. What better time to steal it than when she was being distracted by her confirmation party? Using the wolfmen my brother had accidentally been creating for distraction?

"If they get that blood, it'll shift the balance of power." If blood was the power to create new vampires, and get more daytimers in thrall, I couldn't let anyone else get what was in the transfusion lab.

Meaty's head shook. "It's too dangerous. I won't let you go without a plan."

I reached out and took a trank gun from Gina. "I'll think of something on the way. Where's transfusion?"

Meaty sighed and waited, to see if I had any sudden epiphanies. I didn't. Frowning, my charge nurse took the lab results back from me and drew a quick map at the bottom. The elevator banks were designated by their letters, and floors of stairs were hashed. "This is where you're going—the transfusion lab's at the back. This," Meaty said, pointing to another spot on the map, "is where we'll be. There's an underground tunnel at the back of the accounting department, it leads to the loading docks outside." Meaty took off their badge and pulled out keys, handing them all to me. "I'm not sure if I have access to all the doors. When you're done, come find us. I hope you make it."

Gina handed me a fistful of darts. "If you get into trouble, call." She pecked me on the cheek, like she was letting me go. Rachel shrugged and shook my hand.

They walked out together like a combat unit, Meaty leading the charge. The wolfmen bayed behind me, thumping at their plastic walls.

I looked over at Gideon. "I hope you don't mind staying behind."

Gideon threw his hat on the floor and took off his gloves.

"I guess that means you're in. Thanks." I held up Meaty's map between us. It was a good thing I was familiar with the hospital's general layout, because the map wasn't very clear. The transfusion lab was on the first floor, but it was an entire hospital-length away. We would be safer if we came up to a higher floor, then ran along in one of the basement hallways.

The elevators let us out, and we took a flight down, and I wished I'd popped a Vicodin back in Y4, when I'd had the chance. It was hard to be quiet when each step hurt, and frustrating to be going so slow.

We were in the diagnostics imaging corridors now, limping along beneath sterile lights. There were howls coming from inside the building, and I was glad County had thick floors so I couldn't hear claws scrabbling overhead.

Then the howls were from down the hall. I opened up the door nearest to us, and pulled Gideon inside. We were in one of the many rooms that patients disrobed and waited in before assorted scans. There was the chance they'd just race by—but fucking weres and their fucking noses, the door opened just as I closed the breech of the rifle.

I shot the first one in the shoulder. It was a were with fingerless gloves and dreadlocks. I knew him, I'd seen him on Christmas Day. He was Jake's friend, Raymond—I registered it in half a second, and shot him anyway. The trank gun bucked, and the dart lodged into his chest, pushing a were-dose of suxamethonium chloride inside. I hit him again, just in case, before realizing I'd be screwed if I had to reload.

He dropped as the drug paralyzed all the muscles in his body. A new were ran in after him. Gideon punched it in the face. His tined fingers slid into the were's eyes, and the creature howled in agony for a split second before Gideon's metal fingers skewered its brain.

"Oh, God—" I wanted to throw up, but there wasn't any time. I reloaded the gun, and we went back into the hall, Gideon staying a little behind.

We made it to the end of the hall, but another howl forced us inside a nearby door. I realized where we were in an instant. There was a red line of tape on the floor, and huge medical equipment on the room's far side—this was the room with the MRI.

I moved to stand in front of Gideon. The red line on the floor marked where it was safe to stand with any metallic object. If I crossed over that line, it'd start tugging the metal on me, the buckles on my purse, the grommets on my boots. If Gideon crossed over it, it'd pull Grandfather right out of him.

The room stank like cigarette smoke, and a man stood up from where he'd been sitting, on the MRI's bed.

"Hey, lady. I wondered if you would show up. I heard about you." It was Y4's erstwhile daytimer patient, Mr. Hale, smoking in his hospital gown.

"Who are you?"

"Just another daytimer," he said with a greasy smile.

Gideon started forward and I pressed him back. "No, you're not."

"Okay, you caught me." He clasped his hand to his breast dramatically, as if shot. "I'm from House Grey. I think you already heard of us, from that whining were-brat."

This was the first time I'd ever met a House Grey vampire. "Why are you here?"

"To help control those pathetic were-distractions outside." He tapped his head. "House Grey specializes in fucking with minds. Which I'll show you, as soon as I get near. Without your Shadows to protect you—" He made a tsking sound and shook his head as though I was in trouble. "Did the Rose Throne really think we were going to let her rise go unchallenged?"

"Who?" I pretended not to know.

In the blink of an eye he was two steps closer. Even though he was a daytimer, he'd had vampire blood yesterday. That made him stronger-faster-everythinger than me. He pointed an accusing finger at me. "I witnessed your trial, so don't pretend you don't know who I mean."

I swallowed. I didn't like being reminded of being stabbed by vampires just now. "Anna," I said, taking another step back as he took a corresponding step forward.

"Yes. Her. That's why we're here. For the blood. But I bet you knew that already." He stubbed his cigarette out on the MRI table at his side and gave me a heavy-lidded grin. "Who knows, if I kill you—they might give me some of it."

"You need to stop right there." My gun was down, no way I could lift it before he'd cross the distance between us. I reached into my pocket that had the darts.

"Sorry, lady, but I can't have you interfere." He stepped in front of the MRI.

I backed up again, shoving Gideon behind me. "I wouldn't do that if I were you," I said, trying to look as helpless as possible.

"Why? How are you going to stop me?" He gave me an amused look.

"Because I know something you don't."

"Really?" He laughed. "Lady, I have lived for a long, long time. I survived smallpox and the black plague. I won't be dying here." Then all his humor faded, and his eyes focused on me. "But you will." Gideon leaned forward in warning against my back.

I pulled a trank dart out of my pocket and threw it at him. It raced toward him like a javelin, seeking to mate with the superpowered magnet on his far side. Picking up speed, it punctured him, making a clean hole at the level of his heart. It tinged cheerfully when it hit the MRI.

He appeared aghast, and then he crumpled, joining his own cigarette ash on the floor. I stepped forward to stomp on the pile of dust. "Oh yeah? The MRI is always fucking on, asshole." I ran back and grabbed Gideon's arm. Together we hobbled back the way we'd come into the room.

We got to the end of the hall and came up the stairs to the ground floor. Three more hallways down and we found ourselves at the transfusion lab's back door. I waved Meaty's badge around in front of the access panel, but the lock didn't click. Gideon shoved me aside.

"Edie?"

I turned back and Sike was racing down the hall. "Edie!"

"Shhhh!"

"I came as soon as you texted. What the hell is going on? It's full of weres outside."

"They're after the—" I began, and stopped. Would she help me, or hinder me, in what I was about to do next? I wouldn't know till I knew. The door unlocked for Gideon, and I opened it. "Just come inside with me."

I closed the door behind us, and Gideon set to locking it again. The entire room thrummed with electricity—power running to refrigerators, microscopes, testing equipment— things that a hospital always needed to be on. County was a twenty-four-hour operation. Now it was like a science lab in a ghost town, empty and eerily still except for the were-shadows running back and forth outside. The far wall of the room was lined in skinny 1960s wire-glass windows. Past that, they were protected by metal bars.

"What is this place?" Sike asked, wandering around.

I took Meaty's keys out of my pocket. "You'll see." I skirted the edges of the room, looking for a locked fridge that my keys would open—and found it.

Small, squat—it could have been a medication fridge on any floor. But my key fit in its lock, and inside it was stacked high with small vials and bags of blood. Each one of them was stamped with the same stamp—Y4.

"This is your last chance to fix all this!" I shouted up at the ceiling and down to the crevices on the floor. If this had all been some shitty Shadow-test . . .

But nothing responded to me. "Okay then." I started

throwing the fridge's contents into the sink, fistfuls of plastic at a time.

"Edie, no." Sike caught the first bag I'd thrown before it hit the sink's metal bowl. "I can't condone this."

"All those weres outside? They've all been drinking werewolf paw-print water for weeks. House Grey's controlling them. They're after this." I shook one of the blood bags in Sike's face.

There was the squeal of metal scraping cement outside, and then something—someone—hit the window with a *thump.* Then another *thump.* If it were a bigger window, if the outside of the building weren't concrete—"They want the blood, Sike. We have to get rid of it. This is our only chance."

She looked at the blood bag she'd caught. "How do you know House Grey's behind this?"

"I killed one of them down the hall."

Sike snorted. "That wasn't smart of him then, was it?" She curled in her fingers until her nails pierced the blood bag like an overripe fruit, then wrung it out over the sink, making sluggish blood ooze out.

Up until that moment, there'd been a chance she'd have stopped me. Relief ran through my body in a wave, then another were banging on the window outside made me jump. I focused and tossed another blood bag to her. "I don't think we have much time."

CHAPTER FIFTY

The sink didn't have a garbage disposal. But all sinks at hospitals had one thing in common underneath— industrial-strength cleaners and bleach.

The weres outside were pinging off the window like grasshoppers in July. I emptied out the entire fridge and tossed the small desks in the room till I found a pair of scissors. Then I pulled on gloves and started cutting the bottom ends of bags, while Sike popped off the plastic caps and poured the contents out. I turned the sink on as hot as it would go to denature proteins and started splashing in floor cleaner.

"Damn House Grey. This is a horrible waste." She watched the blood swirl down the sink like Minnie watching the drain of my shower.

"Can't be helped," I said, handing her another bag. "This is the last one." She flipped it over to look at it.

"It would be were-blood." With a sigh, she ripped it open and squeezed the contents out.

I pulled off my gloves and threw them away. She washed her hands with the cleaner. The windows were vibrating percussively with each blow. I tried not to look at them there, slavering, smearing spit and blood on the barred windows.

"We can't stay here," Sike said. "Did you have another plan?"

"There's an emergency exit through the accounting department, down to the loading docks."

Sike inhaled deeply. "Let's go."

Gideon opened the back door for us, and we started running—or hobbling in my case—down the back halls.

I heard a skittering of claws on a tile floor. Sike heard it first. She flung her arm out, catching me in my side.

A wolf turned the corner and ran down the hall at us. Helen's wolf, gray and blond, slowed.

"Helen—Viktor somehow—" But it wasn't Viktor, never had been, all along. Viktor had tried to warn me. And I was wearing Jorgen's blood—Jorgen, who had hit Winter with his truck. House Grey had gotten the werewolf paw-print water from somewhere. From . . . someone.

I stepped forward. "Helen—it's not too late. You can stop this. Call those other weres off."

Helen twisted her head to one side, as if to pity me, then started trotting forward again. Sike pulled me back again.

"Is there another way for you to go?" Sike asked me without taking her eyes off Helen.

"Sike, she'll kill you." Sike was only a daytimer, and Helen was a major wolf on a full-moon night.

"You're just a human, Edie. I've got a chance. Take the gimp and go."

"Sike—" I warned.

"Go!" Sike shoved me toward Gideon, sending me to my knees. Gideon caught me and picked me up as Sike blocked Helen's path. "You know you want a fight, fucking were," she taunted. Helen snarled. I got to my feet and looked back at her, one last time, red hair streaming down her back like arterial blood.

* * *

I ran as fast as I could through a bureaucratic maze, aided by Gideon and Meaty's map. I shinned myself on copier trays, caught my hips on the edges of desks, bouncing down the accounts and billing floor like a pinball.

It didn't matter what I hit or what hit me. I felt numb. Sike was gone. Meaty's directions led me to the end of the accounting floor. I went into a file storage closet and found the shelves disturbed to reveal pieces of flooring pulled off and a hole underneath. I reached inside, felt metal, and undid a latch. I heard a howl behind me—I jumped into the space in the floor. I screamed as I fell and landed on cold cement, then scrambled out of the way just before Gideon climbed down behind me.

"About time you got here!" Rachel reached up, shut the trapdoor behind me, and spun a lock.

Gina put her rifle down to help me up. "It's called a ladder, Edie."

"You all were waiting?"

"Well, I figured on this particular night, a werewolf would have a problem opening the door." Gina gave me a thumbs-up to demonstrate why. "Still bad up there?"

"From bad to worse." I leaned on her. "Where's Meaty?"

"Up ahead."

My charge nurse stood at the end of the hall, where we quietly joined them. It got colder as we neared—I realized we were outside, or heading toward it. The loading docks. We were only safe as long as no one knew we were here.

Meaty shone a flashlight at the thing ahead of us—a glinting wall of ice. "Snowbank. Must not have gotten any deliveries for a few days." Then the light was flashed at me. I threw up a hand to cover my eyes. "Edie—what happened?"

I felt my face crumple. I couldn't say the words and not cry. "A friend of mine just died."

Compassion flowed across my charge nurse's face. "Oh, Edie. You should know by now that we can't save everyone." Meaty reached out, and I folded into Meaty's huge chest and bawled like a child.

We huddled together. Meaty kindly held me till it reached that awkward stage, and I stepped away, but not too far, because it was cold and events were still frightening. Each breath I took fogged the air, made my bronchioles tight.

"We can't stay here all night," I said.

"Want to go back, nearer the angry werewolves?" Rachel said, her teeth chattering.

"I've got us covered. Just wait it out," Gina said.

A paw clawed through the snow ahead of us. I ducked. Rachel and Meaty jumped, reaching for their rifles.

"No no no!" Gina said, stepping forward, waving their guns down. Another paw scissored through the compacted snow, and even colder air rushed in from beyond. She looked over her shoulder at me. "Edie—this is Brandon."

The bear unearthed himself. Rachel and Meaty still had their guns ready, but lowered. Gina ran forward, and I lunged after her. I couldn't take losing anyone else tonight—

The bear caught her, and she snuggled against his chest. His giant head came down and nuzzled the back of her neck, looking at the rest of us with intelligent eyes. Gina turned back to me, smiling.

"Just because he can't text me back doesn't mean he can't read." She patted her cell phone in her pocket.

"I guess he's a Care Bear, after all," I said.

She reached out and hit my arm, exactly where my shot had been.

CHAPTER FIFTY-ONE

Through a series of yes/no questions, Brandon convinced us we probably wouldn't die once we emerged. We followed him out of the drift, and I realized why—he'd brought bear friends. Twenty full bears, different sizes and colors, but massive and shaggy in every way. They formed a diamond pattern around us and led us away from the loading docks and toward the front of the hospital.

I didn't know where we'd go, or how we'd manage to fix things. The contingent of weres was still howling in the hospital behind us—I wondered if Jake was among their number, if the Shadows had stopped protecting him from his folly the second they left town. We headed for the tree line surrounding the visitor parking lot, and as we arrived a shadow separated itself from among their number.

"I had wondered if you'd survive this mess." The voice came from a trench-coated, sickle-bearing vampire with a large bag at his feet—Dren. Almost a sight for sore eyes. Then I realized again that Sike was gone, and my chest got two sizes too small. He began walking toward us, dragging the bag behind him. "I heard it went well for the fearsome child. I believe I have something of interest for her."

Brandon got up on his two hind legs and made a threatening noise.

"Shush, beast. My fight's not with you." Dren put his hand on his sickle's holster and scanned around. Behind him the weres scented us—they began to turn away from the building and lope in our direction. A car pulled up and stopped in the lot beyond us, skidding in the snow.

"Are you with us or with them?" Meaty asked Dren.

"He'll be with you, if he knows what's good for him." Anna stepped out of the car, then she looked to me. "I know about Sike."

I swallowed hard. "I'm sorry."

Grief washed over Anna's face, then was quickly replaced by anger. "I should have made her a full vampire when I had the chance. Which wolf was it?"

The only reason she was asking, I knew, was so that she could kill it. And I didn't care. "Helen—the matriarch. She's yellow and gray."

"And what has been the point of all this?" Anna threw her arm out at the carnage of the hospital behind us. Turning, I could see pinpricks of light growing bolder— the beginnings of fires.

"I believe I have someone who can answer that for you." Dren kicked the bag he carried. "Anna, newly minted member of the Sanguine, meet an emissary from House Grey. He's the one who gave blood to Winter the elder. His own blood, to be precise."

I was glad to see that the drop of blood I'd given Dren had gone to good use.

"Took me a long time to find him without the use of a Hound." Dren reached into the bag like he was producing a rabbit from a hat, and hauled out a suit-wearing man. Gray hair, gray glasses, gray suit, gray tie—he was the color of the sinking moon. "Luckily he was one of the ones who's been running around controlling this were-mob."

"Unhand me, you illegitimate beast," the newcomer

complained. Dren bent him over and kneed him in the chest, then shoved him to kneel on the ground.

"It's rare to see one of you out at night. Or ever." Anna wound her fingers in his short gray hair. "What was the point of this?"

"We play a larger game."

"Fuck you. I lost a friend. Tell me truths now, or you'll pay."

"What can you do to me, little girl?"

"Unless you want to be nailed on my car's hood when the sun next comes out—"

The gray vampire laughed. "When does the sun ever come out up here?"

"Dren, cut off his arm."

"Whatever you say, lady Sanguine." Without a second thought, Dren hauled out his sickle and snicked off the gray vampire's arm at the shoulder. It turned to dust, and the fabric fell to the ground.

"I meant the other one," Anna said. Dren moved and—over the side of the car, where there was a gap in the wall of bear-weres, a wolf leapt into our clearing, bowling Anna down.

It was a yellow-gray wolf, almost the size of the car.

"You—" Anna said in recognition. Helen had bloodstains on her side, meaning Sike hadn't gone down without a fight, but—Anna screamed in anger. She rose and rushed at Helen, who jumped to one side. Helen followed Anna's turn and lunged for her. At the same time Anna turned back, grabbing Helen's front paw. She yanked and there was a crunch as bone crossed bone and broke, jutting out through skin. Helen whined and gnashed her teeth at Anna, who danced back. In a moment the leg was straightened, back in place. Steady on all four feet now, Helen made another lunge.

"You know them all?" Gina whispered to me. I nodded.

Anna ran forward again, so fast I could hardly see, another blur in this crazy night. She bowled into Helen's side, tearing with raw angry force. As soon as she hurt Helen, though, Helen healed. Anna leapt for Helen's neck, trying to get her arms around it to snap it. The wolf bucked like a bronco, flipping Anna around. Anna's teeth were out as she held on, sinking her jaws into Helen. Blood poured out of Helen's neck with each fresh bite, and Anna kept biting, as fast as Helen could heal. I knew how those teeth felt, I'd once been bitten by them—and now Anna kept gnawing, through fur, down to bone.

Anna stood up near Helen's sinking form. The tear in her neck was wider now; Anna had worked her hands inside. The edges still tried to heal, but Anna kept the center from meeting. Helen howled her frustration, lashing her neck from side to side—and a nearby howl answered her.

Jorgen began shoving his way through the circle of bears, howling again.

"Is it a team match now? I can hardly guard Master Grey and also play," Dren asked of no one.

"Enough!"

Anna, Helen, and Jorgen were all forced backward, like they'd been shoved by a wall.

"I will not allow this insolence to continue!" Meaty's voice didn't sound like Meaty—it resonated with something older and more wild.

Meaty reached down and snatched a piece of the shadow of the tree we were near, as though pulling fabric free, and cast it up into the sky above us, saying, "The only magic mine." We would have all been in the dark had not Meaty began to cast an eerie light. Gina and Rachel stepped away quickly. "No moon now. Time to answer for your crimes." Meaty pointed at Helen, and her wolf form slipped away, shedding off her, leaving her naked. Jorgen's form changed too, lessening, the beast flowing out of him, leaving only human behind. "But before that—"

"Who are you?" Anna asked.

"This body is quite old. It suits me well." Meaty inspected both thick arms, as if seeing them for the first time. It didn't look like Meaty anymore. The physical space my charge nurse held was overlapped with light, and that light had a slightly different shape. It was like a sheet of disembodied power draped down, turning Meaty into a glowing Halloween ghost. "In answer to your question, bloodslave—I am an avatar of the Consortium. This body was the only thing nearby large enough to hold me that wasn't wearing fur." Meaty cast about on the ground. I wasn't about to ask what they were looking for.

"You. There." Meaty turned over a rock with a toe. "Get up here and explain yourselves."

Had I seen anyone else talk to the ground, I'd have deemed them profoundly insane. But I had a hunch who we were ringing up now.

More shadows oozed away from the base of the tree, thickening like oil, folding in on themselves till they made a creature waist-high.

"Your Grace, honorable Dr. Swieten—" the tar-like creature said. Despite the fact that the Shadows were amorphous, I got the feeling they were groveling.

"Do not say my name like you know me, dark things." The phosphorescence around Meaty glowed brighter.

"Never again, Doctor, never again. Please, take pity on us." The Shadows thinned, dropping lower into the ground in the face of this brightness.

"You know how valuable this territory is. What possible reason could you have for leaving your post?"

"Santa Muerte escaped. We had to go and find her."

One of Meaty's eyebrows rose, both the glowing and nonglowing one. "And did you?"

"No!" A hundred different tones of wailing combined in that one word. "Should she gather—"

Meaty's avatar cut a glowing hand down. "Your foolishness is no excuse for this. Abort your search, and fix this mess you've made."

I was pleased to see there was something in this world that the Shadows were frightened of—and then realized that if they were frightened, than I almost certainly should be too. The howling behind us had ended, and the surrounding weres were still. I didn't think they were waiting—it was like they'd been frozen in time. I scanned for Jake in vain.

Meaty gestured behind our group, toward the hospital. "Those poisoned people were not meant to become were, Shadows. Heal them or kill them off." The glowing began to fade, and the sense of having another presence there receded.

"Wait!" I called out. Gideon put a hand on my arm to stop me. "What about everything else?"

The light returned, and the Consortium's avatar looked at me through Meaty's face, condescendingly. "Several unexplained fires have been set in the city, to help explain the chaos. The rest, I'm sure you'll deal with." Meaty looked from Anna to Helen. And then the light drained away—although the shadow overhead remained. Abandoned, Meaty stumbled, and Gina caught our head nurse.

Anna walked over to Helen. Her bestial half was gone now, but Sike's blood was still on her hands. Jorgen clutched her to him.

"She fought well, but—" Helen said, the words apologetic, the tone not.

"I loved her."

"Then you are broken. Vampires do not love," Jorgen

said. Muscles rippled under Jorgen's skin—furless or not, he was a force to be reckoned with. He held Helen protectively.

Ominous howls began again.

"What did her blood buy?" I asked aloud, because I needed to know that I hadn't sold it too cheaply.

"House Grey said that if we stole the blood from here for them, they would give us their blood in return. As they had once given it to Winter, prolonging his life." Helen's eyes looked over to the emissary from House Grey. "Their devil's pact with my father cost me my husband's life. How I loved my husband and hated my father for killing him." She freed herself from Jorgen's arms and threw herself at Anna's feet. "Show us mercy. We repent."

The House Grey vampire coughed. "Your sentimentality is unbecoming."

"Dren, please kill him," Anna said.

The Husker hesitated. "To kill him will make you a large number of enemies, Sanguine. Enemies you might not want yet, in your illustrious five-hour-old career."

"I don't think I care."

Dren shrugged and set his sickle to the Grey's throat. "Don't you want to know about Santa—" the Grey began. Anna didn't look up. Dren finished his move and the vampire dusted like a cloud.

The distant howling came nearer. Anna looked down to Helen now. "Such a meal I have not had before. No wonder we used to keep your kind as pets. Perhaps that can be your punishment. I'll chain you to the end of my bed and drain you every night."

Lucas the wolf crouched at the edge of the circle, then bounded in. His wolf left him as fluidly as I knew it had arrived. He landed softly, on one knee, both hands touching down. Two other weres leapt in beside him.

"Their punishments are ours." He stood and turned to

look at Helen. "What were you thinking? How could you shame us so?"

"My father killed my husband to hide his secret, to buy his extra years of life. Fenris—my Fenris—died for my father's secret use of vampire blood, so that no one else would know." Helen picked up a handful of the slush beside her and threw it at Lucas's feet. "Fenris Jr. was too young to lead, and the pack would never pick a woman. I had to let that bastard live until my son's position was secure—then he went and got you to rule us!" Her face curdled in anger. "That was when I made my pact and told House Grey I'd raise an army to get the blood from here. They denied him vampire blood and Jorgen tried to kill him, but the bastard wouldn't die. All of it was going to be ruined. All my waiting, all my patience, and for what?"

Lucas's face held pity for her mixed with horror. "I told you I was only going to be pack leader for the interim. Why didn't you believe me?"

"Have you ever known a man to step away from a throne?"

Lucas clenched his fists at his sides. "I am not like him, Helen."

"That's what all men say."

Anna moved to stand in front of Lucas. "I demand her life. A life for a life—it is the old way."

"We will punish her in our own manner. Take Jorgen instead." The weres beside Lucas moved to grab Jorgen, and he fought back.

"No!" Helen screamed, reaching for him as they dragged him off.

"Is that the one who attacked you, Edie?" Anna asked. I nodded. "We'll accept him then. His death shall be as you prefer."

I took two steps back. "What . . . if I don't prefer it?"

Her eyes narrowed. "Sike did not die so that this one could live."

I waited, unable to speak.

I could use needles on patients; I could debride painful wounds; I could hold a crying child down to push a feeding tube up its nose—and I could bleed a vampire. But could I, with my voice, give the command to kill a man?

"If I may make a suggestion, ladies," Dren said, stepping in. "I've always wanted a were for a Hound."

Anna looked at me, then back to Dren. "Do it."

It was better than death. Right? I didn't fight when Dren took Jorgen in hand. I knew then I would always regret it. Dren pulled him outside the circle, and it was dark, so I couldn't see, but I could hear Jorgen cry out.

"No—" Helen whispered. "Samson, Lars, Nichola—when they questioned how Winter was living so long, he bought some of them off with blood. Take one of them instead!" she pleaded. At the back of the pack, in the shadows, some weres peeled away and ran off.

Lucas snapped his fingers, and other wolves ran off after their traitors. "Who else?"

"No one!" she said.

"All right. Then we decide."

A high-pitched snarl began from inside the pack's group. Helen blanched. "Fenris, no—"

Fenris Jr. ran in, on four legs, then two, crouching in front of his mom. "Don't hurt her!"

Lucas swooped down and scruffed the boy, just like he was a puppy, holding him up by his neck.

"No, Lucas—no," Helen whispered.

"Pack honor demands that your bloodline be punished. That means both of you." Creatures with teeth and paws reached forward into the circle, grabbing hold of Helen, pulling her back into the dark. Lucas tossed Fenris Jr. to the ground.

Fenris landed poorly, a tangle of arms and legs. I ran out to stand in front of him.

"You can't, Lucas. He's just a child."

"Edie—get out of the way."

"I can't let you do this, Lucas." I looked to Anna for help, but she raised her hands as if they were tied. "You'll regret it forever if you kill him!"

"I'll regret it forever if I let him live. I'll be the pack leader who was dishonored."

"So? Who cares? No one cares about that! No one has to care!" I reached around behind myself to press Fenris Jr. tight.

A phalanx of new wolves and wolfmen arrived, and one of them pressed through. It was deep black, with white splotches. When it reached the circle's edge, the wolf skin fell away. Viktor stood there, finally without his hat. "I care. None of your bloodline deserves to lead this pack, not anymore." Viktor moved into the center of the circle, shouting loud enough for all. "I figured it all out. All of it. Only none of you would have listened to me. I brought one of the drug dealers here—I interrogated him. Found out he got his drug—his Lobos Luna—straight from Jorgen." The wolfmen shoved forward a man, who hit the pavement on his knees.

The dealer was Jake. My heart stopped. How come Jake wasn't out there with the rest of the crazed new weres? I couldn't look behind me now to see how the Shadows were "taking care" of things. And Jake was looking down—soon he had to look up and see me.

Viktor continued. "You're not fit to lead, Lucas. Look at all this chaos in your pack. So many traitors. Kill the boy—and then fight me for your pack."

Lucas watched Viktor as the newcomer walked proudly around. "Who are you to tell me what to do?" Lucas asked.

"I've watched all of your fights. I know where all your weaknesses are. To the Viktor will go the spoils!" Viktor said, thumping his chest, stepping aside.

Lucas took three steps toward me, as though he were coming for Fenris. Fenris scrabbled behind me, reaching the edge of the circle at last. I heard the snarls as he changed into a wolf, and frightened yips as he ran away. Lucas made like he'd give chase, then whirled and took two low steps back at Viktor, punching out to shove his human hand into Viktor's stomach, carrying Viktor upward with the force of the blow. Standing, he drew the other were onto his toes, his arm embedded in Viktor's chest. "It seems I have your heart."

Viktor couldn't say anything. His face went red, his rib cage straining the confines of his chest, gasping for air. Lucas went on.

"No one tells me how to lead my pack." He flung Viktor outside the circle, and the black wolf form enveloped him as he left it. "Heal—and heel. Don't offer me counsel ever again."

Lucas looked out at the rest of his pack, held his arms wide. "Is this settled? Is there anyone else?" His pack gave no response. "Good. No one harms a hair on Junior's head. Bring him home safe, to me."

He turned toward me, sitting in the circle with him, and offered me a gore-covered hand. Since I'd already had one were-shot that evening, I took it. "You were born the wrong species."

I sagged with relief and exhaustion. "I don't think so."

CHAPTER FIFTY-TWO

Lucas left with his pack. I couldn't imagine how Fenris Jr. would deal with things tomorrow morning. I had no doubt what the punishment for Helen would be. And what exactly had I condemned Jorgen to, giving him over to Dren? I didn't want to know.

Jake still hadn't looked up. I wondered if the weres had hurt him or if he was fighting the Luna Lobos. "Jake?"

He held his hand up, in a stop. "I'm fine. Just do what you need to do, Edie." Normally, I would have fought him on that, only Anna interrupted us.

"Is there anything else that needs doing tonight?" She put her hands on her hips and stood tall.

I remembered what I'd been doing right before Sike died. "There is one more thing for me to confess to."

"Hmmm?"

"I . . . destroyed a lot of blood. All of it, in fact. I didn't think I could risk them getting it."

Behind her, Gina heard me and pumped her fist in the air.

"Well, that was unexpected." Anna said and looked around, calling out, "Shadows—"

As the moon sank, the shadows of the trees were growing. The nearest Shadow answered her. "We can return the hospital to the way it was, and also many of these people. But we cannot find individual blood cells and return them to their original state. If they were here, perhaps. But they were washed away an hour ago, and denatured before that."

"Denatured by what?"

"Chemical solvents."

Anna's shoulders slumped. From behind, and the side, she must have looked dismayed. But when she spoke next, her eyes were lit up by power. "When the other Houses find out—" She shook her head, mystified at the future she was seeing, with an avaricious smile. "They will all be indebted to me. I will, of course, have to be gracious, and give them pint upon pint of replacement blood. For a nominal fee."

"You have it in you, after all," I said.

"That I do." She gave me a private nod. "So be it, Shadows," she said louder. "Hurry this process. Dawn comes."

I walked over to check on Rachel and Gideon. Gina came over to us.

"I've never seen so many weres," Rachel said in awe.

"I'm glad Charles isn't here. He'd be having a fit," Gina said, crossing her arms. "I miss him."

"Me too." I looked over at Gideon. "Are you okay? You'll need a new hat."

Gideon held up his hand with his one missing antenna finger, and then gave me a thumbs-up.

Nearer the hospital, the weres were queuing. Where they'd once been intoxicated by werewolf water and controlled by House Grey, the Shadows took them over, setting them in orderly lines to deal with them one at a time. A wave of black washed over them one by one—weres with malformed hands and muzzled faces went in, and mere humans came out the other side. The survivors milled about, confused to find themselves suddenly in a hospital parking lot on a cold winter night, before dispersing.

Some that went in didn't come out at all, and others lost the strength to move on the far side—with the were-strength leaving them, some of them couldn't move at all. One fell like a stone, and a second later a woman's voice cried out.

"Don't worry," said one of the horrible Shadow-things, feeling my gaze. "We can hide the dead."

"That's awful—" I said.

"Javier!" a woman screamed.

"Shit." I started hobbling over.

Luz held Javier as he gasped for air like a dying fish. She looked wildly around. "Where are we? How did we get here? What's happening to Javier?"

Oh, God. He was going to die out here in the cold. We were too far from the hospital to try to carry him in. The Luna Lobos that Luz had given him without me knowing had given him his legs back and healed his spine—but only for a time.

"Luz—" I began.

I didn't know if she recognized me or just my bearing. "You! Help him!" She rocked him in her lap while he turned blue.

"I can't." All the emergency services here were gone. All the technicians gone home. Four nurses, one of them incapacitated by merging with blinding judgmental light, were not going to cut it.

"He's going to die!" she protested. "Do something!"

"Shadows?" I knelt down and hit a fist on the ground. In the shadow made by the ridge of a cement curb, I was answered.

"His time has passed. We set things right, we do not change them."

Luz kept crying and rocking him. "Do something! Fast! I would give my life for his!"

"Do you mean that?" Anna said as she arrived.

Luz looked at Anna with fury in her eyes. "Of course I do."

"All right then." Anna crouched and bit her own hand savagely. She shoved her bloody fingers into Javier's lips, and he inhaled. Then she looked to Luz and held her hand out.

"He'll be fine now. Come with me."

Luz looked at Anna's bloody hand.

"You said your life for his. Are you honorable or not?" Anna shook her hand, blood dripping off it.

Luz grabbed it. And when Anna let go, she reached out and stroked a line of blood on Luz's forehead with her thumb.

"Good. Stay with him for now. I will return for you." She stood and began walking away. I hurried after her, and she spoke before I could. "I need a sister, not a child. I'll turn her tomorrow night."

"Anna—Sike's not a pet that can be replaced."

Anna drew up short. "I feel her loss more than you. You merely feel guilt," she said, and I knew what it felt like to be stabbed by a vampire again. Her face softened as she looked up at me. "It is my right now to build my House. I saved his life, and the girl is willing. It's the price of blood."

A group of vampires I vaguely recognized arrived. They were all the ones that'd been serving Anna-blood cocktails at the ascension earlier tonight.

Anna gestured to include them in our conversation. "Normally the loss of so much precious blood would be an offense punishable by death. But you have already been at trial once before, and we both know how that turned out. There is only one suitable punishment left."

"What's that?" Gina asked, taking my side, ready to fight.

Anna smiled at her approvingly, then looked to me. "We will shun you, Edie. No one will contact you, on pain of death. This world will be closed to you now."

"Wait—what?" It was what I had wanted, to get away from all this. But I was still surprised.

She stepped nearer and raised her hand to touch my cheek. "I swore not to hurt you, remember?"

I nodded silently.

"I meant it. I will miss you, Edie." She stepped back from me, and I could almost feel a wall rising between us. She tossed me keys, and I caught them. "Take Dren's car. Go home. Be safe."

"I'll try," I said, my throat tightening. It was the least I could do, after everything that had happened tonight.

CHAPTER FIFTY-THREE

Anna went to hang out with the others of her kind, leaving my co-workers and Jake in the moon's dwindling light.

I'd save Jake to deal with last. He was being so quiet. He must have been stunned.

Rachel engulfed me in a hug, then patted me roughly. "You did it."

Gina was crying too hard to talk. She said it all in her hug.

I saved Meaty for last. Meaty squeezed me tight, then grabbed my shoulders. "Don't look back, Edie. Just go."

After all this, Jake finally stood. "Can I get a ride home, Sissy?"

"Sure." I held out my hand to him, and he took it.

It was good to have a reason to stay composed on our walk to Dren's car. Otherwise, I would have lost it. The Shadows spoke from the shadow of a lamppost that they made look like a scar on the ground.

"Shall we fix him for you?"

I looked to Jake. He seemed baffled. I shook my head. "No. He and I need to talk."

"As you like. No one will believe him anyhow."

The Shadow changed back to a shadow, and I unlocked the doors.

* * *

Dren's car was nicer than mine. I wondered darkly if I'd get to keep it. Jake and I drove along in silence. I almost hoped he'd speak first—I sure as hell didn't know how to start this conversation.

"Jake—"

"Turn here." He pointed at an exit coming up.

"But that's not—"

I looked at the hand. It wasn't Jake's anymore. I gasped, and then realized Jake was transitioning to look like Asher.

"It's the way to my house. I don't have cab fare on me. Plus, I doubt we'd see any cabs," Asher said, in his gentle British accent.

I hauled my car over onto the on-ramp. A fleet of emergency vehicles was sprinting the other way—the Shadows had a lot to fix, before dawn. "You—you! You touched him, didn't you!"

Asher shrugged, as if it wasn't worth making the point. "It wasn't hard. Your brother loves you, deep down inside. I just had to convince him you'd be better off without him, to get him out of town. Four hundred dollars didn't hurt, either."

I beat on my steering wheel.

"Why? He's safe—I saw him before I left tonight," Asher said.

"It's not that, dammit—" I sank forward, shoulders slumped. I was glad the Shadows had kept him clean so far, despite his four-vial-a-day habit of paw-print juice. But who knew if the Shadows would keep him clean, now that I'd been shunned? Also, with the demise of his hookup for Luna Lobos, I had no doubt he'd find harder things to sell. He'd never know that all of its purported health benefits had been a placebo for him, entirely in his mind.

I followed Asher's directions to his house, without saying anything. I pulled up into his driveway, in silence. He turned toward me. "No matter what happens to your brother, she's right. It's safer this way."

"I know. I agree." I stared at my steering wheel. I couldn't deny it after tonight. I'd been struggling to play along ever since I'd gotten stabbed. It was lunacy.

"Edie—being shunned—it's everybody. Shapeshifters too."

I kind of figured as much, but I hadn't admitted it to myself. I nodded at the dashboard of my car.

"Edie—"

I turned toward him and stuck out my hand. He looked blankly at it. "Really? Just a handshake?"

I looked at him in the half dark. "No."

He reached for me, and I leaned into him. Our lips met halfway and I kissed him hard, and he kissed just as hard back. Everything I'd ever screwed up I wanted to let go now, and just think about this, because if I thought about anything else I would cry.

And in thinking too much about not thinking about anything, I missed it. His lips pulled away. He pulled back, studying my face like he was afraid he'd forget it—which I knew, for him, was a lie. He didn't say anything else, just turned, opened the car door, and walked away. He didn't look back. I knew because I watched him, hoping he would.

I started my car back up again and pulled out of his driveway.

It was almost dawn when I reached my apartment's parking lot. I pulled into the first spot I saw and walked my way in. A person emerged from the shadows and joined me.

"I want my keys," Dren said, walking alongside me.

"Aren't you supposed to be shunning me now?" My feet made crisp sounds in the snow.

"Shuns usually go into place at dawn. Gives aggrieved parties a last chance to settle scores."

"I suppose that's type of technicality a Husker would know."

He held out his shorter arm toward me. "You still owe me for my hand."

"Being shunned doesn't dissolve my debts?"

"No. I just won't be able to bother you about them now."

I stopped, and Dren did too. "That doesn't make sense."

He grinned maliciously—it even went up into his grass-green eyes. "Let's just say I have a feeling we'll be seeing you again."

I opened my mouth. I wanted to say, *I hope not.* I thought I'd mean it. But the truth was I really didn't know. I hated where I'd been tonight, but I was scared of the normal life that lay in front of me, too. I tossed his keys up, and he caught them.

"Besides, Edith. You're the type that gets into trouble, or gets dead."

I closed my mouth without saying anything at all. He gave me a flourishing bow and veered off, walking away through the snow.

I arrived at my door and unlocked it. Inside my apartment, the carpeting was still new, and I stepped onto it, feeling like I'd stepped onto the ground of an unknown world.

I took a shower and I waited up. And once dawn came, I slept.

SHAPESHIFTED

Coming Summer 2013

I'd lost fifteen pounds in six months.

Being a nurse, I'd run through the worst-case scenarios first: cancer, diabetes, TB. When I'd checked my blood sugars and cleared myself of coughs and suspicious lumps, I was left with the much more likely diagnosis of depression. Which was why I was here, even though here was an awkward place to be.

"I can tell you anything, right?" I asked as I sat down across from the psychologist.

"Of course you can, Edie." She gave me a comforting smile, and adjusted her long skirt over her knees. "What do you feel like talking about today?"

I inhaled and exhaled a few times. There didn't seem to be any good way to launch into my story. "Hi, I used to work with vampire-exposed humans. Once upon a time, I dated a zombie and a werewolf. So, you know, the usual." I snorted to myself and admitted: "I'm not sure where to begin."

"Anything that feels comfortable for you is fine. Sometimes it takes a few sessions to rev up."

"Heh." Six months was a long time—I should be getting over things already. Things like being fired . . . well, shunned, which felt a lot like firing. Maybe I should have let them wipe my memory when I'd had the chance.

Figures I would make the wrong decision. "I've just been through a rough time lately."

"How so?"

"I had this job that I really enjoyed. And I had to leave it. To go elsewhere. Ever since then, my life just feels . . . plain." I'd spent the end of winter up through July working full-time night shift in a sleep apnea clinic, monitoring patients while they slept. It was dull. My skin was paler than ever, and my social life was long gone.

There was a pause while she attempted to wait me out. When I didn't continue, she filled the gap. "Let's talk about what you used to enjoy. Maybe we can figure out what you enjoyed about it, and think how you can bring those qualities over into your current situation.

"Well. My co-workers were good people. And my job was exciting." I paused, chewing on the inside of my cheek.

"What was exciting about it?" she encouraged me.

I looked at her, at her nice office, nice couch, nice shelves with nice things. It must be *nice* to be a psychologist. I looked back at her. She smiled, and opportunity blossomed inside my heart. We, she and I, had patient-therapist privilege. I knew the boundaries; as a registered nurse, I was a mandated reporter, too. As long as I wasn't a danger to myself, or to anyone else, she'd have to keep what I told her quiet. It wasn't like she was going to believe me, besides.

I leaned forward, my elbows on my knees. "What do you think about vampires?"

The smile on her face tightened for just a fraction of a second. "It's more important that I know what you think, not the other way around. So tell me, Edie. What do you think about vampires?"

"What if I told you they actually existed?" I said. Her smile appeared increasingly strained. "Here, I won't make it into a question. I'll tell you what I think. They do exist. There are quite a few of them out there, actually. They have human servants, some to do their dirty work, and others just to get blood from, like human cattle."

The words just poured out. I knew I wasn't supposed to say anything, and I knew from looking at her that she didn't want to hear it—but it felt so good to finally talk about it. The dam had broken. I couldn't stop now.

"And there're werewolves, too. There were two big packs, but now there's just one, and they race around on full-moon nights in the parks outside of town, and then there're also zombies, and I dated this zombie for reals once—I knew he was a zombie going into things, and I still dated him. You know how I knew? He told me. I was his nurse one night. At the hospital where I used to work."

I sank back into the world's most comfortable couch, and pressed a hand to my chest. "I cannot believe I just told you all that. That felt so good." Looking up, it was clear my confessions hadn't had the same effect on both of us.

She gave me a tight high smile. "Do the vampires tell you to hurt yourself?"

"Not lately!" was the wiseass answer that I wanted to give—but everything I told her was going down into a file. If I was going to abuse her for her listening skills, the least I could do would be to take things seriously, and stay polite. "No. They don't. They're not in my head, either."

She tried a different tack. "Do the vampires tell you to hurt other people?"

"Not anymore!" "No. They're not allowed to talk to me anymore."

I could see her measuring me, weighing my sanity. It was pull up now, and laugh, like everything I'd said had been part of a prank or crazy joke, and wasn't I hilarious?

Or sink like a stone—it could be said I lacked the gene for self-preservation that most people came installed with.

"There was this one vampire that I was really close to. She kicked me out to protect me, after I destroyed all the extra vampire blood in the county. I saved everyone . . . but I ruined everything, too."

The therapist inhaled and exhaled deeply. "Edie, at twenty-five you're a little old to be having a schizophrenic break. But we need to do some reality testing here."

Reality testing. Like everything that'd happened to me this past winter wasn't real. I stared at the patterned carpeting beneath my feet. "That's the thing. It was all real. All of it. But I can't tell anyone about it. You know what'll happen to you when I leave this room? If you believe me?"

"No." Her face looked like she was sucking on an increasingly sour candy. "Why don't you tell me?"

"The Shadows will come out of the ground and erase your memory of everything I said. Maybe even of me." I nudged the carpet with my toe.

"Edie, how long have you been having these delusions?"

I didn't answer her.

"I know you're a nurse, and no one wants to put you on meds less than I do, but my co-worker next door—he's a psychiatrist. We can go together and check in with him. He could get you in as an emergency visit, and then you could go fill your prescription. Risperdal does wonders for people."

"Risperdal?" I startled and looked up. I was crazy . . . but I wasn't *crazy*. "No."

"Edie—" Her voice went low. I grabbed my bag and started walking toward the door. "You're not going to hurt yourself, are you?"

"Not if I don't stay here," I said as I shut the door behind me.

In nursing school I'd done a psych rotation. The nurse I was following and I ate Risperdal-endorsed microwave popcorn out of a brand-new plastic bedpan. It was incongruous at the time, participating in even a small part of the pharmaceutical promotion machine, and eating out of bed pans like they were bowls for food. After that, I'd always made sure to bring my own Tupperware, and had limited any brand endorsement to using whatever Med of the Month–themed pens were lying around.

I didn't want to be on the Med of the Month, though. Even though I knew meds were helpful—and vital, in some cases—for depression. It was just that . . . well, my problems felt situational. You would have thought that it was the stress of working with vampires and were-creatures that did me in, but no, my depression had come after that, with the onset of spring.

I drove home with the windows down, hoping that the wild air flowing over my face would make me feel more alive. It did—until I thought about the fact that I had to work tonight. My stomach curdled, and I finally put two and two together. Working at the sleep clinic was killing my soul.

There're only so many nights you can watch someone sleep on a video monitor and stay sane. I had two years of intensive care unit–level experience, and then I'd spent the last six months watching people sleep, listening to them snore. It was like going from being a fighter pilot to a model airplane captain—the joyless kind glued to the ceiling at a Toys Я Us.

My phone rang. I saw the picture of my mom, and picked it up like you're not supposed to in the car. "Hey, Momma—"

"Hey, Edie! Can you come over?"

A lifetime of being my mother's child meant that I could tell from her voice that something was wrong. "Um, sure. Why?"

"You're not on the phone in your car, are you?" she attempted to deflect me.

"No," I completely lied. "What's wrong?"

"Nothing—I just—" she hesitated. My mother was good at many things, but lying was not among them.

My brain itemized every bad thing it could be, as I waited her out. The list was shorter than it'd been six months ago, since the supernatural community was now shunning me—back then, if she'd called me up like this, I might have panicked and hung up to call the cops, for whatever good they could do.

Thank goodness she'd never known where I'd been working, who I'd been hanging out with, or what I'd been up to.

Now, the first spot on my "reasons my mother could call me in the middle of the day" list was occupied squarely by my brother. Jake had had a brief reprieve from his heroin addiction when I'd been working at the hospital—it was the trade-off for keeping me employed. When I'd been shunned, all of that had ended though, and sure enough Jake had gotten back on the junk. I tried not to think about him, most times, now. Thinking about him only made me sad.

The awkward lull on the phone continued as I stopped at a red light. "I just got some bad news is all," my mother went on. "You're pulled over, right?"